I0635898

MICHAEL ATAMANOV

COUNTDOWN

Wishing you safe travels on your fantasy journey,

Michael Atamanov

REALITY BENDERS
BOOK ONE

MAGIC DOME BOOKS

All books
by Michael Atamanov:

Reality Benders LitRPG series
Countdown
External Threat
Game Changer
Web of Worlds
A Jump into the Unknown
Aces High

The Dark Herbalist LitRPG series
Video Game Plotline Tester
Stay on the Wing
A Trap for the Potentate
Finding a Body

Perimeter Defense LitRPG series
Sector Eight
Beyond Death
New Contract
A Game with No Rules

League of Losers LitRPG Series
A Cat and His Human

You're in Game!
(LitRPG Stories from Bestselling Authors)

You're in Game-2!
(More LitRPG stories set in your favorite worlds)

TABLE OF CONTENTS:

Introduction

First Contact

HOW MANY WAYS have writers, astronomers, philosophers and military theorists imagined humanity's first contact with a celestial intelligence? Earth's observatories receiving intelligible signals from deep space? What about the discovery of interstellar artifacts or even living aliens when excavating ancient burial mounds or pyramids? And the appearance of ominous extraterrestrial starships over our major cities? Heavenly bodies falling to Earth, UFO's crashing? Meeting brothers in intelligence on far-off planets? Invasion? War? The extinction of everything alive...?

But when it really happened, it looked like a stupid joke, hoax or intrusive advertisement, so humanity didn't believe it was the real First Contact. One day, a popup window appeared on many popular websites, blocking off the whole screen. Despite every computer user's habitual and instant reaction, it was impossible to close. It played a video showing a furry humanoid that was somehow distantly reminiscent of the abominable snowman, but with thick dark-red fur. The tall bipedal alien had piercing black eyes, a flat dark nose and a wide mouth. Its clothing was somewhere between a suit of armor and a helmetless spacesuit. The first thing it did was raise a clawed hand and give a friendly wave to its captive audience. With a very strong accent, the humanoid gave a speech adapted to the language of the receiving country:

"People of Earth, by right of first discovery, the civilization of Shiharsa declares its authority and jurisdiction over your planet. We will provide one Tong of safety to your world, but the fate of humanity depends exclusively on what you do with that time. You have now made sufficient progress as a species, and may take part in the great game, the game that bends reality. So, come play and earn the right to take your place among the great spacefaring races!"

That was followed by strange diagrams and blueprints, then the fifty-second clip ended, and the popup window closed all on its own. You surely understand that only stupid people would believe such a primitive and artless sham. Even the most gullible viewers thought it was just an actor in a hairy suit delivering a clumsy advertisement for some new computer game.

But some naive individuals had questions. Television studios invited experts to inspect the "blueprints" from the

2

ad, and they all came to the unanimous conclusion that even the most surface-level examination revealed them to be pure gobbledygook. The technology depicted, they assured us, didn't even have a power hookup, so it could not work even in theory.

Interest in the video of the furry alien didn't last long. The ad kept coming though. Eventually, when yet another movie, news site, or sports broadcast was interrupted by the obnoxious popup, no one cared what it was for, and just got mad. Unhappy internet users the world over installed pop-up blockers and wrote all kinds of complaints to the tech support services of affected sites.

The authorities tried to combat the viral ad and threatened grave consequences to the mysterious hackers who'd played this stupid practical joke. Sys admins learned to quickly block the bothersome video. Data-security specialists tried to determine its source, but it was skillfully masked. They all assured us, though, that they would soon pick up the trail of these impudent scofflaws. And although they were never tracked down, after just a few weeks, the ads stopped coming and the whole earth breathed a collective sigh of relief.

Thus, the greatest event in human history, settling an age-old dispute about extraterrestrial intelligence, came and went as a chaotic flop. Sure, lots of people noticed it, but practically none of them realized what it was.

There were lone enthusiasts, though, who wanted to find out more about "the game that bends reality." Despite the expert testimony calling the designs absurd, these stubborn weirdos believed they had seen a miracle and some even built the device depicted in the blueprints...

Chapter One

Online
Tournament

YES, WE KNEW it was risky and illegal. We understood perfectly well that we'd be booted out of university and fly home with a whistle, if it was discovered that we were hosting these for-profit online gaming tournaments. And especially if they found our gambling software. Nevertheless, we took the risk. Why? Hard to say. At first, it was easy to understand. My roommates and I organized the very first tournaments from our dorm and purely for money. After all, we were borderline-poor university students. But, after we'd earned some cash, we simply couldn't stop ourselves. By then, money no longer played the biggest role. Adrenaline, the thrill of the game, respect among our classmates and popularity with girls were motivation enough.

We understood perfectly well that, as the scale of the tournaments grew, more and more people would find out what we were up to. That would make it harder and harder to hide it from our teachers, the police and university security. All the tricks we used to maintain the anonymity of the players and organizers were primitive. Eventually, serious information-security professionals would investigate, and the gig would be over. We were keenly aware of that. More and more often, my friends and I would say it was time to close up shop or say that the next online tournament would be the last. But that was always followed by another one, then another and another...

This time, our grand PvP tournament had attracted students from every dorm in Moscow. It had begun midday on Saturday and was still underway now, at five o'clock in the morning on Monday. Out of eight hundred players initially, just thirty-two had filtered through the qualifying matches. And I was among them. Yes, unlike my roommates, who handled the servers, encryption software and bookkeeping, I often took part in the online battles. And, a decent chunk of the time, I even won, earning some sizable monetary prizes.

And I never used any "immortality mods," cheat codes or other unfair methods. All I needed was my powerful computer with a top-of-the-line graphics card and good processors, fast ping, knowledge of game maps and weapons and, most importantly, nimble fingers. I always used different pseudonyms and was sure none of the usual players had guessed that the same person had won many of the recent tournaments.

And now, I was playing. With the virtual reality helmet on my head, and my fingers on the buttons of the ergonomic glove controller, I was totally immersed. To me, the outside world just didn't exist...

I was running up a steep spiral staircase to the third and highest floor of a luxurious palace. I stopped to catch my breath. Endurance practically at zero, my thick column legs were shaking, and my sides were puffing out like a smith's bellows. I rasped heavily and opened my mouth like a fish out of water. There was just not enough air. How hard it was to be a giant!

I spontaneously chose an Ogre Fighter just a minute before the start of the final match. The randomly selected map was a medieval castle with huge gloomy rooms, narrow passageways and steep staircases. That would be very disadvantageous for the Drow Archer I'd played in the earlier stages so, at the very last moment, I changed it up.

I had never played such a large character before, and the inconvenience of this heavy body came as an unpleasant surprise. My six-hundred-fifty-pound Ogre was unable to run or clamber up drainpipes. Even a steep stairway was a serious obstacle, eating up all my endurance. Also, there was nearly a second of delay between inputting a command and the character reacting, which was particularly hard to get used to.

That inertia had nearly cost me my life in a recent scuffle with a crafty Human Assassin, who had easily dodged the blows of my huge two-handed pole-ax. I'd had to use an unusual tactic — I'd wound up to swing my weapon but, instead of striking, I'd splayed my arms and jumped forward. That had knocked the crouching man off his feet and I'd luckily managed to pin my agile opponent to the floor. The main advantage of the Assassin class was mobility, and I'd deprived him of that. So, I'd finished him off easily, just by twisting his neck with my bare hands. That assassin was my fourth frag in the final, so I had just thirty-seven percent life remaining. Too little to win. A critical situation.

While my endurance dawdled back up, I opened the leaderboard. After nearly an hour of gameplay, just four of thirty-two players remained: my Ogre, a Human Spearman, an Elf Archer and another unknown character. Since no players had managed to spot them yet, their race and class were listed as a question mark. And meanwhile, this unknown person had racked up three kills. Pretty cool. Must have been some kind of invisible stealth character, attacking people from behind while cloaked.

An alarm rang out, informing me that the tournament would be over in five minutes. I needed to hurry. I opened the map. There was a long straight corridor behind the closed door in front of me. If I were playing an elf archer, I would be keeping watch for my opponents there, shooting them down from afar. A very convenient place. I needed to keep that in mind.

Loudly throwing open the doors, I made a decisive step forward, then took a sharp jump back. And right then, a long arrow with red fletching slammed into the doorframe next to me at headheight! I was not wrong. The Elf Archer had hidden exactly where I supposed. Not wasting a second, I ran forward, giving a terrifying savage roar. A loud shout could sometimes cause enemies to freeze in confusion and fear, which was a real boon. The effect was only increased coming from a huge man-eating giant.

Even the greenest amateur can understand that one arrow to the chest will not stop a massive killing machine. Where was a feeble archer to aim? Obviously, for the head, which would do increased damage. So, just as the elf loosed her bowstring, I blocked my face with the broad blade of my pole-ax.

Clink! I got lucky. The arrow ricocheted aside, and my weapon gave a shudder. Dumb move! She should have shot at my legs and slowed me down. Then she could have got a couple more shots off. But the pointy-eared Elf was acting too predictably. After that failure, she lost courage. Staying in place, she loosed another arrow, then tried to run away. But it was too late! I hacked diagonally down from the right, and the pretty long-eared girl's head rolled along the stones, lopped off by my heavy pole-ax. A fifth frag! And without losing any health!

I stopped and opened the map again. There wasn't much time left. Where could I find two more enemies? Just then, as if answering my question, a distinct yelp sounded out twenty steps in front of me, behind another door. Another enemy down. I wonder who died this time? I opened the player table. The name of the Human Spearman went dim, then the number opposite my last remaining rival flipped to a four. And again, the victim didn't manage to see his killer. Skillful bastard, no two ways about it...

In the upper right corner of the screen, the timer was ticking away, telling me there were just two minutes until the end of the match. If several players survived to the end, a rematch would trigger, and the eight best cyber-athletes of the final would meet again on the same map. Oh, please not that. After the prolonged gaming marathon, I could barely think as it was. What was more, I had an important test in third period today, which I wanted to study for then, ideally, get a little sleep. Well, forward! Nothing ventured, nothing gained!

Throwing the door open, I quickly leapt back, repeating the trick I used on the Archer. But no one attacked me. Strange. Somewhat calmer, I looked around. The gloomy little room was strewn with furniture. It had two exits, one to the left and one to the right, but they both led to the same semi-circular ivy-covered balcony. There was also a round hatch in the ceiling and a rope ladder hanging down. Perhaps the mysterious stealth character was up there. But most likely, my opponent was still somewhere in this small darkened room, hiding in invisibility and waiting for me to slip up. Now, my mission was to discover them without exposing my vulnerable back. Many game classes could land a critical hit by stabbing a rival in the back, and that meant increased damage.

I cut the rope ladder down, then made a crisscross in the air with my pole-ax and abruptly led the blade along the floor a few times. Nothing. Either my enemy was skilled enough to dodge silently (which was hard to believe), or just wasn't here. But then, where were they? Waiting up above? Hardly. After all, they probably also wanted to end this here and now, not play a rematch. Could they really be waiting for me on a sunny balcony? Come on, that was nonsense. Why would a stealth character come out of the shadows?

I looked around again. There was simply nowhere to hide in this small room. Shelves, a little table, an open cabinet with crooked doors. Cutting through space with my weapon again, I convinced myself that my opponent was not here. Another alarm screeched out. Just one minute left in the final. So, I needed to make up my mind. Should I go out onto the balcony through the right door, or the left? My rival must have been waiting for me behind one of these doors. They were probably sitting in invisibility and me agonize right now. Luck of the draw. Would I manage to come face-to-face with my opponent and kill with my advantage in strength, or would I make the wrong choice, get stabbed in the back and lose?

With a heavy sigh, I made my decision and... with all my might, spending all my endurance, I slashed the cabinet with my pole-ax!

My heavy weapon cut into something soft. Bingo! Instead of boards and splinters, blood spattered, and a cloven body fell to the floor. A Shapeshifter. This class sat in waiting to attack an unsuspecting victim from behind, usually killing them in one blow. They were used very rarely in online tournaments because they moved slowly, had to be right next to their victims, and would be absolutely helpless if the first blow didn't kill. Unexpected choice, but I had to admit that it had very nearly brought them victory.

"Hell yeah! Did you see that?!" I shouted joyfully to my roommates, removing my virtual-reality helmet.

And froze...

My dorm room was full of people wearing the dappled gray uniforms of the Moscow Police Department. My friends were pinned to the floor, their wrists cuffed behind their backs.

"Yes, we saw," chuckled a mustached man holding a snub-nose machine gun. He looked to be in charge here. "How 'bout you make like your friends and get on the floor, spread your legs and put your hands behind your back. Don't make me repeat myself, champ."

Chapter Two

Expelled

"**A**M I GONNA be expelled?" ?" I asked when the important investigator finally found the time to interrogate me.

"What do you think?" the middle-aged mustached officer answered with a question. Based on his shoulder loops, he was a captain. He skimmed a stack of papers on the table and signed a few of them. "It would have been just fine if you and your little friends were only playing computer games instead of studying at the best university in the country. Can't say I'd approve, but at least I could understand. But you just had to let people make bets! So, there's nothing I can do here. Russian Federation Criminal Code article 171.2 item 2. Up to four years in penal custody. Kirill, you really did step in it."

I shuddered, then nodded stupidly. Of course, I already knew this, because I had looked last year to see where our illegal enterprise might land us. Four years in prison... I groaned and shuddered, trying to gather my scattered thoughts. I was so exhausted and panicked that my head was working very slowly. Before this, I had spent three unpleasant hours on a bench in lockup at the local police department. My cellmates were a group of unbearably stinking bums, who had also shit themselves. I did everything in my power to stay away from them and not sleep, but I did drift off eventually. A little while later, I was shoved awake by a police sergeant, and he led me down the hallway into this office. I was told he was an investigator, but he didn't ask me any questions, just confirmed my first and last name and the short biography in my personal file.

And I answered his questions eagerly. Yes, I am Kirill Viktorovich Ignatiev, twenty years of age. A native of the small town of Suzdal in the Vladimir Oblast. No brothers or sisters. I don't remember my mother. I wasn't even four when she died. But my father died relatively recently. It hadn't even been three years. He was a geologist, and his group happened upon some illegal gold miners in Eastern Siberia, who didn't want any witnesses to their criminal enterprise. After that, I stayed in Suzdal with my aunt, finished high school and was admitted to the Geology Department of Moscow State University.

The investigator listened attentively, marking something in his papers. Then it was as if he forgot I existed. He turned on his computer and searched for a long time, scanning through screens of text.

"And where are my roommates?" I asked just to break the prolonged silence.

The officer finally tore his gaze from the screen, set the ball-point pen on the stack of papers and looked attentively at me.

"Those two losers? For now, they're being held in a cell and not told what will happen to them. It's the usual procedure. We're trying to make them nervous and fill their heads with horror stories. And tomorrow or the day after, when they're morally prepared, we'll offer them a simple choice: either go to court for the illegal gambling software, or voluntarily join the army. Your sidekicks haven't finished their mandatory reserve-officer training programs, so they'll go serve as privates in the engineering corps. That's usually where students expelled from the Geology Department are sent. They'll serve the Motherland, gain life experience and get a good lesson about what happens to lawbreakers."

I considered it, but it was very hard to think in my sleep-deprived state. On the one hand, it was good that there was some alternative to prison. On the other, I had no idea why the officer was telling me that, and why I was being held separately from my classmates. Former classmates, to be more accurate.

"And why am I being held separate from my friends?" I finally asked.

"Because you, Kirill, are not a mere participant, but the ringleader of this whole illegal enterprise. It's been quite the public fiasco, and someone has to answer before the law.

Although as for you, it isn't decided yet. We need to first confirm some details. Maybe we'll stick you with your friends, then you can all go build pontoons and raise bridges in the Far North or something. Although, it's also possible that you'll have a richer choice than your roommates."

The officer fell silent and again delved into his documents. I meanwhile tried to understand what exactly he had in mind, and what details he might be interested in. I was left in silence long enough that I started nodding off. But suddenly, the telephone on the investigator's table rang and I nearly jumped in surprise. The officer took the telephone, silently listened to a message, then lowered the receiver.

"They've just finished decrypting all of your accounting, and the list of prizewinners and totals from all the past tournaments," he shared, not hiding his self-satisfaction. "Now, all the players can be punished. Some will be expelled, if they're already struggling. The rest will be given a quick kick in the ass to put them back on the straight and narrow. But as for you..." the man stopped sharply, setting a few pieces of paper out before him. He gave a whistle of surprise, underlined something with a pen, then raised his eyes. "Based on the finance reports, Kirill, you played in fifty-three online tournaments. Twenty-seven of them you won, and you ranked high enough to get some money in all the rest. Is that right?"

"Yes, yes it is," I said, not trying to worm my way out of it. "I only fell below prize level in two tournaments. In the rest, I got at least some reward. Although what does that matter now...?"

However, based on the noticeable change in his behavior, my results were important for some reason. The investigator carefully placed all the papers on the table in a plastic folder, covered it and leaned in my direction.

"Strange as it may seem, it really does matter. Just yesterday, we got a very unusual request from the tip-top: compile a list of inveterate gaming addicts from Moscow's student population and send that up the chain. Luckily, we happened to find all the information we needed on your game server."

"Who might want a list of student gamers?"

The mustached officer shrugged and sat back in his chair.

"I only know what I'm told. Some institute in the Moscow District working on virtual reality wants a few experienced gamers to test their programs. I don't know how many vacancies they've got and I don't know the exact conditions but, for you, this is a great alternative to prison clothes or army boots. So think, Kirill. Such a chance doesn't come along very often. You can avoid punishment and get a good job instead. Just think fast. This loophole won't stay open forever."

I considered it feverishly. Work for a bit in an institute in the Moscow District while all this brouhaha settles down? It sounded amazing! Even if the salary was modest, that didn't matter now. What was more, apparently, they weren't going to confiscate the money I'd won, because all my debit cards were still in my wallet. So that meant I had some savings to live on.

"What's to think about? I'm in!" I loudly declared. "Where do I sign?"

Chapter Three

Comrades in Misfortune

I WAS AWOKEN by a girl shouting angrily in surprise.

"So the freaking contract with the institute is for two years?!" the girl moaned, nearly in hysterics.

I peeked open an eye and... finally woke up. I was in an unfamiliar place, a dark room, filled with bags of cement and old furniture. It took me a few seconds to get my bearings and remember where I was. Some hangar or warehouse I'd been brought to directly from the police department in a vehicle with blacked-out windows. To be honest, I couldn't say how long the drive was or which direction it went, because I fell asleep as soon as I hit the seat. I only remembered being pushed out, led into this room and told to "wait for the rest of the group."

My body was aching and numb. I'd fallen asleep in an unmerciful pose on the hard and uncomfortable bench, which was like those usually found in bus-station waiting rooms. The kind with armrests between the seats so bums couldn't spend the night on them. But today, I was so tired I somehow contrived to splay out my extremities and lie down. But when I tried to move, I felt a sharp pain in my numb leg.

"Well, well. The yogi awakens!" someone quipped, which was met with laughter.

I somehow got out of the trap, straightened up and turned to see who else was in the room. Three young men and two young women, the whole group approximately my age. Were they also expelled gamers, taken to work at the mysterious institute?

Maybe, but one of the girls didn't fit the image. She immediately caught my attention. A flashy long-legged blonde with a pretty doll-like face, she had a

mind-blowingly perfect figure and... a clever attentive gaze that immediately undercut the rest and betrayed a high intellect. She had on a stylish travelling dress and shoes, a designer bag and expensive emerald earrings. This elegant beauty didn't look like the kind of person who needed virtual worlds to replace reality.

The other girl, in contrast, was totally unremarkable: short, dark-haired and modestly dressed with a pair of thick glasses perched on her nose, something of a classic plain jane.

"Hey everybody!" I greeted them all with a smile. "Did I miss anything interesting? I heard someone mention a two-year contract?"

"Yeah, Artur," the plain jane pointed at a long-haired hippy-looking boy with a ring in his left ear. "He said that, in his dean's office, he was presented with a two-year contract."

"Yep, totally!" the hippy confirmed. He was dressed in tattered jeans and a black t-shirt with a Pink Floyd logo. "I got expelled today. I was already in my third year! It's a long story, but they had their reasons. I tried to fight it, though, and even wrote a statement to the dean like, I'd learned my lesson and wouldn't do it again bla bla bla... But that asshole said I have to prove I meant it, and work on a special assignment in a paramilitary institute in Moscow. He said they'd reinstate me after I'm done. And he made me sign a contract that said 'two years' in black and white."

Artur finished his speech, lowered his head and fell silent. The others were also silent and looking unabashedly at me.

"What about you? Expelled student, like the rest of us?" asked a squatting boy. His hair cut short, this was the most *gopnik*-looking person imaginable[1]. He was wearing a black leather jacket, track pants, running shoes with no socks, and a newsboy cap. To complete the picture of the

---

[1] Gopnik: in Russia, a street thug or a young low-class criminal

classic low-class Russian, all he'd need was a black eye and a crumpled Belomorkanal cigarette in his mouth.

I had nothing to hide, so I told them my real name and said I had been expelled from the Geology Department of Moscow State University because, instead of studying, I had been playing an online game for money.

"Just like the rest of us," the plain jane chuckled bitterly. "While you were asleep, we all introduced ourselves and figured out that we were all in the same online tournament. What was more, we'd all gotten to the final. Worst of all, I almost won the last round with my archer. I was one of the final four surviving players. I had a stroke of bad luck. I missed a few times and a fighter shredded me..."

"You should have shot at the ogre's legs and walked backward so he couldn't get you," I said, giving some belated advice. The girl exclaimed in astonishment:

"So that was you, Kirill?! It was your ogre that killed me? You won the final! You probably got a ton of money, come clean!"

"Hmm, how the..." I got embarrassed and lowered my gaze to the floor. "Sure, I won, but I didn't get a bean. As soon as I took the helmet off my head, the cops had me in cuffs. I didn't even get up from my comp."

Here, a previously silent muscular boy who looked to be from the Caucasus region cut into our conversation. Until then, he had been trying fruitlessly to get his cell phone to work.

"As for the tournament, I'm telling you — it was the

organizers that called the cops! After all, only they knew all the players IP-addresses. And they gave us all up to the fuzz so they wouldn't have to pay out. They just pocketed all the money, the sons of bitches!"

Everyone there held the same opinion. Curses and abuse flew at the tournament organizers. And I complained loudest of all so no one would suspect me of having a connection to the mysterious conmen. Finally, everyone had said their fill and fell silent. I took advantage of the pause and asked everybody to introduce themselves again.

The blonde said she was Anya from First Medical. She didn't regret being expelled at all, because she couldn't bear the sight of blood, and it was all her parents' stupid idea to push her into medicine in the first place. The second girl was called Masha and, skipping over the details, said she was a grad student at a technical university in Moscow, and was also glad to be out of school. For her, it was a prolonged torture with constant lack of money, and humiliating begging for stipends and dorm rooms.

The gopnik grudgingly squeezed out that his name was Denis, and that we "don't need to know the rest, because that's all in the past." The last guy was more open, though. He said his first name was Imran and that he was a SAMBO expert[2]. Imran had graduated last year from the Athletics Institute at the top of his class but was in no rush to return to his native Dagestan, continuing to live by hook or

---

[2] SAMBO (a Russian acronym for "weaponless self-defense") is a Russian martial art developed in the early 1920s.

crook with his friends in the dorm as he waited for his golden ticket.

"Some friends promised good work in Moscow, but something happened," he said, getting into the details of his failed plan.

Imran spent another minute poking around with his phone, then stuck it back in his pocket, saying:

"Can't connect to the network, the stupid thing! It's probably this damn steel roof."

"That is part of it," came a derisive voice from the darkness. "But this is a military site, so there are also signal jammers."

Along with the rest, I turned to the voice and saw a middle-aged strong-looking man in a dark-blue uniform jumpsuit. On his sleeve, there was an unusual colorful emblem with a gold Greek helmet inside a white circle. Under that was a crest and cursive writing that read "Second Legion." He didn't seem to be armed, but his military bearing and army experience were immediately apparent.

Without letting us think over what he said, the man motioned into the dark depths of the hangar:

"Walk that way, into the darkness. In the very corner, you'll see a stack of roofing tiles. Move them aside and go down the stairs beneath them. Go down into the tunnel and walk until you've reached the dome. The other newbie groups are already here. The intro session will begin shortly. The meeting hall in the dome is not very big, so make sure you hurry. The presentation lasts a few hours, and latecomers have to stand."

We quickly found the tiles. It was a stack of twenty, and they were absolutely immovable. But a light push launched a hidden mechanism and the whole stack slid aside. There was a round hatch underneath, and when we opened there were metal rungs leading down into the darkness. Imran went down first and soon shouted that he'd found a switch on the wall. A second later, a light turned on below, and everyone could see that it was actually quite a short ladder.

But the tunnel, lit sparsely by dull bulbs, seemed endless. We walked for a long time past unadorned gray concrete walls, looking at the pipes and bundles of wire along the floor. A few times, our group's path was blocked by metal doors, but they opened silently as soon as we walked up to them. Despite myself, I was impressed at how sturdy the doors were. Each was ten inches thick at least, if not twelve and made of strong hard metal. Finally, after yet another door, we discovered a ladder up.

I blinked, getting used to the bright light in the small room. A beefy guardsman standing next to a metallic frame, again in a blue Second Legion uniform told us to place our documents, phones, wallets, keys and other objects on the table.

"You won't be needing those for a long time," he

assured us. His partner, standing not far away, gave a chuckle.

Anya from First Medical was standing at the front of the line. She blushed an unexpectedly deep shade of red and spent a long time hesitating about whether to demonstrate the contents of her bag with everyone around. I had no idea what could be so compromising, and I didn't find out, because the guards asked us to walk away and spare her the embarrassment.

But then came my turn, and I also was forced to shake out my pockets. My government ID card, my now invalid student ID, a handful of change, an unopened pack of condoms and keys to my now former dorm room. After that was my wallet with the debit cards that gave access to all my savings... I was made to walk through a metal detector, then quickly and professionally searched. After that, sure that I hadn't hidden anything, the guard returned only the pack of condoms. The rest he placed in a large transparent \ bag and sealed it with a special device.

"I don't even know if that's a good sign or a bad one," Denis commented spitefully on the selective return of my property. After me, it was his turn.

"Don't hold up the line, keep moving into the dome! Remember, your number is one thousand four hundred seventy!" the military man hurried me along, attaching a numbered label to my bag.

Before that, plain-jane Masha had received 1469, while hippie Artur was 1468. So, the numbers went in order.

That meant almost fifteen hundred people worked in this mysterious "dome." The scope was impressive. This must be a very, very serious project!

The guardsman stuck my bag through a little window in the wall and someone immediately grabbed it. Then I walked down the corridor, repeating my number to myself and trying to memorize it: "One thousand four hundred seventy!"

Chapter Four

Subterranean Dome

I HAD HEARD the word "dome" a few times, but I wasn't expecting it to be this large. Just as its the name implied, it was a reinforced concrete hemisphere, but of truly unbelievable dimensions. The diameter at floor level was no less than a quarter mile. The far wall was blurry and lost in a blue-gray haze. The top was about a hundred, and maybe even a hundred and sixty feet high. A vast number of bright spotlights high above our heads created the illusion of a midday summer sun. Under this Dome, there was a little residential neighborhood with apartment buildings, a soccer field, a few tennis courts, a green park and white sand paths.

"Woah, I had no idea there was anything this huge in the Moscow Oblast," said Artur, also impressed.

"And it isn't even all that far from Moscow. Our drive

from downtown took only an hour," Masha added. "Although there are some big hangars along Dmitrovskoye Highway, they are many times smaller than this..."

"Guys, look!" Anya shouted, pointing at a silver cigar-shaped object flying just under the ceiling.

I turned my head and first took the aircraft for a helicopter. However, its strange sleek shape, lack of rotors and total silence showed that it was unlike any flying vehicle I'd ever seen before.

"Is this some kind of joke?!" We exchanged glances in complete incomprehension.

After hearing our surprised exclamations, a blonde in a silver track suit, her skin red from an evening run, stopped next to our group.

"Newbies? It's obvious. They're testing an antigrav built with Miyelonian designs. It's actually the second prototype. A bad pilot crashed the first one a month ago on one of the corncobs."

"Ah, that clears things up. Of course, it's just a normal, everyday antigrav. We should have known!" Denis answered, clearly trying to get a rise out of her. "We see this stuff every day. And no duh it slammed into a piece of corn!"

The girl didn't answer, just sized-up the boor with her gaze, furrowed her brow contemptuously and continued her jog. Her uniform had the number 343 on the back, alongside the skull of a bull with large horns. Below that, in angular Gothic script, there was text reading: "First Legion."

"Based on her number, she's been under this dome

for a long time," I said thoughtfully, advising the gopnik not to start a fight with the locals.

In reply, he swore rudely and said not to try and teach him any lessons. After that, Denis went off the handle and started discussing the body of the athlete in totally vulgar and insulting terms. Then, he began to generalize about all women. He didn't manage to finish, though, doubling over after taking a sharp jab to the gut from Imran, who was standing next to him:

"Don't you dare insult women around me! You have a mother, I have a mother. Everyone has a mother. You must be respectful to those who blessed us with the gift of life."

The conflict didn't continue, although the gopnik spent some time whispering unintelligible threats. We walked down the sand path and stopped at a fork next to a sign with directions. It had three arrows:

Shooting range. Corn. Labyrinth.

There was no sign of a conference hall, meeting room or introductory information session, so we stopped. Fortunately, I spotted two guys playing tennis not far away and hurried to ask them the way. They answered me eagerly and, in a few minutes, our whole group had taken their seats in a small semi-circular room reminiscent of an enclosed summer movie theater. There were already fifty people there and, although there were seats for everyone, we were nearly late. A man tall enough to play basketball wearing an austere business suit was testing the microphone, preparing for his speech.

"Greetings, I am Ivan Lozovsky, deputy director of the Dome and our faction's diplomat," he introduced himself and asked for the light to be turned off.

Then the room went dark, and the screen behind him lit up. There was an anthropomorphic creature looking back at us from the screen with thick brown fur and wearing a bright crimson cloak over a suit of metal armor. It had powerful brow arches, a broad forehead, black eyes with no pupils, a wide nose and a massive chin. Its furry ears were pressed against its head and its tightly pursed lips had the protruding fangs of a predator. Both of the humanoid's hands were gripping the handle of a wide glistening blade.

"So then, newbies, I'll start from the beginning. Before you is Krong Daveyesh-Pir. He is one of the rulers of the powerful space-faring Geckho race, and the all-powerful sovereign of expansive territories in our galaxy. Among those territories, by all interstellar laws, is our home planet of Earth. I understand that may sound unbelievable and shocking, but the fate of humanity is entirely in the hands of this creature. Let me clarify one thing: the Geckho are not our enemies. They're more like our protectors and mentors. In any conflict with another race, they will fight on our side. However, you must always keep in mind that Krong Daveyesh-Pir has the right and power to remove humanity from Earth and even entirely annihilate our civilization if we express the slightest disrespect of or disobedience to our Geckho suzerains."

In the room, not only did all conversations go quiet,

everyone was so shocked they started to skip breaths. The presenter then made a brief pause and made sure that everyone understood the importance of what he'd said, then continued:

"Now that we all understand our political reality, let's discuss why you were all brought here: the Dome, the game the bends reality, and your role in all this."

I was probably the only person in the room seeing the fifty-second clip of the furry alien for the first time. I remembered hearing about it annoying internet users the world over last year, but it just so happened to come at a difficult period in my studies. I had recently fallen in love for the first time, lost interest in school and gotten three failing grades. I was on the edge of expulsion so, I spent days on end in the library, studying textbooks, writing summaries and preparing painstakingly for my tests and exams.

But, like millions of people the world over, if I had seen this clip last year, I most likely would not have believed it was the First Contact, either. Now, however, after Ivan Lozovsky's message about our shaky position, I watched the video with rapt attention. One Tong of safety, how long was that? I was not ashamed to stand and ask the presenter.

"Excellent, very good question!" the diplomat answered, inspired. "We studied the Geckho race's time reckoning system a while ago, and a Tong is approximately three and a half years. But there are two unclear aspects. First of all, we know that, on the Geckho homeworld Shiharsa, time passes more quickly than on Earth, so a Tong there would be somewhat shorter than it would be here. Six percent shorter, and that is no more and no less than two months and seventeen days. Second, we still haven't received an answer about when the countdown began. The clips of the Geckho messengers were broadcast for twenty-three days and, each time, they gave the very same one Tong. Some even believe the countdown started, not when the information was first broadcast, but when the first virtual reality pod was built on Earth and the first human entered the game that bends reality."

"Virtual reality pod?" asked four-eyed kid, his interest piqued by the odd term.

"Yes, that's right, a virtual reality pod. The blueprints at the end of the clips show the general design of virtual reality pods, and how to assemble them. Each diagram is a different element, but it's all fairly logical and fits together. The first one was assembled in South Korea one year and seven months ago. The first person to enter the virtual world was named Kim In-Hun, a young engineer from a South Korean electronics company. He was also the first person to successfully pass the Labyrinth. Fortunately, he had the good sense not to stray far from where he entered and left to tell the authorities what he'd found. Soon, another few researchers entered the game, then a whole group of thirty

Korean soldiers. A month after that, our military intelligence discovered a construction project near the city of Yeongju, a subterranean complex called Nop-Eun Ogsusu, which in translation from Korean means 'tall corn.' Very soon, we also built a couple of virt pods and we started construction on the subterranean Dome base in the Moscow Oblast, which is where we are now located..."

"You mentioned a labyrinth. What was that about?" the nerd interrupted the presenter again.

The diplomat gave a dissatisfied cringe, but still answered:

"Yes, after creating a character, every newbie appears in the center of the Labyrinth. It's supposed to help you get used to the virtual body, train your skills, and test your aptitude. If a new player gets out of the labyrinth within a certain time limit, they will earn extra stat points. It's a very rare chance to strengthen your basic attributes. Other than that, you can basically only level them by training. For that very reason, we have an exact copy of the Labyrinth next to the administration building, and you must learn it by heart before entering the game. Approximately half an hour is given to exit the labyrinth. You must learn to finish it in fifteen minutes. Only after that will you be allowed into a virtual reality pod. Then, when you finish the labyrinth, you are not to spend any stat points. You must take down all your parameters and exit the game. Our experienced mentors will look that over and tell you what skills to take to play effectively and what statistics to reinforce with your unused points."

"And what about this 'corn?'" Our four-eyed colleague just wouldn't shut up, even though some in the hall had begun to hiss at him.

The diplomat finally changed to the next slide and, instead of the furry face of our alien master, we saw a tall cylindrical building that looked quite a bit like a corncob.

"The corn question is the last one I'll answer right now. If you want to know anything else, ask after my speech, otherwise we'll never finish," Ivan Lozovsky said unhappily. "So, the corn and its purpose... One lone virtual reality pod can be placed anywhere, and it will work, drawing energy from the gravitational and electromagnetic fields of our planet. But with multiple pods, it's much more complex. We now have hundreds and must arrange for them to work in concert. After all, a newbie merely entering the game isn't enough. They must appear precisely in the right place and be correctly identified by the system as a member of our faction..."

The diplomat took a quick break and splashed some mineral water into a cup. In fact, due to the number of people in the room, it was getting quite hot, and I could stand to wet my whistle as well. He took a few gulps, then continued:

"By the way, our faction is called Human-3, or H3 for short. That abbreviation will always be shown on your equipment, and it cannot be removed or erased. The Koreans are H0, which means we were the fourth human faction to enter the game that bends reality. Returning to the corn... This arrangement of virtual reality pods was taught to us by the Geckho. It is a tall structure with a central core and separate kernels for each pod. In theory, the height of a 'corncob' is unlimited. But in the Dome, we started with one hundred pods per cob, which results in a twenty-story structure. So, your group will be working in corncob number fifteen. It is ready now. We're working on number sixteen already but getting another hundred people to join our faction is going to take quite some doing!"

I perked up my ears, preparing to listen to the important information about our player limit the difficulties connected with it, but the diplomat's speech was interrupted by the deafening wail of a siren. The sound, which was shrill and rattled my bones, reminded me of an air-raid drill. My ears started twitching, then shivers ran over my whole body. After that, a voice thundered out, filling the Dome:

"ATTENTION, THIS IS THE DOME DIRECTOR. BORDER POST FOUR IS UNDER ATTACK! THE DARK FACTION HAS INTRUDED THROUGH A FOGGY PASS! MORE THAN FOUR HUNDRED ATTACKERS! FIVE ENEMY TOP PLAYERS HAVE BEEN SPOTTED! TO ARMS!!!"

Chapter Five

Entering the Game

AND AT THAT, intro session was put on hold. Ivan Lozovsky said he was not only a diplomat, but also a high-level player, and that it was of vital importance that everyone who could hold a gun went to the front lines. So, the diplomat rescheduled the rest of his two-hour speech to seven AM the next day.

There were lots of questions being asked, some about the Dark Faction, others about how many border posts we had, and some even more general about the overall situation. But Ivan Lozovsky didn't answer of them. Instead, already in the doorway, he turned and told us to head to the residential area and get situated in our dorms, then go to the cafeteria and eat dinner, familiarize ourselves with the daily schedule and rules of the Dome and get some rest. Starting early morning the next day, we were to return for the rest of this presentation, then study the Labyrinth and generate our characters before we finally entered the game that bends reality.

We left the meeting room. The siren was wailing everywhere. Many people were running in the same direction.

"Looks like it's serious. Maybe we should go help?" I suggested but didn't find any support.

They all made excuses, saying we'd been given clear instructions on what to do this evening, and no one wanted to break the presumably strict rules on their first day. I took a heavy sigh and walked off after the others. The path to the dorms passed between the corncobs, and I finally saw the tall buildings with my own eyes. To say I was astonished wouldn't even begin to cover it! They were cylindrical columns two hundred and thirty feet tall, with spiral staircases looping around the outside. The glass kernels protruded from the sides and each housed a metallic germ. Clearly, these were the virtual reality pods.

"Hey, there's ours, number fifteen!" Masha said, pointing at one of the corncobs.

I stopped and, pointing my head up, looked at my future workplace. The height was intimidating. We'd have to go up those stairs day in and day out. Good thing I wasn't afraid of heights, otherwise I had no idea if I'd make it.

Other than the big easily visible number fifteen on a concrete post at the entrance, there were player numbers from 1401 to 1500 inside. I also noticed people rushing into every tower except that one. In a rush to their pods, they were pouring into their corncobs. I looked at number fifteen again. Strange. There were no guards at the entrance. What could stop us...?

I wanted to tell my new acquaintances but discovered that they were already quite a ways down the white sand path. I was all on my own. What if...?

I trusted my intuition. It had practically never led me astray. So now, as with the spontaneous character change in the final round of the online PvP tournament, I could feel in my bones that I needed to learn this new game and not waste any time.

Carefully, expecting someone to shout at me at any second, I headed to tower number fifteen. No one stopped me, and no one even seemed to notice. Now more confident, I started climbing higher and higher up the spiral staircase. Ugh, it was unbearable. Could they really not build an elevator?! By the time I'd reached the eighth story of the tower, my legs started to shiver from the strain. My pod was on the fourteenth floor, though, and when I'd made it up there, I was practically crawling on all fours, with my tongue hanging out in exhaustion. Ugh!

I saw my number 1470 on the wall, and a short corridor leading to a small glassed-in room with a metallic ovular bed in the middle topped by a transparent lid. My virtual reality pod! I stood there, looking at the high-tech device and admiring its smooth flawless curves. The lid easily slid aside as soon as I touched it. The bed, covered with a soft porous material was alluring and called me to lie down as quickly as possible.

Should I take off my shoes? Did I have to get undressed? There were no coatracks in the room, but that didn't mean anything. I looked at the neighboring towers through the transparent glass. In corncob number eleven, right at my level, an unfamiliar lady walked into her little room and, quickly closing the lid, lay down in her pod right in her clothes and shoes. Alright, no need to undress. I carefully stepped onto the springy cover. Alright, it held my weight. I lay down and wanted to stretch my arms for the lid, but it had already started moving on its own. At that, the lid material, which had seemed like glass, became opaque and everything looked totally black. Not like coal, or the color of a raven's wing, but some absolute darkness that didn't reflect any light whatsoever.

"An ideal black!" I thought as the world around me changed.

I found myself in a tiny round room with totally white walls, ceiling and floor. There was just over a step of space on all sides. The source of the dim light was not visible, and it seemed to be streaming in from all directions. The only object other than me and the cold smooth walls, was a large body-length mirror.

Neither glass nor metal, it was some kind of image projected on the wall. Everything I did was reflected in it, but I could turn the image with my mind and see myself from all sides. And I did that, taking a critical look and cringing in dismay.

My hair was far too long. I should have gone to a barber long ago... A moment later, I saw myself in the mirror with a close short cut. Wow! And what if I left it a bit longer, with slanted bangs? The image changed obligingly. And if I change my hair color? No, I don't like that. Let's go back.

I finished playing with my hairstyle and left it a sumptuous shade of black, then moved on to eye color. I wanted emerald green eyes. They were generally considered the rarest! It looked pretty good but didn't go with my hair at all. What about an icy blue? And hey, why not make my eyes glow like a wizard's? It looked fearsome, but I left it that way.

Now for toned muscles. I wanted to be tall, have broad shoulders and all that... I tried to give myself the flawless body of the athlete, so any girl would want me, but I was just a weenie and couldn't change my body composition. In some parts, I could only change the skin tone and remove or add birth marks and scars. Too bad. But alright, what next?

Name: Kirill Viktorovich Ignatiev

The words appeared over my image in the mirror, and I shook my head in dismay. No, that won't do. Anyhow, did I want every random person I met to know my real name?

What if I made someone mad? This would make me too easy to find in the real world.

So... I managed to shorten it to Gnat, but I couldn't remove it all the way. Gnat? That was my nickname in school, so it felt natural. Alright, let it be Gnat. What next?

Available classes: Geologist or Prospector

What the crap?! This was a violation of my rights! Why only two? What if I wanted to be a tank driver, sniper or even starship pilot? I tried to widen the miserly choice in all kinds of ways or go back to a previous menu, but I couldn't do any of it. Only Geologist or Prospector. Dang... So, how were they different?

Geologist. Specializes in discovering and mining valuable minerals, sedimentary deposits and ore veins. As level and skills grow, mineral discovery chance and extraction volume increase.

Primary skills: Minerology, Forager, Explosives.

Class limitations: May not equip heavy or power armor. May not use sniper weapons or rocket systems.

All the information I needed was shown on the mirror above my character. Alright, I see. So then, what made the Prospector different? Instantly, obeying my mental request, the mirror displayed a different text:

Prospector. Specializes in discovering secret locations, anomalies and minerals with electronic scanning devices. As level and skills grow, discovery chance and value are increased.

Primary skills: Electronics, Scanning, Cartography.

Class limitations: May not equip heavy or power armor. May not use sniper rifles or automatic weapons. May not pilot starships or any kind of flying vehicle.

Ugh, dang... the Prospector class had so many limitations! And although I was intrigued by searching for hidden locations and anomalies, being unable to use automatic weapons seemed like a serious handicap. I'd be helpless at sniping range, too. But the Geologist class had similar problems. At medium or close range... I didn't know. I had no idea what kinds of weapons were available in the game. Perhaps there would be something non-automatic, but still totally fine. But maybe not...

I pulled up the information about the Geologist again. Seemingly a more balanced class, and such a path felt right, considering my education and training. I was ready to make my choice, but then my eye caught on the words "mining" and "extraction."

What did that mean? After discovering useful minerals or ore veins, I would be forced to mine them all on my own? My character had a bonus to extraction, so who better? That unhappy perspective threw me. I didn't want to spend the next two years of my life breaking rocks with a pick. I might go mad from boredom...

But the words "secret locations," and "anomalies," on the other hand, were tempting to any gambling man. The Prospector path also seemed to promise other interesting aspects. So, I made up my mind.

The mirror went dim, then I saw a table:

Gnat. Human. H3 Faction.	
Level-1 Prospector	
Statistics:	
Strength	12
Agility	15
Intelligence	17
Perception	19
Constitution	10
Luck modifier	+2
Parameters:	
Hit points	176
Endurance points	114
Magic points	0
Carrying capacity	53
lbs.	
Fame	0
Skills:	
Electronics	1
Scanning	1
Cartography	1

I read it carefully. It was hard to say if it was good or bad, although the low Constitution did upset me. Just ten points. And also, having zero magic seemed less than ideal. It wasn't that I was expecting spell-casting abilities from a Prospector, more like the opposite. But seeing that part of the table meant magic did exist! And if that was the case, my level-1 Prospector had lower magic than someone else.

Anyway, I could read short hints on all the statistics. For example, Strength influenced the amount of weight a character could carry, how far they could throw objects, and damage done by melee weapons. The number of health points, meanwhile, depended on Constitution, level and a class multiplier. About magic, it said that the amount of "mana" depended on Intelligence, level and game-class coefficient. Clearly, the Prospector simply had a zero there.

Overall, I didn't discover anything new. All my character's statistics were as usual, more or less like I'd seen in other games. All I didn't understand was "fame." How was it calculated, and what were its effects? Either it was some kind of "karma," a positive or negative number depending on previous actions, or a modifier that influenced the reaction of other characters in the game world. After all, it's one thing when you're asked a favor by a totally unknown person and, you couldn't care less if they are offended by your refusal. But it's quite different, if the very same thing is asked by a famous figure, respected by all.

I quickly realized I couldn't edit any parameters in the table, and I would have to accept what the game system gave me. The only prompt asked whether I was familiar with the introductory information and ready to enter the game world or would prefer to wait and think.

The right thing to do would be to leave the virtual reality pod, wait until tomorrow, listen to the two-hour introduction, then study the Labyrinth, and pick up from here. But it's so hard to tear yourself from a new toy!

I understood that as soon as I gave my confirmation, I would be dropped into some labyrinth made to test my abilities. I had a perfect idea of how mad the leadership would be if I failed the test and lost the chance to strengthen myself. On the other hand, I wasn't a child. This wasn't my first time in a videogame. I already understood how to move and orient myself. I was a fairly experienced gamer and had seen the darkest depths of many game worlds. I mean, come on, this labyrinth was made for newbies. With all by abilities and experience, how could I fail?!

So, concentrating and wishing myself luck, I confirmed that I was ready for the test.

Chapter Six

Testing by Labyrinth

THE PICTURE CHANGED instantly. The mirror disappeared, and a semi-circular gap in the wall replaced it. It was filled with a glowing blue force field that periodically glistened with sparkles and electricity. And then, one after the other, I saw little bars of different colors. One for life, one for endurance and another for hunger. When each bar appeared, a popup hint appeared before my eyes with a notification, so I had no misunderstandings or questions about the new features.

I turned my head, but the semi-transparent bars remained in the upper left part of my field of vision as if glued there. They didn't obstruct my view or annoy me, though. All the scales were at maximum, and I nodded in approval, speaking aloud for an unknown moderator:

"I understand, no questions. Except one. What am I supposed to do, go through that force field? Is the electricity gonna shock me?!"

Predictably, I didn't receive an answer, but a small icon appeared at the bottom of the screen showing several concentric circles, like ripples left by a stone in a calm pond.

Scanning. Class ability. With skill growth, scanning radius and discovery chances will increase, type of results will expand, and reload time will decrease.

Well, well! What is this? I use echolocation like a bat? But what about the electronic scanning devices mentioned by the class description? I was somewhat confused, especially because I was unable to test my new ability. The little icon remained inactive.

Meanwhile, my introduction to the game abilities continued. A progress bar appeared at the bottom of the screen.

Using skills and performing other actions fills the progress bar. When the bar is completely full, character level will increase. Dying zeroes out the progress bar.

ATTENTION!!! If the progress bar is at zero, dying will cause your character to lose one level, some skills and all unused skill points. Dying again with progress bar still at zero will cause your character to lose two levels and even more skills.

Now that was very important information. First, dying in the game was entirely possible, and it was not final. Beyond that, if the progress bar was even a bit filled, death wouldn't cause any serious or irreversible consequences. However, death with an empty progress bar came with a hefty penalty.

By the way... I looked at the empty bar and my level-one character. What did that mean? If I were to die right now... was there a level zero? Or would I just die once and for all? I started feeling a bit beside myself. I suddenly didn't want to go through the force field and test this out.

Meanwhile, Gnat's inventory opened. A jean jacket and jeans, a turtleneck, a pair of tennis shoes, and underwear. The items of clothing were in their equipment slots and had almost no properties, just +1 armor from my jean jacket, but it was half worn down. Most of the boxes were still empty. No headwear, my belt slot was inactive, no weapon, either main or secondary, no gloves, glasses, bracelets or rings. In my so-called "backpack" there were just six slots, one of which was occupied by a pack of condoms...

Great equipment for a test. No compass, no coil of rope, no set of colored chalk to mark dead ends or turns I'd already been down. Not even a basic flashlight if it got dark or the most primitive knife. I sharply came to my senses and was astonished by my recklessness. What had come over me? Why sneak unprepared into a place I knew nothing about?!

A wave of fear swept over me, replacing my rash self-confidence. I had already nearly made up my mind to try and open the virtual reality pod, but the glowing force-field flickered, went dim and turned off. Just then, a countdown timer appeared in the lower part of the screen. I was given thirty minutes to get out of the labyrinth...

Naturally, I was no longer thinking of exiting the game. Onward! I had nearly walked through the doorway when the scanning icon changed color from gray to violet. I could use my skill! I immediately turned around to see how the gap looked from the other side. But the wall behind my back was totally smooth and stable, without the slightest sign of gaps or holes. A one-way portal! Dang! There was no way back. Now I could only look for the way out.

Anyhow, there was plenty of diffused light coming from the walls, so I wouldn't need a flashlight. But where to go? I could only see smooth white walls everywhere. About ten feet above me, there was a solid ceiling. Perfect time to try out scanning.

I didn't know if it was the scan, but a map of the corridors suddenly appeared at the bottom of my screen, showing a ring labyrinth. And what was more it wasn't only the parts I could see with my own eyes. It also showed behind the walls. Nice! So that's what scanning could do!

But the reload time was a whole ten minutes, and the draw distance on the map was not very large, just fifteen steps or so. I could only see a couple of rings of wall, gaps and forks. However, it was valuable to know that the labyrinth was circular, and that I was in its very center.

Just thirty seconds later, basing myself on the map, I ran down the only corridor leading outward, leaving the revealed part, then stopped at a fork. Right or left? I turned left at random and ran along the wall, as is usually advised for those trying to escape small mazes. Following one wall was a reliable, though fairly slow way of finding an exit. But I guessed that this labyrinth was not large, as it was designed to test the abilities of new players. So sooner or later, this method would lead me out. It was also important to walk quickly so I would exit the labyrinth in the time allotted. What was more, I immediately noticed that, as I moved through the labyrinth, the map grew larger. This was child's play! I couldn't even get lost!

Wait... four minutes after starting, I reached a small round room with a ramp down and a ramp up alongside three other doors. My confidence blew away like the wind. The main difference between multi-story labyrinths and one-level ones, other than their greater complexity, was that following one wall no longer guaranteed exit. What was more, this meant there must have been much more ground to cover than my extremely slow method could handle. I needed to change tactics.

I expanded the map to the whole screen to get my bearings. No hint had told me how to open the map, but it happened automatically, and that surprised me. So, had I gone far from the center of the labyrinth?

Just one look at the interactive map and I began to

howl in impotent rage — all the sections I had already been through were gradually disappearing! The center was already entirely erased, and the other corridors were also going away. So, I had an approximation of how long the map would last: three minutes. Just what I needed! How could I get my bearings in this multi-level labyrinth?!

Leave marks or objects at the forks so I wouldn't duck into a dead end multiple times? Sure, that was an option. I took out the pack of condoms from my inventory, ripped a small piece of colored cardboard from it and threw it down the hallway behind me. It was meant to mark places I didn't need to go again. I didn't delve into the upper and lower floor yet and continued running through the maze.

My endurance points were gradually falling, and I was starting to get tired from so much running. Another five minutes, maybe six and I'd have to change to a walk. In this indefinite nerve-wracking situation, the only good part was that my progress bar was filling up slowly but surely. So, even if my Prospector managed to die in the labyrinth, my character would respawn.

My scanning icon turned purple again. I immediately made a scan and looked at the map. Another circle thirty steps in diameter, including part of the room with ramps I had run through. What was more, based on the map, I would end up back there soon. I'd chosen the wrong hallway. So, a minute later, there were two corridors marked with a piece of torn-off cardboard.

Just one unchecked corridor remained on this level,

but I decided to go up it. I was now running totally at random, ignoring some forks and diving down others. A few times, I saw holes in the floor, which I had to jump across, and another time I had to crawl through a small section of corridor with a low ceiling. Then suddenly... I was in a circular ramp room. What was more, some hallways were already marked with cardboard! How?! I had gone up already!

But there was no time to fill my head with such questions. I was already down to less than ten minutes. I went down a floor and was no longer running so much as keeping up a fast walk with short bursts — my endurance was hovering around zero.

One more scan...

And then, when I had almost no hope left, I saw the outer edge of the maze on the map! The circle of halls and walls just ended on one side! I also noticed a marker on an internal wall very near me. I hadn't seen anything like it before. I got my bearings and turned toward it, then found an unusual section of cracked wall. Probably, this wall was weak, and could be broken...

But what was the point of breaking through if I had already seen on the map that I could also go the normal way?! I didn't break the wall, just ran to the outermost hallway. Perhaps the exit was somewhere there.

Unfortunately, I didn't find an exit in that section. All paths led back to the center of the maze. But I did discover something else — a part of the outer wall with cracks! If I broke the wall here, I'd be outside the maze!

After breaking a hole in the wall, I emerged into a dark void. There were just six seconds left on the timer. I fell painfully face-down from a decent height onto sand, which knocked the wind out of me and made my nose bleed. My clothes were all dusty, my knuckles were bloody, and both of my tennis shoes were now tattered and untied. My health bar was balancing somewhere around thirty percent, while my endurance had been at zero for some time. But I'd made it!

Five stat points received
Scanning skill increased to level two!
Cartography skill increased to level two!
Fame increased to 1.

"Strange way of leaving the maze. I see Leng Radugin finally followed our sage advice and stopped giving his recruits information about the Labyrinth."

This was said just a step from me, and with a strange and entirely unfamiliar accent. The voice was dull, quiet and too distant, as if it belonged to someone who didn't care what happened to me.

Writhing in pain, I raised my head... and found myself gazing at a pair of worn metallic boots about size twenty five if not thirty.

Kosta Dykhsh Geckho. Clan Waideh-Dykhsh. Level-56 Diplomat

An alien! I couldn't afford to give an impression of

weakness and worthlessness. It might reflect badly on the whole human race. I gathered my strength and got to my feet, though I was still stumbling around after the fall. The huge furry humanoid towered over me by two heads, carefully looking with his piercingly black eyes and tusked grin, as I tried to stand upright. He had the very same metal armor as the extraterrestrial from the video clip. And perhaps, this was Kosta Dykhsh.

I bowed respectfully, hoping it would look like a gesture of deep respect, and not an inability to stand.

"Greetings! My respect to the great and powerful civilization of Shiharsa!"

In response, the diplomat made a cough or laugh. It was like a muted bark through tightly clenched teeth.

"I see, Gnat, that you were told about my race. But stop trying to express reverence. It doesn't come across as sincere. But I want to know, did you pass the labyrinth test?"

"It was hard and, I seemingly had an unusual method, but I think so," I smiled with my bloodied lips. "I got five points to improve my statistics."

"Five? Excellent result. That means you didn't know about the maze. Usually, the Leng of your faction prefers not to risk it. One in the hand is better than two in the bush. His words. Recruits learn the way through the labyrinth by rote before entering the game. Sure, they get just two points, but that's guaranteed. I'm glad your commanders have allowed newbies to risk it and test their mettle."

I got embarrassed and lowered my gaze.

"Yes, well, no one said I was allowed. Everyone was busy because of the Dark Faction attack, and I just walked in."

"I was a bit perplexed by your outfit," the humanoid shook his head in reproach like a person. "Oh, your bosses are gonna give it to you tomorrow. What do your people say...? Ah! You'll get knocked into next week!"

"How do you know? I passed the test! No one judges the victors!"

But Kosta Dykhsh was certain my punishment was inevitable. As it turned out, the problem was not only my badly-considered risk. The diplomat told me that, when newbies first enter the game that bends reality, their inventory contains everything they had on them in the real world. It was the only way to bring the things we needed to survive and grow the colony into the game.

Dielectrics and superconductors. Circuit boards and processors. Batteries and molybdenum steel springs. Machine parts and rare materials such as lanthanoid alloys or transuranium elements. Every newbie was supposed to carry useful cargo for the needs of the colony. Everything we couldn't produce or didn't have the resources for. Plus, thermal lenses, optical and collimator sights, hard-to-produce bullets and detonators, and personal weapons...

The more the diplomat told me, the gloomier I became.

First of all, I no longer hoped I might not get chewed out. Now at the very least because I hadn't brought any useful things and had thus disadvantaged our whole faction.

Second, what was I supposed to equip myself with? Just keep running in this ragged jean jacket and torn tennis shoes?

Chapter Seven

First Night

I COULD NO LONGER see the maze. There was just sand, the odd short bush and the somewhat distant treetops of a tall dense forest before the crimson horizon. I shouted in surprise that the Labyrinth was gone, and Kosta Dykhsh explained that the mysterious structure appeared only at the very beginning of the game, was not part of the main world, and was impossible to return to. The Geckho diplomat told me he had been standing on the doorstep of his home and listening to the far-off battle when I just popped into the air ten feet up and splatted into the earth ten steps from his dwelling.

I had already seen the hemispheric metallic structure nearby. It looked like a tent or small yurt, with a dull greenish light emanating from it. It was giving off the tempting aroma of roast meat and aromatic spices. But only after the diplomat reminded me did I also notice the distant flashes on the dark horizon and strange crackling sound.

"The enemies are attacking your main base," the diplomat explained, yawning carelessly and demonstrating his large sharp predatory teeth. "They already managed to get through to the second row of fortifications. I don't remember them ever getting this far before."

"Shouldn't the Geckho be supporting us?" I asked hopefully, which made him truly surprised.

"Whatever for? Both you and your opponents, as well as all other factions on this planet are vassals of the Geckho race. We do not intervene in your internal struggles. We merely trade with all and take our tribute. If your world is attacked by the aggressive Miyelonians, though, or anyone from the Meleyephatian horde decides to found a base here, we will defend you. That is our duty as your suzerains and protectors."

We spent a bit longer standing there, watching the flickers of the far-off battle, then Kosta Dykhsh lost interest and turned around, preparing to return to his tent.

"Tell me, diplomat, are there many races in the cosmos?" I asked somewhat belatedly, and the Geckho stopped.

"There are plenty. And all races are different. They each have their quirks." The diplomat considered such an answer sufficient and was preparing to end the conversation once and for all, but I stopped him again.

"Kosta, how might one learn to speak the language of

your kind?"

The furry giant didn't even try to hide his surprise:

"Gnat, why would you want to do that? You're a Prospector, not a Diplomat or a Translator. You're never gonna have to talk with any Geckho other than me. I know the language of your faction, and that is well enough to communicate."

But those seemed like empty pretexts, and the diplomat was clearly happy to see me expressing interest in his language. So, I answered with a slight bow:

"You are a great space-faring race with a great culture and history. You possess colossal amounts of knowledge in various spheres of science. All that is extremely valuable to me, and humanity as a whole. There are probably a huge number of texts with truly invaluable information for my people, but they cannot be understood without knowing Geckho..."

The furry giant gave a bark of approval and a line of text appeared before me:

Kosta Dykhsh offers you the Astrolinguistics skill. Would you like to take this skill?

Of course! For some reason, I was certain that the Geckho diplomat was nowhere near the only representative of the alien civilization I would meet in the game that bends reality. Understanding their language would be a huge plus!

You have taken the skill Astrolinguistics level 1.

A heavy furry paw came down on my shoulder, which made me somewhat bend at the knee. With a reassuring pat,

Kosta Dykhsh barked in approval:

"Gnat, you're the third person in the whole H3 faction that wanted to study our language. I like that you do unusual things. That's just how the game is played. Don't stay in the confines others make for you. So then... if Leng Radugin and his retinue scold you too much, refer to me. Tell them the Geckho race approves."

After these words, the furry giant wished me a good night and crawled into his tent. I meanwhile blinked in amazement, looking at the lines of text that ran by:

You have reached level two!

You have received three skill points!

Fame increased to 2.

Attention!!! All skill points that have been saved for more than 24 hours will be lost if your character dies.

Well, well! Level two so fast! And I'd met a Geckho diplomat! Now life will get easier!

Walking a bit further from the tent in order not to embarrass the Geckho or disturb his sleep, I sat down on a boulder covered in dry lichen. It was still warm from the daytime sun. I opened my character's stat table and familiarized myself with all the numbers unhurriedly and thoughtfully. I needed to use my stat and skill points to eliminate weak spots and reinforce my strong sides.

Yes, I understood perfectly that newbies were advised against taking this important matter into their own hands and expected to rely on experienced mentors. But in videogames, I preferred to think through my own development plan rather than copying others or taking advice. Also, the Geckho Diplomat had advised me to forge my own path.

Five free points... Very little, if you think about it. Where would they find the greatest use? Above all, I was interested in Constitution — my weakest stat.

A character's Constitution determines the total number of Hit Points and Endurance Points, as well as resistance to disease, poison and radiation. Higher Constitution will speed up healing and decrease bleeding time. Characters with high Constitution can hold their breath for longer, and are also more resistant to corrosion, encumbrance and high gravitation.

Considering how hard it had been for me to finish the newbie Labyrinth, this game must be very difficult and hardcore. There lay a huge number of challenges and dangers before me, and my character's survival would depend on hit points and endurance points, which were derived from Constitution. My pitiful ten points there were not good enough. So, I'd invest two points in Constitution!

My health grew right away to 211, and Endurance to 125. It even felt my lung capacity increase, my ribcage expand, and my turtleneck stretch and rip a bit. Also, the fine abrasions on my hands and face immediately healed over. It was an amazingly pleasant sensation to suddenly feel healthier! It took massive effort, but I resisted the temptation of putting another point or two into Constitution. No, enough. Moderation in all things.

Now, Perception. After all, it was not just the aggregate of vision, hearing and other senses. For my Prospector, it was the most important statistic, as it directly determined the success chance of my scanning. So, I added one point, raising it to twenty. I instantly perceived that change as well. The dusky evening around me became sharper, and the cannonade of the far-off battle was now more distinct.

On to Intelligence. After all, it was not just for mages. My Prospector would have to work with all kinds of electronic scanning devices and other complex high-tech instruments, so Intelligence would certainly come in handy. One more there.

There was just one statistic point left. Increase Strength? It was a good idea. I'd be able to carry more spoils of war. And my muscles would grow visually, which was also a plus. Or should I go for Agility? Or another point in Perception?

But then I realized I was totally ignoring one statistic — Luck Modifier. It could also be improved.

A character's Luck Modifier increases hit chance with any type of ranged weapon, success in gambling and critical damage dealt.

Attention! For the Prospector class, as with any other

class, the Luck Modifier does not increase discovery chance but there is a certain chance the things you find will be of higher value.

It sounded, of course, tempting. But I wished I knew what that chance was, at least approximately. Ten percent or, maybe, just one one-hundredth of a percent? The difference was very, very significant. Was it worth the trouble? By which I meant, was it worth investing in the Luck Modifier?

After a minute of thought, I decided to take the risk and spent my last free point on the Luck Modifier, bringing it to +3.

I finished with the stat points, now onto skills. There were three points to spend here. It was irrational and dangerous to save them up for the future in a game that bends reality. Unlike most games, just one death could burn them up. So, I needed to use them, if not right away, then at the very least within twenty-four hours.

Scanning, as Gnat's main skill, seemed to be the obvious choice. But I could level it simply by periodically activating the icon, which I was already doing every time the skill reloaded. Cartography? That, it seemed, was leveling all on its own...

Probably, it would be wisest to place the points into skills that I didn't yet understand how to level. For example, Electronics or Astrolinguistics.

Electronics skill increased to level two!
Electronics skill increased to level three!

Astrolinguistics skill increased to level two!

Now, with all my points spent, the time had come to go somewhere. I couldn't just sit all night on this stone, after all. I stood up and looked around. It was totally dark. There were bright and unfamiliar stars in the sky. I wasn't such an astronomy enthusiast, but I could find the Big Dipper, Orion's Belt or the North Star in the night sky. But I didn't find anything among the millions of pulsating stars. I also dismissed a thought about the Southern Hemisphere quickly. There was no Southern Cross either. So, I wasn't on Earth...

The warm night wind rustled my hair, thousands of crickets were fiddling frantically, and bats occasionally flitted overhead. If not for the colored bars of life, hunger and endurance, the progress scale, and the map before my eyes, I might have taken the world around me as genuine.

Where to go? There was a scary black forest on two sides, dense as a solid wall. A fearsome howling sound was coming from somewhere beyond those trees. Clearly not the best place to walk at night, especially unarmed. And so, I decided to head toward the distant cannonade where my faction's soldiers were holding the line. I laced up my raggedy tennis shoes, then went to find my allies.

I had no idea what I would say to them or how to explain my appearance. But probably, they would at least hear me out and tell me what to do, where to go and how I could help. I walked straight through a flattened field until I hit upon a road. First, I saw it on my mini-map, then a minute later, I was standing on the dusty well-trodden path with clear tire tracks. Right or left? I chose left at random and saw a sign a quarter mile later at a fork. Two wooden arrows pointed the way to the nearest structures:

Prometheus Technology Complex 2 miles

Shooting Range 0.5 miles

I had no idea what they did at the Prometheus, and I wasn't sure I'd find anyone there at night anyhow. The shooting range was much closer and probably under guard all day and night. That meant there would be people there from my faction, and that I would be able to go to them for help and explanations about the game.

In both directions, there were fields of a tall strange grain. Before I'd managed to go half way to the firing range, two messages cropped up simultaneously:

Scanning skill increased to level three!

Cartography skill increased to level three!

Not bad, not bad at all. My scanning radius grew noticeably. I activated the icon again and, on the roadside one hundred feet away, I saw a group of round red markers. Danger? I crouched down at once and quietly crawled off the road on my stomach into some high grass. A short while later, I managed to see the enemy:

Field Pest. Insect. Level 4.

It was a spiny bug the size of a spaniel. A whole group

of the scoundrels was devouring our crops, destroying my faction's fields! I had to stop them, but how? I understood perfectly that trying to attack the insects unarmed or even with a stick would end very badly for me. A level-2 character had, to put it lightly, very bad chances against seven or eight level-4 enemies, even with a decent weapon. But I was unarmed, so there was no way. I was just six hundred fifty feet from the firing range, though, and I might find support there!

Carefully, trying not to make noise or reveal myself, I crawled in a wide arc around the dangerous insects. To do that, I had to get deep into the field opposite the Pests.

Would you like to take the skill Farmer?

Would you like to take the skill Stealth?

These messages surprised me so much I shuddered. No, I didn't want Farmer, it didn't fit my character. But Stealth? At the very least, not now. These were just a few partially blind overgrown bugs, not enough to scare me into taking a skill.

I refused both suggestions and, further from the bugs, went up on the road and ran to the shooting range at full speed. A few minutes later, I looked over the closed gates and high sturdy chain-link fence. It was totally dark at the exit. The grounds weren't lit either. In any case, I shouted loudly a few times, calling for security. But I already rationally understood that there was no one here. Either this place was not guarded at night, or everyone capable of holding a weapon was on the front lines, fighting back the Dark Faction onslaught.

Had I really shown up here for no reason? I looked through the fence at the dark angular buildings of the firing range. Storehouses, containers, plaques that were too far to read... I spent a long time squinting and tried to make out at least the nearest one on the wall of the covered brick building and seemingly guessed one word: "Arsenal." That's where the weapons were!

Now, I had to get through the fence somehow. My first idea was to simply climb the ten-foot-high chain-link fence. But that was a no-go. There was barbed wire strung atop it and it was affixed with porcelain insulators. I didn't see any warning signs like "Danger!!! High voltage!" But I still didn't risk it.

Instead, I walked up to the locked gates. Next to the nearest post, I found a metal pad with numeric keys. Ugh, I wish I knew the code...

Successful Perception check

I noticed that the buttons: "1," "3," "8," and "0" were more worn than the others. Curious... these buttons had been pressed most of all. And if some numbers in the code were not repeated, then there were only factorial four combinations (1*2*3*4), which gave twenty-four possible options. Not too many. I could try to press them all. The code 3180 worked. The lock clicked, and the gates slowly moved aside.

Would you like to take the skill Break-in?

I laughed. What kind of "break-in" had this been?

Child's play, not a serious obstacle! But this time, I didn't dismiss the message and read the skill description.

Break-in. Allows a character to overcome electronic and mechanical security systems, open locks of any type and take control of automated defense systems. Minimum statistics: Intelligence 15, Agility 15, Perception 15.

Hmm, bit of a mixed bag... The Break-in skill combined hacking, programming, lock-picking, and skill with various other thief's tools. Well if this was the terminology the devs had chosen, let it be simply "Break-in." A useful skill, not for everyone, but also not made for boring gameplay. I had to have it!

You have taken the skill Break-in level 1.

Great! Feeling inspired, I walked through the grounds of the firing range, looking around in search of something useful. My scanning ability reloaded at the perfect time, so I now had a map of all these buildings. After that, it became easier to find my way around.

Above all, I was interested in the arsenal, where I could hopefully find a weapon. But there was a massive lock on the metallic door. I walked up and looked closer.

Your Break-in level is insufficient to open this lock. Requisite level: 18.

You lack the tools required to open this lock.

Alright, I guess I couldn't even try. I walked further into the complex. Soon, my eye was caught by a pile of boxes wrapped in plastic film, and I acquainted myself with the markings on the packaging:

82-millimeter grenade launcher grenades... 122-mm howitzer rounds. That would pack a punch... Power cells, what the heck were these?! Handheld antipersonnel grenades, twenty boxes. I could use these against the bugs, although it may have been a bit overkill. I'd mow down the new plants, and I couldn't use them if the bugs ran at me. Although it still was a good idea not to forget grenades. I opened the map and placed a marker. No hint told me to do that either, I was helped by experience from other games.

Then I left, heading for the firing range itself, with rows marked by little flags, bags of sand and targets in the distance... Under a nearby canopy, there were tables for assembling and cleaning guns, and a large locked safe. This also had a numerical keypad like the other one but, this time, only three buttons were worn: "2," "5," and "6." A three-digit combination? I checked all six possible options quickly, but none of them worked. It wasn't quite so simple...

Successful Perception check

The 5 key was a bit more worn down than the two or six. Perhaps it was used twice in the code and this was another four-digit combo. So it was! The second code I checked, 2565, was correct.

Break-in skill increased to level two!

You have reached level three!

You have received three skill points!

Ha! It worked! I opened the heavy creaking safe. Inside, in even rows, there were fully automatics, a couple of machine guns and a few other weapons. The safe also held boxes of rounds.

Bingo! I was starting to love this game!

Chapter Eight

Quick Death

F OR STARTERS, I wondered what might happen if I tried to use an automatic or machinegun. After all, my class limitations said unambiguously that I could not use an automatic weapon, and I wanted to figure out what that meant. I reached for a machine gun and picked it up:

PKP Pecheneg 6P41N 7.62-mm machine gun (modified)

Statistic requirements: Strength 15, Constitution 16.

Skill requirements: Machinegun 16

Class requirements: Shock Trooper, Machine Gunner, Space Commando

Attention! This weapon contains unidentifiable modifications from a space-faring race.

Attention! Your character has insufficient Strength and Constitution.

Attention! Due to limitations of the Prospector class, you cannot use this weapon.

Ugh, dang! Three whole reasons against it... I could carry the heavy gun, but equipping it in my weapons slot was impossible. That was clear, no more questions. I placed the Pecheneg back in the safe and checked a few different types of automatic. The situation was similar. I couldn't place them in my main or alternate weapon slot.

But as for the rifles, everything was different. I could get the weapon into the slot, but the scatter radius took up my entire field of view. There was no accuracy to speak of. I could shoot it only in a general direction. What the crap? First, I blamed it on the fact I'd checked a shotgun, but the Saiga, which was renowned for its accuracy, was the same.

Not right away, but it dawned on me that I needed to take the right skill to effectively use the weapon. But which one? The answer was in the weapon description. Every carbine, rifle or shotgun had a description that showed requirements. They all needed the Rifles skill, and beyond that, had requirements for Agility, Perception and Strength. So, Rifles:

Rifles. Determines proficiency with non-automatic smooth-bore and sawn-off firearms, rail guns, pneumatic and plasma weapons (except sniper or heavy rifles). Improving this skill increases shooting accuracy and unlocks more advanced weaponry.

You have taken the skill Rifles level 1.

Then, for the first time, I considered how many skills a character can even have. Was there any limit at all? I opened my information and started studying the settings.

Unfortunately, there were limits:

    Below level 10, a character may have up to 8 skills

    Between levels 10 and 24, a character may have up to 10 skills

    Between levels 25 and 49, a character may have up to 12 skills

    Between levels 50 and 99, a character may have up to 15 skills

    Between levels 100 and 149, a character may have up to 18 skills

    Above level 150, a character may have up to 25 skills

    Well, well... How many had I already taken? Scanning, Electronics and Cartography had been with me from the very beginning. Astrolinguistics, Break-in and Rifles I'd already taken. That meant I had just two remaining skill slots, out of eight. Yikes! I had basically just started...

    It seemed Stealth and the rest would have to wait. I'd first talk with my faction and find out what was vitally necessary both for my character and the whole colony.

    Now it would be nice to shoot a bit to level my Rifles skill.

    I took the most basic hunting rifle, which had only one requirement, skill level one. It was called just Old Rifle. I picked up a handful of rounds and walked over to the sandbags. The spread circle was half its previous size, but remained very, very large.

    I aimed, shot, went to check the target and shook my head dejectedly. I hadn't hit once from one hundred fifty feet. I returned a few times for bullets and shot probably around a hundred times, raising my Rifles skill to level three before I got my first hit. After that, I almost immediately hit the target again, and again.

I put all three of my unused skill points into Rifles, then got a significant reduction in my scatter circle. Of the next ten shots, seven of them hit the target at least somewhat. Alright, enough abusing the old rifle. I was at level six now and could use a better gun.

Two more weapons were now available to me: "Simple double-barrel 12-caliber hunting shotgun," and "Simple 6.35-mm PCP pneumatic rifle." Everything was extremely clear with the double-barreled shotgun. There was only one box of 25 cartridges with large leaden shot. Its large spread was made up for by its application: short distances or point blank as the last option in a critical situation. I gave it just one lone shot to test it out, shredding the target sheet from five steps away. That'll do. The overgrown cockroaches devouring our crops would certainly not survive that.

But as for the air gun, I had my doubts. To me, air rifles belonged in children's attractions and carnival shooting games, not alongside serious weaponry. I filled its air reservoir with a special pump and tested the weapon in action. Its accuracy wasn't bad, but as for force, it was predictably somewhat weak. From fifty steps away, it might not even pierce the chitin armor of the large bugs. However, it was the best rifle I could use, so I'd have to risk it and get closer to the Pests.

I took the pump and two boxes of metallic bullets of a hundred rounds, then put the ammunition in my pockets, slung both guns over my shoulders and headed out on my first hunt in the game that bends reality.

Carefully applying the gun's safety catch and locking the outside fence behind me, I returned to the road and unhurriedly started on my first serious mission. The distant cannonade hadn't fully stopped; however, the explosions and gunfire crackle had become noticeably rarer. The battle was gradually quieting down, although I also had no idea who had won.

My ripped tennis shoes were clearly hindering me, and periodically catching on the dirt, making noise and giving me away. So, I removed my shoes and went barefoot. Nearer the bugs, I crouched all the way down, stealing up on my haunches. Taking the air rifle in my hands, I looked excitedly into the dark. I was ready to throw myself to the ground at any second. Step by step, I got closer to where I saw the large bugs before. My heart was pounding. It was quite a tense moment.

Would you like to take the skill Silent Walk?

I was caught off guard by the text. I was aiming and instantly fell to the ground. Dang! I couldn't afford to get startled like that! I stood with a grumble and shook the dirt off my jeans. No, I didn't want that skill, or any other. My mind was made up — nothing new until I'd talked with the other people. Hey, wait, where'd the bugs go?!

They were around here somewhere. Although... I wasn't sure. Ugh, why didn't I mark where I'd seen the dangerous pests on the map? Carefully, waiting for an attack at any second, I started to look for tracks, either the stalks I'd flattened when I left the road to crawl through the grass. Or plants trampled by the Pests. But I didn't find anything. Maybe they'd eaten their fill and crawled away? Or maybe this wasn't the right place?

Fortunately, my scanning ability reloaded, and I activated the icon.

Scanning skill increased to level four!

There they were, the scoundrels! The bugs were noticeably farther from the road than before, practically on the edge of my scanning circle. There were seven. I determined the direction to the targets and walked toward them. I stopped a hundred thirty feet from the nearest Pest and, evening out my breathing, aimed the air rifle. Fire!

A short quiet clack sounded out, and the air-propelled bullet sped off toward the target. No effect. The bug I'd fired on didn't stop devouring our food. I shot again. And again. Nothing. Either I was constantly missing, or the bug didn't care one bit about the tiny metal bullets.

And then, when I was about to get closer to my victim, I hit! Even from a distance, I could hear the clear sound of impact. And the bullet went through its shell!

The contours of the bug lit up an alarming crimson. I saw a life bar over the insect. It was down to half. It spread out its three-foot wingspan and the huge spiny Pest lifted into the air with a heavy buzz. It determined my location, turned and flew at me.

I was hoping the bug would crawl. Then I'd have managed to kill it with the air rifle at this distance. But I had already considered that it might fly and was planning to run away if it did, luring the insect farther from its buddies, then shooting it with the shotgun.

But it was flying much faster than I planned. I couldn't run away from this. And I certainly wasn't expecting all the Field Pests to swarm and race toward me. What was more, there weren't just seven, there were more than thirty!!!

I shot from the hip at the wounded bug and missed again, then put the air gun away and took out my shotgun. I had to shoot practically point blank, just seven to ten feet, but the large pellets from two barrels tore the bug to shreds!

You have reached level four!

You have received three skill points!

But then I realized the tragedy of my situation. I had just barely reached level four, and my progress bar was empty, so my inevitable death would lose me a level, three skill points and some skill levels. And now, with a ghastly hum, there were three enraged beasts flying straight at me!

Surviving in this situation was hardly possible, but there's death and then there's death. If I managed to do something that filled the progress bar by even a hair, then I stood to lose practically nothing. That thought fully occupied my consciousness. It was surprising, but I wasn't afraid of death. I was only afraid of dying stupidly.

I ran headlong for the road, hopping like a hare and dodging the bugs divebombing me. I ducked away from two or three insects, and kicked another like a soccer ball, but then I was knocked off my feet by a blow to the back. It felt like a red-hot knife had been driven under my right shoulder blade.

My life bar immediately sagged to half. Dang that hurts!

Poison! You will lose 5 HP every 3 seconds for 3 minutes.

Bleeding! You will lose 4 HP every 3 seconds for 40 seconds.

Well, that meant death... I didn't have enough health points to survive these negative effects. Strange as it was, I was entirely calm and stuck to a clear goal for my remaining seconds: take at least one enemy with me.

I abruptly rolled onto my back, throwing off the bug that had got me, and sending another back with a punch, then stood back up. I tried to reload the shotgun with my trembling hands, dropping cartridges in the tall crops.

Would you like to take the skill Dodge?

Would you like to take the skill Sprinter?

Would you like to take the skill Hand-to-Hand Combat?

Would you like to take the skill Entomology?

These obtrusive skill suggestions were getting in my face! Would I really be reading this spam in the very last seconds of my life?! With a kick of my bare foot, I sent another bug flying back, finally reloaded the double-barrel and met the next enemy with a shot from both barrels as it sped at my face. Got it! I hit!!!

Rifles skill increased to level seven!

My face was spattered with stinking orange goo, but that didn't matter now. I could clearly see that the progress bar was more than a quarter filled. And then... I suddenly felt better.

Healing effect applied.

Antivenom received.

Your wounds have healed.

As I was reading these messages, I was suddenly stunned by thundering fire. Just above my ear, someone was mowing down the Field Pests from a high-caliber and very loud weapon. On the mini-map right behind me, I suddenly saw a marker, a green circle. Ally!!! However, I would put my head on the chopping block to bet that, just a few seconds earlier, there had been no one there.

I turned around sharply and stuck my nose into a worn sheet of armor with a Second Legion emblem. I looked higher. And higher. And higher. There was a ten-foot-tall armored robot standing next to me spitting fire from a high-caliber machine gun as the Field Pests flew away in panic. To be more accurate, it was not a robot. There was a frail dark-haired girl firing the machinegun, inside an automatized armored suit. She was a young beauty who looked to be no older than eighteen.

Gerd Tamara. Human. H3 Faction. Level-78 Paladin

My team! Not ceasing fire, the girl started rebuking me:

"Who let you out alone at night, newbie? And who said you could waste these rare cartridges?!" Here, the girl lowered her head, met gazes with me, shuddered in fear... and stuck me through the chest with the wide sharp blade on the right arm of her suit, killing my Gnat in one blow!

The world went dark. After that, I saw only bright red words on a black background:

Your character has died. Respawn will be possible in fifteen minutes.

Would you like to review your statistics for this game session?

I was so dumbfounded that I didn't immediately react to the question. The words soon faded and disappeared, then the virtual-reality pod opened. But I spent some time lying on the soft bed and, looking dumbly at the ceiling in disbelief.

An ally killed me, a member of my faction... Why? What for? Could my actions in the game really have been taken so negatively that my character deserved to die? Was I now a criminal?

But first, that Tamara had saved me from the bugs and even healed me. What happened after that to make her opinion turn on a dime? And by the way, from a technical standpoint, how had she healed me? After all, she hadn't given me medicine or made any injections. Alright, that isn't so important. The much bigger question was what I should do now.

Because no one had yet come to arrest me, I crawled out of my virtual reality pod and went down the spiral staircase from corncob fifteen. It was "night" under the dome. The majority of the spotlights had been turned out, which submerged the huge space in partial darkness. Also, I could see sprinklers driving unhurriedly over the park paths.

Once down, I didn't see anyone waiting for me. No one wanted to see me, and what was more, no one was preparing to immediately arrest me. I calmed down and quickly walked to the dormitory complex, asking the night guard where my dorm room was located. The tranquil sweet-looking lady, totally not surprised to see me arrive at three o'clock in the morning, found me o

n her list, gave me my keys and explained in detail how to find my building and room.

I was on the third floor in a four-person room. Three beds were already occupied, and one was empty. I immediately recognized all three boys I had come to the Dome with: Artur, Denis and Imran. I took the towel, soap and toothpaste from my bed, then headed into the bathroom. And there, I looked in the mirror and nearly dropped everything: looking back at me was a boy with close-cut black hair and piercingly blue eyes that glowed in the darkness.

Chapter Nine

Performance Review

"**F**OURTEEN-SEVENTY, Tyulenev would like to see you," said a small boy of around fifteen with a shaved head, tapping me on the shoulder.

Children under the Dome? Startled awake mid-dream, I figured this was just an extension of my fantasy. But no, the bald kid wasn't going anywhere. Standing next to my bed, he continued to try and rouse me. I suppressed a yawn and sat up, now looking around consciously. It was still dark out the window. My roommates were sleeping.

"What time is it?" My phone was the only time-telling device I owned, and they'd confiscated it, so I had no way of knowing.

"Just after seven," the boy answered quietly. "Daytime lighting will be turned on soon. Get dressed quick and go see Tyulenev. He's a serious man and does not appreciate having to wait."

"Who is this Tyulenev, and where can I find him?"

The boy shook his head in reproach, as if I had just asked the stupidest question he'd ever heard. Thankfully, he at least did give a detailed answer:

"Tyulenev is third in command under Radugin, head of the Dome. A real big shot, he develops individualized levelling plans for each team member based on the faction's needs. His office is in the administration building. Don't make Tyulenev wait. He's already in a bad mood..."

I asked the boy what had our third-in-command so uptight, but he didn't answer. He just made sure I was really up and had understood what he'd told me, then quietly left as I stewed in anxious guesses.

But I had some idea why he might be upset if staff issues were his domain. My mindless rule breaking!So as not to annoy him even more, I got up, dressed myself and washed up. I got startled again when I saw myself in the mirror. Hmm... My eyes were still purplish blue, glowing and totally inhuman.

Just five minutes later, I knocked on Tyulenev's office and entered. He was a corpulent man of middling years. Despite his loose clothing, I could see his huge gut sway with every movement. It was quite strange to see such a fat man under the Dome. Everyone else I'd met down here had a fit athletic figure.

"Take a seat," said Tyulenev pointing me to a chair

near the table, "and tell me about it."

My superior then spent a few long seconds staring at my face, studying my eyes, after which he gave a snort of delight and turned his gaze away. I obediently sat down and asked what he wanted me to tell him about.

The man frowned and answered with a now more official and severe tone:

"One thousand four hundred seventy, we received a report about you from a very respected player, Second Legion Commander Gerd Tamara. She said you were loitering around during an official CtA and wasting rare ammunition. Now I need to know: how did you even get there?! So, tell me in chronological order what you did in as much detail as possible."

I had nothing to hide. I felt my motivation was noble and praiseworthy, so I told him I went up the corncob and into my virtual reality pod out of a sincere desire to help the faction. I described how I'd edited my appearance changed my eye color, adjusted my name, and familiarized myself with my character statistics...

"Tell me more about that," the fat man unlocked his computer to enter my data. "Strain your memory. I need all your character's initial parameters for our records."

For my part, I didn't have to try very hard to remember. I could recall my initial stat table perfectly: Strength 12, Agility 15, Intelligence 17, Perception 19, Constitution 10.

"Doesn't add up. Something must be off," the fat man

objected after hammering in the numbers. "Every newbie is given exactly 75 stat points regardless of race or profession, but yours adds up to just 73..."

"And Luck Modifier +2," I added. He nodded in satisfaction.

"Alright then, sounds like a decent character without serious imbalances," Tyulenev commented. "What class did you get?"

"My options were Geologist or Prospector. I chose Prospector..."

The fat man's kindhearted attitude blew away like the wind.

"No, no, no! That was a mistake!" Tyulenev exclaimed and stood up sharply, even damaging the seat a bit.

His gut swinging, my superior headed to the coffee maker. He just kept criticizing my choice and wouldn't calm down:

"You should have exited then and consulted with me! It's too bad. You could have done such great things as a Geologist! That's all down the drain now! You have high Perception and positive luck, so that would have been perfect! We could cover so many gaps in our colony with a Geologist like that! But instead, we have another worthless player... We already have a starship pilot, a space commando, and a paleobotanist. Well, it looks like team useless has four members now. You'll be assigned menial labor like taking out trash and digging ditches."

Extremely surprised by the volatile reaction, I asked boldly what was wrong with my Prospector.

"Everything is wrong with him!" the fat man shouted, his hands shaking in agitation as he dropped cubes of refined sugar into his mug. "The Prospector class is meant to work with electronic scanning devices. But human beings don't have such technology! And I cannot tell you how long it will be before we develop it, or if we ever even will!"

I nearly fell off my chair from the shocking news. We didn't even have the technology?! Well I'll be damned! What could I do now?! All the other players would be able to level their primary skills, but I'd be left behind! Apparently, Tyulenev felt irritated and dejected, just like me. He was sulking and, seemingly, had lost interest in working on my development path.

I was utterly discouraged as well. But I tried to reassure him by saying I'd passed the maze and been given five stat points for my performance.

"Five?" Tyulenev asked, perking up. I told him how I'd spent those points and he marked it down in his computer.

I was expecting reproach or at least commentary, but the fat man had no reaction. I continued with the story of meeting the Geckho diplomat, walking down the road at night and breaking into the arsenal. Tyulenev didn't interrupt me once. He didn't even comment on me taking the Astrolinguistics skill, which I figured he'd also think of as wrong.

Only when I'd finished, after describing the short

battle with the bugs and dying at the hand of the paladin girl, my boss said thoughtfully:

"I understand Gerd Tamara's reaction. She was on duty last night. Her nerves must have been fried. Plus, she got fragged twice. Everyone in her Second Legion respawned at least once, too. The Dark Faction assault was strong and focused. But most importantly, the Dark Faction took two of her soldiers prisoner. Tamara was especially upset by that."

"But can murdering a faction member in cold blood really be justified by the frazzled nerves of that... Gerda? Or Gerd? What is it? I've never heard of a name like that before. Gerd?"

The fat man looked at my strangely and shook his head in reproach:

"I can see right away, Gnat, that you are still inexperienced and practically know nothing about the game that bends reality... Gerd isn't some last name. It isn't a title and isn't a military rank... How to put it... It's more like an achievement or rank. It comes from an ancient proto-language used all over the game that bends reality and means something like 'worthy' or 'esteemed.' It's an achievement that cannot be bought or received by vote. It is automatically placed before the name of a player that becomes widely-respected in their faction."

"Are there higher ranks?" I asked right away. "I think I heard the Geckho diplomat refer to the Dome leader as 'Leng.'"

"Yes, 'Leng' is the next highest rank. It means

'viceroy,' 'faction leader' or, if you'd like a more direct translation: 'master of the fortress.' After that comes 'Kung,' which means 'leader of many divisions.' And highest of all is 'Krong,' top of the hierarchy. So then, there is a clear rule: A Gerd is immeasurably higher in status than simple players and never have to explain their actions. To you, a Gerd is like..."

Tyulenev faltered, trying to come up with an apt comparison and I suggested:

"Like a Geckho?"

"Exactly! Great comparison! Exactly right! You are not always required to obey them, but you must give them respect and not enter into conflict with them. In any dispute between human and Geckho, the Geckho is always right. It is the same way with Tamara. She killed you, so she must have thought that was the right thing to do, and now she has no need to justify herself or apologize to you."

Somewhat strange logic, but I understood that it was useless to argue. Rules are rules.

"But could I at least know why she did it? After all, I need to understand what I did wrong, so I don't do it again!"

The fat man went silent for a bit, then suggested I look in the mirror.

"Your eyes! They're inhuman. Also, glowing eyes are a kind of calling card of Dark Faction mages. They are our most cunning and insidious enemy. Tamara has many unsettled accounts with them. But the leader of the Second Legion is also a splinter in their ass. She is the only one who can use magic in our entire H3 Faction. Perhaps, when she saw you on her way to the arsenal, a person with glowing eyes, she thought it was a trap and acted on instinct."

"But the night receptionist and the page boy today also saw my eyes, and they didn't react!"

The fat man laughed happily and turned the monitor to me:

"So you thought, Gnat! Here, look at your personal file. There are two more reports. Today, two thirty AM. The night receptionist suspected you might be working for the enemy. And the second came at six ten this morning from the boy that woke you up. He requested the Security Service to test you for magical abilities. What were you thinking when you created your character? Ask the supply officer to issue you some sun glasses as soon as possible so you don't cause so much panic."

I had no objections, I just asked him to tell me how many of our players had that higher status, so I could morally prepare and not fall victim to their hot temper.

"In our faction, only three players have the status Gerd. They are a level-88 Sniper, First Legion Commander Igor Tarasov, a member of the Russian army and the highest-level player of our faction; a level-77 Scientist, head of the science complex Valentin Ustinov; and the level-78 Paladin you met yesterday, Second Legion Commander Tamara. And that's it."

Just three? Great. If I memorized these three names, I could behave naturally with everyone else. Meanwhile, it suddenly grew light out. The many spotlights under the Dome were turned on. Daytime here had begun. Tyulenev also noticed the coming of morning, but had a somewhat strange reaction, closing the thick curtain over his window.

"Old habit," he commented. "When I was brought under the Dome, I had stage-five diabetes. And it was type one, which is worse. My doctors said I had two weeks to live at most, and more likely a matter of hours. My retinas had deteriorated, and light gave me a horrible headache. But, like many here under the Dome, the game that bends reality saved my life. A healthy character in the game means a healthy body here on earth. My diabetes went away, and my vision returned to normal, but I still cannot bear bright light."

I kept silent, digesting the valuable information. As it turned out, many people under the Dome had once been hopelessly ill, and the game had cured them. After all, the bald fifteen-year-old who woke me up this morning, had most likely ended up here for a similar reason. Meanwhile, Tyulenev calmed down and we finally returned to the topic at hand.

"I don't see anything criminal in your actions, Gnat. You were acting on noble impulses and, although your gameplay was somewhat chaotic, you did a good job. Sure, you entered the game without permission, but that reflects more on the fact that no one was guarding the corncobs. You didn't study the labyrinth, but you still passed the test, and no one judges winners. Sure, we could have sent forty-five pounds of supplies into the virtual world with you but, in that case, I suspect you wouldn't have succeeded."

I agreed fully with my boss. Even without the extra encumbrance, I finished just six seconds before my time was up, with my endurance nearing zero. If I had forty-five pounds of bales and boxes on me, there was no way I'd have made it. So, Tyulenev continued:

"Your only serious oversight, as I already said, was the improper choice of class. But that isn't as hopeless as I first thought. You have two more skill slots. You must now take Mineralogy and level it as a priority alongside Scanning. Consider that an official order. You will work as assistant to our other Geologist, because Mikhalych is too old, and it would take him ten years to climb around all the cliffs and hills in our faction's territory. And as for an electronic scanner... well, I saw one in the electronics shop at the Geckho base. I can't remember how much it cost. We have a severe deficit of Geckho currency, so we only use it to buy things we really need. But let that be a dream for you in the game. If you save up the funds to buy yourself a scanner, you won't have to languish as a Geologist's assistant, you can be a fully-fledged Prospector!"

Chapter Ten

Initiation

I WAS VERY LATE to Ivan Lozovsky's introductory lecture, but it wasn't my fault. Tyulenev sent me to see the supply officer, and it took me a long time to find him. And when I got to the huge warehouse, he'd plunked along at a turtle's pace to dig out a set of athletic clothes, a couple changes of underwear, shoes, and the rest of the standard kit for a newbie under the Dome.

So, at ten to eight, late by a whole fifty minutes, I quietly stole into the pitch-black room. Crouching down, I walked over to a free armchair near the door. The presenter, passionately speaking about a table on the big screen, didn't even seem to notice.

"Lozovsky told us about your little mishap last night," the girl next to me whispered unexpectedly. Much to my surprise, I'd sat down next to Anya from First Medical. "He said it was a perfect example of how not to play."

"What did he tell you?" I asked. I wasn't so surprised

it came up but hearing it had been cast in a negative light caught me off guard.

Anya, not even trying to hide her mockery, told me the whole story. In it, a newbie had entered the game with no equipment or weapon, and no idea how to find our base. He then wandered around at random and almost got eaten by bugs, but a better player shot him first, just to spare him the torment... A strange retelling, to put it lightly. But I didn't dispute it. Let the newbies believe this tall tale. No skin off my nose, if it's for the good of the faction.

"Say, Kirill, show me your eyes?" Anya asked barely audibly. "They said you made them really crazy."

Why not? I removed my dark glasses. Anya didn't recoil but froze and stared at me with her pupils wide in astonishment. In them, I saw a reflection of a dark blue flame.

"Pretty spooky..." the girl admitted, "but I think it's nice and even cute. I could drown in those eyes. When I enter the game, I'll try to make mine just like that. If I don't like it, I'll just put it back before I start."

The other people around us started looking back and shushing. Our conversation was making it hard for them to hear. I put my glasses back on and concentrated on the speech by our faction diplomat. Ivan Lozovsky who was just finishing a section about, as far as I understood, the history of the Human-3 Faction's settlement in the game that bends reality.

Unfortunately, I missed most of it, but the very end

was quite informative. The diplomat mentioned that recently, our faction had been recruiting too many soldiers and not enough scientists and inventors. It was making it hard for us to understand and reproduce the new equipment, weaponry and technology we got from our neighbors. And that, he said, was why our leadership had ordered approximately fifty students brought in from technical institutes. Character class in the game was, as a rule, related to what the person did in real life. And so, Ivan Lozovsky was confident that our faction would be gaining a few dozen sorely needed scientists, architects and technicians.

What could I say? Now I had a good explanation for yesterday's mass expulsion. Apparently, the alarming situation with aggressive neighbors in the game had caused the need for a large number of soldiers with real-world experience to defend our lands. But there were enough of those in our faction now, and the best our country had to offer were already under the Dome. But even if they did take the Construction, Chemistry or Physics skills, natural-born warriors would be about as much use in laboratories as tits on a teapot. They didn't have the base knowledge, neither the mathematical background, nor the higher Intelligence. Building such a workforce required a different foundation. So, the leaders of the Dome had decided to recruit students from the upper classes of bachelor's programs, graduate courses and science institutes.

I looked at the young specialists around me. All of

them were listening attentively, hanging off every word. I could read sincere enthusiasm on their faces. They wanted to dive headfirst into their work. I was getting the impression that practically everyone else was a volunteer, who had signed up without any blackmail or police pressure. That made my small group of expelled gamers look even more surprising. They must have needed us for some reason, but I couldn't put my finger on it.

I got distracted, because the presenter brought up a new image on screen. Some kind of honeycomb pattern with differently colored hexagons. Ivan Lozovsky adjusted the microphone on his collar and continued his speech:

"So then, we've already got a handle on classes and skills. We discussed the motivation and rewards for your difficult work. We have studied the history of our faction and had a brief run-down of our neighbors. Now is the time to talk about geography."

He zoomed in on the honeycombs and I could see that the hexagons were overlaid on a topographic map of forests, rivers and swamps.

This is what it looked like:

Ivan Lozovsky narrated:

"The Geckho told us that our entire planet in the game that bends reality is divided into perfect hexagons with edges of approximately six miles. These six-sided boxes are called different things: hexes, hexagons, cells, although recently the term 'node' has been catching on, taken from some computer game. Anyway, these nodes form a kind of mosaic that covers the whole surface of the planet. Any faction in the game controls at least one node by definition. Each node has a surface area of eighty square miles — that is easily enough to build a starting base and begin producing a colony's essential survival needs."

"So, can a faction control several of these nodes?" The nerd was back with another question.

However, today the diplomat was not so annoyed and answered eagerly:

"Yes, of course. If they have the forces to capture and hold the territory, why not? All nodes have different climates, landscapes and resources. No one territory contains every necessary resource, but most things can be found within a relatively small area. So, a faction must expand to continue to grow. Our Human-3 Faction currently controls five hexagons. We captured the fifth just four days ago, and that was what allowed us to bring more people into the game that bends reality. Those people are all of you."

Everyone started chattering and looking around. Then the nerd asked another question:

"So, is there a strict formula of how many people a

faction can have depending on the number of these 'nodes?'"

Ivan Lozovsky again reacted fairly positively to the question and answered in great detail:

"Yes, of course. We only figured it out recently. But the number of nodes is less important than their development level. A level-one node allows eighty-seven players. A level-two node allows two-hundred sixty-one. A level-three, then, gives seven-hundred-eighty-three players. We do not yet have a development-level-four node, although such a well-developed hexagon would allow us to bring a whole two thousand three hundred forty-nine people into the game. Right now, we have just one level-three node — our Capital. When you first enter the game, you'll appear right at its center, which is approximately half a mile west of our main base. Beyond our highly developed and fortified Capital, we have another three nodes to the south. Two level-two: Yellow Mountains, and Jungles, and one level-one, the farthest away: Antique Beach. Finally, our most recent addition, the Eastern Swamp, which is to the east of our Capital. We've just finished conquering it from the forest spirits. We are actively building roads and fortifications there now. And so, the Human-3 Faction can have a total of one thousand four hundred seventy-nine players."

Well, well... I didn't understand what he meant by forest spirits, but no one sitting in the hall was surprised, so he must have talked about them earlier. But my attention caught on something else. I was number 1470, and there were just 1479 people in our faction. That meant we had already used practically our entire limit! And until we captured new territories or built up the nodes we already had, there could be no reinforcements. So that's what the diplomat meant yesterday when he said we would not be needing a sixteenth Corncob any time soon!

The lecture continued. From there, though, it covered only narrow and specific topics such as what resources are necessary to construct certain buildings, how many people can work in one laboratory, and what bonuses a good leader can give to science or production teams. It was of little importance to my Prospector and, to be honest, I got a bit bored and barely made it to the end. What was more, I was fearfully hungry. It was scary to think, but I hadn't eaten for a whole day, since right before the final match of the online tournament!

Over breakfast, our group of six sat at a separate table. And though Anya and Masha were trying to memorize the maze, Denis was trying to get under my skin with jibes about my change in appearance. I refused to give the girls any advice, not wanting to spoil their chances of getting a higher stat-point bonus. The gopnik, though, I just ignored, which got him more and more worked up.

We had already finished breakfast, when the same

First Legion girl we'd met last night came to our table. For a second, she just looked over all six of us, then confidently alighted her gaze on me:

"Gnat, you're already in the game, so you're on the schedule. You'll be going with Kisly's group to Antique Beach at ten o'clock for a standard four-hour shift of border patrol."

To say I was surprised would be saying nothing. How could my level-4 Prospector make any kind of border guard, when he couldn't even deal with a swarm of flying bugs?! As if reading my thoughts, she added:

"The border is usually patrolled by the First and Second Legions, but we were working all night, so today we'll rest. That means other people have to take that duty. Antique Beach is calm, prime territory for a newbie to get his bearings. What's more, the leader of the group, Kisly, is a level-40 Machine-Gunner, so he can explain stuff and protect you if anything happens."

The girl with number 343 on her shirt turned around and left. I got the feeling my relationship with my new acquaintances had changed. I now sensed a certain respect and even some envy. They hadn't yet seen their virt-pods, but I was already a fully-fledged player. I was on the schedule and the faction was counting on me. Breakfast soon came to an end, I said goodbye and headed for my Corncob.

"Kirill, tonight, you have to tell us what centaurs are like, alright?" Masha asked. With a confident voice, I promised I would, trying not to reveal my confusion.

What was this about centaurs? Although the name of

the place I was going, Antique Beach, did seem to imply centaurs, minotaurs and various other creatures from Greek mythology. Could they really exist? Was I going to see them today with my own eyes?!

Chapter
Eleven

Getting Ready
for Patrol

THIS TIME, when entering the game, I didn't fall from up high. I just appeared standing on even ground. The place, though, was the exact same — right next to the Geckho diplomat's tent. Kosta Dykhsh himself happened to be there again as well, speaking with Ivan Lozovsky. It was somewhat unusual to see him not wearing an austere business suit, but a spotted camouflage smock over heavy armor. The sniper rifle slung over his back just added to it. But he was at level eighty, which inspired respect.

I walked up closer to the conversing diplomats.

"Kento duho, Gnat!" the furry humanoid greeted me with a slight bow.

"Kento duho, Kosta Dykhsh!" I echoed the Geckho diplomat and gave a bow, which inspired a fit of bark-like laughter.

Astrolinguistics skill increased to level three!

Ivan Lozovsky spilled out a long sentence in Geckho, turning to our resident suzerain, but I didn't understand one bit, just my name, which was repeated a few times. Kosta Dykhsh, clearly justifying himself, answered in his own language. Then he pointed to me and repeated in Russian:

"I didn't make him do it. Gnat wanted to learn Geckho all on his own. I told him not to, but he insisted."

"Why would he need that skill? To study a foreign language, one must speak it with a native. But how can Gnat do that? He's a Prospector and will spend practically all his time hiking around remote cliffs and swamps!"

The diplomats returned to the alien language and argued for three minutes. I even thought I caught a few select phrases in Geckho. Then my Astrolinguistics improved again:

Astrolinguistics skill increased to level four!

Finally, Ivan Lozovsky finished his argument and turned to me, looking critically at my street clothes and bare feet:

"Gnat, you should run to base to get some decent attire. Actually, wait... It'll take you more than an hour to get there on foot. I'll call a driver."

He took the radio from his belt and barked an order:

"Zheltov, get your starship to the furball's house. I

need you to bring someone to base."

In reply, a high-pitched squeal came from the radio then two barely distinguishable words: "Three minutes."

"Furball?" Kosta Dykhsh asked, baring his teeth. I'd seen that expression before, and it wasn't a threat, but an imitation of a human smile.

"Well, I figured your race needs an informal name, and you get offended by Wookie, yeti and abominable snowman!" Ivan Lozovsky chuckled.

"Yeti and Wookie are entirely different races. What's more, they are fictional. Humans using such terms for the Geckho shows ignorance," Dykhsh answered very seriously. Then, he suddenly started barking or coughing through clenched teeth. "Furball is fine. It's mostly an accurate description, so I cannot be mad."

I tried not to be surprised at the casual, and even friendly interaction between the two diplomats. After all, Ivan Lozovsky himself had implored us to treat all Geckho as respectfully as possible. And that was putting it lightly. But Kosta Dykhsh didn't object, and even seemed to like it, so our diplomat must have known what he was doing.

Just then, I heard a strange hum and whistle in the distance, and soon an astonishing vehicle flew in from the forest. It consisted of a set of curved metal pipes welded together, attached to four bucket seats and something that was not quite a steering wheel, not quite a helm. The craft was somehow reminiscent of a racing buggy, but instead of wheels on the ground, it had three horizontal metal disks that made it hover. This makeshift transport was piloted by a young redheaded man covered from head to toe in fresh mud and wearing an old-fashioned racing helmet and leather overalls.

Dmitry Zheltov. Human. H3 Faction. Level-28 Starship Pilot

Starship pilot?! Was this the guy Tyulenev mentioned earlier? I suspected we didn't have a starship, so now he was working as a pilot of this... what was this by the way? The strange machine didn't touch the ground and hovered four inches in the air. It didn't look like an air pillow, or magnets. So, was this an improvised antigrav?

Ivan Lozovsky pointed me out to the pilot:

"Bring this newbie to base, right to Vasiliadi's warehouse. Tell him to give Gnat proper equipment, because he's going on patrol soon. Also, stay on call. There are going to be lots of trips today. We've got a big group of newbies. Fifty people."

The red-headed boy whistled in surprise, then pointed me to the front passenger seat. I didn't need to be asked twice and hopped right in. The vehicle sagged a bit to one side. The pilot abruptly turned the helm in one direction, restoring balance and evening out the flying buggy:

"Wo-o-oah! Careful! Can't you see? We're hovering here. This takes a gentle touch. By the way, make sure to buckle up, otherwise you might fly out when we turn. Also, there are helmets in the back. Put one on.You might need it."

I took his sage advice, donned a protective helmet, sat back in the seat and buckled the seatbelt. At that, I noticed a gnarled word scratched into the back bumper: "starship."

"We've got a couple of jokers in the faction..." the pilot said, when he saw me looking. "As soon as I get it repainted, they scratch it back in. But one day, I'll catch them in the act and then I'll show them!!!"

"Is that because of your class?" I clarified, hoping not to seriously offend him.

"What else could it be...? I was brought in from the Mozhaysky Military-Space Academy. I graduated with honors from a special course to pilot near-space vehicles, successfully passed a harsh selection process and was sent under the Dome. And when I got there, the game offered me just two professions: Starship Pilot, or Heavy Robot Operator. Of course I chose the first... But no one told me how far our faction was from getting actual starships!"

Dmitry grated his teeth and turned the helm without warning, which made the vehicle jerk sharply forward, pressing me forcefully into my seat.

"You in a rush? You care if we go around the forest?" the pilot enquired, not turning his head as he maneuvered between bushes and stones at enormous speed. "It's just that, it rained yesterday and there are little streams everywhere. I got stuck in one earlier and, with two of us, we'll probably hit another. My batteries are low. These pancakes don't have enough power. I'll have to charge up at base..."

Cartography skill increased to level four!

Only then did I notice with surprise how quickly my progress bar was filling. Another minute, or minute and a half at most, and my character would hit level five. I was actively using some skill. Cartography? Seemingly. On the dark unexplored map, a strip was slowly being colored in. So, riding the blisteringly fast buggy, leveled Cartography many times faster than going on foot.

Cartography skill increased to level five!

Scanning skill increased to level five!

You have reached level five!

You have received three skill points! (total points accumulated: six)

Whoo, if I rode around like this a couple hours, just think how much I would level! But, unfortunately, we were already there... He gave the vehicle another sharp jerk and we went around a rather sparse grove, then I saw a tall reinforced-concrete wall with watchtowers. Before it, there were rows of barbed wire, trenches and firing points for heavy artillery. The hovercraft slowed down, took a bridge over a river, then stopped next to the open gates.

Dmitry Zheltov removed his helmet and took his hands off the helm. I followed his example and removed my helmet. A guardsman with an automatic walked up and trained a strange camera-like device on us. His partner meticulously studied an image on his tablet. Clearly, we were being checked. We waited patiently until a command came in from the sentry up above:

"All clear. Come on through!"

The mountain of items on the table before me grew at a frightening speed. A whole camouflage uniform. A helmet strung with mosquito netting. Ballistic goggles. A knife in a case. High boots. A canteen. A belt. Kneepads. A backpack. Tactical gloves... Was I supposed to wear all this???

"You want light or medium armor?" asked Vasiliadi, the huge hairy stock keeper.

How should I know? The Prospector class only forbid heavy and power armor. This was the first I was hearing about medium and light. I asked for medium. He plopped down a kevlar jacket with extra inserts.

"Have you already taken the Medium Armor skill? Otherwise, there's no reason to pack on the extra pounds. It won't do any good!"

By the way, the stock keeper was right... I had already taken Mineralogy as my seventh skill, as directed by my boss, and was busting my brains over the last one. That was right! Protection!

You have taken the skill Medium Armor level 1.

"Don't even ask for 12-caliber cartridges. We haven't had them in stock for a long time. But we've got a ton of air rifle slugs!"

"But what's the use of that...?" I asked in disappointment. But Vasiliadi disagreed:

"Don't say that! Before we had a production facility for automatic bullets, even the First Legion used air rifles. Sure, they had a higher caliber and power than your 'burp gun' but, just so you know, a 9-mm PCP pneumatic rifle can splatter the brains out of a bear! But a weapon like that needs high skill. At least level-30, and preferably higher."

Level thirty? My rifle skill was still just seven, so I had a long way to go... I asked what he had for Rifles thirteen or even ten, which made the hairy stock keeper chuckle:

"What are you talking about, Gnat?! I've got a serious arsenal here, not just playthings. To be more accurate, I have weapons for level-zero beginners, with no skill requirements, but you'll get a better one. Level the skill to at least twenty, then come back and we'll take a look. Or ask our mechanics. They can improve your weapons for some coin. All kinds of modifications are available: accuracy, damage, silence. By the way, you asked about Kisly. Here he comes."

I turned sharply and saw a sprightly old man with his head shaved bald and a full, thick black beard. But I ignored his unusual hair distribution. The first thing that caught my eye was his perfectly square figure. Kisly was not tall, a half a head shorter than me. But at that, his shoulders were those of a real brute. Each arm was the width of my leg, and although his huge fists were not watermelon sized, they were at least as big as a cantaloupe. And Kisly's voice, as immediately became clear, was about as loud as a foghorn:

"Gnat, why the hell aren't you dressed?! We're leaving in ten minutes, and you're not ready!"

"They told me to be ready by ten, but it's just nine fifteen..." I tried to object. But the commander barked in reply:

"You dolt! We're supposed to be at the Border Post Eight on the Antique Beach by ten. But it's a half hour away! Get dressed quick!"

I caught myself off guard with how quickly I changed clothes but, just thirty seconds later, I was standing before the commander with all my items equipped. Kisly nodded in approval, but couldn't hold back a snicker:

"Gnat, what was that? You have experience getting changed in a jiffy? Maybe your girlfriend's parents come home at odd hours? Did you forget you were in a game? Just open your inventory, set the object in the slot and it appears on your body. You didn't have to hop on one leg to get your pants on."

Dang, that was dumb... I really hadn't considered that, in a virtual world, I could just move objects in a window and not have to monkey around with buttons and laces. Meanwhile, the radio on Kisly's belt started sounding. With a sullen face, the high-level soldier listened carefully, confirmed and signed off. After that, he flared up again:

"What is this preschool?! Listen, Gnat, there are another two coming with us. Some newbies. They say you know them. Zheltov is bringing them here right now. But, we've got a few free minutes, so set your respawn point on the base and use up all your skill points, if you've got any. Antique Beach is fairly calm, but you still might die there."

I didn't ignore his valuable advice and dug around in the settings for how to change my respawn point. Ah, there! Some coordinates and even a mini-map. Apparently, my respawn point was right where I'd first appeared in the game that bends reality. I even managed to find the Geckho diplomat's tent on the mini-map.

Would you like to change your respawn point?

Yes, I would! I found a spot on base free of buildings and set new coordinates to respawn at in case of death. Great! Now I needed to spend my skill points up.

All six into Scanning and Minerology, as Tyulenev wanted? I would have done that, but according to my calculation, I would hit Scanning level six any time now. Since arriving to base, I had activated the icon a few times, so it would be dumb to lose the progress. Meanwhile, it would be totally irrational to spend my free points on Mineralogy. The very first levels of a skill always come fast, and I figured I'd first get to five or seven the usual way before wasting any valuable points.

So, hoping greatly that Tyulenev would never find out, I put all six points into Rifles, raising it to thirteen. Patrolling the border was a dangerous and important mission, and with my harmless "burp gun" (as Vasiliadi had disrespectfully called it), I felt very unsafe.

Chapter Twelve

Antique Beach

VEN FOR A MAKESHIFT VEHICLE, this mode of transportation looked very exotic and sluggish. It was a huge wooden box, with sheets of metal tied to the outside and eight wheels plugged right on the frame. Inside, there were four wooden benches, polished to a shine by innumerable butts. The walls had carved firing slits and the canvas roof was full of patches and stitching. And that was all the protection this moving coffin offered from rain and dangerous beasts.

Half of the inside was taken up by cargo space. The driver had to look through a heavily smudged sheet of armored glass, with matte white streaks on the outside. All eight wheels of the hell cart were not rubber, but metal rings, with a contraption of wire and springs stretched over them. Perhaps that would increase their resilience to perforation, but it clearly increased wear, and my poor butt felt each time we went over a rock.

I was sitting on the very first bench next to a level-63 Mechanic-Driver by the name of San-Sanych. A red-headed joker with curly hair, he had already been regularly ferrying members of the H3 Faction to their shifts on his bone-shaker for half a year. The driver turned the donut-shaped wheel, pressed the pedals and jerked the levers, yammering the whole time about himself and his unusual method of transportation.

As far as I understood, the "little bus," as San-Sanych tenderly called his vehicle, was the very first transport our faction had constructed. The diesel engine had been carved and assembled in the Capital, along with the majority of the other parts. The remainder had been bought from the Geckho or brought in from the real world.

"This is the border of the Yellow Mountains node," the driver declared loudly, demanding that the passengers in the back pull on the canvas roof. "Before us is a forest full of nasty predatory flowers. They spit fluoric acid," San-Sanych said, turning my attention to the whitish blotches on the windshield. "Very corrosive, it even eats away at tempered glass. And most importantly, there's no way to get rid of the white marks. We have to change the windshield once a month because it just gets pure white. A loogie from one of those things will kill a person instantly if they're lucky. Either that or they have to walk around with a burn that doesn't heal until they die and respawn."

Anya was sitting behind me. Now a level-2 Medic, she gave a sob and started wiping indignant tears off her pretty face. Today, she had been sulking since arriving to the Capital, just crying and cursing her bad luck. It was easy to understand, though: no matter how Anya tried to distance herself from medicine, the game hadn't given her much choice of profession: either Medic or Veterinarian. And she hated animals even more than the sight of blood, so she had to agree to the role of Medic.

Over the ten minutes we had been underway, we had already heard all the possible ways Anya could lament her hated and, most importantly, useless profession. She asked things like, "why do they even need Medics in this game? It's easier to die and come back in fifteen minutes totally fine!" Group leader Kisly, which I found quite strange, agreed completely. When base is not far away, as a rule, a bleeding or crippled soldier would rather die on the battlefield and respawn, returning with a full store of health points and clips of bullets. The commander's words had a very dismal effect on the already severely upset Anya.

The second of my newbie friends was Imran, a level-2 Gladiator. The Dagestani athlete was in a very bubbly and even motivated mood today, and it was all because of his class. From what I understood, he had the choice of either Bodyguard or Gladiator, made it consciously and intelligently. Imran had even left to get advice from

Tyulenev. Bodyguards were a masters of shooting light firearms off the cuff, had a huge store of life points and could absorb some damage taken by other group members. Gladiators, though, specialized in hand-to-hand combat. To facilitate that, they had a cool unique ability to leap one hundred to one hundred fifty feet, so they could get right next to their enemies and shred them like cabbage with their deadly blade. Imran already had the blade, too. It looked something like a large sickle. And, it should be said that the Gladiator class could also use automatic and semi-automatic firearms, though was forbidden from using heavy weaponry or rockets.

Other than us three =, Kisly's group had another four players at levels twenty to thirty-five. But, from what I understood, they were supposed to get out earlier at a different post. Kisly was going to maintain constant communication with them so that, in case any thing happened, both groups could quickly join together and come to one another's aid.

Cartography skill increased to level seven!

Scanning skill increased to level six!

Scanning had, as I suspected, leveled quickly to six. However, Cartography was growing even faster. In the Capital, Vasiliadi told me all newbies are issued a full map of our faction's territories, but I told him I didn't want it. After all, if there was nothing to discover, my Cartography skill would remain inactive, and that just wouldn't do. And practice was proving me right. Although it wasn't as quickly as in Zheltov's starship, riding in the little bus levelled my Cartography skill at a decent pace. What was more, I was watching the surrounding country not through a narrow gun slit, but through a full windshield.

The eight-wheeled bus passed through the dangerous forest without any incidents with spitting plants. Then, with its engine groaning in strain and bouncing over stones, it started climbing higher and higher up the mountain road.

"You should have seen the battles for these passes three months ago!" the driver continued, bringing us up to speed. "This node didn't belong to any faction but that didn't stop the centaurs, forest spirits and atlantes from regularly sending sabotage and recon groups up here. Look at that burned tower over there. Our faction was trying to build a fort here, but the centaurs burned it down. Then, at another pass, the First Legion torched the surrounding forest with flamethrowers and managed to fortify. After that, we built posts around the perimeter and things settled down."

Eventually, the bus drove up into a gray cloud, and I could no longer make out anything through the damp glass. Together with that, my Cartography skill stopped levelling. I spent a long time staring at the progress bar to make sure. I had no idea how San-Sanych could see anything through this fog. He must have had a secret skill like "daredevil driver" or something because the bus just kept bouncing along confidently, and he kept yammering.

"Let us out here!" The four soldiers threw back the

canvas, jumped out and got lost in the fog.

"This is the highest point in the pass," Kisly commented for the newbies. "There are usually two watchmen here. Now, its cloudy and damp but, when the fog disperses, you can see twenty miles in every direction. With good optics, you can even see the Geckho base on the other side of the gulf. Normally, there are two soldiers down below monitoring the path into the mountains as well, so no one slips through here from the forest."

Perhaps, in clear weather there were excellent views from up here, but now I couldn't even see two or three yards. Now though, we were going down and, a few minutes later, we abruptly emerged from the gray fog.

"Look, the sea! How pretty!!!" Anya shouted out, her bad mood instantly gone.

Far below, I could see the azure ocean starting at the foothills and stretching to the horizon. Our bus, turning for a few minutes on the mountain switchbacks, went down to the very water. There we were awaited by four shirtless sunburned soldiers.

"Hurry up! These guys need to get back!" Kisly sped us along, and we rushed out of the bus.

Cartography skill increased to level eight!

I looked around. The sea was stormy. Heavy waves were breaking on the shore one after the other and shells and small rocks washed up with a rustle onto the wide sandy and pebbly beach. Nearer, past the raging waves, I could see a whole heap of seaweed on the beach that stunk of iodine.

Behind me, there was a sheer rock face, going steeply upward, seemingly to the very sky. From there, it looked so impassable, I had no idea how our unprepossessing bus could have made it across.

"Alright, newbies, everyone listen up! That stone tower over there," Kisly pointed at the massive square construction behind us, "is Border Post Eight. It's got a good firing position, embrasures on all sides and, in case of attack, can be locked up tight until reinforcements arrive. Other than the beach, which is just fifty steps wide, our neighbors can only get here from high in the mountains where our soldiers got out of the bus. So, I'll man the tower with my machinegun. That'll stop the centaurs and whatnot from trying to cross the beach. They've already tried a few times, and always get lit up. They know me and my machinegun well, and they fear us."

A couple seconds later our muscular commander was wearing a suit of metal armor like that of a medieval knight. Another second and a huge heavy machinegun appeared in Kisly's hands. Bluish green light glinted off it, and it had a sophisticated sight and a bunch of little doodads screwed on.

"My favorite toy!" the professional soldier said with tenderness in his voice, clapping his hand on his fearsome gun. "It's based on a mounted Kord, but I invested heavily in modifications to reduce weight and increase firepower. And look what that got me! Once, a level-80 Minotaur came at us from over there, slashed his way through a whole division, but couldn't stand up to my little sweetheart. Watching the bullets go straight through his horned head was a delight!"

Kisly turned around and, slinging the machine gun on his shoulder, headed for the stone tower. The three of us exchanged surprised glances.

"Uh... Commander, what are we supposed to do then?" Imran called out to the machine-gunner as he walked away.

"You?" Kisly turned around in surprise. "Well, I guess do whatever you want. I can hold the tower down by myself, and you three are too low-level to help. If you want, come up on the watchtower. From there, you can see living centaurs. Or walk down the beach and collect shells. Some of them have pearls. But don't try to swim. The game rules are pretty strict on that. If you don't have the Swimming skill, you'll just drown as soon as you get into deeper water. In four hours, the little bus will come to take us back to base. I'll make sure to write in my report that you all did a great job keeping watch."

Well I'll be damned... Kisly thought of us as nothing more than useless ballast. And he didn't hide that. Perhaps he was right, but it stung a bit to hear it out loud. So, what could we do for a whole four hours? I went up the tower after the machine-gunner and looked out an embrasure. From there, I could see pillars going into the sea with barbed wire running between them, though it was torn in a few places.

"The barbed wire doesn't hold them," Kisly shook his head, having noticed my interest in our broken defenses.

"The minotaurs tear through it with their bare hands, and many centaurs as well."

Just then, I noticed that the machine-gunner had taken his armor back off and was now wearing only Bermuda shorts.

"So, where are the bad guys?" Anya asked in surprise, standing behind me.

Fair enough. All I could see past the barbed-wire border was a lifeless beach and some cliffs. In reply, Kisly pointed to some far-away bushes and tall grass:

"The centaurs aren't idiots. They don't hang out under the burning sun all day. Over there, by the bushes, a small stream runs into the sea. They usually gather there in the shade near the cool clean water. Just so you know, that is the only source of fresh water on the whole beach. It's morning now, but by midday, the sun here is so scorching that some soldiers have suffered heatstroke. So, I usually don't wear my armor without good reason. Sure, it isn't regulation, but this thing is like a tea kettle, and it'll boil your brains before a shift is up."

He was right. It was sweltering in this tower. I was afraid to even imagine how blistering it could get in the hotter part of the day. And my canteen was totally empty. I hadn't thought to fill it in the Capital. I'd been rushing and figured I'd have time later. Anyway, I could make it four hours without water, but it would be a lesson for the future...

I walked over to the opposite embrasure. I just saw more beach running along a mountain ridge. Far in the distance, there were some buildings.

"What's over there?" I asked the commander.

Kisly looked where I pointed and, cringing in disgust, answered:

"It's a pier. It is on our land and technically belongs to our faction, but the Geckho run the show. They bring our trade goods and tribute there, then haul it away by sea. We are their vassals and pay thirty percent of every resource we gather: crops, lumber, metals and ore... Ivan Lozovsky assures us that's the way things should be, that we owe it to them for protection, and we could easily be exterminated if we fail to provide for our suzerains. But I don't like it one bit. It makes me feel like we're being occupied and robbed blind..."

Kisly spat loudly through the embrasure, expressing his feelings on the matter. But at that, as if answering himself, continued:

"But you're newbies. You must be curious about the aliens. You can't see the centaurs right now anyway, and if you sit around here with nothing to do, you'll get bored. If you want, go over to the pier. The Geckho won't let you into the warehouses, but you can take a look at the outside. By the way, you can ask the Geckho to fill all your canteens. They're usually pretty good about little favors like that."

Chapter Thirteen

First Patrol

E VERYONE LIKED the idea of walking to the dock. I don't know why Imran or Anya wanted it, maybe they were just curious, but I saw many upsides. First of all, I could level Cartography by walking the nearly two miles of unmapped coastline. Second, our path took us along a crumbling rock cliff, and I was hoping to practice Minerology. Thirdly, speaking with Geckho would increase my Astrolinguistics skill. And of course, I was just curious to see new parts of Antique Beach and didn't want to get bored just sitting in the tower.

Medium Armor skill increased to level two!

The sudden message made me think. The sun was scalding. Following Kisly's example, I was about to stash nearly all my clothing in my inventory and get back into my jeans. I planned on keeping the army boots on though, because the sand was red-hot, and I didn't have any other footwear. But given that just wearing the kevlar jacket was gradually levelling my Medium Armor skill, I decided against changing clothes. I could bear the heat. The Medium Armor skill was very useful and leveling it would not only increase my defense stat, it would also improve the armor bonus of my equipment and let me use better armored vests in the future.

Unlike me, Anya changed practically at once, getting into a bright crop top, short shorts and a baseball cap. She wasn't afraid of getting sunburn here, either. She was tanned bronze, which meant she either spent a lot of time down south on the beach or frequented a tanning salon. Imran stripped down to the belt, demonstrating his athletic body with clear pride, especially showing off for the pretty girl. I even caught Anya staring at his rippling muscles, though she didn't say anything out loud.

And then I got startled by an alarm. My food bar had dipped below half. I'd got some briquettes of dried food from the warehouse in the Capital today, so I dug into my inventory. There was dried meat, bread and some dried green blocks which must have once been plants. Sure, I was glad to have food, but it was pretty hard to chew. I needed water, which I could only get at the Geckho base.

"Let's hurry up!" I turned and shouted at my companions, who had lowered their speed to that of a tortoise, stopping frequently and poking around in the sand.

Anya was crouching down in the surf and looking

closely at something. She stood up and wiped her wet hands on her light shorts:

"Wait, Gnat! The storm brought all kinds of shells here. Some of them are beautiful. And there's something alive in practically all of them. Maybe I'll find a pearl."

"Hey, I just found one!" Imran shouted in satisfaction, having opened one of the shells with his blade and showing us the quarter-inch-diameter pearlescent sphere.

Sea Pearl (trade good)

I walked up and took a closer look both at the pearl and oyster shell. The gnarled outside of the mollusk was a blackish-brown. The inside was white and contained the torn remains of a tiny shellfish. The game system obligingly told me the oyster counted as food. Sure, why not? I tore out the slimy veiny meat and carefully stuck it in my mouth.

"Ick, how can you eat that crap?!" Anya cringed and hurried to run away so she wouldn't have to watch the unpleasant spectacle.

I delicately chewed the mollusk and swallowed. Hmm... Well, what could I say...? The flavor was, of course, unique, but not bad. My hunger bar went up noticeably. I took another look at the shell and activated the Scanning icon, wanting to search for similar ones in the area.

Scanning skill increased to level seven!

You have reached level six!

You have received three skill points!

Oh yeah, sweet! Although, before using the points, I looked to see what the scan had found. Now this was even cooler. There were now a few dozen oysters on the mini-map. That meant I could set priority targets for a scan! A few minutes later, I had shaken out thirty brownish-black shells and tossed them up to Imran.

"I don't get how you open them," I admitted. "It seems too tight to get a knife in!"

The Gladiator chuckled and gracefully opened all the shells with his sickle in just under a minute. Only four of them contained pearls. I wanted to split the bounty evenly with Imran, but he refused:

"No, those are yours. I already took my reward. Opening those shells raised my Blades skill by two levels in the blink of an eye! I got my character to level three! So, throw me all the oysters you can find. I'm more than happy to shuck!"

I didn't argue and, working the meat out of the shells, I started eating them raw. My hunger bar quickly filled to eighty percent, but would go no higher, no matter how much of the slimy meat I forced down. Why? I asked my friends, and Imran explained:

"Gnat, you missed the beginning of the presentation today. That high-level diplomat... I forgot his name... told us about the game menu and interface. Somewhere deep in the settings you can customize the hunger bar display, but there's no real reason. You just need to know that game characters need three kinds of food to live. He called them red, blue and green. Most dishes contain just one type. Red is in meat-heavy dishes, blue in seafood and green is veggies.

It's all relative, but I think you understand."

"I see. You need to eat a varied diet, like the food pyramid," I chuckled.

"Yeah, that's right. By the way, our medic friend Anna said that she was a firm vegetarian and wouldn't eat any meat, even in the game. Or fish either..."

We both turned our heads toward the girl. Anya, who was now at level three, had managed to climb pretty high up the stone slope. Digging at one of the boulders distractedly with her knife, she was trying to pick something out of it. Finally, she managed, straightened up and called us to join her. Imran, using his jumping ability, bounded over to Anya in a second, and shouted to me from above:

"Gnat, come up here! She's found gold!"

Gold?! Very interesting! My level-6 Prospector took a bit longer to get up there but, gracefully jumping from rock to rock like a mountain goat, I ascended the crumbling boulders to meet my friends.

"Here! Gold!" Anna proudly showed me a chunk of golden fine-crystalline nodules she'd worked out of the large stone.

I didn't even have to hold the fragment of stone to realize my friends were mistaken. Nothing to be ashamed of, though. It was a common error. Almost everyone who saw crystalline iron sulfide for the first time thought the same thing. Pyrite, or "fool's gold," as it's also known, looks quite similar to native gold ore. That was what I told my friends.

"Are you sure?" the pretty blonde asked with doubt

in her voice.

She clearly didn't want to part with the dream of striking it rich. I saw a marker over the chunk reading "Unknown mineral." The "prospecter" probably saw the same.

"Yes, I'm one hundred percent sure this is pyrite," I repeated with emphasis and a miracle happened:

Mineralogy skill increased to level two!
Mineralogy skill increased to level three!
Mineralogy skill increased to level four!
Mineralogy skill increased to level five!
Mineralogy skill increased to level six!
You have reached level seven!

You have received three skill points! (total points accumulated: six)

Woah... The game system gave a very generous reward for identifying just one mineral. The sheer number of messages spooked me a bit. A clear explanation immediately came to mind, though. Most likely, a player had to reach Mineralogy level six to identify pyrite, and the game had brought my skill level in line with my real-world knowledge.

"It isn't gold anyway, just some crap," the level-3 Medic threw away the stone, which she considered useless.

I didn't agree and explained that pyrite was used in chemical manufacturing to make sulfuric acid, iron sulfate and many other things. Just in case, I marked the source of iron sulfide on my map. I'd tell the higher-ups when I got back to the Capital and let them decide whether it was economically justifiable to mine and process.

It took us another hour and a half to reach the pier. In that time, I discovered another rich vein of hematite, chalcopyrite and, I believe, skutterudite. To be honest, the game wouldn't identify the matte-white crystals as skutterudite, so I couldn't be certain. At any rate, I managed to get my Minerology skill to level eleven, and I was very satisfied with that.

I also leveled Cartography, Scanning and Medium Armor by one, and reached the Geckho pier as a proud level-eight Prospector! My companions also leveled noticeably during our walk along the Antique Beach and were now both at level five. Anya was especially fortunate to use her primary skill. Imran, training his long-jump ability had once miscalculated and slammed full speed into a granite cliff.

It hurt to even look at his broken body after that. His whole face was bloody, he had a huge dark bruise on half his torso and his left arm was hanging down limp... But Anya took out her big first-aid kit and patched up our friend in just half an hour, even fixing his broken collar bone. Near the end, clearly satisfied with her work, she proudly declared that she had made peace with her profession, and no longer wanted any other.

The Dagestani was very grateful for the aid and,

whether joking or serious, promised Anya to sometimes purposely break his body from now on. He said he liked being cared for by such a pretty girl and wanted to help her level her medical skills.

I used my nine free skill points as well: three in Rifles, three in Scanning, and the remaining three in Astrolinguistics. I figured we would be meeting aliens soon, and it would help us all if I could speak their language.

But, after another bend in the coastline, it became clear that there was a way to go before that. Our path was unexpectedly blocked by a sturdy ten-foot-tall chain-link fence. It was exactly like the one outside the Firing Range, right down to the high-voltage barbed wire on top.

The fence extended far into the ocean on one side, the other end stuck into a tall and nearly sheer cliff. There was no way around. We stopped in indecision, discussing the unexpected obstacle. Anya took the radio off her belt and called Kisly to find out how other players had gotten around this before:

"Commander Kisly, this is Anya. There's a tall fence on the beach and we cannot reach the pier."

In response, we heard a high-pitched squeak and a few poorly audible words:

"What the hell... there wasn't... (distortion)... fence... damn Geckho... (distortion)... come back."

And although we didn't get the full meaning, I got the impression the commander didn't know about this obstacle and thus couldn't tell us how to get around it. Imran noted in dismay:

"How can there be any talk of antigravs and other high tech stuff, if our faction can't even make a decent radio?! We're just under two miles from the Border Post Eight, and we can already hardly hear a thing."

It also seemed strange to me that, if the Dome project was so high-priority and had huge government investment, our faction couldn't even get decent radios. But I didn't discuss it. First of all, I didn't know all the details, and there might be good reasons for the distortion. Second, I had spotted a gate in the fence.

However, it immediately became clear that the door was locked from the other side, and this side didn't have a lock or even a handle. Although... I looked higher. At around eight feet above the ground, there was a device that looked like an intercom with buttons and a microphone. I asked Imran to let me stand on his shoulders, so I could reach it.

I pressed the button for the next four minutes and tried to say who we were and why we were here. At the same time, all three of us were shouting through the gate, hoping any Geckho on the other side might hear us. But it was no use. No one answered, no one opened the door, and no one came to the fence.

"We were screaming so loud a deaf person could hear. I don't think there's anyone there," Imran said.

"I have one free skill slot. I could take Swimming and get around the fence by the sea!" Anya offered, but it seemed wasteful to have her use a valuable skill just for this.

Meanwhile, having tested all ways of communicating with the guards via intercom, I decided to try speaking Geckho:

"Kento duho!" I said the traditional greeting phrase. In response, a Geckho phrase came through the speaker:

"Sabi fsen vari."

Some nearby sand started rustling, and a metal pillar with a square white sensor panel rose up five feet. It was seemingly a sign to identify myself. I jumped off the shoulders of the Dagestani athlete, walked over to the panel and placed my right palm against it:

"Gnat, Human, H3 faction," I introduced myself, but the system didn't like that answer, and the post went back underground.

Hm... No dice. It seemed I was not on the list, or it simply only allowed Geckho to enter. The sensor panel was too large for a human hand, so that seemed only natural. So, I remembered the only Geckho I'd met, a diplomat by the name of Kosta Dykhsh. His huge hand had a hairy palm with four fingers. I hadn't seen any parts free of fur. All his fingers ended in large claws. The scanner couldn't be reading fingerprints through all that fur. What if...

I dug through the sand on the beach, picked up a couple of empty shells, cleaned them off and stuck them on all four fingers of my right hand. I said the Geckho greeting phrase again, calling up the sensor panel. I placed the shell-hand up to it, trying to touch the white surface only with the shells:

"Kosta Dykhsh Geckho. Waideh-Dykhsh."

Electronics skill increased to level four!

Astrolinguistics skill increased to level eight!

Break-in skill increased to level three!

Break-in skill increased to level four!

The gate slid silently aside, letting us through to the pier and warehouses.

Chapter Fourteen

Talking with Centaurs

A S SOON AS we'd gone a hundred steps and turned around the jutting cliffs, we could see the long sturdy dock, some hemispheric hangars and a large stack of containers. We stopped and took a look around.

"Don't touch anything!" I immediately warned my friends.

Imran and Anya nodded in agreement, also understanding that, if we stole anything from the warehouse, our Geckho suzerains would react very badly, and might even destroy human civilization. We walked across the pier to the opposite fence, then looked into the locked hangars. They had stacks of lumber ready for export and many sealed freight containers with incomprehensible markings.

We very quickly realized that there was nothing to do here at the warehouse. There were no living people or Geckho here, and we didn't find any fresh water. And naturally, we weren't going to break into the buildings or crack open the containers. Especially after I noticed the security system. On the building roofs and the fence, there were cameras keenly tracking our every movement and constantly holding us in frame.

It was midday. The sun was burning. A few times, my friends suggested I remove my jacket and dress a bit lighter, but I said I'd rather get soaked in sweat to level my Medium Armor skill. Anya then, as she was planning, took the Swimming skill and went for a dip, diving off the pier. Imran stripped down to his trunks and, right on the pier, started practicing with the sickle-like blade, also leveling his skills and showing off for the pretty girl.

I meanwhile walked the perimeter of the warehouse and used my shell glove to trick the sensor system two more times. My Break-in skill leveled to six, along with Electronics. But as for Astrolinguistics, it didn't get any better. Then my radio turned on. Through distortion, I heard Kisly saying the centaurs had come out of hiding and could now be seen from the tower. Our commander suggested we start making our way back to catch a glimpse with our own eyes. Also, he said we should leave soon just to be at Border Post Eight by the time the little bus came back.

We all turned and started back. But we didn't manage

to leave the fenced-in area before we heard a whistle and hum from over the sea. Flying very low over the water, a strange silver vehicle was speeding along just above the waves. It looked most of all like a fat airplane with miniature wings. When it got closer, I managed to read some information about the object:

Shiamiru. Geckho cargo shuttle.

"We're here illegally. We should move our asses!" Anya suggested, alarmed by the approaching guests.

"It's no use. They probably already saw us. And we'll be in plain sight on the sandy beach. There's nowhere to hide..." Imran objected.

In the end, we didn't run. In fact, we stood on the pier for all to see and watched the heavy vehicle climb higher, flying over our heads and landing in a free space in the middle of the warehouse. The heavy craft didn't entirely quieten down before the doors slid aside. Many strong figures in dark armored space suits poured out. Their furry faces weren't visible due to the darkened helmets, and there was no more information available about these extraterrestrial newcomers — no names, levels or classes.

There were fifteen Geckho but, surprisingly, they didn't pay us three any mind. Quickly, in a business-like manner, the furballs unfolded a crane attached to the side of their shuttle and started loading containers into their flying vehicle. And they weren't loading at random, but very selectively running up to certain containers, attaching hooks and transferring the goods into the cargo bay. Some boxes were negligently shoved out of the way because they were blocking more desirable ones. While they rushed to load the containers, a couple of dark figures split off from the main group and forced open the doors to one of the buildings with crow-bars and hatchets. It took them around a minute to get inside. They took out something in a small transparent bag and threw it into the shuttle.

After just four minutes, the whole team of loaders was folding the crane back up and hurriedly returning to the flying vehicle. It took off vertically at an extreme pace and disappeared into the sunny sky in less than a minute.

"They sure worked fast," Anya commented. "Although it was also quite careless. Look how many boxes they knocked off those piles! And I'm not even talking about the door they broke! You think they were in such a rush they just forgot their keys?"

"Yeah, they were acting weird," Imran agreed. "It was like they were pressed for time, and didn't care if they broke stuff. All that mattered was taking what they wanted."

"Guys, do you think we just witnessed a warehouse robbery?" I suggested, as if I had second sight.

At the same time, both from the sea and the path leading into the mountains, many flying armored vehicles appeared and rushed toward the warehouses. Another couple minutes later, the pier was packed to the brim with armed and very angry Geckho soldiers. We were surrounded, had our weapons confiscated brusquely and were searched, including with some kind of scanner. An enraged dark-brown Geckho by the name of Sysa Kuttsh yelled something, clearly demanding an answer. But my friends didn't understand him at all, while I could only make out at most one word in five, but that didn't add up to anything sensible.

"...Shuttle ...ore... sea... idiot... damn... Geckho..."

I simply didn't have the words to explain what we'd seen, or how we'd gotten near the guarded warehouses. However, hearing his select phrases noticeably enriched my vocabulary, raising my Astrolinguistics skill to nine. Fortunately, another fifteen minutes later, a representative of our faction arrived on a two-seat antigrav. It was Ivan Lozovsky accompanied by the Geckho diplomat Kosta Dykhsh.

They conversed with Sysa Kuttsh in elevated tones for five minutes. At the end, the dark Geckho, seemingly responsible for defending this warehouse, took out a short high-caliber sawn-off and... shot himself, placing the weapon to his own forehead and pulling the trigger!

As soon as his body hit the sand, both diplomats walked unceremoniously over the lifeless corpse toward us.

"Well... Looks like you guys landed yourselves in some shit..." Ivan Lozovsky told us in the dismayed tone of a teacher who'd caught troublemaking students near a broken window. "The security camera footage has been wiped, the safe of monetary crystals was broken into, and there are only human fingerprints on all the entrance scanners... If it weren't for the disappearance of thirty shipping containers,

I can't even imagine how you'd get out of this... But the Geckho, despite being extremely angry, understand that you would not have been able to make off with thirty containers."

"I need to know what the people saw," Kosta Dykhsh said in an even tone that expressed no emotions, not addressing any of us specifically. "And the Geckho will have a look..."

The three of us exchanged glances, and I stepped forward. I started honestly telling why we came to the warehouse, how we got into the fenced-in area, and what we saw in greatest possible detail.

"Show me!" the diplomat pointed his furry paw at the nearest gate.

I repeated my trick with the shell glove, though this time I used a different name: Sysa Kuttsh. The gates opened obediently, and I saw Geckho expressing surprise for the first time. All the furballs around me had their nostrils flare, while their eyes turned into narrow little slits.

Fame increased to 3.

After a second's pause, a heated argument began between the extraterrestrials crowded around the gates using many select and idiomatic expressions. Funnily enough, I partially caught the sense of their argument. Stock keeper Sysa Kuttsh had decided to scrimp on security systems and had either bought or just taken as tribute the very cheapest thing he could get his hands on. And it turned out those systems were totally useless and not even able to distinguish between a human and a member of a different race.

The Geckho seemingly forgot about the humans all around them. Taking advantage of that, Ivan Lozovsky took the three of us aside:

"They aren't going to accuse you of theft. But, unfortunately, your vague description was not enough to identify the true thieves. The Geckho have many clans, groups and independent military divisions. And Shiamiru isn't the name of a single ship, but a very widely-used class of cargo shuttle, which doesn't help the investigation one bit. Nevertheless, Gnat, I'll be expecting you this evening in the real world. We need to have a very serious discussion about your risky gameplay. It threatens problems not only for you personally, but for our whole faction, which I cannot allow! But now, while the Geckho are concerned with other things, I suggest you get back to Border Post Eight as fast as your feet can take you, and don't stick your heads out or get caught up in any new adventures!"

With all the twists and turns, we forgot why we had even come to the pier. Our canteens were still empty, and I remembered that only half way to the border post. Meanwhile, the heat had become totally unbearable. By my estimation, it was no less than one hundred degrees

Fahrenheit in the shade, and maybe more. To even take that measurement, I'd have to find some shade first! In the sun, it was far beyond acceptable. I finally had to put all my kevlar armor in my inventory and strip to the waist. Then I twisted my shirt into a makeshift turban to avoid heatstroke. Levelling be damned, if it meant nearly fainting in the heat! It wasn't worth sacrificing my health!

But I planned to take a different way back to Border Post Eight, going higher up the mountain slope, so I could level my Cartography and my Mineralogy. But in the oppressive heat, I had no energy to scramble up rocks, and time was pressing. There was just an hour left before the end of our shift, so I resigned myself to scanning for oysters a few more times and giving them to Imran. In the end, that netted me ten more pearls, and got my Scanning to twelve. What was more, my character had reached level nine!

I put all three skill points right into Scanning. I didn't want to get scolded tonight for disobeying direct orders on top of the almost guaranteed lecture for my risky behavior.

Kisly was still sitting on the very top of the tower with his trusty machinegun but, despite the heat, our commander was now suited up. The machine-gunner listened to the story of our misadventures on the pier, and didn't hide his dismay:

"I told you to come back! You didn't listen, you wanted to go where you aren't allowed. It's your own fault!"

Imran noted fairly that, with such bad radio signal, we couldn't make out more than a couple disjointed words. Also, the level-6 Gladiator asked why it was like that. Despite himself, Kisly agreed that our communications devices were atrocious:

"All our soldiers complain about that... Our technicians initially blamed it on a lack of pure crystalline silicon to make semiconductors, and how hard it is to make capacitors, diodes and other transistors from scratch. The quality varied a lot. In the end, we just brought in components from the real world, but there were not enough. That allowed us to make okay radios for the First and Second Legions with encoding and other bells and whistles. But newbies are still issued old devices that just barely work..."

The experienced soldier went silent in thought, then changed the topic:

"So, you wanted to see centaurs. There are a couple near the barbed wire fence now."

I looked through an embrasure and saw two centaurs just three hundred feet from our tower! One was a large male with a chestnut-colored horse body that gave way to a muscular human torso. And next to him was a relatively small female with stripes like a zebra. Kisly, holding his sights on the couple, commented:

"They aren't crossing the border, just stomping around their territory. They probably came to trade. They sometimes have fabrics, pearls or forest berries to sell. I'm not coming down from my position but, if you want, you can go talk to them."

Anya was categorically opposed, honestly admitting

that she was afraid. Imran was also hesitant, but in the end decided to stay. He said he'd already had enough adventure for one day. So, I had to go it alone.

"Just put your rifle into your inventory," Kisly advised me. "Centaurs are strong, clever and utterly unprincipled. They'll take your weapon from your hands and run off with it. Then, you'll have to explain yourself to the leadership and ask Vasiliadi for a replacement."

It was reasonable advice, so I followed it, but I couldn't fathom why the centaurs might want a rifle without bullets. I came down from the stone tower and walked unhurriedly to the border and read the information about these mythological creatures:

Ness. Centaur. Antiquity Faction. Level-68 Gladiator.
Phylira. Centaur. Antiquity Faction. Level-48 Archer.

The centaurs were watching me carefully. The male periodically made loud sounds similar to a horse's neigh, while the female remained silent and smiled just like a person. I didn't see any weapons on them, although I understood perfectly that they could take them from their inventory in an instant. I stopped three steps from a gap in the barbed wire and gave a bow.

"Greetings, Gnat!" Phylira said in quite clean Russian. "Don't be afraid, we come in peace. I found a good pearl and would like to trade. Have you got any bullets for sale? Or some of that burning white wine?"

"Vodka?" I suggested, and Phylira nodded in joy:

"Yes! Vodka! I'll give you a big handful of pearls, there

are even some large ones!"

But I didn't have any spare bullets, and especially vodka. Also, I didn't have anything in my inventory to trade other than more pearls and condoms. Should I try and sell them? I took out one packaged condom and showed it to the filly:

"I haven't got any vodka. But I have got something better. This little thing can buy you a magical night of love no foals guaranteed."

The centaur woman either snorted in dismay or chuckled, then cast a sidelong gaze at her four-legged companion and turned back toward me:

"Ness doesn't understand your language, so we can speak freely. So, can it be with any stallion? A magical night of love?"

I realized my unusual trade good had intrigued the lady, and she wasn't trying to hide it. I assured her the miracle item was effective, and Phylira gave a whinny of satisfaction, then extended me her cupped hands full of pearls:

"Gnat, will this be enough? This is all the pearls I have on me. I could add my throwing knife or..." here the centaur lady gave a neigh, "myself. I see how you people look at me. You find me attractive, admit it!"

The bare breasts on Phylira's female torso really were exceptional, prim and perky. She also had a nice face and head of hair. But everything below Phylira's waist was just like a zebra, and I had no idea how she envisioned this going, just from a technical standpoint. Real pervert stuff! Of course I refused. Instead, beyond the pearls, I asked for the right to take water in my canteen from the river behind the centaurs.

"Water?!" Phylira asked in surprise, seemingly somewhat offended. "That's up to Ness. He's in charge here."

The language of the centaurs was a mixture of horse-like neighing, short one-syllable words and many tongue clicks. The male had a very stormy reaction to his companion's request. He neighed in dismay, reared up, and I even saw a short spear appear in his hands. But Phylira was insistent, seemingly even promising something. Ness spent a little while longer being stubborn but eventually allowed himself to be convinced. Both centaurs stepped aside ostentatiously, allowing me through. I politely thanked the border guards and gave a deep bow. Ness gave a contemptuous snort and galloped away.

"Come back tomorrow, Gnat. I'll gather more pearls and we can trade again!" Phylira promised, then hurried off after her companion.

I walked the 100 feet to the dense bushes lining the banks of the small river at a deliberate confident pace and stopped five steps away. I could already see the babbling and tempting water through the greenery, but there was an unnatural silence in the shrubbery. No insects chirring, no birds singing. And that unnerved me

Successful Perception check

My intuition was right. I looked closer and saw a

figure practically stock-still blending in with the leaves. A dryad with a bow at the ready. And not just one! I activated Scanning. Woah! So many red markers! There was a whole squadron of them! For a moment, I met gazes with one of the archers, and gave a respectful bow, saying in a calm quiet voice:

"Greetings, esteemed ladies of the forest! Your border guards gave me permission to gather water."

In reply, I heard a rustling of leaves. On the mini-map, I noticed that practically all the red markers started moving away. Thirty seconds later, only the first dryad I'd spotted remained. It seemed I was being allowed to approach the river. I removed my canteen and started poking through the thick bushes.

Fame increased to 4.

Astrolinguistics skill increased to level ten!

Cartography skill increased to level ten!

Fortunately, it was a fast-flowing river, so it was untainted by salty sea water. I drank some water at my leisure then filled the canteen and clipped it onto my belt. I thanked the dryad, turned around and headed back to my faction's territory with just such a deliberate gait.

As soon as I'd passed the rows of barbed wire that marked the border, Anya flew at me in anger:

"Why did you leave our node??? We were sick with worry! The commander said he'd pummel you into the ground if the centaurs didn't do it first!"

Kisly was so upset he abandoned his post and came

down from the stone tower to give me a piece of his mind:

"Bonehead! Idiot!! Imbecile!!! What were you thinking going that far?! You could have been kidnapped! To be honest, I was sure you'd be attacked. I was holding you in the sights of my machinegun until you reached the bushes to make sure they wouldn't take you alive. I nearly pulled the trigger when you crawled into the bushes! I thought it would be better to shoot you myself than to have the whole faction gather goods to ransom you back from the centaurs!"

Chapter Fifteen

Return to Base

ANYA'S DISAPPROVAL of my thoughtless behavior did nothing to stop her from greedily drinking from my canteen, though. Kisly also stopped frowning fairly quickly and changed back to his usual relaxed and confident face. The commander heard out my story and even chuckled at the negotiations with the centaurs.

"Huh, how didn't I think of trading rubbers with them before?!" the machine-gunner moaned. "But it's too late now. Such a great trade opportunity, and you cut it off at the root…"

"Why do you say that?" I didn't understand.

Kisly gave a wry chuckle and explained in great detail:

"Did you see the wood the centaur stallion was

packing? Below the waist, he's just like a horse with all goods that go with it. A human condom will never fit a centaur! Phylira will think you tricked her after the magical night of love doesn't pan out. And it's too bad, it was such a good idea. It weighs practically nothing, and it would be easy to bring even a hundred from the real world and get a whole handful of pearls for each!"

"And what's the use of pearls?" I asked the experienced commander.

"You can exchange them with the Geckho. The Geckho have been using electronic payment amongst themselves for a thousand years. But with savages like us, they use a special form of currency: artificial red crystals cut in a special way. They'll give one crystal for thirty pearls, and you can use the crystals to buy goods in their shop. But everything they have is expensive. For example, one blaster battery is seventeen crystals while the blaster itself is just under a thousand!"

I just whistled at the sky-high prices. A thousand crystals was thirty thousand pearls, and there was only one pearl per ten shells... I'd have to gather pearls for a whole year to save up enough for one blaster! I said just that out loud.

"Exactly," Kisly agreed, "they're robbing us blind! The Geckho pay us outrageously low prices. A ton of good, sanded lumber is just twelve crystals! When we bought an exoskeleton armor suit for the leader of the Second Legion, our whole faction had to grub along morning noon and night for a whole week to gather the crystals!"

"The leader of the Second Legion? Gerd Tamara?" I clarified, and the machine-gunner confirmed with a nod.

Choosing his words very carefully so he wouldn't accidentally offend the esteemed girl, I enquired what made Tamara so special that the whole faction had worked together to pay for her armor.

"Do you really not know?" our commander was surprised and even seemingly somewhat flabbergasted.

Neither I nor Anya knew, which we told Kisly honestly. He looked around nervously, as if we might be overheard and told me quietly:

"Alright, I'll tell you. But if it comes to anything, you didn't hear this from me. Got it?"

Anya and I nodded in silence. Our commander then, taking another look around, started his story:

"As I'm sure you already know, many terminally ill people were brought under the Dome once it was discovered the game that bends reality could cure them. But no one had a story as gruesome as Tamara's. Her father was a judge, and one day he sent a few high-level drug traffickers to jail. He wasn't afraid of taking them on, but he should have been. They came from a large and influential gang. For years, they controlled a whole city in the Urals. With connections both in the administration and police, they basically ran the place. They barely even had to hide. Higher-level investigators and the prosecutor's office were constantly trying to hook them by the gills, but they never did. Some witnesses would disappear without a trace, others would get scared and refuse to testify. Everyone in the city knew about these drug traffickers, but they were afraid. Plus, city administrators and local police were actively defending them. Tamara's father was also pressured during the trial, and he and his family were threatened many times. But he wasn't afraid of giving them long prison sentences..."

Kisly lowered his gaze and spent a long time in silence before continuing his story barely audibly:

"At night, a group of armed men broke into the judge's house and the whole family was violently murdered. Tamara was tortured while her dying father looked on. They broke her arms, pulled out her eyes, punctured her ear drums, stabbed her in the chest and left her to die. But despite it all, she survived. Her wounds were so severe, the doctors said she'd never make it, but she eventually crawled back from the brink. Even when she got better though, she couldn't see or hear, so she might as well have been a vegetable. That all happened four years back... Tamara spent a few years in a hospital, cooped up with her thoughts until she was brought under the Dome. I didn't see her before her recovery, but I've heard it was a nasty sight. Practically no one believed Tamara would get better. But miraculously, in just a few weeks, she fully regenerated her lost body parts, and her sight returned. After that, Tamara came forward on her own accord and testified against the men who murdered her family. She's been under the Dome for six months now. In the game, she is always on the front lines in the toughest battles. She's garnered a reputation as an extremely strict leader with no patience for anyone who doesn't quickly carry out her every order. The Second Legion adores her. They'd tear their enemies' teeth out if she asked. Also, Gerd Tamara is the only player in our faction who can use magic. When Leng Radugin announced we were collecting funds to buy exoskeleton armor for Tamara, practically everyone in our faction pitched in. And I was one of them. Without hesitation, I gave up all my crystals and spent seven days from morning to night slaving away as a lumberjack."

Kisly finished the story and went silent. After that, I knew no one in our faction would support me if I complained about Gerd Tamara. Her status as a Gerd was not even the biggest factor.

"I see the little bus on the mountain road!" Imran shouted down to us from the tower.

Our commander glanced at his wristwatch, gasped and started getting ready to go. He put his trusty machinegun into his inventory, changed his metal armor for civilian clothing and ordered all three of us to line up in formation outside the tower.

"All in all, I'd say you had a good first patrol!" the group leader declared. "The enemy didn't cross the border, and all the newbies are still alive. You leveled up, improved your skills, and learned something about the game. So, I'd say I did my job. As for Gnat's unauthorized border crossing, I won't not mention it in my report, because it all ended for the best. But don't go wagging your tongues about it.

Agreed?"

My friends and I promised the commander to keep silent on the minor incident. Just then, the familiar little bus came around a bend in the mountain switchback.

"Now that's great! Take your places, let's go back to the Capital. If we don't get stuck on our way, lunch won't even get cold!"

We ate lunch in a dining hall identical to the one we'd had breakfast in this morning. We even sat at the same table. But this time, we were in a virtual game at the central base of our faction. It was a very bizarre sensation. Unfortunately, there were too many people around, so I was too embarrassed to ask my friends whether the virtual food would nourish my real body.

At the table, we were reunited with Masha, Denis and Artur. It immediately became clear that none of them had done any border patrol. Instead, those three had spent the first half of their day in science buildings: Masha in a chemistry laboratory, hidden from prying eyes in the Jungles node, while Artur and Denis were stationed at the Prometheus.

"We're synthesizing explosives in a remote location in the middle of an endless forest, and testing various priming compositions for detonators and capsules. Some are working with lead azides, others with hexogen or peroxides. I was assigned to experiment with mercury fulminate. I even died once today!" Masha boasted, as if that was something to be proud of. "A flask blew up in my hands, and I came back at the respawn point!"

While Masha the level-four Chemist had lots to say, Artur and Denis had nothing to share about their work, saying it was top secret. All I could do was glean some clues from their game data:

Artur Ganin. Human. H3 Faction. Level-5 Constructor.

Denis Tormashyov. Human. H3 Faction. Level-5 Engineer.

Unlike them, Anya and the normally taciturn Imran sang like nightingales, describing our shift on the border with the centaurs. They showed off the shells and pearls they'd collected, and even a piece of pyrite. It was clear that our scientist friends were secretly jealous, though they wouldn't admit it. But I was busting my brains over why the leadership had split us up like this, sending half of us on a combat mission, and the other half to laboratories. Was it due to our classes? Probably.

Then, I felt a wave of déjà vu. Before we were done with our meal, the same fit First Legion blonde walked up to our table. In the game, she didn't wear tight athletic clothes, but a formless baggy camouflage garment that quickly changed color to match her surroundings. Just like a chameleon! I'd never seen technology like this before, so I saw that before paying any mind to the athlete's information:

Svetlana Vereshchagina. Human. H3 Faction. Level-64 Assassin.

Assassin? A murderer?! I was struck by the sweet young girl's class. Gopnik Denis, who was wolfing down a plate of greasy pilaf started choking and couldn't catch his breath. Svetlana gave him a confident slap on the back, immediately shaking loose the piece of trapped rice.

"Thank you," he squeezed out grudgingly through his teeth. Then he immediately groaned: "I didn't ask for help, though. I could have managed."

"No, you would have died and had to run to my fitness class from the respawn point! And you need to save your energy with those smoked-out lungs! By the way, I was ordered to gather all the newbies on the athletic field in ten minutes. So, finish your food quickly, drink your compote and go fall in line!"

We were almost done with lunch, though, so we were practically ready. Anya, who had yet to touch either the meat broth or the pilaf limited herself to salad, so she was done. She stood from the table first, setting an example for the rest. We followed her to the athletic field. There was already a large group of level-three-to-five newbies there. Some of them looked comical in their camouflage military uniforms. Most of them had clearly never held anything more dangerous than a fork before.

"Why schedule exercise right after a meal?!" Imran didn't hide his incomprehension. The PE instructor measured up the muscular Dagestani athlete and gave a good-hearted chuckle:

"Imran, in the real world you'd be right. That is not how it's done. But this is just a game, so don't you worry!"

Anya and Imran, both level-seven, immediately stood out from the motley crew. And it wasn't so much their higher level as it was the fact that they at least distantly looked like they could fight. At level nine, I felt like a hardened veteran, until I was rudely put in my place by the instructor:

"Gnat, I was ordered to keep an especially close eye on you," she said, stopping next to me and not hiding a mocking smirk. "With your ability to worm your way into places you have no business being, and knack for finding trouble, I just hope you don't die before class is over. So, I never want you to leave my sight. Everyone else, run up this path to the stadium!"

To be honest, I was shaken by the mistrust, but I tried not to show it. The whole group of fifty newbies jogged ahead. Svetlana and I walked unhurriedly after them. Just after the last runners were past a bend in the path, my companion said quietly, without turning her head:

"All that is the honest truth. Ivan Lozovsky is very upset with your behavior, especially what happened at the Geckho warehouses. He has spoken with Tyulenev about drawing up an individualized training schedule for you, to make sure someone always has an eye on you, so you don't get up to any more hijinks. But that wasn't the only reason I sent the others away. I've heard a rumor you've got pearls, and you're looking to trade."

I immediately knew the source of this rumor. Kisly must have been blabbing to everyone about me trading condoms with the centaurs. Regardless, I didn't deny it.

"One hundred forty pearls, two large," I confirmed.

"I'll take the standard ones at a rate of twenty-five pearls per crystal. I'll need to see the large ones before I name my price. In any case, it will be a better deal for you than selling them to the Geckho."

Well, why not? I showed the two larger pearls to Svetlana, and she gave her conclusions:

"I'll give eight red crystals for all the pearls. You'll never find a better price. But my character has high Trading, so I get a better exchange rate."

I agreed and received eight identical multifaceted red crystals. They seemed to pulsate with an internal glow. The assassin girl was very satisfied with the exchange and put the pearls in her inventory, then suggested we start jogging to catch up with the rest of the group. Just after the athletics field came into view, I got a few system messages in a row:

Cartography skill increased to level eleven!

Medium Armor skill increased to level four!

You have reached level ten!

You have received three skill points!

Congratulations! You now have two more skill slots!!!

Despite the fact that Svetlana was running two steps ahead of me, she noticed my character levelling up. Did she have eyes in the back of her head or something? Maybe she saw detailed information about all the characters on the mini map. At any rate, Svetlana stopped sharply, and I nearly ran into her.

"So, you've reached level ten in less than a day?" she clarified.

I just nodded, because it was hard enough to breathe after the long run. Talking was out of the question. The instructor commented with clear approval:

"Excellent result, Gnat. You could even try to beat our faction record: thirteen levels in the first day. If you manage, I bet faction leadership will be much more understanding of your risky behavior. You can say it's all been part of your leveling plan. It may be unusual, but they won't be able to argue with your results. Everyone loves a winner, after all."

"So, who set the faction record?" I asked, having just caught my breath, and the assassin grew embarrassed and lowered her gaze to the ground.

"Well, I was actually the first to get thirteen levels on my first day. Another three in our faction have done the same since. You've got six hours left to beat my record."

Chapter Sixteen

Free Time

I T WASN'T THAT I was exactly afraid of getting chewed out by the leadership, but I wasn't looking forward to it either. And so, given there was a way to avoid being picked apart, I needed to try and level up as much as possible in the next six hours. To beat the record, I would have to get another four levels before sunset. To my eye, it was totally possible. Each subsequent level was harder to get, though. To get to level two, I just had to activate scanning a few times and see part of the labyrinth map. For ten, I'd needed to raise a skill seven or eight times.

So then, how could I do this? Scanning? I was already using it every time it reloaded. Cartography worked automatically when my character saw new areas. Medium Armor also leveled on its own, although quite slowly. I just had to make sure not to remove my Kevlar jacket. Those three skills were basically passive and leveled on their own. But I strongly suspected they would not be enough to get me four more levels in the time I had left.

But the rest of my skills — Electronics, Astrolinguistics, Break-in, Rifles and Mineralogy could only be used in certain conditions. And so, I would have to try and bring as many of them together as possible. Ideally, converse with an alien or foreigner somewhere with valuable mineral ore, while soldering an electronic security system and occasionally shooting a rifle. I couldn't hold back the stupid ear-to-ear smile, imagining such a surreal picture.

"Gnat, did I say something funny?" the fitness instructor demanded, peeved.

She was now telling us how to raise our base stats. It was very, very difficult. To raise one's Constitution by just one point required exhausting monotonous work-outs, pushing your body to the very edge for around eight hours. After that, to raise Constitution by another point, you'd have to endure similar torture for around three weeks. And although the Geckho assured us that a third point could be added to Constitution, no humans had yet managed to do so.

"No ma'am, there's nothing funny about hours of torturous exercise," I answered, and she finally stopped boring into me with her dismayed gaze.

"Svetlana, may I ask a question?" I didn't even turn my head. I knew that little nerd by voice. He was asking yet another pointless question. "My character is a scientist specializing in theoretical physics. I'll spend all my time in a laboratory. Why do I need to level Constitution and Strength?"

The assassin was instantly ten steps from the newbie, and I didn't understand how she did it. But just a second later, the nerd and all the newbies standing next to him were lying on the ground, writhing in pain and gasping for air, like fish out of water. Svetlana, not paying any attention to the fallen scientists, turned to the rest:

"Let me tell you all the cautionary tale of why we do not have a player number two hundred twenty-four in the Human-3 Faction. His name was Valentin. He, by the way, was also a physicist. And he assured us that he didn't need fitness training, or any combat skills, because he was not planning to leave the laboratory ever. That stubborn ass also, despite many warnings and even direct orders from leadership, had not spent any of his free skill points since he entered the game. He said he'd use them all after it became too hard to level his skills the normal way."

"But that's a good strategy!" gopnik Denis interrupted Svetlana. "People do that in every game!"

The assassin girl looked severely at Denis, and I thought he would get laid out too. But Svetlana just gave a wry chuckle and continued her story:

"For three months, Valentin insisted on doing things his way, becoming the weakest link in the laboratory, significantly behind his colleagues. It was really getting on our nerves. He just fed us all promises that eventually he would catch up and be the highest level. But then, a group of

Dark Faction saboteurs attacked... The Prometheus is just some four miles from the border, and that's two minutes on an antigrav. Our enemies went straight for it, blew up a few workshops, and a couple scientists were sent to respawn. Among them was Valentin the physicist. And he, by the way, was level thirty-nine. All one hundred fourteen of his unused skill points burnt up. That day, Valentin locked himself in his room and hung himself... And so, like it or not, there's a clear order from Leng Radugin: all skill points must be spent within twenty-four hours. What's more, every member of the H3 faction must undergo basic fitness and military training, so they can hold their own if need be. No one is expecting military greatness from you, but in case of danger, at the very least you'll be able to hold out until the First or Second Legion arrive!"

The next hour and a half we exercised. An obstacle course, strength training, push-ups and pull-ups. But above all, running with weights. Everyone's character had a weight calculated for them depending on their Strength and Endurance. It was hell...

Silent in exhaustion, with a heavy log on my shoulders, I made lap after lap on the tarmac track. The worst part was that I could never say: "I can't, it's too heavy." Svetlana was a sadist and knew perfectly well what I was capable of. What was more, she put us all into a group and, as its leader, she could see everyone's health and endurance bars.

The system suggested I take new skills with my free slots several times: Survival, Loader, Athlete, Long-Distance Runner and, for some reason, Meteorologist. But I read all their descriptions and didn't take any of them. They just weren't for me. It was a good idea to take two more skills, but not just because. I needed to weigh all the plusses and minuses, along with their potential benefit.

After all, who was my character going to be? A Prospector's job was to work with electronic scanning devices and find things of value. So, I arrived at two conclusions at once. First, I needed to pick new skills to help me with my primary ones. Anything that could help me discover better things, farther away, or scan more often. Second, it was important that I be able to sell what I found for as much as possible. Trading those pearls for crystals had proven that, without the Trading skill and knowledge of average prices, I could end up with a lot less.

My endurance reached zero and I was falling over in exhaustion, so I had to take a breather. Using the time, I asked the experienced instructor what skills might allow me to discover hidden enemies, traps and items.

"Are you picking your two new skills at level ten?" Svetlana immediately guessed. "What can I say? You're not wasting any time. The classes Sentry and Spy as well as Assassin have the primary skills Danger Sense, Eagle Eye and

Sharp Hearing. I bet one of those would be of use to a Prospector. But overall, I advise all my students to level Sharpshooter. It works for any long-distance weapon, reducing scatter and increasing chance of critical hits."

I thanked the instructor for her help, put the log back on my shoulders and shuffled off for another lap. At the same time, I called up explanations of the skills Svetlana had suggested. I especially liked Eagle Eye:

Eagle Eye. This skill lets you see farther and have a higher chance of discovering items and creatures in adverse conditions (fog, smoke, darkness, camouflage etc.). As this skill improves, you will be able to see farther, and have a better chance of discovering hidden objects. Minimum statistics: Perception 18, Intelligence 15.

Exactly what I was looking for!

You have taken the skill Eagle Eye level 1.

After prolonged consideration, I followed the experienced mentor's advice again and filled the other slot with Sharpshooter. Sure, Trading would be nice, but I needed to be able to take down enemies and other dangerous creatures to get and keep anything worth selling. After all, Gnat's combat abilities clearly needed work. The example of my recent encounter with a swarm of field pests had shown that clearly.

You have taken the skill Sharpshooter level 1.

Sure, Sharpshooter may not have been the best possible choice to beat the one-day record. However, in the longer perspective, it had clear plusses, especially considering the overlap between Sharpshooter and my high Luck Modifier, which gave a higher chance of crits.

I was in a mental fog for the next half hour of training. I was immeasurably tired. If not for my desire to break the faction record, my only thought would have been collapsing on the grass and lying there for a few hours. But instead, I was keeping careful track of time and planning my next moves. Just ten minutes before I finished my exercises, I got a double message:

Medium Armor skill increased to level five!

Scanning skill increased to level seventeen!

Finally... Although it was quite little for an hour and a half running myself ragged! There was just four hours left until sunset, and my progress bar to level eleven had reached just a quarter of the scale. Not enough, not at all. I placed the three skill points I got at level ten into Scanning just like the last time, raising it to level 20.

I thought up a clear plan of action for the rest of the day and, just as Svetlana told me exercise was over, I ran back to base.

"Gnat, wait! Where are you going?" Imran called out to me, overheated and soaked in sweat.

The level-8 Gladiator was very happy after working out and, based on his present level, had grown quite a bit. But now, Imran was seemingly counting on all of us going somewhere together as a group. But I had totally different plans for this evening:

"I need to find our Geologist right away to discuss our

partnership. Some guy named Mikhalych. They say he can be hard to track down."

"Wait, why are you still working?! On the schedule, we have free time! You can find Mikhalych tomorrow. But now we can do whatever we want! I say we should zip down to the Firing Range. It's right nearby! We'll train up and get ourselves some better weapons!"

But I didn't let him talk me out of my plans. Hurriedly bidding my friend farewell, I ran to the Capital. I was, of course, not looking for Mikhalych. I wanted to find Starship Pilot Zheltov and his fast-moving vehicle. Hopefully they were on base!

I got lucky. Zheltov was in the hanger. He was painting his bumper green, trying to once again cover up the gnarled word "Starship." Based on the mocking smirks on the soldiers nearby, a fresh set of scratches would appear as soon as Zheltov finished painting and walked away.

"What do you want, Gnat?" The pilot could also see the soldiers standing stock still, and probably realized his work was pointless, so he was upset.

"Here," I showed him eight red Geckho crystals in my hand. "I've got a job for you. How long of a ride will this get me?"

"I don't run a taxi service! And as you can see, I'm

busy!" Zheltov groaned in dismay, although his gaze was transfixed by the crystals.

I immediately realized we would come to an agreement despite his grumbling. But I didn't persuade or pressure him, just stood in silence, letting Zheltov make up his own mind.

"I have to pick up a group from a distant sentry tower at six in the evening," the pilot said, thoughtfully stroking the back of his head.

"So, until ten to six?" I forwarded and, not waiting for an answer, sat down in the front passenger seat. "You manage to charge up those pancakes? Or are we just gonna crawl along like last time?"

"What do you mean crawl along? My girl is a speed demon!" The pilot objected, getting in the driver's seat and putting on his old-fashioned motorcycle helmet. "Don't forget to wear a helmet, big talker. These pancakes are one hundred percent charged and we're gonna push them to the limit. Where are we going?"

"First along the outer border of our faction, but stay in our nodes. We don't need to cause problems with our neighbors. Then, I'd like to see all the main and secondary roads. After that, we could drive around the main ridges and mountaintops. I'm trying to build up a complete map."

"We can't do all that before six..." the pilot answered doubtfully, taking out a tablet, calling up a map and marking out a suggested route. "Also, let me warn you, I won't go far into the Yellow Mountains node. My racer can't make it along those steep cliffs... So... I guess, we'll finish the excursion either in the Eastern Swamp near the new base on the central island, or in the central node at a hot sulfur spring near a ridge."

"The sulfur spring is better! Exactly what I need!"

From there, the talking ended and the race began. Seemingly, Zheltov was seriously offended by my disparaging remarks, and the former student of the Military Space Academy did everything in his power to prove the opposite. We raced along at a mad speed, at times making such sharp turns that my eyes went dim. I had read that a normal untrained person could lose consciousness in a Formula-1 race car by the second or third turn, and I could tell this was near that. I suspect that, if I hadn't invested in Constitution after going through the Labyrinth, I'd have already passed out.

Yes, it was hard, but it was worth it! The progress bar was filling up right before my eyes. I was leveling Cartography and Eagle Eye with enviable regularity. My character had reached level eleven in just ten minutes! And I'd hit twelve soon...

We flew into the swamp, spooking frogs and other creatures. A wave of muddy water rolled over me, then I was forced to lurch forward when we came to an abrupt stop in some deep muck. I couldn't see anything, I even had to remove my mud-caked glasses to see.

"Why are you still sitting?! Get out and help pull us out before we get totally stuck!" Zheltov yelled, also caked from head-to-toe in mud.

I would have gladly unbuckled and gone to help, but I was so exhausted my body wouldn't obey. Every muscle was screaming in pain. Also, the seatbelt was too tight, and I couldn't move my arm, which was squeezed against my torso. The pilot had to help me out of the safety belt, then the both of us pulled the ooze-caked starship onto dry land.

"I usually go through here at speed when I'm alone in the vehicle. Sorry, I didn't think we'd get stuck together," Zheltov started justifying himself, but I just waved a hand:

"I don't mind. These things happen. We don't have much time, let's keep going. Plus, I can see a bunch of red markers on the mini-map. It seems dangerous to stay here."

"Yeah, this place is full of swamp creatures, and a bunch of them are poisonous. Let's go!"

And so our mad race continued. Through forest and field, down nice roads and through untamed wilderness, the starship sped confidently onward. Zheltov told me about the local scenery, defensive structures and places where especially fierce battles had taken place. I was only half listening, but still answered sometimes. By the end of the two-hour excursion, I found the speed, turns and buzzing past trees positively exhilarating.

At ten to six, Dmitry Zheltov let me out near a small pond of cloudy green water that smelled like rotten eggs.

"Alright, we've done what we agreed on. I hope you aren't mad at me for the accident in the swamp. Anyway, you can wash the mud off your clothes here," the pilot pointed at the sulfurous spring.

But I, staggering in exhaustion and barely able to stand, didn't have a care in the world other than my level: fifteen. Despite the aching pain in my joints, I wanted to sing and dance for joy. It had worked!

"How could I be mad?! Dmitry, you helped me a ton. I owe you a bottle of good brandy in real life... well, if I can figure out how to buy one under the Dome. And when I'll get more crystals, maybe we can do some more stunt driving!"

Zheltov started smiling, squeezed my hand farewell and pointed to the northeast:

"The central base is that way, just one mile. There haven't been any dangerous creatures here in the central node for a long time. But if you see anything, shout on the radio, our guys will quickly come help!"

I don't know why he told me the direction to the Capital. My map already had every structure of any significance in our faction's territory. I certainly wouldn't get lost as long as I had that and a compass. I bade the pilot farewell, sat down on the shore of the lake and opened my statistics.

So, how was I doing?

Gnat. Human. Faction H3	
Level-15 Prospector	
Statistics:	
Strength	12
Agility	15

Intelligence	18
Perception	20
Constitution	12
Luck modifier	+3
Parameters:	
Hitpoints	480
Endurance points	80 of 285
Magic points	0
Carrying capacity	24 kg
Fame	4
Skills:	
Electronics	6
Scanning	20
Cartography	26
Astrolinguistics	10
Break-in	6
Rifles	16
Medium armor	6
Mineralogy	11
Eagle Eye	19
Sharpshooter	1

Not bad at all! And I had fifteen skill points just sitting there! What a great ride! The idea to take Eagle Eye had justified itself one hundred percent. If my view was obstructed by branches, mud spatter, fog or smoke, it skill leveled even faster than Cartography.

I'd already beaten the faction record, and by two whole levels. What was more, I had two and a half hours to go. I was not planning to just kick back and be satisfied. While I had the time, I needed to build on my success! But what should I do to earn accolades and avoid criticism? I wanted my allies to shake their heads in shock when they saw my achievements!

The upcoming conversation with the leadership no longer seemed so frightening and unpleasant because my record breaking leveling served as proof I was on the right track. I filled my lungs with fresh forest air, although it was somewhat tainted by the smell of the sulfur pond. I lay down in the tall grass. How awesome! I love this game!

Successful Perception check

I seemed to hear voices, and not so far away. Without raising my head, I carelessly moved the grass aside to see who it was. There were three strangers, and all of them were wearing strange dark-gray uniforms that looked to be made of small scales, and chameleon camouflage cloaks on their shoulders. Without a doubt they were people, and they were in our capital node very near the central base. But I was thrown off by several inconsistencies. First, their skin was an unusual ashen gray color. Second, they were walking hunched over, as if sneaking. People normally don't walk like that in their own lands.

Not yet totally believing my guesses, but still trying not to make any sharp movements, I tried to read the information about the nearest unfamiliar person:

Bey-O Tu-Leen. Human. Dark Faction. Level-32 Warrior

Dark Faction!!! A second later, all three markers on the mini-map turned bright red. The game system classified them as enemies!!! They were no more than ninety feet away, and they were coming in my direction. I froze in fear, trying to press myself against the ground. But then I began to crawl up the slope very slowly into the bushes on the edge of the sulfur lake.

Chapter Seventeen

Observation Post

MY HEART STARTED POUNDING against my ribcage in fear. My thoughts scattered in panic. What to do? It was most likely too late to run. As soon as I got up from the grass, I'd be seen. Fight? That wasn't even funny. I had just one shotgun cartridge left, and it was sitting in my inventory, not even loaded into the double-barrel. I had unloaded the gun for safety before the trip with Zheltov. And I couldn't load it now. The sound of a barrel clicking would draw attention. It would be very dumb to put any hope in my weak little air gun, too. It hadn't pierced the shell of a level-4 bug, so it wouldn't even scratch the scaly armor of the Dark Faction soldiers. All that remained was the knife, and I squeezed it tight in my right hand.

Another alarmed thought flickered about my fifteen free skill points. But my progress bar to level sixteen was not empty. I'd managed to fill it to twenty percent. What was more, twenty-four hours had not yet passed since I'd earned them. So, in theory, dying wouldn't be catastrophic. I wouldn't lose the fifteen skill points; my progress bar would just fall to zero.

But death was not the most frightening possibility. It was actually probably the best way this could end. For some reason, I was reminded of the Assassin Svetlana. During our lesson, she was standing pretty far away from her students, yet she managed to get next to them in the blink of an eye and bash them in the chest so hard they couldn't even move. I also remembered hearing that the Dark Faction took two Second Legion soldiers prisoner in the last battle.

From what I'd heard, enemy factions could keep a player captive for an unlimited time. They just had to make sure they stayed alive, so they'd never respawn. It was really the most damage that could be done to a faction. Take an active player out of their ranks and lock them in a dungeon for many months or even years. What was more, this was not our world. Different rules applied here, and the Dark Faction hadn't exactly signed the Geneva Convention, so there was no guarantee I'd be treated with dignity. So, as a prisoner of war, I would be broken physically and mentally. And that was truly frightening.

At that very moment, my mind filled with horror stories, a Dark Faction player appeared on the shore of the forest lake just five steps from me. It took me enormous effort to not scream or move in the grass and sedge.

Minn-O La-Fin. Human. Dark Faction. Level-48 Cartographer.

She was a tall thin girl with ashen gray skin and short silver hair. Clearly of the human race, but I'd never seen anyone that looked like her before. My fear and her enemy status didn't stop me from noticing her uncanny beauty. Now, from up close, I could see that she wasn't wearing armor at all. The thin form-fitting suit, perfectly outlining the alluring curves of her young feminine body was covered with an innumerable collection of tiny ceramic scales.

I had once seen a clip on the internet about future technology describing a suit like this. If I was right, every scale would heat up or cool down to match the temperature of her surroundings, making her totally invisible to infrared sensors and heat-seeking weaponry. The chameleon cloak on her shoulders made her visibly blend in with the grass, stones, trees and surrounding environment. In fact, to a distant observer, she would be entirely invisible as soon as she stopped moving.

"Rosg in kuwi unt ik," the cartographer girl called her companions after her with a shockingly normal wave of the hand, calling her companions and pointing to some tracks on the ground.

"Oni in kuwi 'staasheep,'" said a man, straining to pronounce the foreign word, and all three laughed.

Apparently, the name of Zheltov's fast-moving craft

was funny to them as well. I was in no mood to laugh, though. They'd noticed my tracks! And now, as soon as they looked down to the water's edge, they'd see me!

I had to make sure they wouldn't take me alive!!! With some doubt, I touched my finger with the blade of the knife. I didn't have the Blades skill, so I was in serious doubt it could kill me, even if I slit my throat. After all, I was at level fifteen and had four hundred eighty hitpoints... If I didn't kill myself quickly, the bleeding could be stopped, and they could bring me back from the brink.

So, the knife would not do. I couldn't kill myself in one blow, and they wouldn't allow me to make a second or third. What then? Quickly load a cartridge into the shotgun and shoot myself in the head? Also not instantaneous, and they might not give me time. But if I didn't manage, the lake was behind me and, apparently quite deep. What had Kisly said today? "The game rules are pretty strict there. If you don't have the Swimming skill, you'll just drown as soon as you get into deeper water." Not a bad option.

But for now, the enemies were stalling. Based on the mini-map, two of them were trying to track Zheltov's starship. The cartographer girl was still standing on the shore, though. She took out something that looked like a monocle and investigated the distant forest more closely. As my enemies hadn't yet discovered me, I felt no need to take my life. So, this seemed like a good opportunity to spend my skill points. I opened my character window and hurriedly placed them all: five in Rifles, five in Sharpshooter, five in

Medium Armor. Now, I was mad I hadn't taken Stealth. If I could place fifteen whole points there, there would be a decent chance no one would see me.

But I didn't need Stealth. The men called the girl from far away demandingly and Minn-O La-Fin placed the monocle back in a case on her belt. She took one final look into the forest through her dark glasses, then threw the hood of her invisibility cloak over her pretty head and hurried off. I concluded the two men must have been her subordinates, because they were of a much lower level, thirty-two and thirty-six. She must have been an important person to warrant that. Now, they were hurrying the cartographer girl on, telling her to quickly get off the hill because it made her too visible.

Astrolinguistics skill increased to level eleven!

Tracking the red markers on the mini-map, and giving them a forty-yard head start, I slunk after them up the slope. I was no longer considering suicide. My priority was not letting the enemy spies out of view. And by the way, where were they? Lying down flat in the grass, I looked into the leafy forest on the slope of the hill.

Successful Perception check

Eagle Eye skill increased to level twenty!

They were going up the stream jumping from stone to stone. I placed that point and my location on my map. Letting the enemies get a bit farther away, I activated my radio:

"Come in, anyone! This is Gnat, number fourteen-seventy. I'm tracking three members of the Dark Faction in the central node near the sulfur lake."

"...ar ...bonehead... frequency... tique beach!" Despite the interference, I recognized Kisly's voice, but he was immediately interrupted by another voice:

"This i... ...post One! Gnat, I... can't hear, ple... repeat, over."

I repeated everything, gave my map coordinates, the enemy's trajectory and even their classes and levels. I also said the members of the Dark Faction were going up the stream, jumping on stones in order not to leave tracks on the wet ground.

"The raid ...roup will be handled by the Sec... Legion! Communication on thi... frequency immediately... cease! Everyone switch to chan... seventeen, turn on encoding, over!"

I may have been mistaken due to the distortion, but the last voice seemed to be Gerd Tamara. But I couldn't hear them anymore. I turned the simple radio over in my hands and looked at it: microphone, speaker, talk button and volume knob, plus and an on/off switch. How could I even turn this to another channel? It seemed that my primitive radio simply didn't have that function. It didn't have encoding either. Damn!

And meanwhile, the three red markers were getting quite far away and nearing the border of my mini-map. Considering the high-tech chameleon cloaks the raiders were wearing, I had a serious risk of losing sight of them. So,

I went after the enemies, trying to keep them at the very edge of my vision. A few times, one of the trio turned and looked back, but I managed to remain unseen, taking shelter behind a rock or tree trunk.

Eagle Eye skill increased to level twenty-two!

I kept up pursuit for seven minutes. We were going further and further up the hill. The forest was getting sparser all the time. There was less and less cover, but I didn't stop tracking them. Suddenly, all three of them stopped. Either I had failed a Perception check, or their cloaks turned on, but all three of them instantly disappeared. I quickly placed a marker on the map where I had last seen them.

What to do now? I didn't want to keep going, because the forest was ending, and my enemies would probably notice me if I came too close. There just wasn't enough cover. After waiting a few minutes for my scanning skill to reload, I activated the icon. But no, even with scanning, the enemies were undetectable. I had to go back to the sulfur lake.

I had gone almost all the way back down the stream to the lake when I heard someone call my name. Immediately, several bulky figures in camouflage uniforms appeared from behind the nearest bushes and rocks. I nearly got scared but saw the Second Legion emblem and H3 code on their uniform, as well as the fact that they had green markers on the mini-map, meaning ally.

The high-level soldiers immediately started telling me off:

"Where'd you run off to, Gnat? Why weren't you answering your radio?"

I unclipped my radio from my belt and showed them:

"If any of you can explain which of the two buttons on this thing change channel or turn on encoding, I'd be very grateful. I couldn't figure it out."

"And where are the enemies? Or was that a joke about the Dark Faction? And why is your uniform so dirty?" An armored anthropomorphic robot ten feet in height appeared from invisibility three steps away. I strained to look through its darkened helmet visor and saw the face of a dark-haired girl frowning in dismay.

So, I hadn't been wrong last night. It wasn't just some hallucination. Gerd Tamara or at least her exoskeleton suit could become invisible. I wanted to make a sarcastic quip in reply to her foolish question, but I held back. I remembered the last time I'd spoken with the leader of the Second Legion. It hadn't lasted long and ended very tragically for me, so I decided not to repeat my error.

"I took a ride on Zheltov's starship, and didn't have time to clean my uniform before I saw enemies. I had no way to get in touch, and they were walking away. So, I tracked them through the forest along the stream, then up a slope. There, they must have taken cover, because I lost them. I didn't get any closer so I wouldn't give myself away. Here are the coordinates where I saw them."

I rattled off the coordinates I'd marked on the map. Gerd Tamara gave an untrusting snort, but after a five second pause, pointed at four of her subjects — a level-70 Commando, a level-65 Scout and two Assassins above level 60. Seemingly, the commander had chosen everyone who could move in stealth.

"Check this intel! If you do find enemies, do not engage. Wait for the rest of the group."

They were all wearing chameleon cloaks, while the Commando even had a scaled thermoregulating suit just like the Dark Faction players. They walked in the direction I indicated. After a minute, the towering Gerd Tamara disappeared without a sound but, based on the flattened grass made by her heavy steel feet, I determined that she'd gone after the first group. The other soldiers of the Second Legion, and there were thirty of them, followed their commander.

"What should I do?" I asked the soldiers as they moved out.

They all ignored my question, as if I didn't exist. Finally, the level-55 Shock Trooper bringing up the rear of the column with the strange name Rupor, turned to me and answered:

"Well, you must have been doing something here, so just get back to that. I don't advise you to follow us. A serious battle is no place for newbies. What's more, I can't say for certain how you earned our commander's distrust, but little Tamara will throw you under the bus if anything goes wrong."

Harsh, but fair. Thanks for that. I stood on the bank of the lake, catching my breath and deciding where to go next. The bubbles of hydrogen sulfide coming up from the bottom and the yellowish gray residue on the stones and plants drew my attention. It looked like a sulfur hot spring. I'd have to comb through the nearby hills with our Geologist in search of sulfide metals. It would also be interesting to study the chemical composition of this lake.

But, no matter how I spun it, I was most interested in the stream. Somewhere up the slope, water was flowing out of a cliff. If I had a standard geologist's kit to study water composition, I could learn a lot about the local mineral deposits very quickly. But that was the only place I couldn't go now...

And then my radio started buzzing:

"Come in, Gnat. This is Rupor. You done good, kid! It was all confirmed. The radio won't pick up from over the hill, so call two transports to that green lake from the central base. And, if you'd like to see it all with your own eyes, get up to the spot you pointed us to. It's really worth a look."

"But Gerd Tamara," I started but fumbled, not knowing how to formulate my thought that the leader of the Second Legion was not too fond of me and would not want me there.

"You have my permission!"

Fame increased to 5.

I couldn't believe my ears. The voice, beyond all doubt, belonged to Gerd Tamara! The harsh Second Legion commander had an unexpectedly sweet tone. Before she changed her mind, I called the base and, giving my coordinates, gave an order to send two transports to the lake in the hills. Then, jumping on stones, I raced up the stream and scrambled up the steep slope.

Wow!!! From this stony platform, I had an excellent view of the whole node, even though the Capital itself was blocked by a higher neighboring hill. I could see all the main roads and distant buildings in the Yellow Mountains, Jungles, even the Eastern Swamp.

Cartography skill increased to level twenty-seven!
Cartography skill increased to level twenty-eight!
Cartography skill increased to level twenty-nine!
Eagle Eye skill increased to level twenty-two!
Eagle Eye skill increased to level twenty-three!
You have reached level sixteen!
You have received three skill points!

All those messages made me stumble, then I came to a very important conclusion. Leveling Cartography and Eagle Eye could be done not only from fast vehicles, but also by climbing up to good vantage points. A nice place for some spies. There was nothing surprising in the fact that the Dark Faction had taken advantage of it.

There was a small tent for three or four people, sheltered from view by thick bushes and boulders. Before it was a pot on a gas burner. Nearby they had a powerful radio station with a tall antenna, hidden in the thick foliage of a tree. A tripod stood next to it with a huge telescope practically six feet in length, which also had a laser distance measurer and another couple modifications.

The spies were lying next to their camp on the grass with their faces down. Their naked bodies were spread-eagled with their arms and legs tied to stakes in the earth. The Dark Faction players were only wearing dark impenetrable blindfolds, and thick rubber ball gags, held firmly by a strap around their head.

Right next to them on a flat stone, there were some things the Second Legion had confiscated: chameleon cloaks, dark scaled suits, boots, helmets, strange-looking firearms and clips, radios, grenades, coils of rope and wire, a first-aid kit, thermal underwear and plenty of personal items.

Gerd Tamara was standing next to the sophisticated telescope and carefully studying it. After that, she crouched down in her exoskeleton armor, twisted a few settings and turned the optical device to the northwest.

"Holy crap! What a powerful telescope! I can see First Legion at Border Post Four playing cards instead of keeping watch. By the way, Roman Pavlovich, write down their names, so we can punish them: Headquarters Pen_Pusher, Shoot_To_Kill, Nelly Svistunova and... crap, I can't see the fourth, there's a slab of reinforced concrete in the way."

"The fourth is most likely Gurbin, the group sniper," answered a tall muscular level-72 Grenadier by the name

Roman Pavlovich.

"Most likely it is Gurbin, but I can't see him for certain. And as I'm not one-hundred-percent sure, don't put Gurbin on the list. Hey, get away from her!!!"

The cry of rage tore itself from Gerd Tamara after she peeled herself from the telescope. It was directed at a group of soldiers at the feet of the naked Minn-O La-Fin, who were discussing the amusing spectacle. The soldiers obeyed unquestioningly. The leader of the Second Legion then stood up, searched for me and called me closer with a gesture:

"Gnat, I'll admit I don't know how you did that. And when I don't understand something, I get mad and untrusting. I don't know these two," the paladin nodded her massive helmet carelessly at two of the captive soldiers, "but as for Minn-O La-Fin, this is not our first encounter. She has excellent intuition, with her Perception far beyond twenty and a well leveled Danger Sense skill. Usually, you can't even raise a weapon at Minn-O La-Fin before she's out of firing range or behind cover. How did she not detect you?!"

"I simply didn't think of pointing a weapon at her, because I understood the senselessness of fighting three high-level enemies at once. And I was close to her, and totally covered in wet mud when she looked over the area through that thing," I said, pointing at the unusual monocle lying on a stone among the spoils.

"That is an infrared lens, and a very good one at that. You got very lucky, Gnat, twice. But in any case, you were a great help to the faction. Plus, you helped the Second Legion and me personally. Minn-O La-Fin is a valuable prisoner, and the Dark Faction is sure to want to trade for her. I heard you had a dispute with Lozovsky and Tyulenev. I'll put in a good word for you."

Chapter Eighteen

Lessons Learned

I DIDN'T MANAGE to hit level seventeen before sunset, and it was all my fault. First off, I didn't have the audacity to go use the powerful telescope right after Gerd Tamara was done. I could have seen a lot of territory that way. But, while I was speaking with the leader of the Second Legion, the telescope was taken off the tripod and folded up for transport to the Capital. The radio station was also packed up and prepared for transport, along with the tent and other camping supplies.

After that, I wasted twenty minutes just talking to players and watching the Second Legion soldiers. I should have spent that time leveling! Sure, it wasn't totally in vain, not at all. There were plusses as well: I met mechanics that could improve my weapons and clothes and found out something important about the game system.

For example, if an enemy was stunned or tied up, one could fully remove all their equipment and weapons, and also clear out their inventory. But the same could not be done with a corpse. Worn items and weapons were generally preserved after respawn, and the whole inventory was kept other than the few items that dropped.

I also found out some extremely important information. Apparently, your character stayed in the game for a certain amount of time after exiting the game that bends reality. How long depended on the safety of the location. In any base of one's own faction, or other territories classified as "green, safe," the character remained for around thirty seconds after the player left their pod. But in those thirty seconds, your character was inactive and very vulnerable. It could easily be killed or robbed. Of course, players of one's own faction almost never harmed their allies. Nevertheless, such a thing was possible, and had to be kept in mind.

So, if there was no way to get somewhere safer, and one had to log off in a "yellow, normal" zone, the delay increased to ten minutes. That was very risky, because predatory creatures were especially active at night. Also, enemies could easily kill your immobile and helpless character. And finally, in "red, dangerous" zones, for example with enemies nearby or in extreme conditions (lack of air, poisonous fumes, frost etc.), a character would not disappear after the player logged off and would just be left in a lethal scenario. In the majority of such cases, the character would die.

While I talked with the experienced players of the Second Legion, Gerd Tamara handed out the thermoregulating scaled suits and chameleon cloaks at her discretion. The remaining valuable items were also immediately taken by the Second Legion soldiers and stuffed into duffel bags. There was even a small scuffle over the laser pistols. Anyhow, Grenadier Roman Pavlovich, Gerd Tamara's right hand man, quickly established order.

There was just the cartographer's IR lens left. It had unusual skill and stat requirements and was no good to anyone. Many players turned it over it in their hands, looked at it with pity and set it back. When distributing the spoils of an operation, the Second Legion had a rule that an item had to be used and could not be taken "just because."

"Gnat, take a look and see if you'll be able to use this item any time soon." the leader of the Second Legion suggested. "The lens is worth a pretty penny. What's more it's rare and, as far as I can see, has bonuses. It was clearly made for people, although not by the Dark Faction."

I didn't have to be persuaded and walked up to the IR lens lying in a plastic case with soft lining that looked very similar to felt.

Infrared lens (helmet mod)
Vision radius: 11,500 feet. Target identification

radius: 6,000 feet. Perception +2

Statistic requirements: Perception 20, Intelligence 17

Skill requirements: Cartography 25, Eagle Eye 20, Electronics 8

Attention! Your character's electronics skill is insufficient to use this item.

Without saying a word, I opened my skill window and placed all three free points into Electronics, raising it to level 9. After that, I carefully removed it from the case and, using the attached clamp, clipped it to my helmet over my right eye.

The twilight grew more contrasting. The soldiers of the Second Legion and the captives lying on the ground changed to bright white silhouettes. I even noticed a little fox hiding in the nearby bushes, sniffing around in alarm and studying the people here in the hills.

Eagle Eye skill increased to level twenty-four!

"Now that's great! I sensed that this item should belong to you," Gerd Tamara commented and, turning back to her subordinates, ordered: "Alright, transport is here. Let's pack up!"

The captives had their ankles tied together and their hands cuffed behind their backs, but their blindfolds and gags were left in place. Then, they were carried down to the sulfur lake as if they were fragile porcelain vases. But I didn't follow the Second Legion. I was in no rush to return to the Capital.

For a few minutes, I stayed on the high vantage point

to try out my new IR lens, but the view didn't change much. I should have figured. Even without this device, I could see more than two miles from up on the hill, so my map didn't expand. My progress bar was rising, probably because of the animals I couldn't see before, but the pace was positively comatose. That wasn't good enough. I had to find somewhere else. There was still time, so I decided to go up a taller hill nearby. I could level fastest from there, because I'd be using both Eagle Eye and Cartography.

But that was the wrong move. I might have reached level seventeen on my first day if I'd chosen differently. The swampy wooded thicket in the hollow between the hills took a lot longer to get through than I imagined, and I was caught off guard by a pack of level 30+ Forest Wolves. Fortunately, using the IR lens, I saw them before they saw me and managed to slip away quietly. I tried to take a wide arc around the dangerous predators, but that just led me into a patch of swamp muck so deep I had to turn back. It was all for nothing. The sun was setting, and I had to get back to the Capital while it was still light. The only good that came of all my wandering through the woods was that I leveled Medium Armor to twelve.

A quarter mile from the Capital, there was a bridge over a river. I was surprised to see around forty crack First Legion troops just past it, blocking the road and seemingly waiting for something. I just kept walking toward them, though, until one of them called out to me, telling me to get off the road. I was somewhat befuddled but obeyed, going to stand in the grass nearby.

Then I saw an antigrav. It was nothing like Zheltov's hovercraft, though. This was a long cigar-shaped object that cruised across the evening sky without a sound. The First Legion soldiers saw it as well and formed a large circle one hundred feet in diameter. The silver antigrav positioned itself over the very center of the circle and set down vertically until it nearly touched the ground.

Its door slid noiselessly to the side, and a technician in an orange uniform jumped out. I looked on the mini-map, saw his marker was red, then scanned over his information and realized he belonged to the Dark Faction. The First Legion didn't reach for their weapons, but I could read tension on their faces. They were ready for this to turn hot at any moment. What was going on??? I froze in place, not wanting to accidentally mess up something important.

Meanwhile, the enemy technician quickly ran around the antigrav and extended three support legs, allowing the aircraft to stand stable. After that, the very same technician lowered a gangway and made a low respectful bow. A tall old man walked out slowly in a dignified manner. He had a long gray beard and was dressed in a black robe that went all the way to the ground. In his hands, he held a heavy carved staff capped with a human skull.

Leng Thumor-Anhu La-Fin. Human. Dark Faction. Level-108 Psionic Mage

Level one hundred and eight! God damn!!! I never even imagined there were such high-level bruisers in this game yet. At least not humans. What was more, he had La-Fin in his name, just like the prisoner Minn-O La-Fin. And their facial features were similar, as if they were related. This must have been her father!

And then... as if reading my thoughts, the enemy mage turned unerringly in my direction! Despite the eighty to one hundred feet between us, we locked eyes. It felt as if a gust of air blew over me as cold as outer space. The old man's eyes glowed with an eldritch flame, his gaze boring deep into my psyche. His eyes lifted just a tad. The already frigid stare turned even more glacial. Then a hypnotic voice rang out in my head:

"This man is strong and dangerous. I'd hate for him to have a personal grudge against me. I should walk up to the mage, fall at his feet and return his granddaughter's lens."

Successful Intelligence check

Granddaughter??? I didn't think Minn-O La-Fin was his granddaughter. I figured she was a daughter, though perhaps born a bit late in life. My mind immediately caught on that detail. That thought didn't belong to me. The dreadful psionic's command may have worked on me under normal circumstances. I also may have resisted, hard to say. But with such a blatant error, I had no problem recognizing the implanted thought.

I gave a mocking chuckle, removed my dark glasses and showed the Psionic Mage my eyes, which had a magical blue glow just like his. Then I pulled my glove off my left hand and flipped Thumor-Anhu La-Fin the bird. Sure, it wasn't the smartest thing I'd ever done but, I was feeling ecstatic after my small but significant victory.

The mage grasped his staff with both hands and the skull on top lit up.

"What do you think you're doing?!" Gerd Tamara exploded, appearing from invisibility in her exoskeleton suit. The level-79 Paladin was incensed and aiming her high-caliber machine gun right at the mage's forehead. "We agreed that magic is not to be used during the prisoner exchange!"

Either the grisly Psionic Mage understood our language, or Gerd Tamara's fearsome demeanor spoke for itself, but Leng Thumor-Anhu La-Fin's staff stopped glowing. He said something quietly and pointed at me. The leader of the Second Legion looked over and hissed like an enraged kitten:

"Gnat, if you keep provoking the respected Leng and bungle these negotiations, I swear on my life I will not hesitate to shoot you! And every time I see you after that, I'll kill you again!"

Fame increased to 6

So, my Fame would grow just for being called out in front of lots of people? In that case, I should answer this little hot-head:

"Well, that old fart used his magic to try and trick me into giving his granddaughter's lens back!"

"Ha-ha! Good one! If Leng Thumor-Anhu La-Fin really used his magic on you, you'd be a pile of dust!" the paladin girl disagreed vehemently. "And for the rude language, I warned you..."

Her high-caliber machinegun turned instantly in my direction. I didn't even see it shoot.

Your character has died. Respawn will be possible in fifteen minutes.

Would you like to review your statistics for this game session?

What the crap?! This was the second time in less than 24 hours I had been killed by the very same player of my own faction! That was becoming a fine tradition. Would I ever be able to exit the game without being helped along by this finicky girl? Although, I had to admit it was my fault. I was warned not to argue with Gerds. And the leader of the Second Legion was not known for her patience and hated being defied. I scolded myself for the lack of self-control and loose tongue. I'd have to make sure not to do it again.

But this time, I decided to look over my numbers.

Time in game: 11 hours, 43 minutes. Your character has leveled up 12 times and gained 124 skill levels.

Oh yeah! Pretty badass.

You have earned 19407 experience points

Huh, I guess there was "exp." in this game!

You killed zero players and zero NPC's. Your game

session ended due to: death.

Alright, enough for today. I opened my pod and crawled out of the bed with an old-man's groan. All my muscles and joints were in pain. My body wouldn't do what I wanted. The way down from the tall corncob was torturous. My legs wobbled with every step and could barely support the weight of my body. I guess I 'd played too much today...

Once I got to the bottom, I saw Ivan Lozovsky standing right outside my cob. I was expecting him to be upset and maybe even curse, but he just asked compassionately how I was feeling. In reply, I just cringed in pain. I felt like saying "shitty," or something even worse.

"I imagine. Some newbies can't even walk after their first day. The game puts a strain on your body it just isn't used to. I mean, you spent all day hiking in the mountains, patrolling and running with weights. Don't worry. Today it'll hurt, but your body will get used to the new regimen."

He offered to help me walk to his office, but I refused. This man was as physically tall as he was high up in our faction hierarchy, so I wanted to prove to him that I wasn't some namby-pamby. It was just a hundred yards. I could make it! I limped over to the administration building, then down the hall to Lozovsky's office and collapsed into an armchair with relief. He made me some coffee and set it on the table.

"So, as far as I understand, you set a new faction record for first-day experience gain."

Of all the ways this conversation could have started,

he went with that! That perked me right up. With some surprise, I realized he wasn't going to chew me out. In fact, Lozovsky had no complaints about my gameplay. Instead, he was interested in how I had leveled so quickly. I told him about the combination of Cartography, Eagle Eye and the fast-moving starship.

"Interesting. Somewhat paradoxical even. Refusing to take our readymade map so you could make one yourself... a curious approach. I'll admit, I thought of Cartography as basically a useless skill. Hard to level and with little benefit. Especially for players that sit in laboratories and workshops and never go anywhere. Great idea! Of course, your method requires high Perception, so it won't work for all new recruits, but in any case, our starship pilot will be getting more work."

"By the way," I said, remembering my promise to the antigrav pilot, "I owe Zheltov a bottle of good brandy. How can I get one under the Dome?"

Ivan Lozovsky first looked surprised, then chuckled:

"I see you missed my introductory lecture this morning. Today or tomorrow, you'll all be issued special debit cards and your salary will go to them twice a month. Your pay is determined by Radugin, and it depends on your level, contribution to the faction and other bonuses. What's more, any resources provided to the faction, such as valuable minerals, machine parts, mechanisms, weapons and whatnot, will be compensated with either goods or services in the game, or real money on your debit card. The choice is up to you. Using these cards, you can order anything your heart desires. But if you need brandy right away..."

The diplomat walked up to a cupboard and opened it, showing me a shelf filled with expensive bottles of liquor. He chose one, a French cognac, and placed it on the table.

"Take this. I've got no use for it. They're gifts from relatives of the terminally ill people we have cured under the Dome. Don't be ashamed, take it!"

Feeling somewhat timid, I took the bottle off the table, and Lozovsky continued his speech:

"That trick you pulled on the freight pier, I have to admit, it made an impression on the Geckho. Kosta Dykhsh even said you're playing the game as its meant to be played. Gerd Tamara praised you very highly as well..."

"But in the end, she shot me anyway!" I interrupted, unable to hold back. The diplomat just laughed:

"First, you must agree, she had a good reason. You should never argue with a Gerd, especially with other people around. Your behavior dishonored an esteemed player in the presence of an enemy! Second, there were complications after you died. The Dark Faction negotiator added two last-minute conditions: return his granddaughter's things and punish those responsible for dishonoring her. The problem is that, in their world, Minn-O La-Fin comes from a very prestigious aristocratic family. She is supposed to be treated the proper way, and certainly not like a simple prisoner of war. By shooting you, Gerd Tamara smoothed that problem over. You had been killed, which they found to be just punishment. Also, no one could say where you'd respawn, and they didn't want to wait around just to get the items back. Sure it was radical, but it worked."

Aha... A bizarre perspective. It seemed things were coming together poorly for me, so I asked:

"With the items I get it. I have Minn-O La-Fin's lens. But what did my character have to do with 'dishonoring' her? It wasn't me that captured, undressed and searched her!"

"But the old man found out about the whole thing by reading your thoughts! The only other person who was at both places was Gerd Tamara. Plus, she gave all our soldiers defense against mental magic before the prisoner exchange, including herself!"

"I was in way over my head!" All the gravity of the situation reached me. "Someone should have helped me!"

But Ivan Lozovsky didn't agree. The way he saw it, no one had told me to be there, and I had taken the girl's lens of my own accord. The terms of the exchange were already settled, and everyone who was supposed to be there was adequately protected. So, there was one thing to blame: my astonishing knack for finding trouble.

At any rate, though this hurt me personally quite a bit, the faction saw certain advantages in the situation. But what they were exactly, Ivan Lozovsky refused to answer, saying it was top secret. But I was intrigued by what he said next:

"You have a very busy day ahead of you tomorrow. You'll have to get up at five thirty in the morning. If I were you, I'd have a quick dinner and go right to sleep."

"And what am I going to be doing?" I asked, somewhat worried but also intrigued.

"As far as the whole faction is concerned, you have an early morning shift on the Antique Beach. The very same Guard Post Eight but second shift, from six to ten in the morning. Feel free to tell that to your friends and everyone you know. It's no secret. It'll be written on the schedule hanging next to the dining area for everyone. But as for where you're really going tomorrow morning, only a few people will know."

At that very moment, a voice thundered out so loud the windows shuddered:

"ATTENTION, THIS IS THE DOME LEADER. I HAVE TWO ANNOUNCEMENTS TO MAKE, BOTH GOOD. GERD IGOR TARASOV WAS FIRST IN OUR FACTION TO REACH LEVEL EIGHTY-NINE TODAY! WE CONGRATULATE OUR CHAMPION AND WISH HIM CONTINUED SUCCESS! ALSO, A NEW FACTION RECORD WAS SET FOR FIRST-DAY LEVELING. SIXTEEN!!! THAT WAS ACHIEVED TODAY BY A NEW PROSPECTOR BY THE NAME OF GNAT!!!"

"So now the record is officially on the books. Keep it up!" Ivan Lozovsky patted me approvingly on the shoulder. "And now go get some rest, Kirill. You can't even sit up straight. We can talk more later. I'll answer all your questions then. And I'll give starship pilot Zheltov your present. I need to meet with him anyway to tell him he'll soon be getting more work. He should like that."

Chapter Nineteen

Morning in the Forest

"**G**ET UP, GNAT. It's time for your shift!" said the bald boy from yesterday, waking me up again.

I yawned wide and took a look around. It was dark both inside and out. Artur, Denis and Imran were still asleep. As far as I'd seen in the shift schedule, Imran had patrol again today at Border Post Eight on the third shift, just like the three of us yesterday. I had also seen Anya on the list, but at some other time and at the far post of the Eastern Swamp. As for Artur and Denis, I hadn't seen their names. Apparently, they were supposed to spend all day plugging away on some secret project in the Prometheus laboratories.

I quickly washed up and got myself in order, then

hurried to my corncob kernel. My muscles ached, shooting with pain at every sudden motion. I even had to stop on the steep spiral staircase, sit on a step and massage my painfully convulsing left calf. That felt so good! The spasm quickly passed but, for the last few floors, my teeth were clenched and I was dragging my feet. Finally, floor fourteen... I wiped the sweat off my forehead. I hoped Lozovsky wasn't mistaken when he assured me that my body would soon grow accustomed it such constant intense exercise.

I just hoped this pain wouldn't carry over into the game world. Otherwise, I'd be limping all day. But as far as I could tell, the virtual world had an impact on ours, but the reverse was not true. So then, back into the virt pod to load up the game that bends reality.

Fame increased to 8.

My Fame shot up by two whole points?! That must have come after yesterday's announcement that I set a new record. I couldn't find any other explanation.

I appeared, as expected, at our central base right where I'd set my spawn point. And I wasn't limping. That was good. But my progress bar had predictably fallen to zero, so I felt vulnerable. I needed to raise my progress bar by at least a hair right away. I immediately activated the Scanning icon and saw a bunch of lines and marks on the mini-map. Buildings, fences, stacked boxes, roads, trees, items, living players...

As my skill level increased, the results of the scan became more detailed and accurate. I could see some stuff and even people on the other side of walls, and my discovery radius was noticeably larger. Also, allied player markers on the map now had a bit of information with them — name, class and level. Handy!

Speaking of which... I saw stock keeper Vasiliadi on the map, despite the early hour. I remembered what he'd told me yesterday. My Rifles skill was now twenty-one, so I could upgrade to a more accurate and damaging weapon. I had a bit of time, so I decided to pay him a visit.

Vasiliadi clearly hadn't gotten enough sleep. When he saw me come in asking for a better weapon so soon, he looked peeved and told me to quit joking around. I had no way of proving it, so I had to insist, making reference to how quickly my character level had increased. The morose and untrusting stock keeper eventually relented and went back to find me a better gun, though it seemed to me he didn't fully believe me.

Vasiliadi was gone for a while, six minutes. I even got scared that I'd have to go on patrol with what I had on me. But the hirsute stock keeper came back with a roll of fabric, unfolded it on the table and showed me a short pneumatic rifle that looked like a sawn-off shotgun.

"I have very little in the way of non-automatic weapons that fit the bill. But I did find a Matador that was refitted for the game. It isn't new, and the stock isn't original. We got thirty of these six months ago from the real world for the First Legion, and they proved effective against animals and unarmed enemies like forest spirits and centaurs. It's a trusty pneumatic rifle with a ten-round magazine. The caliber is 6.35 mm just like your burp gun, but the firepower is much higher."

The rifle was so pretty I just had to hold it. But even after a quick scan, I quickly noticed traces of repair. The air tank had been replaced, and I could see a line where the wooden stock had broken and been glued.

Angel Dust. Standard 6.35 mm PCP pneumatic rifle (modified)

Attention! This weapon contains the following modifications:

- *+ 20 trajectory flatness*
- *+3% chance of dealing critical hits*
- *+40% damage done by critical hits*

Attention! This weapon was named Angel Dust by its first owner. Name cannot be deleted or changed.

Statistic requirements: Agility 13, Strength 12.

Skill requirements: Rifles 20

Attention! This weapon has been damaged and repaired. Firing power reduced by 17%

I had my doubts about the repaired rifle, and I turned the air gun over in my hands, looking critically at its new tank. It was quite a good repair job, but clearly not up to factory spec. Sensing my doubts, the hirsute stock keeper intervened:

"It's got bullpup configuration — the bolt, trigger group and heavy elements are set back for comfort and lower profile. Sure it isn't new or flashy, but who cares? It got dinged up in an explosion, but our boys remodeled it and sawed out a new stock. Sure, it isn't as pretty as the original, but it shoots just fine. This air rifle used to belong to Lozovsky himself!"

"What does the name do? And why Angel Dust?" I enquired, already having decided I'd take the air rifle, even if it was a bit beat up.

"It does nothing," Vasiliadi grumbled unhappily. "All these custom names are just window dressing. This rifle was just one of many, and Lozovsky wanted his to stand out. But I have no idea where the name came from! Ask Ivan! You want it? Just so you know, this is the best I've got for Rifles level twenty!"

I handed my old air rifle in to the stock keeper and hung Angel Dust on my shoulder. I also took its special pump and a few boxes of lead 6.35-mm slugs and stashed them in my inventory.

"Could I get a couple of fragmentation grenades?" I asked in curiosity. Seeing the dismayed look on the hard-fisted cheapskate, I hurried to add: "Yesterday, only a miracle kept me from being taken prisoner by the Dark Faction. And, unfortunately, I had nothing that could definitely send me to respawn. I didn't want to get taken alive. So, I thought of grenades. That way, I could kill myself and take some enemies with me..."

"Gnat, you just grew significantly in my eyes..." I heard notes of respect in Vasiliadi's voice for the first time.

He went into the back again, but this time came back

almost instantly:

"Take these. Four RGD-5 fragmentation grenades. Here are the fuses. They're good, brought in from the real world. Also, there is no decent replacement for your shotgun yet, so I dug up some more cartridges. There are twenty-five in this box. But they are the last we've got! So, don't go using them up for nothing — we've got a lead deficit, and no in-game production facilities for shotgun cartridges."

I thanked Vasiliadi. Just then, the little bus pulled up. The canvas lifted and the Kisly waved me into the back:

"Gnat, step to! It's time for us to head to Antique Beach!"

I jumped into the bus, and the group commander set the canvas back down. The eight-wheeled titan belched out diesel fumes and tore off down the well-worn road. I did my best not to reveal my confusion. Was I really being sent to Antique Beach? But what about the secret mission Lozovsky told me about yesterday?! But, as soon as the little bus was a few miles from the Capital, deep in the foggy forest, Kisly told San-Sanych to stop.

"Gnat, this is your stop! I don't know why, but I got an order to let you out at this fork in the road. You shouldn't really be at Antique Beach now anyway. Last night, a pissed off centauress by the name of Phylira came by. She was asking for you and demanding you return her pearls. That magical night of love didn't quite work out the way you promised."

"Didn't fit?" I suggested with a smirk.

"Worse! No centaur had ever seen a condom before. You really should have told her what to do with them... Phylira invited the eldest son of the chief of her herd to the open plains last night and had him swallow your rubber. It got stuck in his throat and the lusty stallion keeled over. It was quite the scandal. Phylira was accused of poisoning him and nearly got ostracized from the herd. But she blamed it on you, saying a man by the name of Gnat had tricked her and she didn't know it was poison. So, if you ask me, you should keep your distance from the centaur lands... Oh yeah, I almost forgot! For your safety, they told me to tell you to stay right here."

I didn't ask questions. I knew I wouldn't be getting any answers. Out the door was a huge puddle. I had no choice but to jump right into it, I cursed a bit, then walked up to a sign with two arrows: Yellow Mountains and Capital. There was another road, clearly less used, but it wasn't marked. Leaving me in a cloud of gray smoke, the bus sped off down the forest road, leaving me all alone.

Five minutes passed, and nothing happened. It had just started getting light out, and the forest was coming to life. I heard early birds singing. Some extravagant grasshoppers, despite the fog and damp were already trilling out their songs. A woodpecker had gotten up at the crack of dawn and was poking holes in a rotting tree. But all these sounds were far away. There was a small zone of silence around me, and that made me suspicious.

Successful Perception check.

My intuition was right again! A soldier was hidden ten steps from me and gave himself away with a passing motion. He moved his leg out of an uncomfortable position. Just a few inches, but I caught the slight movement with the corner of my eye. Then, I turned to face him and made out a human figure in the pile of mossy branches.

Shoot_To_Kill. Human. H3 Faction. Level-71 Scout

Familiar name. Ah, right! One of the First Legion soldiers punished for playing cards. And he was probably not alone... My scanning ability had just reloaded, so I tried emphasizing suspicious mounds, bushes, and people in camouflage. I knew it! There were another three faction allies nearby, all high-level First Legion bruisers, the best of the best.

Scanning skill increased to level twenty-one!

Eagle Eye skill increased to level twenty-five!

I lowered the IR-lens and gave a whistle of respect. The First Legion group was well equipped. They were all totally invisible in the heat spectrum! They were probably wearing temperature-regulating suits like I had seen on the Dark Faction. I wondered what they were waiting for?

The obvious conclusion was that I was being used as live bait. But who were we fishing for? Enemies or... allies? All the suspicious secrecy around my patrol duty was leading me to the second option. I really hoped it wasn't allies. And it would be really bad if these "allies" wanted to harm me, whether they just disliked me or were working for the enemy.

Realizing the importance of my mission, I didn't expose the hidden soldiers. I even purposely looked away. But time passed, and nothing happened. Then, when the morning chill had made me totally stiff, and the biting insects had covered every inch of my body, I heard a strange sound from the road leading to the Yellow Mountains.

I got off the road and hid behind a fallen tree, loaded my shotgun and hurriedly screwed the fuses into my grenades. I again lowered the IR-lens and saw three large bright spots approaching in the fog. They were clearly vehicles, based on the humming and metallic clang. I thought for a second, stashed the useless shotgun and equipped a grenade.

"Gnat, don't be stupid! Put the grenade away, they're allies!" Shoot_To_Kill shot out, revealing his presence, standing to his feet and brushing the twigs and debris off his camouflage smock.

"Yeah? How am I supposed to know that?!" I objected, but still put the grenade away. "I saw your whole group sitting in ambush, all four with weapons at the ready. What was I supposed to think?"

"Wait, you could see us? But we were camouflaged. We have nice equipment, and high Stealth... And hey, how did you know we're a group?" the scout asked, growing tense.

I snickered, happy with the reaction. Apparently, the First Legion soldiers had no idea I knew they were there. Spreading my arms, I shrugged my shoulders and twisted my face into a guilty grimace:

"Well, sorry. No one told me I wasn't supposed to see you. But if you're being serious, my character is a Prospector, so I'm supposed to be able to find hidden things. My Perception is twenty-two, plus I have a bunch of skills that help me discover stuff. And as for your group, that's no secret either. Yesterday, after Gerd Tamara caught the Dark Faction scout group, I was there when she saw you four playing cards through a telescope. She told me your names and ordered her assistant Roman Pavlovich to take down three of your names."

"Son of a bitch!!!" came Nelly Svistunova, level-69 Saboteur, also giving up and standing to full height. "So that was why Tarasov made us do four-hour weighted CrossFit yesterday!"

I didn't reply to the angry young girl's sharp words. She had a fine figure, and the baggy camo couldn't detract from that. Her pretty little face was painted in green, black and yellow stripes. I had been punished for insulting high-status players before, and I had taken that painful lesson to heart. What was more, an armored mechanical vehicle had just come lumbering around a turn. It was somewhere between a truck, armored transport and hovercraft. And there wasn't just one, but three of the steel monsters.

From what I'd seen so far, I assumed my faction had nothing but dumb-looking makeshift vehicles. This respectable craft proved just how wrong I was. These things had sheet armor, thick reinforced windshields, four pairs of metal mesh wheels, high-speed cannons mounted on spinning towers, spaced armor, and reactive armor bricks. And on the underside, there were powerful antigrav plates to provide extra thrust and mitigate their many-ton weight.

Peresvet. All-terrain armored cargo transport.

These armored vehicles had very little in common with San-Sanych's little bus. That must have just been a prototype. But there was a remote resemblance. This was some serious tech. And the three combat vehicles were identical, which made me think they were being made on assembly lines. And the number "8" painted on the lead vehicle seemed to mean there were at least five more. Cool! If of course that wasn't just to mislead our enemies.

The first Peresvet came up to me and stopped. The side door opened, and Ivan Lozovsky waved me inside:

"Come on Gnat, hop in. You must be getting eaten alive out there. There were Dark Faction saboteurs after you in the Yellow Mountains, but we already took them out. The little bus didn't get so lucky, though. The enemies torched it. They say it's too damaged to be repaired..."

"What do you mean torched?" I had already set my boot on the running board, preparing to climb inside, but the diplomat's last words shocked me. After all, just half an hour ago I was sitting in the little bus with a few other soldiers!

"It got ambushed and blown up. San-Sanych was shot and Kisly's whole group was executed. The commander put up a good fight, though. He managed to take three of them down with his machinegun. But we thought that might happen. The Second Legion was standing by. They got there quick and killed the six enemies. We even took two alive. So, we'll exchange them for materials and build a new bus for San-Sanych. It'll be better than before, don't you worry! But you're coming with us to the Geckho base. We're buying you an electronic scanner, Leng Radugin approved it himself. He said you've earned it! So get in and close the door. It's time to go. And we can talk more on the way. You've probably got a bunch of questions."

Chapter Twenty

Around the Bay

H E GOT THAT RIGHT! I had a truckload of questions and enough to fill an economy-sized car after that. I didn't even know where to begin. On the mini-map, I saw the four First Legion soldiers hop into the other two vehicles, so I decided to start by getting the details of our current mission:

"So, I assume the faction didn't send three armored vehicles all the way to the Geckho base just to buy me a scanner."

The driver of the Peresvet gave a happy chuckle, and Ivan Lozovsky couldn't hold back a smile.

"Of course not," the diplomat replied goodheartedly. He filled me in on all the relevant details. "Our faction just sold a large shipment to the Geckho. Mostly rare steel alloys, rolled metal, and high-tension glass..."

"Palladium ingots..." the level-54 Mechanic-Driver named Vadim threw out. But that was all he said, intimidated by the diplomat's fearsome gaze.

"Yes, palladium as well," Ivan Lozovsky confirmed after a long pause. "That was supposed to be top secret, but apparently the whole faction already knows. We've got just sixteen tons of cargo, but it's worth fifty-five thousand crystals. This is our highest-value trade yet. It's a point of pride for our faction, but a huge responsibility for us. Our suzerains have already paid for the goods, so now it's a matter of honor that we reach our buyer."

"Wouldn't it have been easier to send it by sea?" I asked in surprise. "We could just drop it off at the Geckho storehouses by the pier."

Ivan Lozovsky gave an unhappy chuckle and shook his head.

"It isn't all so simple. You see, Gnat... How can I explain it...? The Geckho are a very populous space-faring race, but their society is multifaceted. The Geckho have many leaders of different varieties and levels. And those groups don't always have trusting and warm relationships. You see, the Geckho responsible for the pier on Antique Beach, and the ones buying this cargo..." he got stuck trying to choose his words.

"I get it. In that way, the Geckho are just like us. If some extraterrestrials wanted to sell platinum to, say, North

Korea, they might think it reasonable to drop it off in South Korea. But even though they are neighboring countries, and speak the same language, it would never reach its intended destination."

The diplomat clearly found my example funny, and even laughed:

"This wouldn't be quite as hopeless as that, but you get the idea. We can't send it by sea, so we have to go around the bay through three neutral nodes. That's twenty-nine miles each way through swamps and forests. By the way, this is the first serious test of our Peresvets. We've driven this route a few times before with somewhat more basic trucks, but we had an order of magnitude less cargo, and it was of lower value."

The diplomat went silent, because a man in a camouflage smock appeared on the road ahead. But I saw on the mini-map that he was an ally. A First Legion scout, he had some recon for us. Our driver clearly knew the man, started smiling, lowered the armored glass on his side and stopped. The acquaintances exchanged handshakes, and the Scout extended a tablet to the driver:

"Vadim, here's the route. It's basically the same as before, but the pass near the Harpy Cliffs is blocked by a landslide. You'll have to take a two-mile detour. We've marked it on the map. We checked the whole length of the road and cleared a few fallen trees. Also, we dug out the boulder you got stuck on last time and rolled it away."

Here the scout saw Ivan Lozovsky sitting next to the

driver, stood at rigid attention and hurried to issue a report:

"Deputy director, sir! Late last evening in area 22-40 we observed an army jeep of terrestrial origin at the Geckho space port. It came to the Geckho base from the north via a gravel road. It was carrying four members of the H1 faction. A diplomat, a driver and two bodyguards. Our soldiers didn't reveal their presence and the vehicle left the area unharmed."

"Well done, soldier! I suppose that was the Chinese coming to apologize for the low-quality security-system sensors. I imagine they let 'em have it..."

The driver and soldier both snickered, but the diplomat put a damper on it:

"I don't see what's so funny here. The Chinese will take it into account and quickly correct the faults in their system. But them producing one piece of bad technology doesn't diminish the fact that the H1 Faction is significantly ahead of us in semiconductor and electronics technology."

The scout turned serious and, placing his hand on his helmet, wished us a pleasant ride. Our Peresvet raced off into the thick fog. Three minutes later, Ivan Lozovsky, having led his gaze over a crooked leaning pipe, commented to me:

"We've just crossed the border into neutral territory. This node is strategically important for us. It has access to the sea and provides the shortest path to the Geckho base. And there we can trade, acquire new technology, access the space port and improve our development. Overall, our faction is very lucky the Geckho base is so nearby, and that we have smooth trade relations. I can't imagine how we'd get by in this difficult world without the technology they've provided us."

Perception raised to 21.

That short message made me shudder. What? Why? I checked Gnat's stat table, and made sure Perception really was one point higher. I was reminded that, during the Assassin's fitness class, Svetlana had said that any statistic could be improved, and the first increase would come after eight hours of intensive use. That meant that I had been using my Perception actively for eight hours already. Cool!

Meanwhile, the diplomat turned the settings of his sophisticated radio and sent a message to Border Post One that our scouts had spotted members of the Human-1 Faction. After that, he turned off the radio and turned back to me:

"Unofficially, we already consider this node to belong to our faction. We call it Karelia due to the similar climate and landscape. It borders three of our territories: Capital, Yellow Mountains and Antique Beach. We always have a few scout groups here, and our military divisions often comb the area. Also, our Geologist Mikhalych sometimes comes here to work. There are no organized hostile factions here. The only threats are a large pack of man-eating wolves, lone bears over level 100, and lots and lots of poisonous snakes. But all the animals won't stop our faction from founding a base here."

"But then why haven't we done so yet? Especially if

the Karelia node is so important to us!"

"Gnat, we have less than fifteen hundred people in our faction, and it isn't enough to do everything we want. It's scary to think, but we have just one capable guardsman for every square mile of territory, and that's barely enough to secure our external border. Due to the lack of manpower, enemies occasionally break through our lines, and can remain in our lands unnoticed for weeks at a time, as you've already seen. So, expanding our territories and extending supply lines is a huge risk."

I lowered my head, downcast by the alarming news. No, I had already understood that we didn't have many people. But I didn't even come close to understanding the scale of the problem. Seeing my disheartened state, the diplomat tried to perk me up:

"Don't worry, Gnat! In a few weeks, if everything goes according to plan, we'll get the Antique Beach node up to level two, then we can bring another hundred seventy-four players into the game. But, to be honest, we'll have to build two new corncobs first. Still, I hope everything goes smoothly both in the real world and the virtual one. Then, the situation will improve, and I'll ask Radugin about building a base in Karelia. Before we expanded into the Eastern Swamp, I suggested this might make a better choice, but I was in the minority. All other faction leaders voted for the Eastern Swamp because it has oil. What's more, the Eastern Swamp node borders the Dark Faction, so it was very important to occupy and fortify the land before they got to it. Perhaps my colleagues were right. In the last couple days, wev've got an oil refinery up and running, and now we have plenty of fuel to send our vehicles on longer journeys."

Cartography skill increased to level thirty!
Scanning skill increased to level twenty-two!

I dismissed the popup messages. Not bad, not bad at all. I felt lucky I was being taken through three nodes I'd never been to. By the end of the trip, I suspected I would get at least one more level in Cartography, and maybe even two! But I still wanted the deputy leader to explain why I'd been scheduled for patrol. So I asked.

"You see, Gnat..." I could sense the diplomat straining to find the words again, as if he was afraid of saying too much. "We have long suspected, and are now quite certain, that one or more of our people are working for the Dark Faction. We've had a string of failures in scouting and combat operations that are hard to explain otherwise. Also, they know about our secret inventions and negotiations."

Seeing a lack of understanding on my face, the diplomat clarified:

"You see, Gnat, this is a harsh world. And there's too much riding on this horse. If they win, humanity as we know it will be wiped out. So, we torture prisoners. We need all the information we can get, no matter the cost. Sure, it's barbaric, but they do the same to our soldiers. Anyhow, most of what we get is useless, but sometimes we glean surprising tidbits. For example, before we finished building some 152-mm howitzers at the Prometheus, the enemy already knew not only about the top-secret production project, but exactly where we were going to install them!"

Holy crap! I whistled in surprise. That meant there had to be a leak. And this wasn't the kind of information every H3 player would have, either.

"And there's another cause for worry. There have been strange rumors swirling recently that the Dark Faction is quickly gaining power and is already head and shoulders above us in technology. Very soon, according to this rumor, resistance will be futile. They say our days are numbered, all our nodes will be captured, and we'll no longer even be able to enter the game that bends reality. But supposedly, our players who join the Dark Faction and earn their gratitude will be given asylum and can even leave their virt pods not under the Dome, but in their world. After that, they can supposedly change sides and play for the Dark Faction."

"Yeah, I've heard that a few times," our driver clenched his teeth angrily and gripped the wheel so hard his knuckles went white. "We all understand that these aren't even our thoughts. It's just enemy mages trying to muddy the waters. Cheap propaganda like the Nazis used back in the war. 'Russian, surrender, there's plenty of food and shelter in our camps.' History tells us what happened to those who believed them. My great grandfather was surrounded by the nazis near Kiev in '41, and he surrendered. He and a hundred thousand other captives were tortured to death in a concentration camp."

That time, the diplomat didn't interrupt the driver

and let him say his fill. After that, Lozovsky continued:

"And so, Gnat, you did something rude to Leng Thumor-Anhu La-Fin. With many people around, you either gave him the finger or showed him your bare ass. Various stories have reached me. After that, you called him an especially bad name, something along the lines of 'impotent dotard.' You said his magic was worthless and no match for you. And before that, you brought shame upon his granddaughter, stripping her naked and taking her clothes and lens."

"What?! I didn't even do a tenth of that!"

"Gnat, it doesn't even matter now whether you did it or not. I'm telling you the story the way I heard it. And believe me, that exact story is what our enemies heard as well. After all, Leng Thumor-Anhu La-Fin is a big mucky-muck in the Dark Faction. In his homeworld, he's part of a ruling Triumvirate. So, the old mage cannot simply ignore an insult and pretend nothing happened. His own people just won't accept it. They'll start doubting his right to rule. Beyond that, as with any high-status player, he has an Authority stat, and your insults brought it down a good deal. And now, put all that together. What do you think you were doing in the forest just now?"

I thought very briefly and gave him a full answer:

"I could tell right away I was being used as live bait. But it's not like the traitor was going to come get me himself. More likely, he would simply tell the Dark Faction where to find me. So, you were using me to test someone you suspect by selectively feeding them information. The whole faction thought I was headed to the Antique Beach. Just a few people knew better. And even less were aware that I'd be going to the Geckho base."

"Wait, wait!" Ivan Lozovsky interrupted me. "You're basically right, but the last thing is not part of the plan. That was a spontaneous improvisation on my part. In fact, Dmitry Zheltov was supposed to come and bring you back to the Capital. We told him you'd be in the forest to scan territory and determine the boundary of a water-flooded cave system that is inhibiting construction."

Seemed like a thin pretext. Who would believe such crap? But the diplomat proved me wrong:

"Those waterlogged caverns are a real thorn in our side. Two days ago, we had a group of people digging a ditch get eaten by cave monsters when they accidentally broke it open. So, that part looked natural. But the Dark Faction informant must be a lower level player because the enemy attacked the little bus after you got let out. We were ready for that. The Second Legion was on the scene in a matter of minutes."

Chapter Twenty-One

Harpy Cliffs

THE PERESVET DASHED first through a forest clearing, then some swampy hollows and meadows with grass as tall as a person. The all-terrain transport confidently overcame shallow streams, stones and rocky slopes. I kept a close eye on the road and surroundings, expanding my map the whole time.

Cartography skill increased to level thirty-one!

Eagle Eye skill increased to level twenty-six!

Everything was coming together just perfectly! I liked this trip more with every minute. Also, this was an excellent chance to find out about the surrounding world and its laws. Ivan Lozovsky wouldn't pipe down for a second and told me something about every part of Karelia we passed through.

But mostly, the diplomat told me about the structure of Geckho society, which he had spent a long time studying.

They had many outposts throughout the cosmos, and many powerful space fleets. He also told me about meeting several significant furball leaders. Ivan Lozovsky also told me that he was the only person in our faction to have visited the Geckho planet Shiharsa. As the official representative of a new vassal, he was officially introduced to Krong Daveyesh-Pir himself, one of the highest leaders of the Geckho and the official sovereign of our Earth.

All that was very interesting, but I was interested in more earthly matters. I decided the time had come for a very important question. I really should have started with it, but I kept putting it off. What exactly was the Dark Faction? After all, it clearly wasn't one of our usual governments, nor some top-secret special service or representatives of a highly important corporation. Magic, strange technologies, unusual social structure, a language unlike anything I'd heard on earth... All that spoke to them being totally alien to our world.

"That's right," the diplomat agreed. "They come from a parallel world, an alternate reality, another version of our mother Earth. Call it what you like. We share a common history with roots in the darkest depths of time. But at a certain point, our worlds split and became incompatible with one another. We cannot say for sure why. Now we can encounter the inhabitants of that alternative Earth only in the game that bends reality. In this game, we can access a primeval Earth. A sort of blueprint for the planet. But, no matter how many alternate Earths are out there, there is only one in here. Also, events in the game impact not only our world, but all other versions as well."

"Hey, hold up," I got caught on the diplomat's last words and decided to delve deeper. "How can the game contain a primeval Earth if the Geckho just discovered it?"

"Well, the Geckho didn't create the game that bends reality. It has existed long before them. The Geckho discovered it themselves around three hundred tongs ago. That's a bit longer than one thousand years in our reckoning. What's more, even then, the game had other inhabitants. For example, there are the Trillians, an ancient race of space nomads, wandering from one planet to the next. And the Meleyephatians, a warlike and extremely aggressive race of conquerors that enslave planets one after the next, making them obedient vassals and members of their horde. And the Geckho have discovered evidence of much older races that no longer exist, the Precursors, Mechanoids and Relicts. The Geckho have learned a lot about this game. But even a thousand years later, our wise suzerains don't know all the mysteries and laws of the game that bends reality. All the same, we can say for sure that the Geckho introduced our planet to the game."

Again, he went to his favorite topic, the Geckho. But I asked Ivan Lozovsky to return to the Dark Faction.

"We first encountered them four months ago. We know for certain that they are also newbies in the game and built virtual reality pods after seeing a video clip just like the one we got. And now, they are actively expanding their holdings just like us. Our territories have bordered one another for the last two months. Ever since then, our conflict has been heating up. We keep sending more and more soldiers of higher level, but there hasn't been much headway. Now, it is truly a struggle not for life, but to the death. By the way, you should find it interesting to know that they call us the Dark Faction. To them, the Koreans, Chinese, Russians, Americans, Japanese and whatnot are one and the same. And the game identifies us as such, 'Dark Faction.'"

"Interesting, but does the Dark Faction have one initial base or a few like our world?"

"Now that we, unfortunately, don't know. The Geckho refuse to answer that question, maintaining neutrality so as not to influence our conflict. And wev'e yet to take any prisoners from the Dark Faction of a high enough level to have such information. Perhaps Minn-O La-Fin, who we captured yesterday, may have known the answer but Leng Radugin forbade us from using enhanced interrogation on her. Also, she was instantly ransomed, exchanging her for two of our soldiers. Our only clue is that, three months ago in the Poppy Fields node, which is to the northeast of Karelia, our scouts witnessed a firefight between two Dark Faction squadrons. So, it is possible that our opponents also have various sub-factions."

"But that isn't for certain," the driver added. "I've heard that, the poppy plants are predatory and release intoxicating vapors. First, reality starts to glitch, then you fall into a deep sleep and the poppies entangle you in their roots and suck out your blood."

"Yes, that is true," the diplomat said. "Its possible the Dark Faction soldiers were under the influence of the poppy fumes. But that isn't the only evidence for other human factions. For example, take that captured IR lens... Can I have a look?"

I unclipped it from my helmet and handed it to Ivan Lozovsky. He turned the item over in his hands and squinted, trying to read the miniscule script. Yesterday, I had also tried to figure out what was written there but didn't encounter a single familiar character.

"Mhmmm... Quite a curious little item. Too bad I didn't get a chance to talk with its owner yesterday," the diplomat said, handing it back to me. "You see, Gnat, that is not the language of the Dark Faction. But the lens was clearly made for humans because no other race I know of has the proper anatomy to use it."

"Gerd Tamara said the same thing yesterday," I reminded him. "She said it was made for people, but not by the Dark Faction."

"Yes, I have never seen letters like this before. That isn't the Geckho alphabet, nor Miyelonian symbols. It's all very strange... By the way Gnat, up ahead are the Harpy Cliffs, the next node on our journey. Its main feature is a wall of nearly impenetrable cliffs, which are inhabited by a huge number of birdlike humanoids. And a lot of them seem to be flying around today..."

Successful Perception check.

Eagle Eye skill increased to level twenty-seven!

He was right. I could see no less that one hundred of the strange winged creatures wheeling around above the cliffs and looking down in agitation. The harpies looked spooked. Maybe it was some kind of predator or other threat. I told my companions.

"So it seems. Fortunately, we aren't going there," the driver answered, also looking at the flock of dark-colored bird-men. "We generally take a shortcut through those cliffs but, as you heard, its blocked today. We need to go around. And I say that's a good thing — I hate those assholes! They shit on our windshields, throw rocks at us and shoot us with their crossbows..."

"The harpy are fairly intelligent," the diplomat replied. "They can use missile weapons and firearms, are willing to negotiate and quickly learn foreign languages. They even can be enticed to trade from time to time. But the foremost rule that must be observed when talking with harpies is that one must never believe a single word they say! They disdain everything that cannot fly. Also, in the harpy lexicon, there aren't even such concepts as 'honor,' 'debt,' or 'agreement.' To the harpy, tricking a trusting neighbor and breaking one's word are considered marks of great honor. And mocking the weak and wounded is their favorite pastime. They've made problems for us before. Fortunately, the harpy have no weapons that can damage our Peresvets."

Then, one thousand feet from the cliffs, our truck and two others took a sharp turn to the left down a road parallel to a ridge of high overgrown hills. I was surprised to see the flock of mythical creatures start quickly flying in our direction! And although Ivan Lozovsky assured me the harpies were powerless against our vehicles, that put me on guard.

Before that, I was watching the road and surroundings closely, leveling my skills. But now, I was darting my eyes in every direction, utterly paranoid. The harpies were intelligent, so they must have known our vehicles were too strong for them. But they were coming in our direction nevertheless. Suspicious! They clearly had some plan of action, or they saw something from above we hadn't yet guessed. I spent a few seconds waiting impatiently for my scanning ability to reload, and quickly activated the icon.

Scanning skill increased to level twenty-three!

I saw many markers on the mini-map and took a closer look. They were all expected, although... in front of us, there was a narrow space between nearly sheer cliffs with a huge deep puddle. At the very narrowest point, our path was blocked by a chain of red markers. I zoomed in on the suspicious part of the map and read the description:

Antitank mine

"The road is mined! Next to the puddle! Brake!!!" I screamed in a voice not my own, warning of the danger.

But our driver answered in a surprisingly calm voice that betrayed no emotion:

"Yes, I know..."

And he pushed the pedal to the metal, turning our armored car right toward the chain of mines!

I had to admit, I didn't understand what was happening right away. At first, I thought the experienced driver wanted to speed up to get around the mines through the deep puddle to the left or (I mean, who knows what antigravs are capable of?) up the practically vertical surface of the cliff to the right. Then the diplomat grabbed the wheel and tried unsuccessfully to turn it. I only realized the full gravity of the situation when he shouted at the top of his lungs: "Help me, you bonehead!!! Can't you see, his mind is under control!"

Vadim was pushing the gas pedal all the way to the floor with a glassy look and holding the wheel firmly with his iron grip. Most likely, I should have tried to find a hand break or to pull the key from the ignition. But in my panic, I totally forgot about such humane methods of stopping the armored vehicle. The seconds were ticking away, and I needed to act decisively. So, I took out my shotgun, placed it to the driver's temple and shot with both barrels.

Sharpshooter skill increased to level seven!

Rifles skill increased to level twenty-two!

Most of the windshield and the whole left door were spattered in blood and flesh. The lifeless and practically headless body of the driver fell to the side. I was deaf, but the most important part was over. The mad driver had stopped resisting and Ivan Lozovsky managed to turn the wheel. Just twenty-five feet from the deadly obstacle, we turned sharply to the right and flew off the road. At our high speed, the transport first tried to go up the steep slope, but fairly quickly slammed into a double-trunked tree and came to a stop.

My forehead slammed painfully into the armored glass, reducing my health by half.

Bleeding! You will lose 3 HP every 3 seconds for 20 seconds.

Despite the damage and pain, I exhaled in relief. I had 310 hitpoints of 518, so the bleeding wouldn't lead to anything serious. The diplomat sitting next to me also looked somewhat disheveled and bruised , but it looked like he'd be fine too.

Placing his right hand to his cracked lips and making sure all his teeth were still in place, Ivan Lozovsky looked at the blood on his fingers and winced in pain:

"I'm afraid this is not the end of our misfortune. There must be an enemy Psionic Mage very close, as he managed to take Vadim under control. We can't stay here. Mages don't travel without support. Here you go, Gnat." The diplomat put his chair back, opening a passage to the covered trunk. "There's a highspeed cannon mounted back there, get into firing position. I'll get on my radio, tell the others what happened and try to get the car back on the road."

"I'm a Prospector. I can't use an automatic weapon!" I remembered in time and added that I couldn't pilot flying vehicles either, which probably applied to the antigrav.

"Damn! Out of all the game classes, I had to join up with a Prospector!" Ivan Lozovsky lamented, not hiding his annoyance. "Wait! Gnat, where are you going?!"

I had opened the side door and was jumping out of the vehicle. Ivan Lozovsky was totally right. We absolutely couldn't remain in the immobile vehicle. I also sensed that. The enemy's main forces must have been waiting in ambush on the main road at the narrow pass. I suspected that was exactly what had the harpies so worked up. But our column took a detour. The enemy wasn't expecting that but, just in case, they'd mined the detour as well. The flock of harpies after us had been following the enemies on the ground. They knew the road was mined, and we couldn't get out. So, if my thinking was right, this place would soon be lousy with enemies.

With just such unhappy thoughts in mind, I scrambled up the steep rocky slope to get a better view and help my allies find the hostile troops. I heard a deafening thunder from behind me. It was the second Peresvet. It had turned its cannon and was firing practically point blank at our third vehicle. This was probably also that enemy Psionic Mage!

I also noticed that two soldiers had run to the leading Peresvet from the second vehicle. Ivan Lozovsky opened the door for them and the first soldier took shelter in the cabin. But the second didn't manage. I didn't see the shots or even hear them. I just saw a pair of bright flashes reflect off our vehicle's armor and the soldier fell to the ground, already dead. Another bright flame lit up a bush next to the Peresvet. Clearly one of the shots meant to kill my ally had landed there.

I quickly ran to some thick bushes and lay down behind them. I tried to follow the firing trajectory from the burning bush above the corpse, and that led me to some thick vegetation somewhat below my position fifty feet away. Most likely, the enemy sharpshooter was crouching somewhere over there. But no matter how closely I stared at the dense thicket, whether with the IR-lens or without it, I could not see an enemy.

But then I saw something more interesting. Not far from me, there was a tall old man on a rocky outcropping wearing a dark hooded robe and holding a long, crooked staff. He was standing in the open just above the second Peresvet. He was waving one hand and the skull atop his staff was glowing.

Leng Thumor-Anhu La-Fin. Human. Dark Faction. Level-108 Psionic Mage

The very same Dark Faction Psionic Mage who'd attacked me during the prisoner exchange! My heart started pounding. He was the last thing I needed!

Chapter Twenty-Two

Grandfather and Granddaughter

THE SITUATION had come together very badly. The third vehicle of our column was already on fire and spewing black smoke. The surviving three or four soldiers were scattered among the nearby bushes. The high-speed cannon from the second Peresvet was still hacking away at the bushes our soldiers were hidden in. After that, the tower turned, and the cannon started filling our leading vehicle with lead, trying to turn it over on the steep slope. I had to help my allies now before it rolled down on top of us. And the best I could think to do was take down the wizard!

I don't know if the ghastly mage had the Danger Sense skill or not, but I tried to abstract myself from the situation and not think about hurting him. I figured that might help. I was reminded of the S.T.A.L.K.E.R. games. One of their most striking monsters, the Controller, took control of its enemies' minds and killed them methodically. The most effective method against those monsters was two, or better three fragmentation grenades...

Totally on autopilot, without a thought in my head, I tossed a grenade onto the rocky outcropping. Bingo! It landed just right, right underneath the old man!! And it went off with a bang!!! The ghastly mage dropped his staff and made like Icarus, waving his hands like wings and flying down from the cliffs. I don't know how many hitpoints the Psionic Mage had at level one hundred eight, but one RGD-5 grenade and a forty-foot fall was not enough to do him in. But my second and third grenade landed just in time, and the flickering red silhouette of the mage went dim. Hell yeah! I got him!!!

You have reached level seventeen!

You have received three skill points!

You have reached level eighteen!

You have received three skill points! (total points accumulated: six)

With the death of the ghastly mage, the battle sharply broke in our favor. Apparently, not all the soldiers had left the burning third Peresvet. They must have been inside fighting the flames this whole time. They quickly extinguished the blaze. The gunman on the second armored vehicle stopped shooting at our guys as well. And now, all our soldiers had taken cover and were lighting up the road and distant forest with gunfire. I couldn't see the people my allies were firing on through the bushes and hilltops, but the harpies circling above showed where they were.

I then stood up to full height and hurried over to the outcrop where Leng Thumor-Anhu La-Fin had been standing. I had seen the psionic drop his staff there, and I was hoping I might find it. The stones and earth there were blown to smithereens and soaked in blood. But I did find the twisted staff of a dark practically black color topped with a human skull.

Wrath. Large mage staff (???)

Attention! Your character has insufficient Intelligence to determine the properties of this object. Minimum Intelligence: 22.

Attention! This weapon was named Wrath by its first owner. Name cannot be deleted or changed.

Statistic requirements: Intelligence 25, Constitution 16

Attention! Your character's Intelligence and Constitution are insufficient to use this weapon.

Attention! Due to limits of the Prospector class, you cannot use this weapon.

I transferred the valuable object to my inventory, and

the game system found room for it in my backpack, despite its nearly six feet of length. It did occupy three whole slots, though. From the cliff, I had a great view. I could see everything. The enemy was taking heavy losses and retreating in panic. I saw fifteen dead bodies on the road and hillside as well as six or seven far-off figures flailing to repel dive-bombing harpies.

Successful Perception check.

Eagle Eye skill increased to level twenty-eight!

You have reached level nineteen!

You have received three skill points! (total points accumulated: nine)

I had totally forgotten about the sniper that had shot our soldier at the beginning of the battle. And meanwhile, they must have been hiding in the bushes where I couldn't see them before. I had a great view from my new position above them, though. There was a group of three soldiers lying in the thick bushes just watching their allies lose. What was more, I recognized them — the cartographer girl Minn-O La-Fin and her two companions. Old friends! Now they were hidden and clearly trying not to give themselves away.

It was quite a distance to their positions, something like one hundred and fifty feet, so I doubted I could lob my last grenade all the way there. But they were below me, so it was worth a shot. Plus, I mainly wanted to draw the attention of our gunmen to them, and what could do that better than a bright and noisy explosion?

I pulled out the safety ring, and swung with all my

might, flinging the grenade as far as possible. Unfortunately, I didn't make it. The grenade landed fifteen feet from their bushes and rolled down hill. But that drew my allies' attention. All three of the Peresvet towers turned sharply toward the blast. A second later, both the cartographer's companions were dead.

But before my grenade even made it half way, Minn-O La-Fin had darted away, abruptly dashing up the hill and taking cover behind a scattering of rocks and thick vegetation. And that saved her. By the time the gunmen saw the explosion and turned the cannons, she was already hidden. That Danger Sense skill was impressive!

However, I could still see Minn-O La-Fin. I drew Angel Dust and opened fire on the fleeing enemy. Miss! Miss! Miss! It was as if she had a spell on her, dodging nimbly from side to side. Miss! Miss! Another few seconds and she was behind some thick bushes. Miss! Miss!

And then I hit! I clearly saw the lead bullet go through the girl's leg somewhere around knee level. Minn-O La-Fin stumbled and fell but gathered her strength and quickly got up. She was limping and dragging one leg, but still walking away. Another miss! With the tenth and final bullet of my clip, I hit her in the right shoulder. She could no longer stay on her feet and fell again, even dropping her pistol. But a few seconds later, she was back on her feet and behind another bush.

Sharpshooter skill increased to level eight!

No! Minn-O La-Fin was too valuable as a prisoner and

could answer many important questions both for our whole faction and me personally. Above all, she might know the identity of the traitor in our ranks. And so, I ran after her at full speed, switching Angel Dust for the double-barrel hunting shotgun as I went and reloading it with trembling hands.

There were no more than one hundred yards between us. Considering her wounded leg, I was expecting to catch Minn-O La-Fin in short order. But she wasn't behind the bushes where I saw her hide. How? She can't have gone far! I stopped in confusion and looked around. I was surrounded by almost fifty feet of thick thorny shrubbery. She might have been hiding just three steps from me, I wouldn't have been able to see her. The IR-lens didn't help one bit and scanning gave no results either. Had I really let such a valuable prisoner slip away?!

I started examining the ground inch by inch for drops of blood, shoe prints or matted grass. But I didn't find anything of the sort. Five minutes of fruitless searching later, I was about to admit my defeat as a gumshoe and return to my group, when I saw a huge winged shadow dive down from the sky. A huge strong harpy landed just forty steps from me almost immediately followed by a woman's cry.

Getting a better grip on the double-barrel, I walked toward the sounds of struggle and shouts of pain. Damn these thorny bushes! It took me three whole minutes getting through them. Finally, I emerged at a small field and stopped abruptly in shock.

Vali-all Kalli. Harpy. Antiquity Faction. Level-68 Instructor.

The huge male harpy looked to weigh around four hundred fifty pounds. He was balancing his gigantic twenty-foot wings and pressing Minn-o's good left arm firmly to the earth with a clawed talon. The second foot of the enormous beast, covered in red feathers, was on Minn-O La-Fin's waist. She was lying face-down, crushed by the weight. The monster's clawed hands were brutishly ripping off the helpless girl's clothes— her invisibility cloak was already on the ground, as was the empty holster, knives and some buttoned cases. And now, the beast was cutting the black scaled thermoregulating suit off Minn-O La-Fin's back with his razor-sharp claws, not giving a single thought to whether he was ripping into living flesh as he did.

I was reminded of what Ivan Lozovsky had said earlier, how the harpies love to humiliate the weak and wounded. Apparently, that was exactly what I was seeing now. What was more, based on the winged beast's throbbing crooked penis, the helpless victim's troubles had just begun... The flying sadist was so caught up in the process, that he didn't even notice me.

"Hey, get out of here you overgrown horny rooster!" I shouted, firing a warning shot from one barrel of my shotgun.

The male harpy jumped in surprise and flew a hundred feet up with just a few flaps of his huge wings. However, the high-level monster was in no rush to flee, and was just hovering there, watching me carefully. I understood that perfectly. I was a fairly weak human, but I was holding a dangerous weapon.

I spent some time staring the harpy down, but the winged beast was just biding his time. Not letting the flying enemy out of my sight, I carefully walked over to the wounded Dark Faction girl. Minn-O La-Fin had already managed to sit upright and, not taking her eyes off me, felt with her left hand where she previously had a belt with holster and knives. Unlike her ghastly father, her eyes did not glow but had a rich emerald color that harmonized perfectly with her ashen-gray skin. Finally, it dawned on her that her belt was gone and she was unarmed.

"Ti livo yen mi! Un tivi ron mekhsh!" Minn-O La-Fin said distinctly. The girl's voice contained some pleading or even begging.

But I didn't understand and was not moving, so the green-eyed beauty repeated the strange phrase, but this time pointed with her left hand first at my shotgun, then at her heart.

Astrolinguistics skill increased to level twelve!

Even an idiot would have understood that. Minn-O La-Fin was begging me to shoot her so she would respawn somewhere safe. But I was in no rush. After all, she wasn't just any terrified wounded girl. She was an enemy — clever, implacable and very dangerous. What was more, she possessed a huge amount of highly valuable information, which could help my faction and all of my world's humanity.

And so, I was more inclined to think that I should keep her alive, use her belt to tie her hands and drag my valuable prisoner back to the Peresvets.

But then Minn-O La-Fin began to cry... Before that, the girl hadn't let slip a single tear even when the ghastly harpy had painfully twisted her arms and ripped into her back with his sharp claws. As it turned out, she was much more afraid of being taken prisoner than the beast with barbarous appetites. So I gave in.

"Alright, have it your way. But if my allies find out I let you go, I'll be drawn and quartered..." with these words, I lowered my weapon to the girl's chest and shot her point blank in the heart.

Rifles skill increased to level twenty-three!
Sharpshooter skill increased to level nine!

Minn-O La-Fin, with a huge smoking hole in her chest, spent another second or two sitting and even looking consciously at me with her pupils wide in pain. But then she fell on her side, and her emerald eyes closed.

Fame increased to 9.

It took me a while to come back to my senses. It isn't every day you have to execute a pretty girl. But just five steps away, that huge harpy male landed heavily. Well damn, I'd totally forgotten about him! And unfortunately, my double-barrel was now unloaded. Nevertheless, I didn't let myself show any fear or lack of confidence. Instead, I turned the shotgun toward him and said with a dismayed and rude tone:

"What'd you land here for? Can't you see? I'm in no

mood to talk with you! And if you take even one step in my direction, I'll shoot through both your wings and you'll have to walk out of here!"

He clearly understood me, because he immediately folded his wings behind his back. Then I aimed a bit lower, this time right at his flaccid masculine dignity. The huge male got even more scared and hurriedly covered his manhood with both hands.

"No shoot. Trading!" the monster hissed out and showed me a laser pistol awkwardly squeezed in his hand, clearly picked up during the recent struggle.

Trade? And why not? Without turning my weapon off the harpy, I opened my inventory and took out a briquette of dried rations.

"Tasty food! Very tasty!" I demonstrated him my goods.

"Not enough," the harpy turned his clawed talon and showed me four fingers.

"Four? You've lost your mind!!! Did you fall off a cliff when you were a baby?!" I exclaimed, acting falsely indignant. "Four briquettes of this tasty food could buy your whole flock! Three!"

Fame increased to 10.

The huge monster spent a few seconds in fevered thought then nodded in agreement. I placed three dried rations on the ground and walked back, letting the dangerous creature leave the laser pistol and pick up my food. After that, I gathered all the things from the clearing and hurried back to my people. There were many harpies circling up above, but I was sure they wouldn't touch me. Those creatures really did despise the weak. But at that, they recognized confidence and strength, and I managed to demonstrate those qualities.

Chapter Twenty-Three

Geckho Base

FROZEN STOCK STILL at the first Peresvet, my allies were not happy to see me. Apparently, Ivan Lozovsky figured I'd got cold feet and turned tail. And now, he'd told the other soldiers that. They wouldn't even listen at first, but when I told them I'd killed the ghastly psionic, I saw their reaction turned indignant:

"It wasn't you that killed him. Gerd Tarasov sniped the enemy mage when he jumped off the cliffs and came down to melee us!" one of the First Legion soldiers pointed at his vaunted commander.

Gerd Tarasov. Human. H3 Faction. Level-89 Sniper

The bald, highest-level warrior was very short but had the broad shoulders of a bodybuilder. Wearing a formless ghillie suit and holding a sophisticated sniper rifle in a pair of calloused hands, the leader of the First Legion looked like he was born for this role.

A Gerd... I took a heavy sigh and counted to three to calm down, gathering my thoughts and forming my sentences just right so I wouldn't accidentally wound the ego and interests of the high-status player. Clearly, I shouldn't dispute this statement head-on. Maybe Tarasov had shot the mage, but what happened before that?

"Jumped down?! He dropped his weapon and fell flat off that elevated outcropping like an unconscious mannequin after I hit him with a grenade. And you say he was coming down to melee you?! I leveled up three times! Do you think that was just from looking at harpies? And I suppose I bought this mage staff at a local market!"

Although my speech was heated, every word was calculated. I took out the staff from my inventory and showed it off. The First Legion soldiers had clearly seen it before. But still they exchanged unconfident glances, not yet able to accept that a day-two newbie could have killed one of their most dangerous enemies. But I continued my fervent speech:

"If you still don't believe me, go up on the cliff and see for yourselves. The rocks are all broken and covered with that mage's blood! Lots of other people in my position might have been afraid and run away, but I hit him with a grenade! And the sniper that killed our soldier," I pointed to the corpse of our ally next to the wheel of the first Peresvet, "I tracked her down and took her out as well. It was a nimble cartographer by the name of Minn-O La-Fin. I just barely managed to hit her. Boy can she dodge! I can show you her body if you like. Her whole chest was blasted open by my shotgun! And her two bodyguards, who do you think showed our gunners where they were with another the grenade?! I suppose they were leaving cover up there to melee you as well?! I've got one of their laser pistols, too. And a belt and chameleon cloak that fell off Minn-O La-Fin."

Ivan Lozovsky motioned toward one of the soldiers to have him check. But Gerd Tarasov stopped him:

"No need. Friends, I can admit I may have erred. Either I shot an already dead enemy, or my bullet was not the last. I was actually surprised to see that my progress bar practically didn't move after the mage died. This explains a lot."

The group opinion of me instantly changed. All of their faces mellowed out and gave way to smiles.

"Great job, Gnat! Congratulations on your first real battle!" Ivan Lozovsky walked up and slapped me approvingly on the shoulder.

Gerd Tarasov also congratulated me and added:

"Get your level up to sixty, go through group training then we can talk about you joining the First Legion. After all, from what I've heard, the Second Legion will never be an option for you."

Everyone around started laughing, as if that was a great joke. I also smiled, but I didn't understand what they found so funny. I guess everyone already knew about my complicated relationship with Gerd Tamara.

Fame increased to 12.

Just then, from the cliffs in the distance, I heard a powerful explosion. The earth underfoot even started shaking. Hundreds of harpies took off with frightened cries and a black stream of smoke appeared in the morning sky. Every radio around me started up at the same time. A hoarse voice said with distinct notes of pity:

"This is Artyomov. We weren't able to capture the Dark Faction transport. Looks like we triggered a security system. As soon as we started clearing the branches off the thing, it self-destructed. Fortunately, none of us were harmed, although we're all a bit deaf now. Looks like a thermite device. All that's left of her now is a puddle of molten slag..."

"Understood. Artyomov, return to convoy," Ivan Lozovsky commanded. "It's time to get moving. We're already behind schedule. Just have the sapper remove the mines. At the end of the day, they're valuable items and might come in handy. And our engineers will want to study the Dark Faction tech."

I was worried they might take the valuable items I'd captured from the Dark Faction on the pretext that I didn't have the skills to use them. But the First Legion had a different set of rules than the Second. Here it was "finders keepers," so no one even tried to contend for the wand or cloak. And no one tried to get the details of my encounter with Minn-O La-Fin, which was perfectly fine with me. As soon as Artyomov's four-person group returned, they hopped into the back two Peresvets and we got on our way.

I was in the lead vehicle with our diplomat as before, but we had a new driver now. It was the guy who'd doubted my ability to kill the enemy mage before. He went by the nickname Bonesetter, and he was a Medic by class. When I got to know him, he was a good guy, although a bit skittish and verbose. But maybe that was just evidence of the recent battle.

The rest of our drive through the Harpy Cliffs node went without incident, although a certain tension could be felt. The crews of the various Peresvets often communicated by radio both amongst themselves and with scout groups further afield. One time, they spent nearly half an hour on the bank of a small lake, waiting for our scouts to check a suspicious section of road. I had already raised Cartography to level 33, Eagle Eye to 30 and Scanning to 24. It looked like I would hit character level twenty before the end of the drive.

When we crossed into the next node, Desert, everyone looked relieved. The cliffs, impenetrable vegetation and sticky mud immediately gave way to a parched wasteland with the odd spiny tree and small wind-swept hill. There was no cover from the scorching sun, though, so the temperature in our Peresvet started climbing mercilessly. But we didn't have to fear enemies or ambushes here, which was much more important that our physical comfort.

Taking advantage of the diplomat's good mood, I asked the origin of my pneumatic rifle's name. Why Angel Dust? Because it would turn enemies to dust? The deputy faction head cracked up:

"Ah, so you got my old air gun! Well, it's no secret. Many in our faction know the story. Gnat, didn't you see the letters PCP in the rifle name?"

Of course I had, which I immediately told him.

"Well, the abbreviation PCP doesn't only stand for Pre-Charged Pneumatic. Those letters can also refer to a narcotic, phenylcyclohexyl piperidine, also known by the street name angel dust. It's a nasty little drug that blocks all your mind's information receptors and causes very severe hallucinations. Phenylcyclohexyl piperidine is eliminated very poorly by the body. A drug test can detect angel dust even a year after you last used. And that was why my career in the Ministry of Foreign affairs went down in flames. They don't allow drug users. But what's much worse is that angel dust is ten times harder to kick than heroin, and practically everyone who takes it ends up in the nuthouse eventually. And that's if they don't jump out a window first. There are plenty of cases of that. But I got lucky. Before I lost my marbles or did myself in, I was brought under the Dome. That cured the physical addiction immediately. But as for the mental... I have to admit I'm still afraid that one day, I'll have to leave this underground base, end up with my old friends and fall right back into it..."

"Geckho shuttle up ahead!" our driver interrupted the diplomat's confession.

I turned my head to look and saw a crescent-shaped flying object shooting over our column.

Sindirovu. Geckho surface and near-space destroyer-interceptor

Ivan Lozovsky also looked closer at the flying machine, even took out his binoculars to get a closer look and started smiling:

"Those are the buyers of our palladium. They don't want to go through the space port so they won't have to report it. Well, what can I say? They warned us. Stop the vehicle, Bonesetter. Looks like we'll be trading right here in the desert."

"Smugglers?" I guessed and, much to my surprise, our diplomat didn't deny it.

"Most likely. But our faction doesn't have much of a choice right now. They'll pay a good price for palladium, and we need as much space currency as we can get to buy technology and manufactured goods, so we can't be picky. But don't go wagging your tongue about our little side hustle at the Geckho base."

Something had clearly gone wrong. Just after our convoy left the Desert node and reached the first rows of automatic laser turrets guarding the Geckho base, a patrol of armed furballs came out to block our path.

Ivan Lozovsky climbed out of the Peresvet to figure out why we'd been stopped and bicker with the guards. I didn't understand what they were arguing about, but I definitely heard the words "sindirovu" and "undimeh" a few times. The first was the name of the Geckho smugglers' interceptor, and the second meant palladium, which I'd learned during Lozovsky's recent negotiations.

Astrolinguistics skill increased to level thirteen!

You have reached level twenty!

You have received three skill points! (total points accumulated: twelve)

"We're gonna have to undergo a complete inspection!" the dismayed diplomat returned to the Peresvet and ordered our driver to follow a light Geckho buggy. "Also, I told them I'm the only one here who speaks a word of Geckho. None of these Geckho understand our language, and if they ask questions in theirs, just play dumb and keep quiet. Especially you, Gnat! I'm sure no one else will gab, but now is not the best time for you to reveal your Astrolinguistics skill. Got it?"

Although I was offended by his mistrust, I told him he

had nothing to worry about.

"But what if the Geckho call Kosta Dykhsh to interrogate us?" I shuddered in fear, to which the diplomat answered that I shouldn't worry.

"He won't be coming. In fact, it was Kosta Dykhsh that introduced us to the palladium buyers. They're his friends, and I strongly suspect the diplomat is also getting a cut."

Our armored trucks drove onto a concrete platform the size of a football stadium, which was surrounded by tall walls of reinforced concrete. The automatic doors closed behind us. I started to get worried, but Ivan Lozovsky demonstrated nothing but calm and confidence. After calling the leader of the First Legion, the deputy faction head ordered us to form an armed perimeter around the Peresvets and not let anyone through.

The diplomat then went off, in his own words, to "make friends with these Geckho and figure out which wheels need greasing." Before leaving, the diplomat opened one of the boxes in the back and placed its contents in his inventory: a dozen bottles of vodka labeled "Made by the H3 Faction using time-honored techniques." He also took a transparent bag of monetary crystals from a safe.

Ivan Lozovsky was gone a long time, nearly three hours. But all that time, despite the unmercifully scorching sun, we took shifts guarding the trucks and looking vigilant and confident for the Geckho who occasionally looked down from the wall.

Finally, the gates slid aside, and a whole delegation of ten important furballs came out with our diplomat. Based on their staggering, big smiles and slurred grumbling Geckho laughter, they had found a common tongue. Ivan Lozovsky, having changed his camouflage smock for an austere business suit, looked flawless as usual.

The diplomat spent a long time bringing the Geckho up to speed, showing them our armored trucks and demonstrating the bullet holes and burns on our armor. After that, he crawled into the back of the Peresvet and handed the furballs a sealed box, which they accepted with favor. After that, the delegation left, and our diplomat called us over with good news:

"Alright, guys, everything's fine! These Geckho already knew what we were up to. But I managed not only to smooth over all our misunderstandings, I also found buyers for the rest of our metal. Unload all sixteen tons right here. The Geckho will help us. They're sending two heavy robot loaders. After that, you have free time until evening. We're waiting on an orbital transport. After it lands, we can load our composite materials and solar batteries into the space port and go back home by ferry. I've already arranged for it. We'll be back in the Capital before nightfall!"

Everyone shouted happily. The soldiers began to smile and look lively. I was glad too. Taking a different route back meant I could keep leveling Cartography. But, I was celebrating prematurely. Ivan Lozovsky started looking for someone and stopped on me, then called me closer.

"Gnat, I've got something for you. It's risky, maybe even too much, but it's right up your alley. In the electronics shop where I bought your Prospector equipment, a Geckho approached me. His name is Uraz Tukhsh, he's the captain of a Shiamiru-class shuttle and will by flying to the asteroid belt in an hour and a half. He has an automatic resource processor and is hoping to score some minerals. But his crew, as far as I understood, hasn't managed to find anything of value yet, just junk like ferroalloys, cobalt and other cheap metals. Seeing me buy a Prospector scanner, Uraz Tukhsh was very intrigued. Basically, he made a spontaneous offer to take you with him on their next voyage so you can help him find valuable minerals."

My jaw simply dropped. No, I mean just imagine what it's like to find out that, in an hour and a half, you might be flying to outer space! Awesome, of course, but... how would I get back? I didn't manage to voice my doubts, but fear or hesitation must have shown on my face because he hurried to add:

"His Shiamiru will return to the space port tomorrow and you can go. Your reward is that, whatever you find, you can take as much as you can carry. And the captain will pay for scanner supplies himself."

"What 'supplies' does it need?" I didn't understand.

"Yeah, I just found out how the whole thing works myself. I figured, you buy the Prospector equipment and that's that. As it turns out, it's all much more complicated. As for the scanner itself... here it is." Ivan Lozovsky took it from his inventory and handed me the rectangular object. It was reminiscent of a folded laptop in a shock-proof case.

Basic scanner (Prospector tool)

Detection range: 5,000 feet. Atomic battery life: 3 years.

Statistic requirements: Perception 18, Intelligence 15

Skill requirements: Scanning 20, Electronics 16

Attention! Your character's electronics skill is insufficient to use this item.

Attention! This device requires geologic analyzers to receive data.

"Gnat, this is the most basic model. The Geckho also had more advanced models in their catalog. But, first of all, they went for simply cosmic prices. And second, I wasn't sure you'd have the skills to use more advanced scanners. By the way..." the diplomat asked if I even had the ability to use the model he had bought.

"Yes, of course," I answered in a careless voice, as if it were something rudimentary.

But actually, after seeing the scanner's requirements, I opened my skill window and put seven points into

Electronics, raising it to sixteen. My remaining five points I decided not to touch for now. What if I had another urgent need? Ivan Lozovsky gave a satisfied nod and continued his explanation.

"As it turns out, a Prospector scanner is just a monitor that displays scanning results which is fitted with a panel to adjust the settings. Anyway, this computer gets results from special single-use devices. I saw them in the shop, they're these three-foot-long antennas you screw into the ground. When activated, they create disturbances... or like a magnetic field... or I don't really know what exactly, but your computer will get results. This method allows things to be found deep underground, all kinds of minerals, ore veins, empty pockets and whatever else... By the way, these pieces of crap cost fifty crystals a piece."

Holy hell! Fifty red crystals for just one lone scan! I began opening my mouth to object to the extortionate price, but Lozovsky stopped me with a raised finger and added:

"Yes, it's expensive, but Uraz Tukhsh promised to pay. And the most intriguing part is that the captain said he has a light spacesuit on his shuttle made for a person. He is not planning to give it to you for keeps, just temporarily so you can work on asteroids. I'll admit, I have no idea what it is, and who can make them. But I know we can't make them. I suspect that our scientists would give up a year's salary without a second thought for the chance to look at a spacesuit of extraterrestrial design! Anyhow, if you're interested, Uraz Tukhsh is sitting in the space port restaurant right now."

What did he mean "if I'm interested?!" Was there any person who would ever find such an offer uninteresting? What doubts could he have?! The ability to fly into outer space comes once in a lifetime, and not nearly to all. Even if it was on a ship of an alien race with a crew that didn't speak my language, I just couldn't say no!

"I thought as much. With all your risk-taking, I knew you'd never let such an adventure pass you by," the diplomat smiled happily, but quickly grew serious and continued. "Just so you know, this journey is important not only for you personally, but to our faction as a whole. Gnat, you will bring us new knowledge, and there is nothing more valuable in the game that bends reality. We have been in total isolation for almost a year with just low-tech neighbors like forest spirits, centaurs and harpies. Meeting the Dark Faction proved how seriously behind we were."

The diplomat went silent and turned, wanting to make sure no one was eavesdropping.

"Yes, Gnat, the situation really is grave. The leadership of the Dome and our outside analysts have come to the same conclusion: the Dark Faction is developing faster and better than us. We cannot hold out on our own. So, we must change our strategy, refuse isolationism and talk with other players of the game that bends reality. Recently, we've been establishing contact with different groups of Geckho but as you see, even at their base, our faction is quite poorly known and treated with caution. So new contacts are very important. Anyway Gnat, here is your mission for the voyage: get to know Uraz Tukhsh and his team, prove yourself a reliable partner, and hopefully get them to hire you long term. Got it?"

I repeated the mission aloud: get to know Shiamiru Captain Uraz Tukhsh and his crew, prove myself a useful Prospector and, ideally, find more work.

"That's exactly right. Try at the very least not to get in any trouble or start any conflicts. The race of Shiharsa is not known for their patience, and they are even less restrained with vassals than Gerd Tamara is with disobedient allies. And you must never change your respawn point. That's your guaranteed way home."

Chapter
Twenty-Four

Journey
to the
Asteroids

WHAT DO YOU THINK of when you hear the words "space port?" Probably a futuristic location where starships of the most unbelievable shapes and designs take off into the heavens with boards showing arrivals and departures, signs in dozens of languages, crowds of aliens, cargo robots scurrying about, fuss, noise and chaos. That is what I was expecting when I went up the smooth spiral ramp to the tall dispatch tower which contained both customs and all other services of the Geckho spaceport.

From outside, the dispatch tower looked like five enormous flat disks, each larger in diameter than the next, with a long thin spire running through them. The structure looked very flimsy, but I suspected that antigrav devices were giving it some extra stability. Most of all, it looked like one of those children's toys with colorful fat rings stacked on a stick, just upside down. Ivan Lozovsky didn't go with me, staying to make sure the cargo was unloaded smoothly. So I had to find Captain Uraz Tukhsh in the restaurant on my own.

The ramp made seventeen or eighteen spirals in the dark concrete cylinder before it led me out into a spacious round room with panoramic windows.

Cartography skill increased to level thirty-four!

There were no scurrying crowds of extraterrestrials, nor fast-moving robots. Also, this establishment could only be called a restaurant if you were stretching it quite a lot. It had three little tables, some hovering semicircular sofas and an automatic panel to order drinks and food. The spiral ramp continued to the next floors and, in the center, there was a closed metal door on every floor — either an elevator, or an employee-only closet.

The room was practically empty. But there was a hirsute Geckho sprawled out in an armored space-suit sitting at one of the tables and looking bored. It seemed to me that the space pilot was either asleep or drunk because he was sitting with his eyes closed and nodding over an empty tray. But I was less interested in the Geckho than the spaceport out the window.

I walked right up to the glass and found disenchantment. The space-ship landing zone was just a rectangular patch of wasteland around a mile in diameter surrounded by a cement wall. It even had all the bumps, bushes and mounds of the surrounding countryside. There was no hard cover, and the withered yellow grass had visible traces of landings: a few burned circles and one long black strip.

Eagle Eye skill increased to level thirty-one!

The only starship on the enormous field was a Shiamiru-class cargo shuttle, which just happened to be at the end of the black strip of burned grass. The space ship was reminiscent of a plump airplane with no tail and short triangular wings. The shuttle was slanted at a severe angle, practically touching the earth with its right wing. There was a brigade of Geckho technicians swarming around the spacecraft arguing amongst themselves. Apparently, I was about to head on my first space flight on that very shuttle. So, I was greatly hoping the strange angled state of the ship and frenzy around it were totally fine, and not caused by technical problems.

"Gnnnat?" the growl of the alarmed space pilot carried throughout the empty room and I turned sharply.

Uraz Tukhsh. Geckho. Clan Waideh-Tukhsh. Level-51 Aristocrat

Aristocrat? What a strange profession?! Why not Starship pilot, like Dmitry Zheltov or "captain," as our furry diplomat called it? Nevertheless, I set my questions aside for better times and politely greeted my employer:

"Kento duho, Uraz Tukhsh!"

In the long minute that followed, I only made out a few words of his two sentences:

"... low level... speak... Shiharsa... good... Shiamiru..."

Seemingly, Uraz Tukhsh found my level very doubtful. I don't know what our diplomat had promised him, but the Geckho was clearly expecting a much higher-level Prospector. In the end, I understood I had been asked a question, but didn't know what the captain wanted from me. But the Geckho was expecting me to answer, so I nodded. I hoped greatly I was not agreeing to sell myself into slavery or donate my body to alien vivisectionists.

Uraz Tukhsh, without standing from the hovering couch, said something else incomprehensible, turned and pointed at his ship. It seemed he was suggesting I follow him to the ship although... I wasn't sure. No, couldn't be right. I opened Gnat's skill table and set all five free Astrolinguistics points there, thus raising it to level eighteen.

It became somewhat easier. I even understood the captain's next question: he wanted to know if two single-use geological analyzers would be enough, or if it would be better to take three. Clumsily, to the best of my ability, I suggested we get three. Just to be clear, I showed him three splayed fingers.

"It's expensive here... damn... boondocks... backward planet... damn... fifty per... totally... damn... just... damn..."

In that matter, I was in complete agreement with Uraz Tukhsh because I was still in shock after hearing the price myself. Fifty crystals for just one!!! What could I possibly find to compensate such huge expenses?!

"Gnat... elevator... landing zone... go Shiamiru... buy three... hurry."

Uraz Tukhsh considered the conversation over, got up heavily from the table and headed up the spiral ramp.

So, for now, I understood what to do. The captain had ordered me to take the elevator and go to the starship, while he went off to buy geological analyzers without me. I didn't argue and headed to the elevator in the middle of the room, although I of course would have liked to go up a floor to take a look at an alien electronics shop.

But, when I reached the elevator doors, I was stumped. Was this some kind of joke? The wall didn't have any panel of buttons with floor numbers like I expected, just a small flat slit, perhaps for a narrow plastic card or some kind of key? I didn't want to go find the captain to ask. Such a small issue wasn't worth looking dumb this early. But there was no one else around.

If I went and asked the captain for help, his first impression of me would be that I was ignorant and bad at taking orders. That was off the table. I considered going down the spiral ramp, leaving the dispatch tower and just climbing the landing field wall. But I figured that was too risky. After all, what if the Geckho guards took me for a thief and shot me?! But what other options did I have? Stand here and wait like an idiot? Or just go up after the captain? What if...

I looked around and didn't see any security cameras,

so I took out my knife and tried to pry up the panel. It was held to the wall with simple snaps and fairly easily broke off the wall, so I removed the whole panel with its electronic circuit and wires. So, what do we have here? I carefully studied the device.

Electronics skill increased to level seventeen!

The way the security system worked, the proper key would connect the wires and form a circuit. Was that all?! With the knife blade, I completed the circuit and immediately heard the elevator go into motion. It worked!

Break-in skill increased to level seven!
Break-in skill increased to level eight!
You have reached level twenty-one!
You have received three skill points!

Quickly putting the panel back in place, I entered the elevator doors as they slid aside. Inside, instead of the usual buttons, there was just a slide lever that moved along a slit in the wall. But this didn't take much thought. I needed to go down, so I moved the lever to the very lowest position. The doors gradually closed, the elevator went into motion and soon took me to the landing field.

Hell yeah! It worked! Now time to go to the starship!

I was expecting the crew to be intrigued by me, but their reaction was surprisingly reserved and even insultingly careless. After hearing that Uraz Tukhsh sent me, and that I was flying with them to the asteroids, the Geckho lost interest and got back to business. The technicians were readying the shuttle for take-off, checking the systems and fussing around with the tools next to the right thruster. The high-level Navigator and Supercargo on the ground next to the gangway phlegmatically led their gazes over me, not asking any questions. The guardsman, draped head to toe in weaponry, also simply stepped aside, letting me onto the starship.

They just took me at my word, and I got the impression that anyone who wanted could enter. What could I say? I didn't insist on being tested, just went aboard the Shiamiru.

Inside the shuttle, conditions were very cramped. There wasn't enough space even for me. I had to walk down the main corridor hunched over. In places, I even had to go sideways. I simply could not imagine how the larger Geckho moved through these halls or let others pass! In fact, the whole crew area was no larger than a typical intercity bus, even though it was meant for sixteen crew members!

The four tiny living quarters branched off from the main hallway, each with four bunks. The residential area had two, other smaller offshoots as well — one into the locked cargo hold, and a second leading to the captain's bridge. I stopped in indecision, not knowing where to sit.

"Gnat can go here... enough... things," one of the crew members noticed my confusion and (here I didn't understand) was either inviting me to stay in his bunk room or angrily demanding I make way.

Vasha Tushihh. Geckho. Clan Tushihh-Layneh. Level-62 Heavy Robot Operator

Seemingly, he was inviting me to join him, as the red-furred giant, huge even by Geckho standards, wearing an armored space suit and an unbuttoned helmet stepped aside, making room for me. I immediately took him up on that and sat down on the very edge of the plastic bench. What was this? I felt like I was seeing double. An identical Geckho was sitting opposite me and polishing his helmet with green paste and a rag.

Basha Tushihh. Geckho. Clan Tushihh-Layneh. Level-63 Heavy Robot Operator

Twin brothers? That seemed to be the case. My other roommate was a short Geckho with huge yellow eyes and thick black fur, striped with an unusual white forking pattern in white. Nature could hardly have created such a bizarre, geometrically-perfect coloration. I was probably more likely seeing an artificial dye job.

Uline Tar. Geckho. Clan Tar-Layne. Level-56 Trader

Our bunk room couldn't have been larger than a standard train compartment. It was quite cramped. I took a look around at the place I'd be spending the next day. Dim lighting. The walls and even ceiling were festooned with boxes and bags, which were seemingly attached by magnets or something sticky. My roommates personal items were crammed under the two benches. There were two more sleeping shelves folded above us. If they were down, none of us would be able to walk.

I greeted my roommates one after the next in Geckho and added: "Happy to meet you!" To which the trader grumbled through his teeth, not hiding his annoyance:

"Last trip... damn... loser... didn't find a decent Prospector... I'll leave Uraz Tukhsh for another... damn... is gonna get it!!!"

Seemingly, it wasn't only the trader upset by my low level. But I soon realized that I was not the only reason for Uline Tar's dismay, nor even the most important. The Trader was calling the captain a loser, and I assumed such angry words must have had some basis. I caught less than half of what my talkative roommate said, but I got the general picture. Our captain Uraz Tukhsh was from an ancient aristocratic house and, according to Geckho tradition, before receiving territory or subjects, he had to prove himself either in military service, or some other field.

Uraz Tukhsh decided to try his hand as a trader, seeking adventure and fortune. It was apparently quite a common choice. He got some starting capital from his family, enough to buy a cargo shuttle and hire a crew, then headed off into the cosmos, seeking his lucky star. He couldn't hack it on the more crowded routes. The traders there were too crafty. So, the young aristocrat headed to the edge of the known universe, hoping to find success out on the frontier. That had led him to a recently discovered system, the projection of our Solar System in the game that bends reality.

Trading with the native tribes (one of which was my Human-3 Faction) had not been quite as profitable as he hoped. We simply didn't have the currency to purchase high-tech goods from far away. The local goods, meanwhile, were mostly cheap raw materials that needed further processing and were of interest only in massive quantity. But that niche was already occupied, and the Shiamiru was too small for that anyway.

Now, Uraz Tukhsh had been trying his best to process asteroids for twenty days and had even bought an automated mineral processor. But he hadn't found anything of value in this system yet, and the cheap metals he had collected just barely recouped his ship upkeep expenses. What could I say? This confirmed Ivan Lozovsky's story and explained why the captain had a sudden need for a Prospector.

Astrolinguistics skill increased to level nineteen!

"We're taking off! Everyone get ready! Navigator, set a course for the previous coordinates. Hopefully we'll find something better this time and put our mobile ore processor to good use!" the captain's voice thundered down the corridor. I understood every word!

A howl and a whistle blasted out. The walls vibrated. I looked at my neighbors in alarm, but Basha Tushihh was still polishing his helmet lens, while Uline Tar just kept complaining. The vibration was getting stronger, even surging. My back was pressed against the wall, but it was bearable.

A bag fell off the wall onto the floor. The Trader remarked in dismay that it was an insignificant occurrence:

"Our captain's just trying to save on the gravity compensators..."

"Well, we broke one gravity compensators during landing," Basha Tushihh finally looked up from his helmet and joined the conversation. "I told the captain, enough ore containers in the hold already, we're already nearly one and a half times over capacity. But no, he didn't listen..."

"And most importantly, the risk wasn't even worth taking," Uline Tar found more fodder for her dismay. "All we found was practically worthless. It couldn't even pay for the repair..."

As I listened to Uline whine, I was walking on air. I had

begun to understand them! Cool! What was more, the engine overloads began to gradually weaken, then came to an end. Things were looking up!

But my rose-tinted glasses flew off when I took out my scanner and switched it on. YIKES! On the dark screen, there was a complete mess of abstract colorful flourishes. What the heck??? I didn't understand a single symbol. My level-19 Astrolinguistics skill and understanding of spoken Geckho were no help with written texts... How could I do my job if I couldn't understand a single bit of the scanner's output?!

Just to test, I dumped another point into Astrolinguistics, raising the skill to level twenty. It didn't help. I might as well have been reading Chinese. Actually, this was worse. I at least had a tentative grasp of how Chinese writing worked. Here I didn't even understand where to start. How did these variously colored geometric patterns work? I had to ask my roommates for help.

Uline Tar, not hiding her negative opinion of me, the captain and our expedition as a whole, predictably refused. But Basha and Vasha agreed. It was more likely out of boredom than a desire to help, but still the twins started teaching me their writing.

Our practice was already entering its fifth hour. I had to admit, my brains were already fried from the abundance of new information, but I was still trying diligently to memorize more and more sequences of curves, broken lines, spirals and loops. The Geckho symbols didn't correspond to sounds or even separate words. In their language, every sentence or phrase was depicted with a single line, wiggling, looping and spiraling depending on the meaning, but always closed at the end, indicating the end of a semantic unit.

At a certain point, seeing my obvious strain and even limited success, the Trader also started trying to teach me. And eventually, I reached the point of being able to write "Uline Tar, space trader." Part of it looked nearly identical to another phrase they'd taught me, "pretty lady," and clearly that was no mere coincidence.

Astrolinguistics skill increased to level twenty-five!

You have reached level twenty-two!

You have received three skill points! (total points accumulated: five)

I told my teachers I thought the two different phrases looked similar. And at the same time, I asked whether I had understood correctly that Uline Tar was a Geckho lady.

"Ha! He finally got it! Took you a while," Uline frowned.

She stood up and walked into the corridor. It seemed

she was offended. I suspected that Uline considered herself irresistibly attractive, so she was offended that I couldn't tell the difference between her and the two huge twin brothers.

"You know, it's actually pretty obvious," Basha told me, lowering his voice to a whisper. "The ratio between arms and torso are different, the height is somewhat less, the ears point back, the figure is different and women have unique fur patterns. Didn't you notice?"

I didn't try to excuse my ignorance, apologize or justify myself. I just wasn't up to it. Uline was already back, carrying three folded metal tripods and a silver envelope.

"The captain told me to give you these geological analyzers and this spacesuit," the furry lady remarked.

Above all, I was interested in the suit. The whole silver jumpsuit was made of rubberized fabric with metallic coating. It also had clip-in gloves and a ball-shaped transparent helmet that folded back. The back of the suit had a fairly heavy thick metal container, clearly an air tank.

Light spacesuit (suitable for thin air, vacuum or noncorrosive gasses)

Radiation defense +12, Armor 1.

Air tank refill time: 12 minutes.

Single tank duration: 2.5 hours.

Statistic requirements: Constitution 6, Strength 6.

The statistic requirements were very forgiving, appropriate for practically any person. And the fabric easily stretched, so the light space suit was practically unisize. I opened my equipment window and equipped the suit. A moment later, I was totally inside and ready to work in the vacuum of space.

Everything was fine and dandy, but I was embarrassed by two clear protrusions from the front of my suit. What was that? Was this made to be worn over a woman's breasts!? This was a woman's space suit!!!

When I told my companions in confusion, both brothers and the girl started rumbling very loudly through their teeth, which was the sound of uncontrollable Geckho laughter. Soon, other furballs also appeared in the hallway, attracted to the sound of amusement. And soon, everyone in the crew had heard the embarrassing story.

Fame increased to 13.

What was I to them, a clown to lighten their collective mood? I changed the space suit into my usual clothing. Alright, in one way or another, everything with the space suit was clear — it was perfectly fine, even though I looked somewhat awkward. The time had now come to sort out the geological analyzers.

I took one of the heavy tripods and turned it in my hands. Lozovsky had said something about screwing the metallic rod into soil, but I didn't see any threading on any of the feet. It was simply three smooth yard-long metal rods, now folded together, all attached to a rectangular plastic box. Maybe this was a different model? And by the way, where was the on button? And how did they synchronize with my scanner? I grabbed one and unfolded a leg in search of a hidden switch.

Something clicked...

The lights turned off not only in our bunk, but down the whole corridor, in the neighboring bunks, and seemingly in the entire starship. The Shiamiru sharply jerked and started spinning on its axis, which threw me into a wall. The only source of light remaining in the starship was my scanner screen. I was happy to be able to read the text, though:

"Signal detected. Data collection underway"

Scanning skill increased to level twenty-five!

I heard screams of fear from all directions. None of the Geckho understood what was happening or why. Through all the clamor, the captain's voice thundered out:

"Gnnnnnat!!!"

Fame increased to 14.

Chapter Twenty-Five

Space Anomaly

I WAS SAVED from grueling punishment only because the reserve power flipped on in short order, and the automatic systems evened out the Shiamiru's flight. All the same, I was not spared a long and obscene dressing down from the captain. Thankfully, Uraz Tukhsh didn't accuse me of intentional sabotage, but I heard a lot of assertions on the low intellectual level of the human race as a whole, and Gnat in particular. But the captain was more outraged by the fact that we had wasted one of three analyzers than the power overload. He even threatened to shake my faction down to recoup his expenses after we returned.

Haunted by visions of the faces of my faction leaders

if that came to pass, I tried to offer Uraz Tukhsh compensation in the form of my Dark Faction laser pistol. But the captain, without even glancing at it, advised me to "use that primitive weapon to shoot yourself through your worthless brain." Fortunately, the storm gradually settled, and I wasn't even thrown overboard without a spacesuit. Uraz Tukhsh had been screaming about just such a punishment, though. I was even morally prepared to respawn back at my capital base in shame.

Over all the screams and commotion, none of the crew even noticed that I had saved the scan in my device's memory. However, my thoughtless action had netted me a highly-detailed three-dimensional blueprint of an alien starship!

When the captain calmed down, and my roommates drifted off, I turned on my scanner and carefully acquainted myself with the saved file. It showed all the key sections of the Shiamiru-class ship along with its control systems and power sources, rooms, corridors and technical components. Practically every rivet could be seen in my highly detailed 3D-model! I had even detected a safe in the wall of the captain's chambers, which looked to contain just over three pounds of platinum and approximately the same quantity of iridium. Naturally, I didn't tell Uraz Tukhsh and the other crew members about my discovery because I was afraid the Geckho would demand I delete the valuable data.

And, by the way, I was very surprised to see that the Geckho didn't leave the game that bends reality to rest, seemingly ever. Before that, I honestly thought the small size of the shuttle bunks was because there was no need for more room. After all, an astronaut who grew tired and wanted a rest could exit the game into the real world, then their character would disappear and no longer take up any space. However, all three of my bunkmates were still logged on even when sleeping. That was strange, but there was probably some explanation. I made a mental note to ask my friends when possible.

Unlike my bunkmates, I was in no mood to sleep. For a start, I looked carefully over my spoils from the battle in the Harpy Cliffs. Before that, I hadn't had a chance.

The Dark Faction laser pistol didn't have any exorbitant stat requirements, but it did need the Pistols skill to work effectively. I turned the unusual weapon over in my hands and stashed it back in my backpack. It wasn't right for me. Minn-O La-Fin's belt was nothing extraordinary on its own, just a common wide belt made of artificial leather with two small cases for storing little trinkets. Inside one of the cases, I found a folding fork and spoon and a spool of surprisingly resilient thread. The second contained a replacement laser pistol battery. But the chameleon cloak had me intrigued:

Dark Faction camouflage cloak
Character detection distance while in motion -23%
Character detection distance while immobile -77%
Battery life: 18 hours.
Statistic requirements: Agility 18, Intelligence 15

Skill requirements: Stealth 16, Electronics 16

Attention! Your character has insufficient Agility to use this object.

Attention! Your character lacks the Stealth skill, which is required to use this object.

Conclusion: a fairly useful item, but not right for my Gnat. Sure, I could take the Stealth skill when my character reached level 25 but raising Agility by three points... that would take at least half a year of intensive training.

Placing it back into my inventory with pity, I gave a heavy sigh and tried to distract myself, getting back to studying Geckho writing. Thankfully, there was plenty of incomprehensible scribbling on the monitor, and every little lever, access door and panel on the ceiling and walls of my bunk.

I also had many questions about my scanner's settings. It was possible to change them, but I didn't risk experimenting any more on the Shiamiru. I was too afraid to mess up again and ruin my reputation both among my crew and faction. I had already failed the mission Ivan Lozovsky had given me, to prove I was a qualified Prospector. In fact, I had given them cause to doubt the intellectual abilities of the whole human race.

My self-castigation was interrupted by an abrupt repeating signal that rolled through the shuttle. Accident? Danger? But my roommates, although they awoke, didn't demonstrate any alarm or panic. It very quickly became apparent that it was just a wake-up alarm. Our shuttle had arrived at the destination, and the crew was going to have to work.

We suddenly saw captain Uraz Tukhsh in the shuttle doors. Throwing a long attentive gaze over my bunk, he stopped on the Trader:

"Uline, look after our newbie. Make sure he doesn't forget to put on his space suit or fill his air tanks or something. Show him how to use the airlock, set up his radio, and just keep him on a short leash. After the wasted analyzer, I don't know what to expect from Gnat. He might push off too hard and fly off into open space. After all, the gravity on this asteroid is practically nil. It wouldn't really be a problem if he just flew off and died. No huge loss, but he has our expensive equipment, and losing that would be a real pity."

All three of my neighbors started rumbling through their clenched tusks in satisfaction, cackling at the captain's joke. I just bore it in silence, not wanting to argue or curse. I would have to prove the opposite by my actions and, right now, the facts were not in my favor. Finally, the captain turned to me:

"Gnat, your mission, while we unload and unfold the automatic processor is to find valuable minerals on the asteroid. The ship's detectors show the presence of heavy metals and even elevated background radiation. But it's weak and indistinct, as if the deposits are at quite some depth. So, your mission is to determine the location of these ores. I have a good feeling about this!"

Uraz Tukhsh, could already taste the high-value minerals, started rumbling in satisfaction, turned around and walked back to the bridge. As soon as the captain was out of earshot, Uline Tar voiced her doubts:

"Every time I heard Uraz Tukhsh say he had a good feeling, we ran into trouble. Either our price got undercut at auction, competitors squeezed us out of a good route, or pirates took all our cargo. So, I don't have much trust in our captain's intuition!"

Nevertheless, Uline didn't contradict her boss, or argue with his orders. She demanded I take out my space suit and fill it with air. I have to admit, without the help of the much more experienced Geckho lady, I might have had trouble activating the built-in battery with the valves and pumps and setting up my radio. But Uline helped me figure it all out. The radio was working, the air pump hummed to life, and the gauge on my metal satchel showed increasing pressure in my tank. At the same time, I checked the gauge on Angel Dust and discovered that my PCP gun could stand a bit more air.

"Do you really not have anything more modern, just that ancient air rifle?" Basha Tushihh asked in surprise when he saw me filling the tank with a hand pump. Meanwhile, his twin brother justly asked who I thought I'd be fighting on the asteroid.

Nevertheless, despite all the taunting, I loaded Angel Dust with air, and checked the battery in my laser pistol. Sure, I didn't have the right skills, and the scatter circle was huge. The game rules baffled me here though. How could a laser beam have scatter??? But the battery was full, and I could at least fire it, so it was perfectly serviceable as a backup.

There was no viewport in our bunk, so I could only tell we'd landed by the change in tonality of the Shiamiru's thrusters, and a sharp vertical impact a few seconds later. We landed so hard I fell onto the floor. My Geckho neighbors had more foresight and, as soon as they heard the changed sound from the thrusters, they grabbed for the side handles. Immediately after we landed, all my roommates had helmets on their heads, and the Geckho spent some time looking and listening in alarm. But there were no signs of emergency, and everyone sighed in relief. Uline swore elaborately, then started grumbling again as usual:

"Uraz Tukhsh doesn't have the skills or experience, so he should have done the professional thing and hired a decent pilot! As it is, every landing tests the structure of the shuttle and my nerves! I'm telling you, this is the last time I'm flying with him! I've had enough rough landings!"

The eternally displeased trader was interrupted by an alarm signal and order from the captain:

"Lead crew roll out tech! Fasten down the shuttle and open the cargo bay! After that, haulers activate cargo arms! Gnat and Uline last. You take the third levitator and buzz the hell off at least two thousand steps from the Shiamiru before scanning! Gnat, got that?"

"Yes, captain, understood," I confirmed shortly, again

trying not to take his mistrust to heart.

Four minutes passed before both twin brothers left down the corridor to the nose of the shuttle. I couldn't hold back and even stuck my helmeted head out the door to see the two giants slip through the narrow corridor. They did it with surprising grace, clearly evidence of their past experience on the Shiamiru.

"Gnat, our turn!" Uline's voice rang out in my headphones.

I started fitfully for the exit, but was stopped by an armored hand packed into a space suit:

"Wait! First attach this to your carbine strap."

With huge effort, I suppressed a stream of curse words. I felt like a dog on a leash being taken out for a walk! Plus, the Geckho lady was much larger than me, which only reinforced that sensation. Despite this being my first spacewalk, my mood was ruined. However, all my negative emotions left me as soon as Uline and I passed through the airlock and found ourselves outside the Shiamiru.

Eagle Eye skill increased to level thirty-two!
Cartography skill increased to level thirty-five!

Wow! The scenery was just as fantastic as it was unearthly. The brownish and bright-red surface was dappled with craters and sharp peaks. Meanwhile, there was a black sky up above with millions of stars stretching into infinity. Apparently, we were on the dark side of a very large iron and stone asteroid. The main sources of light were bright spotlights from the Shiamiru, and other lights on an enormous cylindrical object one hundred and fifty feet from our shuttle. Clearly this was the automatic ore processor.

The thermometer on my sleeve showed minus one hundred twenty-six degrees Fahrenheit, and that was next to the recently landed Shiamiru! I suspected that, further from the shuttle, things got even more extreme. The barometer screen also on my sleeve was showing pressure of less than one point five Pascals. Although this was no deep vacuum, it was close enough. I wasn't even surprised the instruments on my spacesuit, made by an unknown race, displayed in units familiar to me. I suspected the bars and numbers were actually totally different, but the game system was translating all the information into a form I could understand.

Probably, I would have spent a long time at the gangway with my jaw hanging down in astonishment as I admired the unearthly beauty of space, but I was checked by Uline. The trader pointed at a flat metal object in some way reminiscent of a surfboard, just crescent shaped:

"Gnat, get on the levitator and make sure your boots are clipped in. As soon as we get away from the Shiamiru, the artificial gravitation will abruptly drop off!"

I obeyed the Geckho's sage advice and, standing on the flying board, clipped my soles into the special bindings. Uline did the same, then asked:

"So, where are we going? Where will you conduct your scan?"

Her strange way of putting the question left me

hesitating. I have to admit, until that point, I figured I would simply be shown where to scan for minerals. But it turned out that the rest of the crew was relying on me to know. What could I say...? I pointed confidently at some sharp peaks in the distance. That way!

The Geckho lady slightly inclined the levitator, and it smoothly and gently moved from place, gradually increasing speed. It was a lot like riding a skateboard but hovering around four feet off the surface. As soon as we got fifty feet from the Shiamiru, I no longer felt any gravity. The only thing holding me to the board now was the bindings. Uline, steering the levitator, commented:

"It's not true weightlessness, because the asteroid under us is fairly large, but the gravitation here is hundreds of times lower than on your earth. I adore this feeling!"

And just then, she sharply increased our speed, pushing it to that of a Formula-One race car. To the left and right I saw the steep cliffs flickering past, sometimes just an outstretched arm away. It started reminding me of yesterday's race on Zheltov's starship. We probably didn't have to go on such a dangerous ride, but I didn't stop Uline. She was clearly enjoying the thrill.

We flew confidently over deep crevasses and doubled around outcrops. At the very end, we hit our top speed and flew right at a stone spire that shot up into the starry sky. When I was sure we would die by smacking into the cliff, Uline sharply angled the board back, aiming the levitator practically vertically up. The microphone in my helmet gave a satisfied rumble from the Geckho lady, then an elated scream:

"Whoo, hell yeah!!! You have to agree, Gnat, this feels awesome!"

A few seconds later, the trader stopped the flying board at the very end of the spire of protuberating rock, and from the peak we had a view of the whole unevenly shaped asteroid, and the blindingly bright sun.

Eagle Eye skill increased to level thirty-three!

Cartography skill increased to level thirty-six!

You have reached level twenty-three!

You have received three skill points! (total points accumulated: eight)

I finally managed to look around. The asteroid was twenty miles in length and around eight across, with a slightly curved shape like a kidney bean. It was all pocked with craters, cracks and peaks of the most monstrous forms. Three miles behind us, I could make out the tiny Shiamiru, but even my Eagle Eye skill and high Perception didn't allow me to see any crew members.

Carefully unclipping from the levitator hovering a foot and a half over the rock, I smoothly lowered my boots onto the asteroid surface. Uline was a bit alarmed and even grabbed for the line connecting us, as if I might fly away from her into open space. But I reassured my partner and started looking over the side of the cliff.

It was about what I was expecting to see. Pallasite with fragments of olivine — the most common composition of iron meteorites that fell to the surface of Earth. To put it more plainly, iron and nickel with deposits of iron silicates and magnesium. This asteroid was composed primarily of pallasite, but there was plenty of iron and nickel here as well. I approximated the size of the asteroid... Around eight hundred billion tons of iron and one hundred fifty-two billion tons of nickel. On the one hand, it sounds like a huge amount but, considering the cost and difficulty of getting it anywhere, it wasn't financially justified.

The olivine was similar. It was close to the mineral composition of chrysolite, a semi-precious stone, but all the crystals were microscopic, and had no value to any jeweler.

Mineralogy skill increased to level twelve.

Mineralogy skill increased to level thirteen.

So, it looked to be nothing on first glance. Uraz Tukhsh had mined nickel and iron on this asteroid before, so I didn't see anything new. On the other hand, the captain mentioned something about heavy metals and radioactivity, and that was more interesting.

"This is a spike of rock from the very depths of the asteroid, so let's do a scan here," I suggested to my partner, and Uline Tar didn't argue.

The Geckho lady pressed a row of keys on her space suit belt and confidently got off the board. I suspect that her armor suit had, among other things, magnetic soles. Very convenient for walking on magnetic asteroids. Unfortunately, my light space suit lacked that function.

I opened my scanner and asked Uline to translate the

setting panel. The trader readily read the scribbles next to the variously-positioned sliders:

"General metal search. That is also for metals, but it searches by nuclear gamma resonance. That is also for metals, search by gravitational response. That is for superheavy materials. Search by temperature differential. Neutron scanner. Beta-radiation search. Nuclear-magnetic resonance search for non-protein organics. Empty space detector. Motion detector. Heuristic method. Echolocation. Structural analysis. Electromagnetic field search..."

Astrolinguistics skill increased to level twenty-six.

I have to admit; her explanations didn't make it any easier. In fact, my head was spinning from the fearfully complicated words. I tried increasing metal search intensity to maximum, but that made the other sliders go down. Clearly you couldn't just search for everything at once. Well alright, I was only interested in valuable metals anyway.

Seeing me get out a tripod, Uline hurried to turn off her levitator. She must have been afraid of the EMP. This time, I carefully unfolded the tripod legs and, after hearing a click, pressed the geological analyzer into the surface of the asteroid.

Scanning skill increased to level twenty-six.

As soon as my computer had processed the information, I took a look at the results. Very high peaks for iron, nickel, magnesium and silicon — these elements were literally everywhere. A bit less cobalt and aluminum, but also on the order of hundreds of millions of tons. There was also some antimony and bismuth — a small local vein a quarter mile from the cliff base. Germanium was present as well, and some copper and even gold in trace amounts. Many traces of other metals, but it was all a bit vague and uncertain.

"Nothing to write home about," Uline confirmed my conclusions. "Gnat, let's fly over to the other side of the asteroid. I saw another peak over there!"

But I refused and suggested we try another way. This time, I was interested not in protuberated outcroppings, but craters or very deep crevasses. I wanted to try to reach the very depths of the massive stone hurtling through the cosmos. And sure, maybe it wouldn't be to the very depths (with scanning radius 5250 feet I wouldn't reach the core), but still as deep as possible.

"Three miles from here, there is a huge crack on the sunny side of the asteroid," I said, pointing at the distant crevasse. "Let's fly there and try to go down!"

My partner turned on the levitator, placed me on it and clipped in my bindings. This time, Uline didn't go as fast, and was behaving fairly cautiously. Either the sun was blinding her, or her spirits had fallen.

Right before the crevasse, Uline gracefully turned the flying board parallel to it and started riding to the bottom. She switched on her powerful helmet flashlight, and we smoothly descended the 900-foot vertical wall, which was glittering in the light of her headlamp.

"Get going, but faster this time,," she said, agitated for some reason. "If the asteroid collides with something, this crevasse will cave in on top of us..."

"Come on! It just seems like the asteroid belt is packed with flying rocks. You yourself saw that there are thousands of miles between us and anything dangerous. Everything that could have collided with this thing has already hit it in the past millions of years. So don't chicken out, we'll be fine!"

After saying that, I grew afraid that my new Geckho acquaintance may not like my tone. But Uline Tar didn't react, too wrapped up in her worrying. Did she have claustrophobia? That would be strange for a character who spent so much time cooped up in a spaceship where even I found it cramped.

I took out my last analyzer and gave a heavy sigh. Alright, this was my last shot. Make or break! I have to admit, I was very nervous. I was trying not to show it, though. Anyhow, it would feel bad to remain in the Geckhos' memory as a loser human, remembered only for screwing up.

I opened my skill window and placed all eight of my skill points into Scanning, raising it to 34. No reason to sit on my points if I needed results right here and now! I closed my eyes for a few seconds, and even mentally prayed to the admins of this strange game for luck. At the very last moment, I changed the settings, choosing not to search only for metals. Instead, I placed all the sliders approximately in the middle. I didn't react to my partner's surprised exclamation and, with an abrupt exhale, I took out the last tripod and activated it.

Hundreds of results appeared on the screen. Iron, nickel, other chemical elements. But something else caught my eye.

"What is that?!" the bright yellow spot on the three-dimensional diagram had also caught Uline's attention.

"Some kind of anomaly," I answered vaguely, familiarizing myself with its preliminary description.

My heart stopped stock still. I zoomed in on the curious map section. It showed open spaces deep under the asteroid's surface with corridors, hotbeds of intensive electromagnetic field, and sources of strong radioactivity. I increased the scale even further. On the monitor, there was a subsurface complex: hemispheric rooms and a network of corridors connecting them. What was more, the entrance was not very far away. In fact, it was just six hundred feet from us, at the other end of the crevasse.

"This is no mere anomaly, Gnat!" Uline exclaimed, not even trying to hold back the panic bursting out of her. "This is a Relict outpost, a remnant of a long-extinct ancient race! A depository of unique technologies and equipment! I remember the news when some Miyelonians discovered a subsurface complex like this on the outskirts of the galaxy. I was just a girl, it was five tongs ago. I'll contact the captain at once and tell him what we've found! Finally, fortune smiles on us!"

Chapter Twenty-Six

Hostile Reception

THE NEWS OF OUR FINDING excited the entire crew. They immediately stopped unloading the nickel iron ingots from the automatic processor. What was more, in expectation of finding unique treasures in the Relict base, Captain Uraz Tukhsh ordered the Shiamiru's cargo bay entirely cleared.

The captain demanded to see a schematic of the subsurface base. He showed it to the navigator and senior engineer as well. They spent a long time arguing and poking their clawed fingers into the screen of my scanner. From what I heard, I had not discovered the main entrance to a subsurface Relict base, but some kind of back door. And perhaps this wasn't even a door, but simply a corridor that got exposed by the forming of the crevasse. In any case, the Geckho knew no other way into the subsurface complex, so they decided to clear the partially collapsed passage.

The captain and his senior assistants spent a long time deciding the most efficient way of clearing the cave-in and removing artifacts. As far as I understood, before we got into the outpost, we would have to somehow overcome thirty-five feet of rubble. What was more, the path was blocked not by pliable stone, but a hard metal alloy.

They first considered using explosives to clear the passage but decided against it in fear of causing the unstable asteroid to collapse even further, perhaps even caving the whole complex in. That would be a true catastrophe. Clearing the resulting billions of tons of nickel-iron ore would be a titanic endeavor.

So, the Geckho decided on the less risky plan of boring a hole. Our mechanics removed a drill from the ore processor, transported it and lowered it into the crevasse with a crane. I thought Uraz Tukhsh would move the shuttle closer to the crevasse. But instead, he ordered the twin brothers Basha and Vasha to bring two heavy robot loaders to the excavation site.

The drilling had every crew member busy except Uline and me. We were ordered to keep our distance, so our only insight into the process were the rare messages on the common channel. What was more, I was already out of air in my space-suit tank. I asked Uline if we could go back to the Shiamiru to refill it. My partner answered that she would be happy to help, but she didn't have permission to open the airlock, and I would have to ask the captain, navigator or senior engineer.

And just then, it happened...

"They're through the collapse!" came the inspired voice of the drill operator. "There's a round tunnel, then a thick stone wall."

"Bore through that, too!" Uraz Tukhsh ordered.

A high-pitched squeal rang out, then a whistle, and the surprised drill operator said:

"Strong airflow! It looks like air pressure was maintained in the old base this whole time... Captain, there's something moving! Ahhhhhh!"

For the next minute, Uline and I stood frozen in horror as we listened to the intensive gunfire, explosions and fearful shouts from our crewmembers as they died one after the other. We understood very little from their unintelligible screaming. Just panicked yelps, cries of pain, and demands for explanation. Apparently, almost no one managed to even see what killed them. In all the chaos, we heard just one indication. One Geckho shouted before death that he saw a metal hemisphere flying overhead. After that, everything went silent...

"Like I said, whenever Uraz Tukhsh says he has a good feeling, something bad happens!" Uline got wound up again, but I stopped her grumbling with a gesture and asked where the crew members' respawn points were.

"On the Kasti-Utsh III space station, I guess. At the

very least, that's where mine is. It would be dumb to set respawn on your home planet. If anything were to happen, we'd have to wait many, many days for the next ship going our way. Meanwhile, it's too dangerous to put a respawn point on the space ship — you could die once and for all like that if the ship is destroyed. So, probably Kasti-Utsh III."

"What exactly is Kasti-Utsh III? I've never heard of it," I enquired.

"A Miyelonian star base. It was our initial jump point to this distant system. It's a large and well-developed station, a true center of civilization in this region of the galaxy. But flying from Kasti-Utsh here takes two ummi at the very least. So, we're both doomed. There's not enough air, the Shiamiru is locked. First, you'll die of suffocation, then me..."

Astrolinguistics skill increased to level twenty-seven!

I already knew an "ummi" was a unit of time used by the Geckho and several other races. In our standards, it was approximately five and half hours. Mhmm... this was not the most pleasant situation. Apparently, help would not be coming any time soon. In eleven hours, we'd be long dead from suffocation, both reborn at our respective respawn point.

Just then, a familiar voice rang out in my helmet intercom:

"This is Basha Tushihh, my brother is standing next to me. We were bringing the heavy loaders from the processors to the excavation site and, seemingly missed something important. Should my brother and I, like, kill ourselves to get back to the others?"

"Yes, you understand perfectly," Uline Tar confirmed fatedly. "Us three have to commit suicide right now and respawn on Kasti-Utsh III with the whole crew. Otherwise, the others will find a ship coming this way and leave without us."

The three Geckho were speaking so calmly of suicide, as if it was a near daily ritual. That put me beside myself. What was more, I personally found that option absolutely unacceptable. The Geckho would all respawn together on the far-off space station, hire a ship coming this way, and fly back for the invaluable treasure, taking their failure into account and responding appropriately. But after the oxygen in my space suit ran out, I would die and respawn at my capital base. And I somehow doubted that Captain Uraz Tukhsh would deign to fly down and share the spoils with me. Also, how would he do that if he didn't even know where my base was?!

This space suit was very dismal compensation compared to the unique treasures of the secret base of an ancient mysterious race. And so, before the Geckho managed to kill themselves, I would have to change something.

"What is this?! Come on, friends, has fear made you lose your minds? As soon as you meet resistance, you turn coward? You are the proud and brave Geckho, not some sniveling cowards! You know no equals in the universe and, for my race, you are an example to be imitated. Why give up so easily? We haven't even seen what killed our friends. Maybe we can take it down!"

Perhaps, I overdid it because the Trader sharply turned, clearly pretty mad. But Uline took a breath and lowered her shoulders:

"What else can we do, Gnat? We're not warriors. I'm a simple trader. My job is to know prices and the particularities of various interstellar markets. Vasha and Basha are just peaceful loaders. How can we defeat an enemy that even our guards couldn't handle? And how will that help us if we suffocate anyway?"

But then I found an unexpected ally:

"This is Basha Tushihh. Actually, Gnat is right. All is not lost yet. The Shiamiru's cargo hold is open after all, and we can get food from there and use it to access the inside of the ship. Do you remember two flights ago when our lock got jammed, and the mechanics opened a hole in the cargo bay? We could try to repeat their trick. We have tools, so we could try to fool the mechanism! If we get through to the ship, we'll have air and food! And we can wait for the others there!"

"That sounds good," Vasha Tushihh agreed with his brother. "I just got to level sixty-three, so I don't want to go down and lose skills..."

The three Geckho were standing inside the depressurized cargo hold patiently waiting for me to study the magnetic locking device and figure out how to turn it off. I was using a set of electronic probes and screwdrivers unscrewing the massive lock and cutting wires one after the next, trying to ignore the delirium brought on by my rapidly depleting oxygen levels.

"Ready! All four magnetic bolts are undone, and these bars just need to be pulled out manually," I pointed my enormous assistants to them and walked away from the door.

Just like humans, with crowbars in their strong hands, hooting and cursing with every burst, the two huge Geckho started carrying out my order. It wasn't right away, but the obstacle gave. They worked out all the bars and the door into the airlock opened.

Break-in skill increased to level nine!
Break-in skill increased to level ten!
Break-in skill increased to level eleven!
Break-in skill increased to level twelve!
Electronics skill increased to level eighteen!
You have reached level twenty-four!
You have received three skill points!

A minute later, now in the familiar hallway of the Shiamiru, I removed my sweaty helmet with untold joy and took in a lungful of oxygen-rich air. What a joy!!! How little a person needs to be happy. Sometimes it's just a matter of breathing. My head started spinning like I was drunk. I walked to an empty bunk and fell back into someone's cot right in my spacesuit.

Fame increased to 15.

I had hoped this message was positive and because we'd saved ourselves, not because I had taken someone else's bed without asking. Although, even if it was the latter, the cot owner would not be back any time soon, so I wasn't planning to get up.

"I'll heat up some food for everyone," Uline Tar challenged herself. "We can discuss what to do next over a meal."

Just in the nick of time. Gnat's hunger bar was also down in the red zone, and my Prospector had long needed to eat. But I couldn't satisfy my hunger, because I'd used all my dried rations trading with the harpy for the laser pistol.

Uline walked further up the corridor, while Vasha and Basha pulled out a small table from the bunk wall. Just three minutes later, the trader returned, carrying a tray with four deep metal bowls of dark-red spicy-smelling slop.

I lowered my spoon into the thick pottage and raised it to my mouth. The extraterrestrial stew was unbearably spicy. I barely managed to swallow the burning glop, because it got stuck in my throat. Tears welled up in my eyes. I could barely breathe and even took out my flask to chase the blistering concoction. My first thought was that they were playing a joke on me. However, their bowls had the same stuff.

Both twin brothers grumbled through their tightly clenched teeth, obviously taking pleasure in my discomfort.

"This is a traditional vegetable soup of our people, made with a burning underground nut," Uline explained warmheartedly. "Usually, two-thirds of food packets on all Geckho starships contain this stew. I don't know what men see in it. To my eye, it's inedible."

"Woman, you simply don't understand all the charms of the male cuisine," Basha intervened in the conversation. "This dish makes the soul of a true Geckho man sing. It eliminates weariness and multiplies potency."

In reply, the trader snorted in dismay:

"Not to upset you, Basha, but there have been less barbaric methods of increasing male stamina for hundreds of years. If you're having problems, I can send the names of at least ten effective medicines. There's no reason to burn the stomach with this red swill."

Both brothers rumbled again. Apparently, a sharp tongue and ability to joke at others' expense was valued on the Shiamiru. I also smiled and risked trying another spoonful of soup. But this time, I was morally prepared and managed to swallow the nuclear vegetable glop. Actually, it was more than edible. I even found it tasty. But the abundance of burning spice made the vegetable soup a true ordeal for the tongue and throat. Fortunately, I had a canteen of water so, after every spoonful, I took a small swallow and gave my throat some respite.

Constitution raised to 13.

Yes! That was the best improvement I could imagine. The last remnants of the slop went down much easier, entirely filling my hunger bar. The traditional Geckho stew was not only burning, but also very nourishing. And my exhaustion also passed. I felt full of energy and ready to get back to work. Following my crewmates' example, I overturned my empty bowl, demonstrating that I had overcome the trial.

Fame increased to 16.

"You must be tough, Gnat!" Basha Tushihh snarled in approval. "I'll admit, I wasn't expecting it. I even had a bet with my brother. Not all Geckho appreciate our burning stew, which is to say nothing about members of other races. Before you got here, there was a human woman in our crew. That spacesuit actually used to belong to her. Anyway, she couldn't handle our cooking, and quit after the first trip."

Like a hunting dog, I got the scent and tried to find out about this mysterious lady. What was her name, where was she from and what was her profession? The answer surprised me:

"Yeah, who knows? I didn't ask... Members of your race can be found in the whole galaxy, though they are quite rare. There are some people in the Meleyephatian horde. The Miyelonians also have some human vassals..."

"She was from Tailax, a Tailaxian," Uline joined the conversation. "A psionic, I don't know why the captain brought her along. She had a bodyguard with her, also human. And a predatory animal that could turn invisible. But they all left the Shiamiru long ago. It was a bad fit."

I spent some more time trying to find out about these extraterrestrial humans, but my Geckho friends didn't really know much. I understood one thing for sure. The humans living in those distant star systems were totally different, neither of my Earth, or the Dark Faction's.

Time passed. There was nothing to do on the Shiamiru. Basha and Vasha were entertaining themselves by gambling at what looked like three-dimensional holographic checkers. Uline had opened the folding bed and lain down for a rest. But I didn't want to sleep at all. In fact, after that nuclear meal, I felt like I'd taken steroids.

I walked around the whole shuttle and even looked into the bridge, but all the panels were inactive and the screens were dark, so there was nothing to do. The captain's chambers were locked. Although the number pad by the door didn't look too complicated, I had enough sense not to try and force my way into Uraz Tukhsh's room.

What to do? Sitting in a locked shuttle for another ten hours would be boring and useless. What then? Leave the game into the real world? Make a report to the leadership, get some sleep and come back in ten hours when there would be some action. A lot of landing ships would be arriving, and there would be hundreds of Geckho soldiers who would take the Relict base by assault. The Geckho would leave me mere crumbs at best. Most likely, they wouldn't even let me get near their unique treasure. I had no doubt that was exactly what would happen. A total wash, and I really had no idea why I had even broken into the Shiamiru.

Should I risk it and try to fight my way into the subsurface base? I suspected I wouldn't be able to convince my companions. Now, death from suffocation was no longer a threat, so all three Geckho were sitting peacefully clearly intending to wait for help to arrive. Go out alone? There was a high chance I would die there, like many crew members before me and reappear on the H3 base, again with nothing to show for it. Also not an option...

So, hoping desperately that I wasn't doing something impossibly stupid, I changed my respawn point to our bunk on the Shiamiru. After that, I declared to my neighbors that I was going off for recon to see whatever had killed our crew members with my own eyes.

Chapter
Twenty-Seven

Relict Base

HE GECKHO REACTED with surprising restraint. No one tried to talk me out of it or appeal to my sense of reason. Both the brothers stayed silent. The trader just mocked me: "Do as you wish, it's your life. I'm not your nanny." Basha Tushihh helped me open the door out of the air lock into the cargo bay and gave a miserly goodbye wave before immediately losing interest. Apparently, none of the Geckho thought I had any chance.

I had to admit, I also had my doubts, but it was the only way for me (and humanity as a whole) to squeeze any artifacts from the base of the ancient race, so I made a conscious, calculated risk. After all, if I died, I had little to lose. I'd just zero-out my level-twenty-five progress bar, but that was nothing at my relatively low level.

So, I walked into the cargo bay and cautiously set my

boots on the asteroid. I was no longer lashed to Uline, and my space suit had no magnetic soles. It was clear that there was artificial gravitation near the shuttle, so I didn't have to worry. But further away, there was quite a high risk I might fall off the asteroid into space. The crevasse was around 2 miles from the Shiamiru, but I was planning to ride one of the remaining levitators there. I placed the flying board horizontally, turned it on and tried to snap my soles into the bright yellow pilot's circle.

But no:

Attention! Due to Prospector class limitations, you cannot use this mode of transportation.

What the hell?! This was just a skateboard! I could skate pretty dang well in the real world. When I was still in high school, I even learned to do all kinds of tricks to impress girls. Could I really not use those skills in the game?

But the game rules were strict and unyielding. "May not pilot starships or any kind of flying vehicle," meant exactly that — any type, including levitators.

I got very discouraged by that and very nearly gave up. I almost banged on the wall of the Shiamiru to ask them to let me back inside. Could I really walk two miles on the uneven surface of the asteroid? It was covered with craters, cracks and steep cliffs! Plus, gravity would be so low that one false move could send me flying into space until I died of suffocation.

But my eye caught on a large, many-wheeled armored all-terrain vehicle. It was the heavy loader Basha and Vasha had ridden back to the Shiamiru. Carefully approaching the alien craft and climbing up on its front wheel, I studied its control system.

Electronics skill increased to level nineteen!

Electronics skill increased to level twenty!

Not too complicated. To my eye, even simpler than in a terrestrial automobile. One button turns on power. And the control column sets vector and speed. There was a button to increase floor magnetism for those with the special boots. Just the thing for asteroids with weak gravitation. It had a knob that lowered supports for loading. And a handle that... I don't know... ah, written right next to it... released the crane. I wouldn't be needing that. This button turned on autopilot. You could set a dot on the display, and it would go straight there. Nothing too complicated all in all. All that remained was to look at skill requirements:

Tiar 62 heavy loader (standard equipment of the Shiamiru cargo shuttle)

To use this loader, character class must be: Heavy Robot Operator, Mechanic-Driver, or the following statistic requirements apply: Intelligence 16, Agility 10, Strength 12

Attention! This loader has been damaged and repaired. Movement speed reduced by 4%

Great! I had the skills to use it. There was no lock on the door, so I walked right inside and plunked down in the driver's seat. The power button didn't work right away for some reason. I had to push down hard with my finger, even slam it with my fist before the instrument panel lit up.

Break-in skill increased to level thirteen!
Break-in skill increased to level fourteen!
Break-in skill increased to level fifteen!
Electronics skill increased to level twenty-one!
You have reached level twenty-five!
You have received three skill points! (total points accumulated: six)
Congratulations! You now have two more skill slots!!!

Despite all the positive messages, I was afraid. Why had Break-in leveled so much? What had I broken into? The only explanation that came to mind was that the loader had some kind of antitheft function, and that explained why it was hard to turn on. So, I had to press the button in the right pattern, maybe even holding it or varying pressure.

Also, I suddenly realized that the twin brothers Basha and Vasha might not like that I had taken their loader. Especially if I died far away from the shuttle and left it a few miles away. And although there was an identical loader next to the ship, and one of the brothers could take a levitator to collect the vehicle, they wouldn't exactly be patting me on the head for stealing and losing their loader.

But it was too late to change course. The ATV was dashing at a lively pace over the holes and cracks. A few minutes later, I saw a landmark in the distance — a strange massive device on the very edge of the crevasse, which had been used to lower the drill. As far as I understood, it was a "gravitation crane," a device that created a zone of artificial gravitation at a certain distance to move objects. That was the method the Geckho used to move ore containers and whatnot around the asteroid, where lifting and lowering containers by traditional methods was impossible due to the weak gravity.

I stopped the loader thirty feet from the precipice, tying a free end of cord to a metal clamp on the vehicle just in case. I tied the other end to my carbine strap. After that, I moved step by step, very carefully, even laying on my belly at the very end and crawling the last few feet.

Due to the very bright sun and lack of atmosphere, everything was very contrasting. The cliffs around me were bright, practically white and below me was impenetrable blackness. It took my eyes three minutes to get used to it and be able to see. But even after that, I saw only glimmering on the stones, blackness and a few dark spots of a different color. That must have been the drill.

But then I saw movement...

Eagle Eye skill increased to level thirty-four!

Something flickered past just for a moment. After that, I spent another few minutes staring down into the monotonous the black hole as the sun glimmered off the tiny crystals. I even took out my IR-lens and tried to use it, but that only made matters worse, so I put it back in my inventory.

More movement! This time, I had an approximate idea of what to expect, so I got a better view of the small strange object as it flickered past the drill and raced further down the dark crevasse. It was small, approximately the size of a basketball and flew at massive speed.

Now I was ready to identify the weird thingy with my IR-lens. After three minutes, I got my chance. There it went! Got it!!!

Small Relict guard drone.

Hmm... That didn't clear up too much. Although it did confirm that the underground base was made by the mysterious Relicts. It was also valuable to know that the object was artificial, served to patrol and provided defense. I wish I knew how many there were... Hopefully, I could also think up a way of taking it down.

I understood that trying to shoot it was pointless and even stupid. The drone moved too fast. I'd never hit it. Also, which of my weapons could damage a metal drone? Certainly not the air rifle! I mean, it was intended for use only against animals and unarmored targets like centaurs. It just could not harm a metal robot. I'd just draw its attention. Shooting with the shotgun at this distance was not an option either. And it probably couldn't pierce the drone's armor either. But if it detected me, that meant certain death...

I supposed I had to admit I couldn't do this alone and ask the Geckho for help. I activated my radio and told them what I'd seen. Uline advised me to return to the Shiamiru and wait for reinforcements. The twin brothers agreed. Basha just added:

"You could try to target it with a laser using your good vision, then we could shoot it with homing rockets. But you'd need to hold the laser on the target for a couple minutes for the homing to work. You said you only see it for a second at a time, so it sounds impossible..."

Would you like to take the skill Targeting?

I hadn't been offered a new skill in quite a while. I'd even grown unaccustomed to them. Targeting? That might have been interesting for an eagle-eyed Prospector in a combat group. But I didn't rush the choice, my interest piqued by the Geckho's words:

"Basha, wait. Do you mean to say that you and your brother have weaponry, and the problem is only holding the drone long enough to target and destroy it?"

"That's exactly right," Uline answered instead. "High-speed projectiles from a Geckho plasma-grenade launcher can blow any enemy to shreds, regardless of armor. But the target has to remain visible, or at least have someone pointing a laser at it for the grenades to home and hit."

Hold up! I was struck by an interesting idea of how to stop the speeding drone long enough to target it.

"Do you think the gravitation crane would be strong enough to slow down a small drone?"

There was no reply to my seemingly fairly simple question for quite some time, and I even thought I might have said something stupid. But then Uline, not hiding her astonishment, answered:

"Gnat, these guys are saying you're a genius! The force of the crane's gravitational field can be regulated. And they could make it so the small drone wouldn't merely slow down but come to a complete stop! I'll fly out on the levitator right now. Gnat! I'll never forgive myself if I don't play some part in this!"

Then Basha Tushihh's voice rang out my earpiece:

"Wait, Uline. You're not the only one that wants to go. Fame will increase even if we don't manage to catch the guard drone. But if we do, and we're the first to enter a Relict base, they'll hear our names on every news channel in the galaxy! So, to hell with the safety instructions, my brother and I are also moving our respawn point to the Shiamiru and joining Gnat!"

When I took the heavy loader, I guess I had nothing to worry about. My companions didn't even remark on it. They were too distracted preparing for the unusual combat operation. Both large Geckho twins clipped some huge backpack-like devices over their space suits. Those must have been the heavy plasma-grenade launchers that could destroy the guard drone. On each brother's right shoulder, there was a short three-barreled turret that turned in syncopation with their helmet. There was a flexible pleated hose as wide as my arm running from the backpack to the turrets — either the round feeder or a power cable.

"We could try without laser targeting, because the target will be held in the gravity field, but a laser will make sure it hits. Here's the targeting system. Have a look. It's probably perfect for a Prospector." With these words, Vasha handed me a strange device that looked like a pair of large army binoculars with a distance measurer and a whole set of tubes and foldable antennas:

Targeting system (standard element of the Geckho infantry plasma-grenade launching systems Avashi, Avashi-II and Avashi Shock)

Can set targets for up to six systems.

Minimum acquisition time: 4 seconds. Target duration: 3 minutes.

Homing-grenade radius: 5500 feet. Plasma installation radius: 800 feet.

Class requirements: Saboteur, Spy, Sentry, Grenadier, Prospector, or Shock Trooper.

Statistic requirements: Perception 15, Intelligence 15

Hmm... I could use this object, and I didn't even need the Targeting skill. Nevertheless, I read the skill description:

Targeting. Determines proficiency with target selection, marking, acquisition and management systems for individual or group applications. This skill allows the player to receive experience for a marked target destroyed by allies. Higher skill level will not increase this experience but does speed up target acquisition, increase hit chance and unlock more advanced equipment.

There could hardly be a skill in the game more appropriate for my Gnat. Help the whole group in battle, increasing the chance that all my allies hit, and get some experience from every kill? Want! Want!! Want!!!

You have taken the skill Targeting level 1.

So, I was lying on the very edge of the crevasse giving directions to Vasha, who was sitting in the gravitation crane and skillfully pulling the handles:

"Lower, lower... To the right! Stop! Down more!"

I had sacrificed my bright flashlight to mark the epicenter of the gravity field, which Vasha was now carefully lowering into the narrow forking crevasse. We started lowering it right after the security drone flew by, and we planned to have the light in place three minutes before it would return.

The flashlight was approximately half way down when I saw a metal ball in its light. The drone?! So early? Clearly, the bright moving light had drawn its attention, and it was rushing in to figure things out. The robot guard didn't attack but did get closer, hovering ten feet away from the bright light.

"Stop! It's here!" I whispered barely audibly, but I immediately realized that I was being too cautious. Sound doesn't carry in a vacuum, so the Relict drone had no way of hearing me. "Wait, Vasha, don't rush it... It's getting closer to the flashlight all on its own... Let it come closer..."

It was a thrilling experience, like when you're fishing and see the bobber flutter. But fishing is generally quite relaxing. My anxiety level was off the charts, and my heart was thrashing in my ribcage like a terrified bird, slamming into my ribs.

"A little bit more... Get ready... Turn gravitation to

full!!! Got it!!! We caught the bastard!!!"

Fame increased to 17.

Targeting skill increased to level two!

The drone was instantly pulled toward the bright flashlight, which immediately went out. Either it broke in the impact or was crushed by the sudden increase in gravitation. I heard the Geckho screaming in exhilaration in my earphones. Their unbearably loud shouting even had painful ultrasonic notes. I was also screaming with my full throat, though. And why not? It worked!

A minute passed, then another. The deadly drone was hovering helpless midway down the crevasse, unable to move. I calmed down and took out the targeting system. The twin brothers started to prepare their weapons. I didn't have any experience targeting, but Uline helped me adjust the settings to detect and synchronize with the two plasma-grenade launching systems.

So, I was lying on the edge of the crevasse again, this time carefully setting a distance and target. The drone was five hundred seventy-nine feet away. My device told me the target was eighteen inches long. A countdown ticked by, then a colored frame clamped down around the trapped ball.

"Got it! Target acquired! It won't get away now!" Both of the twin brothers launched their plasma grenades practically vertically upward.

The rocket-propelled homing explosives left a trail that evaporated almost instantly. I wasn't able to track them in the vacuum. But at any rate, the missiles must have turned and raced down the crevasse because, a few seconds later, I heard a series of explosions from below.

Targeting skill increased to level three!

Targeting skill increased to level four!

You have reached level twenty-six!

You have received three skill points! (total points accumulated: nine)

I first realized the target had been destroyed based on the sharp increase in experience and leveling up. After that, I visually confirmed it. Instead of an intact spherical drone, there was a formless blob of small compact debris.

"Me first!" As soon as I said the target was destroyed, Uline Tar started off, racing practically vertically down the crevasse on the levitator to the Relict base.

That rush and drive to enter history at all costs by being first to enter the secret Relict base played a nasty joke on the trader. The crane's powerful gravitational field was still on, and she was pulled into it along with her flying surfboard. Vasha, Basha and I didn't manage to stop her before it was too late. All I heard was a cry of pain and despair that rang in my ears for several seconds.

"What should we do now, Gnat?" the giants asked me. I answered that it would look bad if we went alone without Uline, and we should wait for her to respawn. After all, she wanted to be among the first to enter the mysterious base.

"Good choice, very noble," Basha praised me. "After all, we are the only four left of the whole crew. We worked together, and the reward should go to all four of us."

Vasha Tushihh sat back down in the seat of the gravity crane, raised the field and turned it off, then the metal debris, little bits of stone and undifferentiated fleshy bits descended slowly to the asteroid's surface.

Then, I saw more movement at the bottom of the crevasse! Another drone! If it hadn't been for Uline's rush, all four of us would now be at the bottom of the crevasse and probably would have been killed by this second guard.

We did the same thing as before. I helped lower the gravity crane, this time using a signal flare from a Geckho emergency kit as a light source. The flare would work in a vacuum, and even under water, so I could see the center of the gravitational field and give directions to the crane operator.

Not even a minute later, the light source caught the attention of the guard drone. And our strange fishing maneuver started again.

"Don't rush it. It's getting nearer on its own... Just a bit further... Alright, turn it up!!!"

Targeting skill increased to level five!

Eagle Eye skill increased to level thirty-five!

After prolonged discussion, we decided not to destroy this drone. Initially, I had suggested we shoot just to get experience and skills, but both Geckho were against it. Functioning Relict technology was of huge interest to scientists so they wanted to capture this guard drone intact. It would certainly be worth more this way than a lump of twisted and melted debris. I agreed with their conclusion, so we decided to keep it as a priceless gift for Captain Uraz Tukhsh. Basha drove the loader back to the shuttle and returned ten minutes later with a metal container, bringing Uline with him after she respawned on the ship.

The drone was held down tight. We lowered the ore container to it very carefully and maneuvered it inside. The doors closed and locked, but we didn't turn off the gravitational field, just leaving the container hovering with its dangerous cargo until the captain returned. After this complicated and dangerous loading job, both twin brothers leveled up to sixty-four almost at the same time.

But then there was a hitch. It was entirely possible that there were more drones down there, but no one wanted to sacrifice their own hide to find out. I couldn't see any more movement from up here. But that didn't mean anything. The guard could have been waiting in ambush inside the underground complex, or hidden unseen in the darkness of the crevasse.

I figured this was the right time to take my last possible skill for now: Danger Sense. After Minn-O La-Fin's clear demonstration of its usefulness, I had decided it was vitally necessary.

You have taken the skill Danger Sense level 1.

After that, I spent a long time listening to my inner feelings but didn't feel anything. Either the skill worked another way, or there simply was no danger around me.

For around a half an hour, I scanned the many-mile

length of the crevasse, watching for more guard drones or other hidden dangers. Uline brought me around the crack on the levitator so I could look from different vantage points. After I was sure the coast was clear, we headed down. In that time, I raised my Targeting skill to 7, Eagle Eye to 36, Scanning to 35, and Astrolinguistics to 28. Danger Sense stayed at one, though.

During my prolonged observation, my progress bar practically filled up. I needed just a few percent more to get to level twenty-seven.

The three Geckho, not wanting to risk it and die stupidly, patiently awaited my final verdict. Finally, I gave the go-ahead, and the four of us went down to the drill site on two flying surfboards. The corpses of the dead crew were already long gone. Just a few dropped items remained to mark the site of the tragedy. We didn't touch their things. Let the owners pick them up when they came back.

An ideally circular hole had either been drilled or burned into the wall. The beginning of the dark corridor was filled with caved in rubble, and the walls were covered with blocks of porous white stone. Before we entered, Uline stopped us:

"Friends, I beg you not to rush. We need to record this historic moment on video. It's the first time any living creature has been in this Relict outpost in tens of thousands of Tongs."

Uline clipped a camera on the shoulder of her space suit and started adjusting the color of her headlamp. We stopped, lighting up the corridor ahead and looking at the incomprehensible symbols on several of the wall tiles. If this base once had breathable air, after the hole was drilled, practically all of it got sucked out. The air gauge on my sleeve was showing a pressure of less than four Pascals, thirty thousand times less than what humans can survive.

Finally, we were ready, and I heard Uline cry out in a celebratory tone:

"Based on these ancient tiles, it's been ten thousand Tongs since intelligent life has been here. We once thought the mysteries and knowledge of the Relicts had been lost forever. But now, it's been rediscovered! Four valiant explorers enter the Relict base! Remember the names of these fearless heroes: the Geckho Uline Tar, the Geckho Basha Tushihh, the Geckho Vasha Tushihh and the Human Gnat! What mysteries and dangers await us?"

Fame increased to 18.

Fame increased to 19.

You have reached level twenty-seven!

You have received three skill points! (total points accumulated: twelve)

Chapter
Twenty-Eight

Gnat's Luck

WE WERE WALKING extremely carefully. We expected traps, combat drones or security systems at every step. The long corridor gradually curved to the left, leading us into a small round room with a caved-in ceiling, half filled with large multi-ton chunks of nickel-iron ore and scattered with shards of strange complicated technology.

"I'm getting the impression the catastrophe that happened here and the formation of the crevasse are somehow connected," the Geckho woman posited, looking around at the mess. "A strong impact must have destroyed this whole underground base and nearly shattered the whole asteroid."

We were walking through the debris, squeezing in the cracks between stones and pushing aside some twisted structures, when Uline suddenly exclaimed in fear, pointing with her gloved hand in the darkness. I immediately turned and shined my flashlight.

Crushed by a tile, in an unnatural and deformed pose, there was a being lying there. It was entirely impossible to make out what it had looked like initially. The flesh was too dried out by the preceding centuries then deformed by the more recent vacuum. Some bits of skin or flesh, a broken armored suit... or was that bones? I walked up closer.

Listener remains.

So, this, I guess, was a Relict "Listener." I wondered what exactly a Listener was. Profession? Rank? Or maybe just a name? It told me nothing, but I immediately noticed that I could open its inventory window and take items.

A strange flat metal disk engraved with symbols...

Attention! Your character has insufficient Intelligence to determine the properties of this object. Minimum Intelligence: 22.

A smooth unadorned bracelet made from what seemed to be bronze.

Attention! Your character has insufficient Intelligence to determine the properties of this object. Minimum Intelligence: 28.

A short wand, that looked approximately like a silver pencil.

Attention! Your character has insufficient Intelligence

to determine the properties of this object. Minimum Intelligence: 24.

And... here my breathing stopped in excitement. I could not only pick up the armor or spacesuit of the ancient creature, I could read about it:

Relict energy armor suit (primary Listener combat armor)

Radiation defense: +32

Armor: 54

Reactive force field: 2800 points (inactive)

Built-in filtration system (inactive)

Single air tank duration: 6.5 hours.

Statistic requirements: Constitution 13, Strength 13, Intelligence 19.

Skill requirements: Medium Armor 40

Attention! Your character has insufficient Intelligence and Strength to equip this apparel.

Attention! Your character has insufficient Medium Armor skill to equip this apparel.

Attention! This object is for the Relict race and cannot be used by Humans.

Attention! Critically low nuclear battery. Current charge: less than 4%! Some of the energy-armor suit's functions are unavailable. Replace the nuclear battery to use fully!

I read the text again and again and, every time, I stopped on the race limitation. None of the other requirements were impossible to meet. I could raise

Strength and Intelligence by intensive physical and mental training. I could also level Medium Armor, and probably even drum up a nuclear battery. But changing race was absolutely impossible in the game that bends reality...

My companions, meanwhile, were digging up treasures of their own. I was just standing in muted astonishment, looking at the old Relict suit when an unfamiliar and authoritative voice suddenly boomed out in my earphones in Geckho:

"This is Waid Shishish! Attention, all members of Uraz Tukhsh's crew! Your captain has sold me the rights to take treasure from the Relict complex, so I order you to immediately leave the excavation zone and return to the Shiamiru!"

The twin brothers exchanged surprised glances, then looked at Uline and I. The Geckho woman swore barely audibly, then said loud and clear, understanding perfectly that we would be heard:

"We have all heard the esteemed Leng's order. We will leave the base at once and return to our ship!"

Then I saw Uline Tar and both twin brothers rush to place anything that might be of value into their inventories: metal parts, bronze disks with symbols, fragments of broken technology... Seeing that, I stuck the large armored suit into my backpack. There simply wasn't room for more. All my inventory slots were full. I could put the bracelet on my wrist though, which I did. The disk with symbols and silver wand I handed to Uline, and the Geckho woman silently transferred the valuable artifacts to her inventory, then placed a hand to her spacesuit helmet at mouth level, which clearly meant "we can talk about this later."

The Geckho were hurrying to the exit. Based on what they told me, Leng Waid Shishish was known for his very unforgiving mannerisms, and they didn't want to give him even the slightest reason to be upset. I ran with the others down the corridor to our levitators near the base exit, feeling aggrieved that we'd managed to see only the first of the many rooms, and only partially at that. Ugh, if only we knew the future, we would have acted totally differently. We'd have moved swiftly and intently, trying to see as many rooms in as little time as possible all while cramming everything of value in our backpacks. We hadn't encountered any traps or hidden dangers in the underground base, and we wasted an inordinate amount of time looking for them...

Near the exit from the Relict base, we met a large group of Geckho soldiers in identically adorned screamingly red heavy armored assault spacesuits. They were all armed, some of them carrying boxes of equipment. When the four of us appeared from the tunnel, all the shocktroops went on guard, turning on their force fields. Their twenty barrels were instantly trained on us. They were especially worried by me. At least half of the red shocktroops were holding me in their sights.

My heart was gripped by panic. I understood that any sudden movement could instantly be the end of me.

Danger Sense skill increased to level two!

So, that's how it worked... I froze, as did all three of my companions. A pregnant pause arose. They must have been consulting with their leaders. Not long after that, one of the red soldiers lowered the huge bazooka-like cannon from his shoulder and ordered us to leave the area as quickly as possible.

Both levitators were still in place, so we used them to head straight for the Shiamiru. We'd barely gotten to the surface when I noticed a colossal disk-shaped starship that blocked the sun. It was hovering just a few miles over our asteroid.

Tinakuro. Geckho combat cruiser.

Uline also saw the combat ship and clearly grew nervous, taking a risky route on the levitator between cliffs. While on our way to the Shiamiru, I noticed that there was fervent work underway next to our shuttle. Our technicians were preparing the ship for launch. They had already folded up the ore processor and stashed it in the cargo hold. Apparently, we were just about to take off. But what about the drill we'd left at the bottom of the crevasse? And the gravitational crane with the invaluable drone? One of the heavy loaders was also there...

I asked Uline that question, but again instead of answering, she placed a hand to her mouth. "We can talk later, now's not the time." Alright. That all was strange, but I could bear it, as long as I could satisfy my curiosity later. After we landed, Uline stored the levitator and advised me not to stand in the way and block the scurrying crew members. I went to our bunk, but Trader headed to Captain Uraz Tukhsh to figure out why we had to leave, and why we were in such a hurry.

In the Shiamiru's bunk area, I finally removed my spacesuit, replacing it with my terrestrial camouflage and Kevlar armored vest, sat down in exhaustion on the bench and stretched out my tired legs in satisfaction. Not three minutes later, Uline joined me. Pulling off her helmet in exhaustion, my roommate complained:

"Uraz Tukhsh is despondent. I can't get a word out of him. I've never seen our captain like this. He had me place an order to replace the stuff we left by the Relict base. Leng Waid Shishish didn't give approval to remove it. Basically, he ordered us to leave everything near the crevasse. The Leng must have been afraid we'd try to sneak something valuable out of the underground complex. It's actually strange that, despite his pathological mistrust, the upper aristocrat let us leave the base alive..."

"What, did Leng Waid Shishish buy the exploration rights?" I enquired, to which Uline waved her hand just like a human:

"Gnat, I've told you a hundred times that Uraz Tukhsh is a chronic loser. And he just proved it yet again. That place was full of invaluable treasure, but he was dumb enough to let it slip through his fingers. After the guard drone took down the captain and crew, they all respawned at the Kasti-Utsh III space station, as I supposed. And there, Uraz Tukhsh couldn't think up a smarter plan than to ask for help from his protector and distant relative Leng Waid Shishish, whose cruiser happened to be docked at the station. The Leng promised to help, got the information about the secret Relict base from our naive captain, and made a harsh offer in reply. The option being either Uraz Tukhsh sell him the base coordinates and exploration rights the easy way for six million crystals, or Leng Waid Shishish would interrogate his crew for the information and not pay a dime. The captain chose the first option... Uraz Tukhsh and the crew were brought here and given a quarter ummi to get off the asteroid, otherwise Leng Shishish's cruiser would destroy our Shiamiru."

Everything became abundantly clear, both the captain's annoyance and the rush to leave. And although six million crystals was a lot, the artifacts, equipment and technology of the ancient Relict race were probably worth several orders of magnitude more. And a quarter ummi was approximately one hour and twenty minutes — very little time to pack up the automatic processor and prepare the ship for take-off. Seemingly, the Leng was simply mocking his distant relative and showing the young captain who was in charge.

The huge Basha and Vasha entered our bunk, and it got cramped again. By the way... I took advantage of the opportunity and asked my companions why they didn't go into the real world during space travel.

"There's no sense," Uline answered for everyone. "Space is a red zone, and a character will never disappear from the game that bends reality here, so you'll just have to worry what might happen while you're gone..."

The trader's speech was interrupted by the captain's voice thundering down the corridor:

"Everyone get ready! We're taking off! Navigator, set a course for the space port we left from. We'll load up the new equipment and let Gnat off on his home planet. Just try not to hit that cruiser when we take off... It's hovering right over the Shiamiru..."

The thrusters whistled to life, the walls of the shuttle started vibrating. The tone of the whistle changed, and I immediately felt a high G-force. About a minute passed before suddenly...

I strained up and grabbed for the handle, though I couldn't say why. A second later, our shuttle shook hard. Many of the things stuck to the walls couldn't bear the force and fell to the floor. The light went out for a second, then changed to emergency mode. A siren roared down the Shiamiru's corridors. My first guess was that Uraz Tukhsh had messed up piloting and we'd run into Leng Waid Shishish's cruiser.

But it must have been something totally different, because the captain's peeved voice, amplified by the speakers, sounded out throughout the ship:

"Gnnnnat! Uline! Both of you report to the bridge at once!!!"

Not wanting to make the captain wait, Uline and I instantly raced onto the bridge. What I saw on the huge semicircular screen made my jaw drop.

The asteroid where we'd spent so much time no longer existed. Instead, in the blackness of space, there was now a huge unbearably bright cloud. There were thousands and thousands of bits of debris flying out of its depths. The Shiamiru had escaped miraculously and was speeding away from the cataclysm, but I could not see the Tinakuro cruiser...

"Is this your doing?" the captain asked severely, pointing a clawed hand at the huge blast. "Admit it, what did you touch in the base?"

Naturally, Uline and I categorically denied everything. We told him that we had just managed to get into the hallway nearest the crevasse, and a badly ruined room just off it, and weren't even considering going further before we were ordered to return. I also turned the captain's attention to the fact that we saw Leng Waid Shishish's shock troops, and they were about to go deep into the Relict base dragging all kinds of equipment.

"They probably got further than us, and set off some guard system that initiated a self-destruct sequence!"

The captain thoughtfully tapped his claws on the armrest of his luxurious rotating chair, then shuddered:

"What can I say, Gnat? That's a very believable explanation. That's probably what happened. When Leng

Shishish respawns he will have nothing to reproach us for. I'll send the esteemed Leng an official statement that my crew had nothing to do with this explosion. But that means," Uraz Tukhsh bared his teeth in satisfaction and started growling, "that we just got very, very lucky. If you had made it any further into the base, you'd have set it off yourself. But you didn't, and we were far enough from the epicenter not to be hurt!"

I also thought we were very lucky the shuttle wasn't damaged. But us four were especially lucky, as we'd moved our respawn point to the Shiamiru. For Basha, Vasha, Uline and I, if the shuttle had been destroyed, we'd be out of the game for good... Ghastly!

Just then, I understood just how serious the safety instructions were and promised myself I'd never do it again... just no... NEVER, NEVER EVER PLACE MY RESPAWN POINT ON A STARSHIP!!!

Chapter
Twenty-Nine

Gnat's
Triumph

AFTER HEARING OUR EXPLANATION, the captain's mood sharply changed for the better. Uraz Tukhsh sat back in the pilot's seat, looking stately and rumbling in satisfaction, placing his huge legs up on the control panel. After asking the trader how much it would cost and how long it would take to replace what we'd lost on the asteroid, the captain asked our mechanics for a parts list to repair the gravity compensator that died last trip. After that, he and Uline spent a long time doing calculations. Finally, Uraz Tukhsh grinned in satisfaction and commented with clear pride:

"My finances are in the green for the first time since I bought this Shiamiru. I'd begun to think that would never happen. I nearly lost spirit with the constant misfortunes. You know, this merits celebration!"

Uraz Tukhsh turned on the microphone and said through the loudspeaker that fortune had finally smiled on him and he could now pay all the debts he owed his team from past voyages. What was more, the captain promised to pay the whole crew double for the last trip. From the corridor, I heard shouts of elation. The captain listened to the praise and gave a growl of satisfaction. Finally, closing the door to the corridor with a remote, he turned to Uline and I:

"I think the video clip you made at the Relict base can be offered to news agencies all over the galaxy, and we might even be able to shake some money out of them for the broadcasting rights. But first, you'll have to include something saying that I am your captain, and we are all part of Leng Waid Shishish's political clan. Otherwise, I'm afraid my influential relative may cause problems. He's gonna be furious that the artifacts slipped through his fingers and reminding him of that and taunting him would be dangerous. As it is, the Leng will get some of the glory, and that is quite important for politicians."

I guessed that it wasn't only Leng Waid Shishish who wanted the glory. Most likely, my captain wanted to show off as well. I think Uline also immediately realized that.

"I agree, I'll add that in a voiceover," Uline Tar said, and the captain rumbled happily.

"And now, I'd like to take a look at what you found," Uraz Tukhsh forwarded, as if it was a given we'd have taken things. "After all, I'd never believe you left the Relict base without a few... souvenirs."

I'll admit, I was very tense at that moment, but my companion began emptying her pockets and backpack without hesitation, setting the artifacts on the table before the captain. There were metal disks with unknown symbols, an unusual but functioning short-barreled gun with seven finger-grooves on the little handle (or maybe they were for whiskers, tentacles, or some other appendage), a fragment of a complicated device that looked to be a computer chip and... the craziest thing, a desiccated skull covered in tightly stretched blackened flesh. Uline placed that right in the center of the table.

"This disk and wand belong to Gnat," Uline said as she separated her part of the spoils, "he just asked me to carry them for him."

Uraz Tukhsh glanced over the disks, wand and chip fragment without much interest, turned the strange snub-nose in his hands, but almost immediately set it back down. As for the old skin-covered skull, though, the captain was intrigued. He asked permission, then carefully took the Relict head in his hands and turned it over for a long time, looking at it from all sides. Staring at it, I guessed how the ancient race might have looked. It had long jaws without normal teeth. Instead, there was a single curved and very worn slab for chewing food. All the bones were very thin and looked quite fragile. Were those even bones? Maybe some kind of chitin? There were no nostrils on the skull, but the sides had two huge holes, as if it had enormous peepers like a nocturnal animal or the faceted eyes of an insect.

"An invaluable find, Uline. Congratulations! Scientists of all races will be tripping over one another for the chance to study these remains!" the captain said in delight, carefully setting the skull back down. "And you, Gnat. Got anything interesting?"

Seeing my hesitation, Uline chuckled happily, rumbling through tightly clenched tusks:

"Gnat, in any other case, your doubts would be justified. But you clearly have a bad understanding of Geckho society. Our captain is an Aristocrat, a member of a ruling family. And that not only makes his life easier. It is also a massive responsibility and a ton of limitations. For example, an Aristocrat cannot break their word, otherwise they may lose all privileges and be shamefully disowned by their family. I know about your agreement with the captain. You were promised whatever you could carry off the asteroid. So, you can be sure that our captain will not try and take your property."

What could I say? It was very convincing, so I cleared a place on the table and set out the armored spacesuit and bracelet. Only now could I see it in all its glory. Before this, in the dark, with the cramped conditions and turmoil, I simply didn't have the time or opportunity to pull out my prize and look at it.

It was a black matte armor suit made of a strange cast material that didn't look like metal, plastic or stone. Made for a bipedal creature with one pair of upper appendages and two pairs below. The Relicts also had either a long thick tail, or a huge abdomen like that of an ant. The helmet was made to be worn on a head very similar to the skull on the table with eyes the size of a small melon. Also, the gloves on the upper pair of hands had seven fingers each.

Uraz Tukhsh spent a long time looking over this artifact, then said thoughtfully:

"It seems I've understood what the Meleyephatians based the design of their famous force-field armor suits on. Perhaps they also discovered a Relict base and simply remade one of these for their kind... Shame it's too small for a Geckho... Maybe a Human could get one of those on, but you'd need to remove the extra legs and that thorax bit..."

At these words, my heart started jumping out of my chest in excitement. Carefully choosing my words, I asked the captain if I had understood correctly that this armored spacesuit could be refitted for use by a Human.

"Yes, that's right, Human. An experienced mechanic could do such a thing, although they would need time and good tools," the captain confirmed. "What's more, you must understand that this would be specialized work and would cost a lot... a ton in fact... although..."

Uraz Tukhsh went silent midsentence and started pacing the bridge, thinking feverishly. Finally, the captain came to a decision and turned to me:

"Gnat, I've got an offer for you. You've proven yourself a capable Prospector and crew member. What's more, Uline thinks you have good luck, and I trust her opinion. So, I offer you a two-journey contract. I think these two voyages will be easily enough to see if she's right. The conditions will be the same: you take as much as you can carry. If you agree, I'll give the armor to Yoongeesh right now. He's my best technician. I'll have him do all the refitting and, by our next flight, it will all be ready. I will pay for the work with my own funds, and all I ask in return is those two artifacts Uline was carrying. Plus, if there is any material left over from the armor suit, I'll take that as well. How does that sound?"

Was I dreaming?! I'd managed to complete Ivan Lozovsky's assignment. I had proven myself a useful crew member and even secured more work! I was ready to jump for joy, although I tried to appear unmoved and demonstrate something like consideration. Finally, I gave an answer:

"I agree, but with one clarification. When the Shiamiru is ready for another flight, you fly to my base and pick me up. Otherwise, my bosses might not let me go. You see, the road from my Human-3 Faction's territory to your spaceport is long and dangerous. You'll also need to buy new materials for my scanner, because I'm all out."

"Undoubtedly," the captain confirmed and let me know we were done talking.

As soon as we were in the corridor, Uline turned to me in anger:

"Gnat, what was that?! He just cheated you like an uneducated primitive, willing to give up his tribe's greatest riches for a couple shiny beads! Although... you don't actually know much about this world, so I guess that's what you are. Do you really not know how hard it is for players of noncombat classes to get experience and level up once they 'hit the ceiling?'"

Seeing how new I was to the game that bends reality, I didn't suspect anything of the sort. I honestly admitted that. Uline gave a growl of dismay, clenched her teeth, then lowered her tone and explained what I did wrong:

"Just know this for the future: many mechanics would sell their mother into slavery just to be able to work with an ancient artifact. You see, that gives new knowledge and guarantees a few level ups. You would have easily found an experienced mechanic to do all the work for free. Heck, they might have even paid you. The only way to improve crafting skills in this game is to do something you've never done before and, after a while, that becomes damn near impossible. But you just paid the captain two artifacts and some excess material for it... I'll admit, as a Trader, I'm disappointed. You could have negotiated a better contract, too. Do you really think you'll carry off a full inventory of artifacts after every trip? Most likely, it will be just another mineral run, and you'll come away with just a bit of iron and nickel."

"Uline, I'm not worried about compensation. I would have agreed to do it for free," I admitted. "You yourself said that getting leveling up and gaining experience takes new knowledge. Well, the same is true for a Prospector. I need to visit new locations to grow and, back at home, I have already seen almost everything. Add to that the fact that my faction doesn't have any scanner supplies, because for us 'primitives,' they are too expensive. So, this is the only way for me to use my class skills."

"By the way, speaking of supplies," the trader interrupted me. "Before talking with you, the captain asked me to order ten geological analyzers, so they would come with the rest of the equipment. It seems he had no doubt you would agree to his offer. Also, on Kasti-Utsh III, geological analyzers go for eight crystals a pop, and on the Waino-Tu station they're just six. So..." the huge furry lady placed a heavy clawed hand on my shoulder and rumbled in satisfaction through her tusks, "I have decided to stick with Uraz Tukhsh's crew for now. I mean, I still think our captain is a born loser, but now you're with us, and you're good luck. Plus, it's more fun now, and that tipped the scales!"

On the way back, I had more Geckho writing lessons. It was at my request, because it was pretty boring in the cramped room otherwise, and I wanted to give everyone something to do. This time, crew members from other bunks joined us as well. The furballs explained the subtleties of writing all the sweeping and broken lines, gave examples and taught me exceptions. They were all happy to see that I was fairly good at absorbing new information and time and again impressed the Geckho with my good handwriting and increasingly complex phrases and constructions.

Sometime later, even Ayukh the level-98 Navigator joined our lesson. The Shiamiru was on autopilot, so he had nothing to do, and wanted to see what was making half the crew crowd up in the corridor. Basha Tushihh reverently ceded his place to the respected Navigator, and the wise short Geckho with deep black fur, set about teaching me enthusiastically.

After Ayukh joined, the lessons became an order of magnitude harder, but my progress started going much faster. As it turned out, the Navigator had the Pedagogy skill, which allowed for faster transmission of knowledge. In the next few hours, I raised my Astrolinguistics by three levels to twenty-eight. My brains were fried by the end, though.

Intelligence increased to 19.

With that popup, I figured I could stop studying and begged the strict Navigator for mercy. Also, my head was splitting, and it was getting harder and harder to concentrate on the screen.

"Of course," Ayukh agreed easily, standing up from the bench. "We can continue our lessons when you've digested this information and feel ready for another portion. Overall, I'm surprised you lasted as long as you did at that pace. Usually, my students don't learn that fast, and end their lessons earlier."

The crew started buzzing in approval. Receiving

praise from the strict and always cranky Navigator was seen as something of a miracle.

Fame increased to 20.

After that was meal time, with more of the burning hot Geckho stew. I could sense my crew watching me closely, but I took down my portion and overturned the empty bowl just like the rest. The food gave me a second wind. I returned to my bunk and was even thinking about asking for more writing lessons when my heart suddenly jumped out of my chest in fear. I grabbed a wall handle, then the thrusters changed tone and started issuing a high-pitched whine.

Danger Sense skill increased to level three!

"Seemingly, the second gravity compensator is messed up as well," Basha said gloomily, lowering a soft protective bumper from the wall just in case, buckling up and donning his helmet.

I followed the example of my more experienced roommate and was grateful for it. The strong vertical impact a few seconds later nearly knocked the wind out of me. My health fell by half. Luggage fell next to me. The floor shook and we came to a stop at a severe incline, just under forty degrees.

"May our captain get sucked into a black hole!" Uline touched her sprained side and groaned.

The other crewmembers started shouting obscenities as well. Nevertheless, Uraz Tukhsh hurried to reassure the crew there was nothing to worry about and the Shiamiru had just slightly hit its tail stabilizer on the ground.

"More repair costs... A tail stabilizer is forty thousand crystals minimum," Uline remarked. "I heard three crew members are leaving in the nearest spaceport to find another employer. I can sense I'll regret that I kept up my contract with this loser, probably a few times!"

Sensing the team's mood and wanting them to forget the uncomfortable landing, Uraz Tukhsh announced that he would be treating every crew member to a meal in the spaceport. Maybe he also just wanted to celebrate the fruitful journey as well, how could I know? A few Geckho shouted enthusiastically in reply, but it really was just a few.

"Let's go, Gnat. We can celebrate your first space flight!" Basha Tushihh suggested, and I didn't refuse.

It was awkward to walk on the slanted floor, but I managed. There was a long strip of burning grass on the landing pad, marking our recent trajectory. At any rate, none of the crew members or spaceport employees were alarmed by the fire, so it must have been a minor issue.

Only a few technicians remained with the shuttle, trying to get the tilted starship to stand upright. The rest of the crew formed a raucous crowd and headed for the dispatch tower. I was surprised that no customs officials came out to meet us. There were actually no checks at all. We walked to the tower unimpeded. Just after we reached the large elevator and started going up, I felt like I was doused in ice water.

Danger Sense skill increased to level four!
Danger Sense skill increased to level five!

I looked around to see this danger but found nothing. Nevertheless, my stress was only growing with every second. To the shocked gazes of the Geckho accompanying me, I equipped my armor helmet, took out my shotgun and quickly started to load it. I knew that I looked strange and awkward, and couldn't rationally explain my actions, but I felt I had no choice. I was impressed by the Shiamiru crew. They didn't question me, just put on their combat armor and drew their weapons.

When the elevator doors opened on the restaurant floor, I cannot say who was more surprised — me when seeing the ghastly Dark Faction Psionic Mage, Leng Thumor-Anhu La-Fin, right in front of me, or the fearsome old man seeing fifteen barrels trained at his head.

But I came to my senses first and even found it in me to give a polite bow. Though he was an enemy, he was a player of respected status. Thumor-Anhu La-Fin did not greet me, just held out his empty hands, showing the agitated Geckho he was unarmed. Then, he spoke in Russian with just a barely noticeable accent, saying:

"Gnat, so there you are... We've been searching every node for three days looking for you..."

"What is going on here?" the captain enquired.

"This man is my personal enemy!" I explained to Uraz Tukhsh and the rest of the Shiamiru crew, pointing my shotgun barrel at the Psionic Mage.

"This is Geckho territory, and conflicts between vassals are strictly forbidden!" Uraz Tukhsh barked loudly.

The old mage seemed to understand, because he again demonstrated his empty hands and said a short phrase, after which his retinue put away their weapons and left. But the old man wouldn't take his ghastly glowing blue eyes off me.

"I am familiar with the laws of the Geckho race, and wish no quarrel with our esteemed suzerains. You're safe in the spaceport, but you cannot stay here forever. The rules say you can only stay in a safe zone for twenty-four hours, then you lose the status of protected guest. No, we will not keep watch for you at the gate. That would be too great an honor for a simple player. I'll just wait until we meet again. My intuition tells me it won't be long. But, seeing how fate brought us together, I have a proposal. I've asked around, and many people say you have my staff. It is valuable to me for many reasons, and I am willing to pay a good price for it."

I held a resolute expression on my face, but internally I was laughing at his naivete. Did this mage really think I would agree to return such a powerful weapon to an enemy? Sure, simply refusing would be the wrong move. At any rate, he was a Leng, a respected player. I should name such an insane price that it would at least be economically justified. But I wanted it to be beyond what he could afford to make him look foolish! One thousand crystals is the price of a great blaster. I'd have to ask for no less than that. Fifteen hundred? Three thousand? What about five? No, five thousand was too much...

"I'll pay five thousand crystals," said the ghastly man,

clearly demonstrating how easily he read my thoughts. "I'll have you know, Gnat, that no one else would give up even a tenth of that for that stick."

"Three thousand, and you swear to call off the hunt," I said, making a counteroffer. But the old man just shook his head.

"No. My granddaughter's honor and my reputation are worth more than that. Five thousand, and the hunt will continue. But first..." the mage snickered, showing a row of teeth that were unexpectedly even and pristine for such an old man, "change your respawn point."

Cold sweat ran over me. How was this psionic reading such secret information so easily?! If I died now, I would reappear... actually, where would that be? In the midst of the asteroid debris? Or on the Shiamiru on the landing strip? In any case, I didn't want to find out. Not wasting a second, I opened the settings and changed my respawn to the spaceport waiting room. A bit more secure than before!

Uline walked up and asked why I was so alarmed, and if I needed some help. I took out the staff Wrath. I still hadn't even determined its properties. But I asked the trader to act as a broker for this potentially problematic trade. The Mage unhurriedly counted out five large red crystals and handed them to Uline. These were very different from any crystals I'd seen before. I didn't even suspect that Geckho crystals came in different shapes and values. But I didn't want to reveal my ignorance, so I kept silent. The Geckho woman turned the precious stones in her hands, looked through them at the light and said confidently:

"They're real. Each is worth one thousand crystals, so this is five thousand."

I thanked our broker, returned the frightening mage his staff and stuck the valuable crystals in my inventory. Thumor-Anhu La-Fin gave me a scant nod, walked toward his minions, who were holding the elevator for him, and turned to say one last thing:

"Thanks for the thing with the harpies. If it wasn't for that, I would have ordered one of my servants to kill you and pretend it was their own idea. And your Geckho friends wouldn't have been able to help. Gnat, you can't even imagine how eager I am for our next encounter!"

Chapter
Thirty

Return
to
Base

I**T HAD ALREADY** been half an hour since the enemy mage left the room, but I couldn't calm down. Sure I was surrounded by Geckho friends, but I just couldn't bring myself to believe the old man when he said there wouldn't be Dark Faction soldiers waiting at the spaceport exit to ambush me. In fact, I was practically sure he was lying. I always trusted my intuition, so throughout the boisterous feast, I was considering my next move.

I didn't even think of going back around the gulf alone on foot. That would be nothing short of suicide. I also couldn't spend more than a day in the dispatch tower. I asked my furball friends if I could stay in the Shiamiru, but that was also a no. The Geckho didn't want primitives loitering about their spaceport, so their laws said I had to leave the protected zone within twenty-four hours. Thumor-Anhu La-Fin hadn't been lying about that. If I were an official documented member of the Shiamiru crew, I might be able to reach an understanding with the administration but, as it was, there was no point in even trying.

Not far from the space port, there was a small hotel in the Geckho village, where I could theoretically spend several days, but they didn't have armed guards, so that wouldn't do either. The hotel was a green zone, though, so I could leave the game there and consult with the Dome leadership. The spaceport, on the other hand, was yellow and my character would remain in the virtual world for ten whole minutes after exit. That might seem like nothing, but the whole Shiamiru crew had just seen the Psionic Mage give me the five thousand crystals, and some Geckho had even asked me about it. Plus, there were Geckho in the restaurant not from the Shiamiru crew. So, there was a large risk I would be robbed to the last thread if I exited the game here.

I needed to reach my faction somehow. That was clear. But how? Contact one of my faction's recon groups that kept watch over the space port, and ask them to take me to our territory? They would probably agree to help, but how could I get in touch with them? I didn't know the radio frequency or encryption codes, and my basic radio didn't have the complicated hardware and software to use encryption, so no one would hear me.

I could also go by sea, though. After all, Ivan Lozovsky said the Peresvets were going back on a ferry. Still, I had no idea where to catch a ferry, how much it cost, or who I would have to find to make such an arrangement. Also, I would need to leave the protected zone to look for the ferry, and I couldn't afford to do that.

Without having thought up a way out of the dead end, I shared my woes with Uline Tar. The Geckho woman was almost totally disengaged from the revelry and was even sitting at a different table with a many-layered cocktail in a tall glass. Staring at the screen of her electronic tablet, if any crew members bothered her, she asked to be left alone. When I walked up to her, Uline first grunted in dismay and hurried to cover the screen with her hand. But after hearing me, her demeanor changed.

"Why didn't you say so, Gnat?! Of course I'll help you. Sit here, don't go anywhere. I'll figure it all out."

She was gone for forty minutes, and I even started to worry she had forgotten. But in the end, Uline came back and plopped down heavily on the bench next to me:

"This spaceport and village are such a mess. No one here knows anything... I had to drag myself to port and figure it out there. There is a freight ferry that leaves once a day, stopping at the opposite shore to pick up cargo containers from the natives, then returning to Geckho territory. But they have a rule against taking passengers... That's officially, though. Under the table, the whole ferry crew will turn a blind eye for fifty crystals. I warned them a person would be coming and even paid in advance, so no one will be surprised to see you. Anyway, they depart in a quarter ummi, don't be late!"

A quarter ummi? One hour and twenty minutes. I thanked Uline from the bottom of my heart and promised to compensate her after I figured out how to exchange the crystals worth one thousand for lower-value ones. The girl rumbled happily, then grew unexpectedly serious:

"I saw a group of people not far away on the road that leads to the Geckho village and port. I do not know if they are your friends or enemies, but I decided to warn you just in case."

Well damn! There was no way I had friends here. The Geckho node was too far away from my faction's borders. More likely, Leng Thumor-Anhu La-Fin had left a group of minions to keep watch over the only road to the village, hotel and port, cutting off all potential escape routes.

I turned toward the raucous Shiamiru crew, still celebrating the successful voyage. I wanted to ask one of them for help. But now was not the time... The most popular drink of the feast was our fire water made "using time-honored techniques." Many boxes had been unloaded from the Peresvets into the large customs warehouse, and some had turned up here. Apparently, vodka worked approximately the same way on Geckho as it did on people. A third of the crew was already three sheets to the wind, while the others were conducting deep philosophical conversations like "do you respect me?" or "what space race has the sluttiest girls?" Captain Uraz Tukhsh himself, his furry legs up on the restaurant table, had already dozed off with an empty glass in hand.

I lamented that fact, and Uline noted reasonably that, even if the crew members were stone-cold sober and well rested, they wouldn't help me.

"Gnat, you must understand that, regardless of personal opinion, no Geckho will intervene in a conflict between vassals. The risk of causing serious and unpredictable political consequences is too great. In the past, it has even led to wars between Geckho clans. So, helping you would be strictly illegal."

"I understand, Uline, and I won't ask anyone to break the law. But I need a decent weapon. Can you show me how to use your store?" I turned to the Geckho woman, who sympathized with my plight, understanding that she would not refuse me such a small favor.

Following the huge Geckho up the spiral ramp, I went one floor up. The "shop" was just a few touch screens on the wall, which showed a catalog. You could use it to order items and pay in either crystals or various interstellar currencies. After the totally automated restaurant a floor below, this is basically what I was expecting.

I probably would have eventually figured out how to use the shop without Uline's help, but I appreciated the experienced Trader's explanations. After all, time was of the essence, and I couldn't make out all Geckho writing yet.

Above all, I was interested in light firearms with the Rifles skill. And I didn't care if it was laser, plasma, conventional or any other type. It just had to be more powerful and reliable than the antiquated shotgun I'd taken back at the beginning of the game.

There were so many options my eyes were spinning. All kinds of blasters from miniature to heavy. Both combat and stun resonators. Rail guns that shot tiny wolfram balls connected by a microscopic monomolecular mesh that could cut a perfect square out of any unarmored target. But the prices stung. Even the cheapest blasters were eight hundred crystals. But something else caught my eye. Everything I wanted had a note I couldn't read... I asked Uline to translate it for me.

"Gnat, that means: 'Not in stock on your planet. If ordered, will be delivered by the next transport ship.' No offense, but your planet is on the edge of the known Universe, so there are no regular routes here. Shipments only come occasionally. So, the prices here are... strange to put it lightly. To me personally, as a Trader, it just hurts to see the huge markup you have to pay to arm yourself. Maybe you can just take mine for now, then give it back when we meet again?"

I couldn't believe my ears, but Uline unclipped the holster from her belt and handed me a shock blaster. I thanked her but had to return the weapon. Due to my class limitations, I couldn't use an automatic weapon.

"Ah, what am I doing...?" my friend grumbled and

took another gun from her inventory. "Take a look at this one then. Can you use it? Let me warn you, though: you have to give it back! If you lose this valuable item, I'll take your Listener's armor suit as compensation!"

Barely glancing at the weapon, I gasped in astonishment. This was the gun Uline had taken from the Relict base!

Relict Annihilator (Listener close combat gun)
Statistic requirements: Agility 15, Intelligence 15
Skill requirements: Rifles 40, Sharpshooter 15.

Attention! Your character's Rifles and Sharpshooter skills are too low to use this weapon effectively. Accuracy penalty with current skills: -59%

Attention! This object is for the Relict Race. Penalties when used by a Human: firing speed -25%, effective range -25%

Attention! Critically low nuclear battery. Current charge: less than 7%! Replace the nuclear battery!

Ugh, what huge penalties! I opened Gnat's skill window and placed six of fifteen free points into Sharpshooter, so I could at least meet the requirement there. The accuracy penalty went down from 59% to 43%. That was still enormous. Invest my remaining nine points in Rifles? But I would need to level Medium Armor to put on the Relict energy armor suit... That was a long way off, though. After all, I'd have to increase Strength before then, and I may need to use the Annihilator today.

Decisively placing the nine points into Rifles, I raised

it to 32, which brought the accuracy penalty down to 15%. Much better. Although...

I suddenly realized I had entirely lost the will to tangle with the unknown number of enemies blocking the road. Now I risked losing not only the Annihilator, but the armored suit as well. Uline laughed:

"I'm glad you realized that, Gnat. After all, there are simpler ways of getting to port than trying to blast through a group of enemies. You want me to call a loader from the Shiamiru by radio and ask one of our technicians to bring you in a vehicle? No one will see you in the closed trunk and, once in port, you'll be safe!"

Strange that such a simple method hadn't occurred to me. I asked Uline to call for transport from the shuttle. If there was a loader, it would be stupid not to use it. I turned back to the store panel. What did the Human-3 Faction need? I remembered that our technicians lacked sufficiently pure silicon and other semiconductors necessary to produce high-quality radio parts. What else? High-temperature superconductors, molybdenum steel springs, light reflecting paint, super-strong magnets, fiberoptic cables, all kinds of premade radio parts: diodes, triodes, resistors, connectors, a couple geological analyzers for my scanner... I skimmed the catalog and ordered a couple of everything we might need if it was at a more or less acceptable price.

The store didn't have everything in stock, but plenty of it was affordable. I spent two thousand crystals all told and received my order a minute later. A little door opened in the wall, and two large sealed boxes came out on a conveyor belt. Uline and I couldn't lift even one of them together, but I ran down to the restaurant and got Vasha and Basha, who were roaring drunk, to help. The four of us just barely managed to drag the heavy boxes to the freight elevator, but it was easy after that. The loader had just come out from the Shiamiru, and we placed both containers in the trunk with its crane.

I only risked going on deck when the ferry had already made it a significant distance from shore. Before that, I was hiding by my boxes. The sea was stormy that evening. Black waves shook the ferry. The sky was heavy with dark clouds just about to pour. The Geckho node was lost in the fog and already barely visible.

Cartography skill increased to level thirty-seven!
Eagle Eye skill increased to level thirty-seven!
Medium Armor skill increased to level thirteen!

The ferry was powered not by underwater propellers, but antigrav disks mounted on the sides and underneath, which made seemingly bottomless whirlpools in the water around the ship. They made the sea foamy and angry, like a shaken bottle of cola. I was looking over the side and admiring nature's fury. There were huge waves running into the whirlpools, throwing splashes of the salty water on deck.

Due to the bad weather, there were no crew members out here.

That made it especially surprising when I saw a fleeting movement on the bow of the ferry. A vague shadow just flickered for one second. But no matter how long I looked in that direction, I couldn't see anything. Was it just an illusion? Entirely possible. At any rate, it was night and it could have just been a splash or some illusion made by the nasty weather. Nevertheless, I felt alarmed and did a scan.

Scanning skill increased to level thirty-six!

You have reached level twenty-nine!

You have received three skill points!

But I ignored the popup messages because, on the mini-map, I could distinctly see three red triangles on the Geckho ferry. And as a matter of fact, one was on the bow of the ferry hiding behind a few large bales of waterproof fabric. And there were another two behind me. Actually, just three steps behind me.

Danger Sense skill increased to level six!

Straining not to show that I'd noticed, I opened my inventory window and got ready to set the Annihilator into my main weapons slot at any moment. After several seconds, the game system identified my three enemies and even showed me brief descriptions. My eye caught on the triangle on the bow. It was marked:

Minn-O La-Fin. Cartographer. Level 50.

An old friend!

Chapter Thirty-One

Battle for the Boat

I DON'T KNOW why I didn't see them before. This wasn't the first time I'd run a scan. Maybe it was because I was in the hold then, and there were too many other objects and containers around me to detect. Or maybe they knew about my ability and were intentionally keeping their distance. But now I was up on deck and out in the open, so they decided it was time to get me in a pincer. They were going to attack without warning.

I had no doubt their intentions were aggressive. And if a battle was inevitable, I didn't want to give my enemies any more time to prepare. I had to attack first. I slowly turned around, as if I just wanted to go to the other side of the and to look over the deck. Then, I made a sudden jump around the corner and shot the Annihilator at the nearest Dark Faction soldier before I even landed. I was shooting from the hip, and had that accuracy penalty, but I was only four feet away, so I didn't miss.

Rifles skill increased to level thirty-three!

Sharpshooter skill increased to level sixteen!

Like a true gamer, my first thought was "headshot!" And what a shot it was! My enemy's skull was just obliterated above the lower jaw. And his headless body slumped onto the deck. I immediately took another shot at the soldier standing slightly farther away while he was stock still and gaping in surprise.

Miss! I put a neat six-inch circular hole in the skirting behind him. How?! I was only nine feet away! I pressed down on the unusual trigger with four fingers again, but this time didn't miss. Although not in the head where I was aiming, I hit him in the chest and it was also fatal. No one could survive a hole through their heart and lungs, even with Dark Faction technology.

Sharpshooter skill increased to level seventeen!

Then, I got an unbearable sensation of pain in my chest as if disaster was impending. It made me automatically jump forward and somersault before I could even consciously register the thought. A second later, a viscous green substance spread out on the wall like an ink blot right behind the place I was just standing.

Danger Sense skill increased to level seven!

I didn't know what kind of weapon Minn-O La-Fin was

using, but I wasn't interested in finding out what it was like to be shot by one. It was dangerous to stay here. I was oddly certain of that, so I jumped sharply, taking cover around a corner. Then I ran full speed down the deck to some stacked containers sixty feet away. Behind them was a hatch that led inside the ferry, which is how I had initially gotten on deck.

While running, I saw my first kill. He was now flat on the ground lying next to a dropped snub-nose gun. I looked closer at it, and the game system told me it was called a Paralyzer.

Paralyzer? They wanted to paralyze me and take me alive, not kill me? That didn't make me feel any better. For me, being a prisoner of the Dark Faction was a hundred times worse than quickly dying and respawning in the safety of the Geckho dispatcher tower. I didn't go back and pick up the Paralyzer. I had no need for it now. The red triangle of the enemy on the mini-map was quickly approaching. Minn-O La-Fin was following me. I got another piercing feeling in my chest, and sharply changed direction, letting another glowing ball of green slime fly past me.

I made it! I took shelter behind the containers and glanced at my weapon. The Annihilator's nuclear battery was at just one percent. I hoped it would last for even one shot. But I wasn't about to shoot it. With my skills, the chance of missing from sixty feet was so high it wasn't worth trying.

"Gnat! You is to take Sensing Scaries! So jump like you mad! I just laughing!" came Minn-O La-Fin's mocking voice.

"Well, it looks like you also took a new skill when you

reached level fifty, Astrolinguistics. You couldn't speak my language before," I called back, trading out the useless Annihilator for Angel Dust.

According to the mini-map, the girl with ashen-gray skin was now next to the bodies of her companions. Her marker was not moving. Perhaps, my enemy was reloading or changing her weapon to something more effective, but she was out in the open, and that was an opportunity for me. Concentrating on my breath to relax, I tried to abstract myself from the situation. "No, I don't want to harm the pretty girl, we're just... playing!" With these thoughts in mind, I stuck my head out of cover and shot the air rifle.

Miss! Miss! Miss! I had been trying to avoid thinking about harming Minn-O La-Fin so I wouldn't trip her Danger Sense. Apparently, it hadn't worked. Miss! The graceful girl, surprisingly agile in her scaly suit and chameleon cloak, could foresee where my bullets would fly and dodged every shot like Neo in *The Matrix*! Miss! Miss! Now here was something new. Minn-O La-Fin ran five steps vertically up a wall and flipped backward to dodge my last two shots. Miss! Miss! Miss!

My clip emptied, I took cover again to reload, picking back up in the conversation:

"Look who's talking about Danger Sense! You were just jumping like a mountain goat!"

Minn-O La-Fin didn't answer. But I heard a strange sound, as if she was pulling the pin from a grenade.

Danger Sense skill increased to level eight!

Not wasting a single second, I sharply hopped up, ran three steps and jumped down the open hatch. I nearly broke my legs in the rough landing and even lost ten percent of my health. But that was nothing, because I had escaped near certain death. I heard a plunk above me. A bright light lit up the darkness of the overcast evening, and a piercing sound somewhere between a creak and squeak, cut painfully into my ears. For a few seconds I was stunned, even though I was outside the flashbang grenade's radius.

Fame increased to 21.

Fame increased to 22.

Fame increased to 23.

What the crap?! I might have understood if my Agility or Danger Sense had gone up, but how did Fame come into this? It took me a few seconds to realize that these system messages were totally unconnected with this battle. Most likely, the video clip of our group entering the Relict base had just been broadcast on the intergalactic news. All the same, it made me freeze. Just for a few seconds, but that was time I didn't have...

It was too risky to go up the nearest stairs now. Minn-O La-Fin had probably already made it to the containers overhead. Yep, she was almost right above me. I saw her red triangle. One very useful aspect of the Targeting skill was that, even after losing an enemy from view, I could still see their marker for some time, even through a wall. I heard the sound of a pin being pulled again. My enemy was about to throw a grenade down the hatch.

I ran down the long straight corridor. Based on the mini-map, there was a second way up at the other end of it. I heard a loud plunk behind me, the corridor lit up with a bright flash, but I was far enough away and was unharmed. While running, I changed the clip of the PCP rifle, reached the opposite set of stairs and was about to go up when I sharply stopped. What I saw just couldn't be.

Next to the stairs on the floor, there was a dead Geckho with its throat slit lying in a pool of blood! I suspected the other ferry crew members had also been killed, which is why no Geckho had reacted to the sound of our firefight, grenades and just general chaos. The fact that the Dark Faction wanted to take me prisoner was enough reason to panic, but now I was terrified.

"You is already to find other door? I here too. You don't climb up now. Too slow," in the hatch over my head, Minn-O La-Fin's smiling face flickered past, and immediately took cover.

Well damn! I was hoping to trick the nimble girl and sneak up on her from behind. But she easily predicted where I'd be. She was now just waiting in ambush by the hatch above me. Although... a cold sweat washed over me. Why did I think she predicted anything? What if she could also see my marker? She probably had a bunch of similar skills and abilities, so it seemed she was tracking me as well.

That was frightening. Minn-O La-Fin was more than twenty levels higher than me, had much better skills and a better weapon. My only advantage was that Scanning and

Targeting allowed me to track her. I guess that wasn't such an advantage after all...

"Why did you kill the Geckho?" I shouted, changing out my long-range Angel Dust for the close combat shotgun.

"No, Gnat. You no understand how genius is we plan. It you that killing four Geckho on ferry. Only you is buy ticket. My group sneak on ship and kill quiet. No one Geckho is see. But when they is respawn, they be very angry and immediately to know who do all this murder. Only can be Gnat. They finding you and know. Is no question."

The girl's face flickered by in the hatch once again, but this time I was ready, immediately shooting from both barrels. Based on the painful shout and yelling in her language, at least one ball had hit.

Targeting skill increased to level eight!

Sharpshooter skill increased to level eighteen!

Astrolinguistics skill increased to level thirty-three!

You have reached level thirty!

You have received three skill points! (total points accumulated: six)

Listening to the muted groans and first-aid kit being ripped open up above, I unhurriedly reloaded my shotgun, then opened the skill window and tossed three points into Medium Armor and three into Rifles.

Now, it didn't seem so hopeless. There were bodies of two Dark Faction soldiers and the signs of a pitched battle. That would immediately tell the Geckho that there were stowaways on board. I just had to leave more clues to attract their attention. I took out the laser pistol and put the weapon into constant beam mode. I burned a complex Geckho phrase into the metal wall over the corpse:

"Minn-O La-Fin, granddaughter of Leng Thumor-Anhu La-Fin did this."

Putting the overheated pistol back in my inventory, I told Minn-O La-Fin what I'd written. To make her even madder, I said it couldn't be washed off or erased. I also added that the corpses of her allies wouldn't disappear before the ferry reached my faction's territory. Once there, I said, a large group of Geckho would fly in to investigate. So actually, the beauty of the situation was that my allies and I would never have to answer for this quadruple murder and property destruction. It would all be pinned on Leng Thumor-Anhu La-Fin and his granddaughter, and the Geckho would be foaming at the mouth when they figured it out.

The Cartographer didn't answer, but her marker started gradually heading for the center of the ferry. Did she want to get rid of her companion's corpses? No such luck! I won't let you destroy evidence! I dashed up the stairs, but just before I reached the top, I stopped sharply, wanting to test whether Minn-O La-Fin really was tracking me.

And I stopped just in the nick of time! Just a few inches over my head, a flash blasted out. The cartographer was expecting me again and decided to greet me with a whole series of laser pulses. Strange that Danger Sense hadn't warned me. On the other hand, I wasn't planning to stick my head out, so it made sense.

I was not in an especially great situation. My enemy was tracking me to make sure I couldn't come on deck, and it wouldn't take her too long to throw the bodies overboard. Most likely, she would then leave the ship herself. She might even jump into the water and respawn somewhere safe. And there was nothing I could do to stop her...

Her marker soon disappeared, and I had no idea what Minn-O La-Fin was doing or where she was. Most likely, she had gotten rid of the bodies like I expected. Perhaps, I should risk it and try to go out of one of the hatches. But that was a very dangerous plan and most likely would end in my death or paralysis.

Then I got a brilliant idea. I knew how to get iron-clad proof that other people were on the ferry. Just run a scan like on the Shiamiru!!! That would give me a detailed three-dimensional diagram of the ferry, along with all living creatures and dead bodies! I could present that to the Geckho, if I needed to prove that there were other people on the ferry. It would at least show Minn-O La-Fin, and maybe her two henchmen's bodies as well!

I hurried down into the hold and quickly found my two containers. An unexpected problem arose, though. Which one contained my scanner supplies? There was nothing written on the packaging. Also, both hard-sided containers were sealed, so opening them was another complication, especially without tools...

I stood there and thought over the problem. Suddenly, the ferry shook, and the antigravitational thrusters went silent. What the crap? Had she stopped the boat?! Most likely. After all, Minn-O La-Fin's greatest problem was a lack of time. As it was, the ferry would be arriving to the pier in the Antique Beach node in twenty minutes. And I had reminded her it was controlled by a hostile faction! I couldn't hope for help from my allies now. Also, the Cartographer girl had an unlimited amount of time at her disposal. Well, well... what a female dog!

On the other hand, with this action, Minn-O La-Fin had revealed her location. The ferry was controlled from a booth on the upper deck, so she must have been there. And that meant I had time to break open the boxes and search them for my analyzers. How to open the hard-plastic containers? If I were on a normal human ship, I'd look for a box in the wall reading "in case of fire, break glass." That would get me an axe or crowbar and, with something like that, I'd be set! But would there be such a thing on a Geckho ferry?

I walked through the gloomy hold to look. On the far wall, I found a panel with a red alarm button. I headed to it and tried to figure out the complicated text.

Hold pest control system. Warning!!! This will release a poisonous gas. Before use, put on a defensive suit or gas mask!!!

Astrolinguistics skill increased to level thirty-four!

I supposed this was the longest and most complicated thing I had ever read in Geckho, so I the pride I felt was well deserved. But I was also disappointed that this was not a fire emergency box and couldn't help me open the containers.

Then, standing in the gloom, I started looking for something more useful. My eyes caught a vague movement in the far end of the hold.

Successful Perception check

I froze, looking into the gloom. Aha! It was Minn-O La-Fin! She had come down from the control booth on the upper deck into the hold so quickly! Crouching with a weapon, she was looking around carefully. But I ducked around a corner before she saw me. I could see her though.

After Minn-O La-Fin made sure the coast was clear, she started doing something very strange. One after the next, every few yards, she was sticking round metal pucks to the floor and pressing down to activate them, making them glow red. She was mining the ship!

Throwing the corpses overboard, erasing security camera footage (if this ferry even had such a thing), cleaning up the traces of battle... those were all half measures. This was the most radical solution to her problem: no ferry, no clues leading back to the Dark Faction! In the end, there would just be four extremely angry respawned Geckho, all placing the blame squarely on Gnat, the only other living soul on the ship!

I clenched my teeth in rage. Alright, if she wanted to up the stakes, I had a surprise of my own! I put on my light space suit and placed my hand on the red button. Although it hadn't worked the last time, I tried to put all thoughts about harming Minn-O La-Fin out of my head. I even stashed my weapon, to demonstrate my peaceful intentions to the game algorithms. No, I didn't wish any ill on this girl. She had nothing to do with this. I had just seen some rats and bugs in the hold, and they needed to be exterminated. Minn-O La-Fin was still mining as if nothing had happened, so I figured I was on the right track, at least for now. And if that was so, now was the time!

I pressed down hard on the red button.

Chapter Thirty-Two

Breaking Protocol

"**U**NT URO FI?" My attention was drawn by a timid voice. I stopped studying the switchboard panel and turned around.

Minn-O La-Fin had come to her senses and was now looking around trying to figure out how she'd ended up in the ferry's electrical room. There were no portholes here, so the only source of light in the pitch blackness was a flashlight I had stolen from Minn-O La-Fin after losing my own while taking down the Relict drone.

The girl squinted when I pointed the bright beam at her face, then looked closer, met gazes with me, and shuddered in fear, remembering everything at once.

"Gnat?! What is be? What you doing to I?" Splayed

out on the floor like a starfish, the naked captive stayed stock still, as if to evaluate her wellbeing. Then, she started thrashing to try and break the ties.

I saw no reason to conceal the truth. After all, I hadn't used any top-secret methods, so I told Minn-O La-Fin in detail about what had happened:

"While you were mining the ferry, I turned on the pest control system and filled the hold with poison gas. Then I dragged your body up and, while you were unconscious, tied you up and took your weapon. But given that your health bar was almost at zero, I was afraid you'd fly off the handle and deprive me of the most obvious proof you were here. So, I used my Prospector tool to get... how to explain... something like a three-dimensional diagram showing everything aboard this ferry."

"So you are bad, take picture of I naked?" Of everything I said, she plucked that one detail out and got indignant.

"*Not just that!*" I thought, amusing myself, although I didn't say anything out loud.

I set my device to scan for organic matter, so all living creatures and corpses came out on the diagram in great detail, with all the bone structure and internal organs, enough to get a full picture of both human and Geckho anatomy. By the way, Minn-O La-Fin had recently broken the radius of her left arm and it had healed. There was also lead shot in her right shoulder, most likely from my shotgun.

I could easily explain the shot, although the girl

healed so fast I was impressed and even scared. Just an hour after getting shot, the marks on her skin were barely visible. And the fracture also made me seriously think. When respawning, all injuries and whatnot would disappear. And I knew she'd respawned no more than two days ago, after our encounter at the Harpy Cliffs. That meant Minn-O La-Fin had broken her arm since then and fully healed! The stuff of fiction! Either the residents of the alternative Earth had amazing innate tissue regeneration abilities, or their medical technology was of an order of magnitude better than ours.

I had also studied the other physiological details of the alternative-earthling, but I had enough tact not to discuss that with her.

"It's not important what was in the image. But I did get indisputable evidence that there were other people on the ferry, including the two corpses. But a side effect of the scan was that it overloaded the ferry's electronics. I didn't have to even do that, though. You have high Constitution and good tissue regeneration. Your bullet wound healed, and you recovered from the poison."

"Me rather to die, than be shame naked prisoner of you!" the girl shouted out angrily and again started flailing.

I hadn't undressed and tied her up to humiliate the girl. It would have been stupid not to do both of those things because, in this virtual game, dying and respawning in a safe place meant guaranteed freedom. Dark Faction technology was highly advanced, and she might have had a miniature weapon, poison, explosive or antimatter capsule hidden in her clothes that could be triggered by words, and that would stop me from bringing my prisoner to port.

But now, I wasn't the least bit worried because I had tied her wrists and ankles tight with strong ropes, fixing their ends to sturdy metal structures in the room. Basically, I had followed the Second Legion's example, although I set her face up, and didn't blindfold or gag her.

I watched her struggling fitfully for some time to make sure she was tied down firmly, then lost all interest and returned to the fuse box. I was studying the bundles of wire, trying the many breakers and trying to figure out why there was no light. In the darkness, I could hear heavy waves beating on the side of the drifting ferry. There was also Minn-O La-Fin huffing and puffing as she tried to pull her arms or legs from the ropes. I tried not to pay those sounds any mind and became engrossed in my difficult task.

But a few minutes later, I heard the Dark Faction girl make an offended demand:

"Gnat, you no can do this! Untie fast, fast! I nobility Princess and no can be such in shame!"

"Oh yeah, you're a real noble princess? With a shaved crotch and painted nipples?" I answered mockingly, not holding back. "By the way, when you were first captured in our node, I don't remember any of that. Did you do all that for me? Or maybe the harpies?"

I heard outraged wheezing from the darkness, then a few long and very emotional phrases spewed out in her language, probably including many vulgarities and bad names. But I didn't react to her righteous indignation, which just made her madder.

Astrolinguistics skill increased to level thirty-five!

I finally understood a phrase in her language, "greasy hooker's ass." It was somehow connected with my name, but I was unable to make out any other words.

Finally, my prisoner said her fill and calmed down, changing to a business-like tone back in my language:

"Gnat, you no is right. You no can insult I. You come close. Offer you for negotiate. I scary in dark."

Minn-O La-Fin was afraid of the dark? It was strange to hear such a thing from the ruthless and calculating warrior, who had at least given an order to cut the throats of four Geckho and perhaps even done so herself. Nevertheless, I walked up closer and sat on a box next to her.

"No you look, prying eye!" the naked captive got offended, following my gaze.

Still, having noticed that all her hysterics, attempts to command or refer to her noble origin had no effect, the cartographer got to business: "I wanting to know price for ransom. Three thousand crystals, is be good?"

I didn't even laugh. Her offer just looked so stupid:

"Your grandfather bought his crooked stick back from me for five thousand. Do you think he values you less than an inanimate object?! But the issue isn't the price. No amount of money could make me let you go this time. First of all, the faction leadership would tear me to pieces. And second, enough easy outs. They got you before and let you go as the granddaughter of a respected Leng, but the lesson didn't stick. So, now you'll be a common prisoner. Maybe that will teach you."

"I no is common prisoner! You no can treat I like that!" Minn-O La-Fin tried that routine again, but I ignored it as usual and continued:

"You know very much and have a very high value to my faction, so I will turn you over to our investigators and they will conduct a very thorough interrogation. The information in your head is worth a lot, somewhat more than three thousand crystals!"

The girl again started testing the ropes and even tried slamming her head into the metal floor. I realized then why the Second Legion tied up their captives face down. It was so they couldn't kill themselves by hitting the back of their head on a hard object. It was too late to tie up the rebellious girl any other way, so I simply placed her underwear beneath her head and threatened:

"You cannot kill yourself. I have a first aid kit, and I'll heal you. But if you don't stop jerking around or bite your tongue, I'll stick a gag of lacy underwear in your mouth. Is that what you want? Or will you behave?"

Minn-O La-Fin went silent and just grumbled angrily. But when I reached for her panties and started balling them up, she looked scared and started talking:

"Alright, Gnat, I promising not to get out. No cripple, no suicide. Princess noble word!"

I stopped and sat back down on the box. The

flashlight had rolled away, and I moved it back. It just so happened that its beam passed a different part of her anatomy on the way. She tried in vain to cross her legs, then Minn-O's ashen gray cheeks started to blush in embarrassment.

"Gnat, why is you shame I? Military secret I is not know, value big only because Princess. If granddaughter is be dishonor, Thumor-Anhu La-Fin is take I title. And then no more worth."

It was a fair remark. But I wasn't trying to mock her. I just wanted to show her how inappropriate her pomposity was for this situation. Anyhow, I turned the flashlight and even offered to give the girl her underwear back and untie her, leaving just her wrists cuffed behind her back.

"Just like that? For free? Not for many thousand of crystal?" Minn-O La-Fin was extremely surprised at my unexpected mercy. But of course she didn't refuse.

"Gnat, you is act nobility. Now telling, what is you title? Or you have military rank?"

Strange question. It even made me chuckle. Did Minn-O La-Fin really think that common decency was a trait reserved for the nobility and military? I answered honestly that my homeland got rid of its aristocracy a long time ago and, although we did respect our military, I was more of a science type.

"How is this be?" The girl looked sincerely surprised. "But I am hear from Leng Thumor-Anhu that you is to be in many, many army tournament and winning all time!"

How could she know that?! Very few members of the H3 Faction were aware of my past, so hearing about it from an enemy was extremely surprising. My heart started jumping in my chest, but not because of impending danger. I felt I might be getting to something important. Minn-O La-Fin had seemingly slipped up and revealed secret information.

But I tried to pretend it was nothing, changed the topic and asked her to be quiet so I could concentrate. Then, while I dug around in the electrical system, the long-legged beauty sat in silence with her hands tied behind her back, shivering in the cold in her thin underwear.

Finally, I managed to figure out the correct arrangement of breakers, and all the lights turned on.

Electronics skill increased to level twenty-two!

Electronics skill increased to level twenty-three!

Great! Now I could turn on the engine and get back underway. Just then, my captive asked what I would do next, especially curious about her own fate.

"When we get nearer the shore, I'll call for help on my radio. On shore, I'll hand you over to our faction leadership, and my diplomats can decide what to do with you. Maybe your grandfather will pay your ransom again if he can agree on a price. But if they cannot agree, you will be given to the Geckho to explain the four murders on the ferry. Our suzerains will most likely have a ton of questions, so I cannot imagine how you'll squeeze out of it..."

Minn-O La-Fin jumped sharply off the box, raised her

voice to a scream, and started justifying herself:

"My people here is not involve! This suggest is my personals servant! Only he is blame! Only he is Geckho punish!"

"Mhm, they might even believe you if you say it like that!" I replied sarcastically. "If two random soldiers killed a few Geckho, only they would be punished. It would probably barely reflect on your faction. But you, a Princess, were mixed up in this. You're the granddaughter of a coruler, so there can be no doubt that this operation was both planned and agreed-upon by your grandfather."

"No! Not be! Leng Thumor-Anhu La-Fin is not know! This is my slave suggest plan for revenge Gnat, and I agree! You bring shame for noble girl before, and I need be to revenge Gnat to keep honor! Is law of my people!"

"And how did that go? Feeling avenged?" I chuckled mockingly. "I've taken so much from you in the last few days my inventory is full. And yet you came back for even more revenge... Do you think your grandfather will be happy when he sees how it turned out this time? Now you made Leng Thumor-Anhu La-Fin look like a big-talking oath-breaker."

"How? No, this no be!" But now the Cartographer girl was afraid. Clearly, the threat of her being interrogated by people or Geckho was not so frightening to her as angering the strict Psionic Mage.

"Leng Thumor-Anhu La-Fin promised in very bombastic terms with many Geckho around that your faction would not ambush or track me as I left the spaceport. But not only was I tracked, you snuck onto a ferry, killed some Geckho and tried to pin it on me. What are the promises of a Dark Faction Leng even worth if they cannot be trusted?! When the Geckho find out about this, your grandfather's reputation will fall very, very far..."

I had never before seen such authentic horror in Minn-O La-Fin's eyes, even when she was being attacked by the lusty harpy. She started shaking and said with resignation:

"If grandfather authority is to fall, rage of old man be terrible... I can even losing title. This shame worse than to die."

I decided to take pity on the pretty noble girl, and tried to reassure her even if she was from a hostile faction:

"Minn-O, I am not planning to raise this topic with the Geckho, so if you do not mention it, nothing bad will happen with your title. After all, I realize that you are not only a warrior, but a member of a ruling family... whatever that means in your world."

"Gnat," she sighed, her emotions overflowing. She paused, trying to find the words. "I am to hate you so, so bad before. This same amount I admire you nobility now. When your faction to lose war soon, I say word for take you on our side! Your glowing eyes be so pretty. You is find girl my planet fast-fast and live happy!"

Probably, Minn-O La-Fin meant that as a compliment, but I really didn't like her confidence in her side's impending victory.

"My ass! That will never happen!" I turned as serious as possible. I steeled my voice, looked right into her eyes and said, "Minn-O, I will do everything in my power to defeat your faction. I swear it! But as for you..." I took a decisive step toward her and, taking advantage the Princess's cuffed hands, embraced the girl and kissed her right on the lips.

Minn-O clearly was taken aback by my audacity, and spent a few seconds frozen, not stopping me. But that didn't last too long.

Danger Sense skill increased to level nine!

Feeling her knee heading for my crotch, I easily dodged and, smiling in satisfaction, walked away from the spooked girl:

"That is just a down payment. It seems like, every time we meet, you end up totally or partially naked. This is the third time and its making me think. And if your peculiar attempts at 'revenge' don't stop, I'll think you're trying to set up these situations on purpose. This time you even painted your breasts and shaved your pubes. So, are we clear? Great. And now let's go upstairs. You will show me how to turn on the ferry's engine."

Chapter Thirty-Three

Radugin's Bunker

DESPITE THE LATE HOUR, my return to the Capital didn't go unnoticed. Dozens of faction members came out to see me get out of the Peresvet. It met me at the cargo pier in the Antique Beach and brought me right to our central fortified citadel. Somehow, all these people knew that a Prospector by the name of Gnat had returned from a two-day space flight on a Geckho shuttle, and not empty-handed. I was met with shouts of greeting, given approving slaps on the shoulders and asked all kinds of questions about space.

Fame increased to 24.

All the attention and kindness were great, but I couldn't stay and chat. I was expected by Dome leader Leng

Radugin and both of his deputies, Tyulenev and Lozovsky. They were in the Leng's office deep under the fortified citadel. I didn't want to keep them waiting, so I hurried to the meeting, despite the fact that my legs were shaking in exhaustion and my mind could barely think.

The muscular First Legion soldiers brought my heavy cargo containers into the headquarters, and the prisoner, hidden under opaque fabric, was taken by the arms and legs and brought somewhere else. Accompanied by two high-level First Legion troops, I took an elevator deep under the earth to our holiest of holies — the command center for all the H3 Faction's nodes and combat divisions.

I walked past a few guard posts and armored doors until I found myself in a huge brightly-lit room. In the middle of it, there was a huge ovular table with an eerily glowing surface. I walked up closer.

Well, well! This wasn't a table at all, but a huge screen, divided into a bunch of equilateral hexagons. It was a map of our territories and the neighboring nodes in greatest possible detail. It showed all the buildings, fortifications, hills, forests, roads, divisions, moving vehicles and even individual soldiers! As soon as I realized what it was, I turned away before anything stuck in my memory.

"Good move, Gnat! That could spoil your whole Cartography-leveling tactic," chuckled an unfamiliar man standing across the table from me. His face was strange, but he had Tyulenev's voice.

Unlike the portly bald man with a huge beer belly in

the real world, Tyulenev was a normal person in the game, a slightly chubby man with a thick head of red hair and a bristling red beard. It was fairly unusual to see such a large difference. After all, every other person I'd met in the game looked more or less the same as in the real world. But there must have been a reason for this. The Dome's third in command was wearing a scratched-up heavy armor exoskeleton. The laser rifle on his belt, though, was nearly pristine.

The game avatar of diplomat Ivan Lozovsky was standing next to him. He was not much different from the real man. But I was most interested in Dome leader Radugin, because I had never seen him before.

Leng Radugin. Human. H3 Faction. Level-84 Administrator

I don't know how this person looked in the real world but, in the game, he was a forty-year-old dark-haired man with the appearance of a typical academic, very gaunt and with slightly slumping shoulders. Unlike his deputies, Radugin was not wearing armor, and not even military-style clothing. He had on a civilian suit, a white shirt and even a tie.

"Mission complete, sirs! The voyage with the Geckho crew was a success! I established personal contact with the Geckho and proved my worth as a Prospector. They also hired me for two more flights! On the asteroid, I discovered a Relict outpost and took some ancient artifacts! On the ferry back, I was attacked by the Dark Faction, but I fought them off!"

"Great, Gnat! Sit down," Radugin pointed me to the edge of the interactive table, because there were no chairs or even stools in the room. "And now, we want to hear every detail."

My tale lasted more than two hours. I was brutally tired and about to collapse, but I couldn't make it any shorter no matter how hard I tried. They were constantly asking me to clarify details, and some parts had to be retold many times. They wanted to know everything — how the Geckho crew functioned, their numbers and professional makeup, flight time, overload tolerance, whether the air was breathable by humans, the inner structure of the shuttle...

My high-detail scan of the Shiamiru was a real coup. My three leaders spent at least half an hour looking over the three-dimensional diagram, changing the angle to see different parts and discussing animatedly. Lead scientist Gerd Valentin Ustinov was even called to the meeting to try and copy the three-dimensional render to another computer. It took him a while, but he managed, then dashed off to the Prometheus with the invaluable data and a full inventory of supplies from my containers.

Also, Ustinov took the light spacesuit I'd been issued by Captain Uraz Tukhsh. I tried to protest and explained that it was only temporarily issued to me and I would soon have to return it, but I couldn't stop him. My three bosses were on his side, so there was nothing I could do. Gerd Ustinov just gave me a vague promise that he would do his best not to damage it, but he wouldn't go so far as to make any guarantees.

After that, I didn't even mention the Annihilator. The last thing I needed was to have that priceless item taken from me and potentially lose the armored Listener's suit!

Landing on the asteroid, studying it and drilling, the automatic processor, levitators, the Relict base, the guard drone, the gravitation crane, the artifacts, the Listener's suit, the bracelet... I showed them the bracelet, but the extreme Intelligence requirement immediately chilled their enthusiasm. As far as I understood, no one in our faction had an Intelligence of twenty-eight, so we couldn't even determine its properties. I got the bracelet back and continued my story.

At the part about the asteroid explosion, Leng Radugin grilled me about whether Leng Waid Shishish's cruiser had survived, but unfortunately I didn't know.

"Well, that fact is extremely important to us and our Earth as a whole," Radugin explained. "Leng Shishish was recently appointed viceroy of a large sector of the galaxy for his service to Krong Daveyesh-Pir, and that includes our home planet. And his *Tinakuro* star cruiser is the flagship of the Geckho fleet meant to come to humanity's aid if we're invaded."

Ivan Lozovsky agreed that the condition of the cruiser was of great importance to humanity and promised to ask Kosta Dykhsh about it.

But I continued my story. The flight back, landing in the spaceport, breaking the gravity compensator, the tense encounter in the restaurant, my purchases in the shop, getting on the ferry...

Just then, we were joined by Gerd Tamara. Security let the leader of the Second Legion right through and the severe paladin just stood there in her armor suit, listening attentively to my story.

Meanwhile, I described last night's battle. Three members of the Dark Faction tried to take me prisoner and killed some Geckho. Then I had a firefight with Minn-O La-Fin, she'd tried to mine the ferry, I stopped her with poison gas, took her prisoner and made a scan. I replaced the Annihilator with the shotgun in my story, though. Other than that, it was the pure truth.

They all listened attentively, although the scan of the ferry was not of much interest. As far as I understood, our scientists already knew how to build such technology, so it didn't have much value, given we already had other proof of who killed the Geckho on board.

When I told them that Minn-O La-Fin and her powerful grandfather knew about my past before the Dome, though, there was a storm of discussion. As far as I understood from the pitched dispute that followed, Leng Radugin himself didn't know this, which was to say nothing of common faction players. They came to the conclusion that the only people who might know worked in staffing, which left us with Tyulenev and the curators of the Dome project, who were not in the game. The third in command went pale and hiccupped out that he was not involved but would certainly figure out how it was leaked.

Leng Radugin was in a very decisive mood and pressured his subordinate:

"Tyulenev, this is in your own best interest! I give you two days. After that, I need the names of the traitors! For the duration of this investigation, you are forbidden from leaving the Capital!!!"

Finally, I finished my narration with Minn-O La-Fin helping me turn the thrusters back on and docking the ferry in a severe storm, just barely scratching it. Sure, a few of the Geckho pier's posts had to be reset, but that was nothing in comparison with my saving the ferry from being blown up or sunk.

"This is all coming together very well for us," Lozovsky said when I finally finished. "First, we can drag the Dark Faction through the mud face first. Killing four Geckho is a very serious crime, and our suzerains will demand extravagant compensation."

Gerd Tamara cut into the conversation for the first time:

"If it was officially approved, then yes. But Leng Thumor-Anhu and the other corulers can easily claim they were not involved and place the blame on insignificant pawns. Knowing the Dark Faction, the scapegoats will be quickly executed in the real world. That will simultaneously prove how upset they are and destroy evidence. But the Dark Faction as a whole will be relatively unscathed and only have to pay a monetary penalty. I can even imagine its maximum amount. Remember when our soldiers accidentally shot Kosta Dykhsh when he was poking around where he shouldn't have been? They made us pay eighty thousand crystals. It should be less for a common Geckho, but even if it is the same, that comes to three hundred twenty thousand crystals. The Dark Faction is loaded, so that's like birdshot to an elephant!"

Lozovsky and Tyulenev agreed with the leader of the Second Legion that such a financial penalty wouldn't be a huge burden to them. Leng Radugin heard them out and asked about the situation with Minn-O La-Fin. Ivan Lozovsky answered thoughtfully:

"If it can be proven that she took part in killing the Geckho, Minn-O La-Fin will be punished severely in her world. She'll either lose her title or be sentenced to death. But it isn't hard to see that her influential grandfather will say she was not involved, and it was all her companions' idea. Perhaps, the Leng will manage to protect her reputation. At any rate, it makes no difference to us whether she is charged with a crime. This issue will be settled purely between the Geckho and Dark Faction. It won't come back on us."

The Dome leader spent a long time in thoughtful

silence, then voiced his decision:

"Alright, Ivan. Get in touch with Leng Thumor-Anhu La-Fin to discuss a ransom for his granddaughter, and how much he's willing to pay us to keep quiet. Your first offer should demand building materials worth forty thousand crystals and the complete removal of Dark Faction divisions from the Poppy Fields node. Let's see what the old geezer has to say to that. Treat our prisoner as delicately as possible. Feed her, give her decent clothing and provide her a place to rest in a green zone. Alright, on that note I suggest we end the meeting..."

But I couldn't hold back and asked what I thought was a very logical question:

"Are we really going to just let Minn-O La-Fin go without interrogating her?! She probably has such valuable information! This isn't right!"

Danger Sense skill increased to level ten!

I realized what would happen as soon as the paladin girl's huge robot suit started moving in my direction. Then, a painfully familiar many-barreled machinegun appeared in Gerd Tamara's armored hands:

"Gnat, weren't you warned never to doubt the decisions of high-status players? There is a Gerd here, and even a Leng. So, this is on you..."

"Go to hell! I'm sick of you killing me!!!" With these words, I moved the Annihilator to my main weapon slot.

Rifles skill increased to level thirty-seven!
You have reached level thirty-one!

You have received three skill points!

You have reached level thirty-two!

You have received three skill points! (total points accumulated: six)

Fame increased to 25.

I got off the first shot, spending the last of the Annihilator's battery to kill the leader of the Second Legion.

Chapter Thirty-Four

Tumultuous Reception

THE SILENT SCENE after I killed Gerd Tamara was enough to make directors of Gogol's famous comedy *The Government Inspector* jealous. Everyone was frozen in panic and didn't move for several long seconds. It seemed I could even read frightened thoughts that nothing could stop me now, I was off the rails, and either working for the enemy to kill the leadership of the H3 Faction or destroy their command center. Finally, I slowly and smoothly lowered the Annihilator, then put it back in my inventory.

"Gnat, you have exactly one minute to explain your actions," Leng Radugin said in an ice-cold emotionless tone. Also, his business suit was immediately changed to a suit of armor that shimmered with a force field.

No one took out any weapons, but I understood that these three such high-level players could instantly kill my level-32 Prospector if I misspoke or made one wrong move.

What could I say? It would be wrong to blame it on her bias against me. I understood that perfectly. According to the game rules, a high-status player like Gerd Tamara could do whatever she felt right with simple faction members like me and didn't have to explain herself or ask permission. So, if she decided to teach me another lesson and shoot me dead, she had every right and must have had a good reason. But as a gut reaction... here I really needed to try to justify attacking the high-status player.

Could I make the excuse that my respawn point was still in the dispatch tower at the Geckho spaceport, and my death would put me in a tight spot? That was an option, yes. But that would lead to another set of questions and punishments. Why had I disobeyed an unambiguous order to leave my respawn point inside H3 territory? I didn't want to give more fodder to the idea that I was disobedient, especially in front of the leadership. I needed to try something else... What if I tried an excuse based on game rules?

"After the clip of me entering the Relict base was broadcast to the whole galaxy, I am famous as a member of Leng Waid Shish's faction. And he is a powerful Geckho, viceroy and master of our Earth. He also has a very hot temper and is famed for his lack of restraint. Killing me to teach me a lesson might lower the authority of Leng Waid

Shishish and that would cause a harsh response. All I was doing was taking preventative measures against Gerd Tamara for making a crude political error and bringing down the wrath of the Geckho race on our faction."

"And how does that line up with what you screamed before shooting?" Tyulenev asked spitefully, giving a mocking chuckle and looking to his boss for support. "To be honest, this looked most of all like a personal scuffle. Gerd Tamara really should have asked permission, though. This is the Leng's office after all..."

Still, the Dome leader cut him off with a gesture, stood in thought for a few seconds, then turned to our diplomat:

"I don't even know... Ivan, in your opinion, are Gnat's fears justified?"

Ivan Lozovsky shrugged his shoulders unconfidently, which looked somehow comical given his armored vest, and tried to answer:

"I personally don't know Leng Shishish, but I have heard tell of his vindictiveness and lack of restraint. He wouldn't take a fall in his authority lightly. Leng Shishish rules a huge number of subjects. Most likely, he doesn't even suspect that a Human Prospector named Gnat exists... Although, that depends on fame."

"Gnat, what is your fame stat?" Radugin turned to me.

I told them it was twenty-five... actually, twenty-six now, because it just went up a second ago. Clearly, the news of my killing Gerd Tamara had spread quickly.

In response, I heard gasps of surprise from all three leaders. Seemingly, none of them had expected such progress. Tyulenev and Lozovsky looked at Radugin, awaiting a decision. Our faction head spent a long time wavering before giving his final verdict:

"Twenty-six... That really is a respectable Fame... Beyond a shadow of a doubt, Leng Waid Shishish has heard of you. I believe Gnat's fears were well founded. My decision: we will fine Gnat however much it costs to repair Gerd Tamara's armor suit. Look at the big hole he put in it! By the way, I'd like to look at the weapon that can do that!"

In the chest plate of Gerd Tamara's heavy exoskeleton, there was a gaping hole big enough to fit a soccer ball through. I suspected it would cost more than one hundred crystals to repair, but I nodded in agreement, realizing I was getting off easy. I was much more worried about the Annihilator. I took it out, but immediately warned them it was not mine and it was critically important that I return it to the Geckho.

Fame increased to 27.

My fame grew again? Hey, keep it coming! It can't have been from the weapon, though. All three leaders had seen it before. Most likely, it was an echo from killing Gerd Tamara. Now I was getting scared.

My terrible fear that the invaluable Annihilator might be confiscated was not brought to fruition, though. Yes, they were very interested in the weapon. If it still had any power, they would probably want to test it on something or someone. But the battery was empty, which seriously limited what they could do, so I was quickly given the Annihilator back.

"Gnat, you are free to go. I can see that you're staggering in exhaustion, so go get some sleep. Tomorrow, I expect you to give me a detailed written report in the real world about your voyage with the Geckho. We cannot afford any more omissions like this Relict weapon. Gerd Ustinov will calculate the value of the supplies you bought us, and you will be compensated in real money or favors from faction members in the game. Naturally, we will subtract the cost of repairing Gerd Tamara's armor."

With those words, the meeting was over, and I was escorted out of the underground command bunker. The first thing I did back on the surface was to change my respawn point to the Capital, so I wouldn't find myself in such a vulnerable position again. I also put all six free points into Medium Armor, raising it to twenty-eight.

Alright, looks like I'm done. I found the "Exit Game" button in the menu and pressed it. For the first time since I started playing, I was just leaving the game, not dying. I dismissed the prompt to review the results of my game session. I was in no mood and was so tired I could barely think. I'd been gaming nonstop for almost three days!

The first thing I saw after opening my virt pod were some dark figures looming over me, then brass-knuckled fists flying at my face. After that, there was only darkness...

I came to my senses on a gurney in a small brightly lit room, with the characteristic smell of chorine-washed floors, isopropyl alcohol and medicine. Almost immediately, I guessed that I was in the Dome infirmary. I had seen this small medical building from afar before, while walking up the path from the residential buildings to the corncobs. Now, I had seemingly landed myself inside. I remembered the punches clearly, but what happened after that was a mystery.

My whole body ached, my head and the right side of my chest especially. My nose was bandaged and, when I tried to turn over, I discovered that my leg was in a cast from foot to knee and elevated in a sling. Boy, I really got it...

"Kirill, you're finally awake!" Anya's familiar voice drew my attention. I turned to look, but the huge bandage on one eye kept me from seeing her without turning my head ninety degrees.

"How long... was I out?" My throat was very dry, so it was hard for me to speak.

"Thirty hours. The doctors say it wasn't all because of the beating, though. You just needed sleep badly. And you were given enough sedatives and painkillers to put a horse under."

I raised my right hand carefully and touched the bandage on my face. Ow! Dang that hurts!

"Your nose is broken," Anya told me. "I saw you when they brought you in. Your whole face was bloody, and your nose was smashed. It was horrible! The surgeons put the small bones back in place, but you shouldn't breathe through them yet, so they stuffed your nostrils with cotton."

"And what about my leg?" I pointed to the cast.

"The meniscus of your right leg tore, and your fibula is fractured. Your left knee was wounded as well, but it isn't critical. They also broke two right ribs, and three fingers on your left hand. Someone beat you severely and professionally, trying to maim and wound but not kill. Do you happen to remember who attacked you?"

I shook my head. I could remember that there were several people, and at least one had brass knuckles, but nothing else. Anya sighed in regret:

"It all happened in eight minutes. That was the exact amount of time the video cameras on corncob fifteen were turned off. Someone knew that would happen and was waiting at your virt pod. Then they beat you up and ran away before they turned back on. Leng Radugin has been throwing a fit for the last two days, demanding they find out who attacked you and why the video cameras malfunctioned. He threatened to punish whoever did it as severely as possible. Investigators have come under the Dome from outside. They're crawling everywhere and interrogating everyone. But I'm not sure they'll manage to figure anything out. As far as I know, the Second Legion usually works security under the Dome, and that speaks volumes. They all hate you for attacking their living legend, so none of them are talking. No one knows anything, everyone is protecting everyone else..."

So that was it... The Second Legion, Gerd Tamara's henchmen... They had a motive for the attack. Anya continued, her eyes turned away:

"I'm not gonna lie, lots of people are mad at you. A few times, pissed off players came to see you in the clinic, both Second Legion soldiers and others. They all wanted to have a serious man-to-man conversation about attacking a girl and faction legend. Imran didn't let them in, though. Our Dagestani friend acted as your bodyguard. A few guys were especially stubborn, and he had to beat them up. You should have seen the pretty shoulder punches, flip kicks, heavy knockouts and even broken bones. No one else tried anything after that. Then Radugin placed First Legion soldiers here for security, alongside normal Russian military. The situation has been under control for some time, but I'll be honest. Two thirds of the faction hates your guts..."

Anya went silent and started listening to a strange sound from the hallway. It quickly attracted my attention as well. Then came the sound of doors opening, and the girl went pale and jumped away from the gurney. I turned my head to see who it was. In the doorframe, I saw a frail dark-haired girl of fifteen or sixteen with a surprisingly calm and emotionless demeanor.

I hadn't seen Gerd Tamara in the real world before, and she didn't quite resemble her game avatar. But I immediately realized who it was. Flanking her, as if in contrast to the frail girl, there were two towering musclemen, each a walking mountain with shoulders as wide as a barn door.

"Wait in the corridor," the girl whispered to a terrified Anya. "Don't worry about Gnat, I won't eat him. I just want to talk. You two also wait for me outside."

Tamara was using a fairly quiet and calm voice, but it also contained boundless confidence that she was immaculate and could order people around. I couldn't imagine who could stand up against her will. Anya couldn't, that was for sure. In her place, I wouldn't have been able to either. She walked up, stopped a step from my bed and spent a long time just staring at me in silence.

I tensed up inside, having no idea what to expect from the severe paladin. What she eventually said surprised me so much I didn't know how to react:

"Your eyes are so beautiful... now that I'm used to them."

What?! That was the last thing I was expecting her to mention. Honestly, I was tired of hearing about them at this point, but I was used to the remarks.

"From our very first meeting I knew you were not a person. More accurately, you're not a normal person like the millions and billions that live on our planet. There's something alien and dangerous in you. And now I'm entirely certain of that."

What was she talking about??? Did Tamara seriously suspect I was an embedded agent of our arch enemies? How else could I understand her words? The girl continued:

"Your distant ancestors were wizards or shamans. At any rate, they had magical powers. And in the hundreds of generations since that time, their gift was passed down to you. If you were born in a different place, you'd have become a mage also. But there is no magical training on our home planet, so your gift revealed itself in the form of risk taking and elevated luck..."

Despite my prejudice against Tamara and natural skepticism, I was listening with greater and greater interest. It was very bizarre, but for some reason I believed her without question, like she was telling me a dogma or inviolable truth. And it wasn't hypnosis, more like a talent for eloquence or speaking self-confidently.

"You've probably heard plenty of things about my past." Here the girl went silent, waiting for me to react. I nodded in silence. "Well, it's all true. I spent several long years in total darkness, balancing on the edge of madness in an endless dream. I was paralyzed, blind, deaf, broken, and all alone. I heard voices in my head that told me wild stories and encouraged me not to give up."

"Voices?" I asked incredulously. It sounded like delirium.

"Yes, voices. I understand I really shouldn't talk about that. It might make people think I'm insane. But it is true. These voices told me that I needed to stay strong, and my time was yet to come. The voices also gradually told me the history of my kind. For centuries, my ancestors were mage hunters. They ruthlessly exterminated all those with magical abilities and eventually they were all gone. And I have inherited their powers. Not only can I sense magic, I can defend people against it. This may come across melodramatic but, if not for my abilities, we would have already lost the war with the Dark Faction."

I had heard several members of the H3 Faction say: "When Tamara's around, I'm not afraid." Clearly, they were referring to her ability to defend against psionic magic. But was that any justification for her unbridled behavior? And was the great and fearsome Gerd Tamara really here just to tell me her story?

"Gnat, to many people in our faction, I am a beacon of hope. I bless and lead the troops into battle, stand on the front lines and embolden our soldiers with my example. I didn't ask for this role, and I wouldn't wish it on anyone. Things just came together this way... it's hard to even say how... Think of me like an Orthodox Icon or a guardian angel. And some players, due to my young age, think of me as a daughter and project their parental instincts onto me."

That was all true, beyond a shadow of a doubt. I had seen that most soldiers of the Second Legion regarded Tamara as more than a simple commander. The austere muscle men were ready to die for her, and not only in the virtual game.

"But everything on earth has an opposite. Gnat, I understand the mood of our people. They're on the edge of despair. You shot me, their Icon, their hope, their holy protector, their angel and even daughter. I swear by my abilities that I did not attack you and did not order it, but still I caused you to suffer. Yes, Gnat, I know who is behind the attack. It was three Second Legion soldiers, no matter how much that hurts me as a commander. I have already given this information to the investigators and Leng Radugin, and immediately expelled all three from my group. And although I have given an order not to harm you, I'm not sure everyone agrees. So, I see only one way out of the present situation. Gnat, I officially invite you to join the Second Legion! Let everyone in our faction know that I approve of your actions and have taken you under my protection!"

It was a tempting offer, but I didn't doubt myself for even a second. I immediately refused:

"Tamara, I respond badly to rigid order. I have already been punished a number of times for disobedience. I often act intuitively, disregarding logic and common sense. In your team, I won't be able to be myself and will become a symbol of bad discipline. I'll probably spend more time waiting to respawn and being shot by you than actually playing."

"What a pity..." Seemingly, Tamara was upset by my refusal. "Although, you're probably right. It wouldn't be right to stuff you into a rigid frame. The leadership of the Dome values you for your unique way of thinking and unpredictability. You know how to benefit the faction in situations where other players would not only fail to do so but would fail to even see the opportunity."

Well, well! Had I really earned praise from the great

and fearsome Gerd Tamara?! Despite the pain, I tried to smile. The girl watched my fruitless attempts with calm detachment, then noted:

"Gnat, you're bleeding through the bandage. Don't move your facial muscles until the stitches are healed. And really, take my advice. Get back into your pod as quickly as possible. In a few hours, you'll come out right as rain. Believe me, I know what I'm saying!"

The dark-haired girl turned and headed for the exit. But in the doorway, she stopped sharply and turned around:

"Gnat, you'll probably be interested to hear that, thanks to your supplies, and Minn-O La-Fin's ransom, the Antique Beach node has reached level two ahead of schedule. Our faction is bringing another seventy-four people into the game that bends reality! A group of newbies is arriving under the Dome as we speak. The Second Legion and I are heading to the Karelia node. After neutralizing the threat of Dark Faction attack from the Poppy Fields, faction leadership has given the go-ahead to expanding into Karelia. Gnat, that's all thanks to you! Until we meet in the game! And when you enter, go right to stock keeper Vasiliadi. He has a gift from me to you."

Chapter
Thirty-Five

Loyalty Test

T HE DOOR DIDN'T EVEN CLOSE behind the leader of the Second Legion before Imran and Anya ran into the room alarmed. The Dagestani athlete, gently but determinedly moving the girl out of his way, walked up to my bed with a big grin:

"Gnat, I'm so glad to see you better! You scared me yesterday, brother! Don't do that again!"

The huge muscular guy bowed gracefully and, afraid to harm me, gave me a careful hug. After that, as if embarrassed at his show of emotion, he stood sharply and walked away, letting Anya through.

"What did Gerd Tamara want?" she asked quietly, looking suspiciously at the closed door. Then she bent over and gave me a quick kiss on my bandage-free cheek.

I tried to smile, but again felt a sharp pain and

stopped trying to show emotion.

"It's a long story... She said she helped find the people who attacked me. She told me about her dreams, invited me to join the Second Legion and complimented my eyes..."

"Gnat, your eyes really are..." Anya was seemingly ignoring everything I said but, after hearing about my eyes, snorted in embarrassment. She then gathered the courage to look me in the eyes, revealing her true feelings... "It's hard to find the right words... First, it's scary to see the blue glow, but it's also so alluring... When I stare into them, it's like drowning in a bottomless blue ocean... It's like magic... I could dissolve in that blue... It's so nice..."

And suddenly, I was looking at myself from above. I saw the bandaged face of a young boy on a sunken hospital pillow. Dark short hair. Face swollen and black with bruises. A huge bandage over a broken nose, side strips of bandage over the forehead and cheeks, spots of blood visible through the pure white fabric. The right eye was swollen and red and there was an ugly scruffy beard on the chin and cheeks. And the blue eyes were glowing...

"How did he even make them like that? I didn't have that option in the character builder. I tried every setting! Glowing eyes like that would be irresistible on my face. Too bad, I must have missed something. Anyway, Kirill is a nice boy with good prospects. Sure, he isn't the most athletic, but he is intriguing. And lucky. Or maybe not lucky, but smart? In the final match of the online tournament, how did he find my shapeshifter and cold-bloodedly end me in the last few

seconds? I wouldn't have been able. I'm actually glad I was asked to look after him, I really shouldn't have refused at first. When Kirill is better, I should try to carefully put the idea in his head of us moving into a separate room together."

The stream of personal thoughts scared me, so moved my gaze away, sharply breaking the strange mental connection. My forehead started to sweat. I took a heavy sigh, not understanding what had happened.

"Ha! Kirill, you just lost the staring game!" Anya laughed happily and carelessly. "Wanna try again?"

Seemingly, the beautiful girl hadn't even sensed what happened just now. I'll admit, I didn't understand exactly what had happened either, but the images and thoughts in my head definitely didn't belong to me. Listening in on others' thoughts... Geeze! That was even lower than peeping while someone showered or looking at someone's phone messages without asking. Not wanting to suffer from a dirty conscious, I tried to convince her not to repeat the experiment:

"Anya, there's an ancient belief that, if a girl stares into a boy's eyes too long, especially blue ones, she shares her hidden thoughts and fantasies. Aren't you afraid?"

Anya furrowed her brow in disbelief and answered that she had never heard about such a "silly superstition," but she still didn't ask to play the staring game again. By that time, I had totally come to my senses and even decided to test what I'd just heard to make sure it wasn't a hallucination.

I reminded Anya of our conversation at Ivan Lozovsky's introductory lecture when she said she wanted to give her character glowing eyes as well. I asked why she hadn't done it. Didn't she like it?

"Are you kidding?" The beautiful girl frowned unhappily. "I spent a half hour trying to find eyes like yours in the character editor! There was nothing like it!"

So, that one was real! Just to make sure, I should check something else. For example, was she asked to look after me? I sighed and spoke sadly:

"So, I've just been lying here for thirty hours... Were you seriously with me that whole time?! What about your daily patrols and training sessions? Did they just let you skip, or were you here only between shifts? And how did you find out what happened?"

Anya got embarrassed and it took her a while to answer, first casting an inquisitive gaze at Imran, as if looking for support or permission. The bodyguard delayed a few seconds and said:

"Tell him the truth. Honesty is the least we can do for our friend Gnat."

Anya shrugged her shoulders and sat on the very edge of my bed.

"Sure, I guess it's no secret. Imran and I were returning from a patrol in the Yellow Mountains on the sixth shift, which goes from ten PM until 2 AM. By three, we were back in the Capital. We immediately climbed out of our virt pods, looked around and saw lots of action in our corncob.

There were a bunch of security people looking around with flashlights, and there was blood on the floor. We overheard that something bad happened to you, and both ran to the medical unit. The first night was scary... well, like I told you. Then in the morning, we both had to meet with Radugin, but he didn't do much talking. There was a strict woman with him in the office wearing glasses... a psychologist... I don't remember her name. And it probably doesn't matter."

The Dagestani athlete walked up closer and grabbed the thread of the story:

"That woman was called Irina Chusovkina. She is a professional psychologist, who wrote her dissertation on gaming addiction and the unique relationships formed between social groups inside video games. Now, she is responsible for the mental wellbeing of the people under the Dome."

"So, the psychologist lady said," Anya picked back up, "that our small group of bad-student gamers had been brought under the Dome for a reason. It was an idea by project curators to break up our faction's fossilized atmosphere. The rest of the team lives by strict rules and regulations. They thought they'd add an element of liveliness and risk-taking to make us less predictable. That was exactly what she said. Her group of psychologists predicted that there might be friction when we first joined, because we were of a different character. For example, Denis Tormashyov had a conflict with the other engineers at the Prometheus, and the psychologists settled it. But no one was expecting such a cataclysmic rift in society as what happened to you..."

Anya sighed in sorrow and went silent, so Imran took back over:

"Mr. Radugin said you were very beneficial and did more for the H3 Faction in just a few days than many have done in half a year. Unfortunately, lots of our players don't get that, though. Lots of people don't like you, and not only because of the Gerd Tamara situation. Many faction members are upset that you don't have to go on patrol, miss training sessions, don't look for minerals and stuff, interact with the Dark Faction, and have a suspicious amount of money. Gnat, I've heard this talk first hand!"

I could see that Imran was seriously alarmed. I had to admit, this was food for thought. Just yesterday, no one gave a damn about me. Few people even knew I existed. But today, there was antipathy all around. It seemed like a conspiracy, but who could be behind it? And again, how did the common players know my character had three thousand crystals? I hadn't been blowing my horn about it on every corner, just Radugin and his two deputies should have known. Nevertheless, the information had leaked...

"The leadership is seriously afraid that, after what happened, you won't want to go back into the game," Imran continued. "They think you'll get mad at the faction and withdraw. Radugin is much more afraid you'll leave our faction. Not that you'll join the Dark Faction, they're not afraid of that. But they're worried you might fly off forever with the Geckho in search of adventure in the infinite cosmos."

What?! The Dome leader suspected me of wanting to desert? He thought I intended to abandon my faction at a critical point in a war for survival just for personal enjoyment? Hmm... Today was full of surprises...

"So, we were asked to stay with you until you woke up," Anya chimed in. "The psychologist thought you would be happy to see friends and know that not everyone in the faction is against you. It's supposed to help make you want to keep playing sooner. The leadership is afraid the Geckho will come to pick you up before long and they don't want to explain why you're not in the game... That would be a whole fiasco and might make the Geckho see the H3 Faction in a negative light. And also," the girl lowered her voice to a whisper, "we were told top secret information that your character is progressing very quickly and, at this rate, will become a Gerd someday. A Gerd does not walk alone. He always has a posse of like-minded individuals, a team. Imran and I were advised to stay by your side for our own good as well as yours."

"But most importantly," Imran took back over, "we were told to follow you and immediately kill you if the psychologists were wrong and you were trying to run or join the Dark Faction!"

After these extremely frank words, a long period of silence fell. My friends were being totally honest, even about the unpleasant parts. Now they were waiting for my reaction. I just laid on the bed, staring at the ceiling and thinking in agitation. These psychologists, my friends, the leadership... None of them knew what kind of man I was! Run? Betray? Don't hold your breath!!!

Seemingly, the heated war with the Dark Faction had made our faction forget our broader goals. The earth had been given a very limited period of guaranteed protection, and it was inexorably coming to a close. We couldn't afford to waste even a second on internal squabbling. And I was here under the Dome not out of some sense of loyalty to the H3 Faction, and certainly not for the money. The only purpose I had in mind was to defend against the enslavement and total destruction of all I held near and dear in the real world — my friends, country, planet and humanity as a whole!

But I didn't know how to express that simply. It would either come across as dramatic, or self-serving and false. But I didn't have to.

"ATTENTION, THIS IS THE DOME LEADER. THE DARK FACTION HAS CROSSED THE TOXIC MARSHES INTO THE EASTERN SWAMP NODE! MORE TROOPS THAN EVER BEFORE. MORE THAN ONE THOUSAND SOLDIERS! BORDER POSTS TEN AND TWELVE ARE UNDER ATTACK! THE EASTERN SWAMP BASE COULD BE DESTROYED! AND THE SECOND LEGION IS UNDER SEIGE IN THE KARELIA NODE AND REQUESTING HELP! THIS IS A VERY SERIOUS SITUATION! EVERYONE TO ARMS!!!"

I confess, my first thought was a false alarm and a test of my loyalty. Would I stay in bed in the clinic and make excuses? Or, like the ancient Achilles, angry at the injustice and ingratitude of my own people, would I calmly watch my faction be defeated? Or would I stand and go carry out the order? After all, "everyone to arms" meant exactly that: everyone. But after entering the virt pod, I would leave all my fractures and pains in the real world. And after exiting the game that bends reality, my condition here would be significantly improved. After all, many people had been treated like that before.

The siren continued to wail. I heard shouts and commotion. All the players under the Dome were flooding into their corncobs. It was looking less and less like a drill. After all, I wasn't important enough for this big a production.

"Kirill... we have to go, you heard it yourself," my friends said, worried. They started hurrying away, but I stopped them.

"Where are you going?! Wait! Help me get dressed and go to my pod."

With Imran's help, I somehow pulled my track pants on over my cast, then buttoned my number 1470 shirt over my bandaged chest shoulders and back. Anya helped me lace up my tennis shoes. We couldn't find any wheelchairs or crutches, so my friends had to grab me under the arm and carry me out.

In the corridor, the two soldiers keeping watch over my room led a surprised gaze over us but didn't tell us to stop. I didn't see any legion emblems or player numbers on their equipment. These were probably the soldiers Radugin had brought in to maintain order. With the help of my friends, I left the medical unit and, limping and hobbling, headed down the path marked "Corn."

Soon, I witnessed a surprising scene. Next to the recently completed corncob number sixteen, which we had to walk past, a severe guard had stopped a group of players from getting inside. Based on their uniform numbers, these were the fresh batch of newbies from yesterday, or maybe even today. They were six muscular boys and one younger girl, either athletes or students from a military academy.

"But we can help! The faction needs us!" the newbies clamored. But the guardsman wasn't having it:

"Not allowed! You are not on the list. You haven't taken the introductory course or memorized the training Labyrinth."

They quieted down when we walked up. We just looked too bizarre: a bandaged person hanging off two others by the shoulders.

"Let them through!" I demanded. "They're acting on sincere and noble impulses. Don't cut that off at the root."

"Yes sir, Gnat, sir!" the soldier gave me a respectful salute and stepped aside, letting the group of newcomers onto their spiral staircase.

The newbies immediately ran in. For a little while, I heard their diminishing voices shouting in joy: "That was Gnat," "Yeah, I can't believe it," "The one they told us about!" I don't know what Lozovsky told them, but my character being so widely known even among green newbies surprised and somewhat alarmed me. I hobbled over to corncob fifteen and asked a strong guardsman there to help my exhausted friends get me up to the fourteenth floor.

Ugh, why couldn't they just build an elevator?! It took seven minutes to get me to my kernel. I could sense the valuable time ticking away. But I finally reached my virt pod. I thanked my friends and the unfamiliar strongman for help and, nearly having forgotten due to the sharp pain in my broken leg, stretched out my limbs and laid down on the soft springy bed.

"I'll meet you in the Capital next to Vasiliadi's storehouses!" I shouted after Imran and Anya as they hurried to their kernels. Then I closed the lid.

Gnat. Human. Faction H3	
Level-32 Prospector	
Statistics:	
Strength	12
Agility	15
Intelligence	19
Perception	21
	+ 2

Constitution	13
Luck modifier	+3
Parameters:	
Hitpoints	873
Endurance points	500
Magic points	0
Carrying capacity	24 kg
Fame	29
Skills:	
Electronics	23
Scanning	36
Cartography	37
Astrolinguistics	35
Break-in	15
Rifles	37
Mineralogy	12
Medium Armor	22
Eagle Eye	37
Sharpshooter	18
Targeting	8
Danger Sense	10

Sure, not yet a beast of a man leveled high enough to induce horror, but a decent soldier nevertheless. I was certainly good enough to help my faction in battle. My fame in the game had gone up by two points during my prolonged absence, and that could have been for so many reasons, I didn't even think about it. There were more important things now: my faction was under attack! The Eastern Swamp base could be destroyed! I had no time to waste!

Chapter Thirty-Six

Virtual SMS Emden

THE CHAOS AND HULLABALOO under the Dome was just a weak reflection of the reality in the video game. The Capital was like a batted bee hive. There was a siren wailing here too. High-speed buggies roared in from afar with messengers. Hundreds of armed soldiers clamored here and there and, at first glance, seemed to be moving chaotically around the central base. The commanders were trying to bring order, splitting up the soldiers into platoons and hurriedly loading them into Peresvets and other vehicles.

There were obviously not enough vehicles and we needed a lot of things on the front other than manpower. I saw technicians dragging endless boxes of rounds and explosives into huge heavy trucks armored with steel sheets. Some of the trucks had long-barreled antitank cannons on trailers. Escort vehicles mounted with flak machineguns were waiting off to the side.

All this fuss was fully justified though. I could hear the cannonade all the way from here, just around eight miles away. The whole eastern horizon was shrouded in heavy black smoke from the burning oil derricks and refinery, which had been torched. I heard rumors our faction was behind it. It was hot in the Eastern Swamp both literally and figuratively.

But what should I do? Stand in line for a better weapon? There were lots of people waiting in front of the warehouse already, and I only saw unfamiliar faces. They were all in a rush, trying to cut ahead and looking tense. What was more, they were shipping out in platoons. But I had never been trained in a group and, to my great shame, didn't know which platoon I was assigned to, or if I was assigned to one at all. Honestly, I was worried and didn't know what to do.

Fortunately, I saw a familiar face just then. From out of nowhere, right in the middle of the square, I saw the leader of the First Legion Gerd Igor Tarasov. I hurried to greet him.

"Ah, Gnat! I'm glad you're back!" the level-90 Sniper recognized me and held out his hand for me to shake.

Someone in the group asked about the situation, and Igor Tarasov's answer was short and packed with meaning:

"Total shit." Many heard that, and the conversations went quiet. The leader of the First Legion hurried to give a more detailed answer:

"What's to hide? It's a bad situation. Border Post Ten fell fifteen minutes ago. I was its last defender. It's a miracle Border Post Twelve is still holding out. The Eastern Swamp garrison is encircled, and we cannot say how long they'll last. If the base is taken, we will lose the node, and all our oil production along with it. But it's too early to give up. There are more than forty capable soldiers in that garrison, and defense is being led by our veterans Shoot_To_Kill and Headquarters Pen_Pusher. They are both from the army special forces and have been stationed in a number of real-world hotspots, so there is hope. And the scientists from the chemical laboratories mostly managed to take shelter in the fort. They're giving support to the defenders, though it isn't much..."

Gerd Tarasov sharply went silent midsentence, because Shoot_To_Kill had just respawned ten steps away. Seemingly, the situation was much more serious than the leader of the First Legion had led us to believe. The high-level players exchanged a couple quick phrases and headed determinedly past the crowd toward the warehouse. Our allies respectfully parted ways before the famed soldiers. I hurried to take advantage of this and went after them before the crowd closed ranks.

"I'm with them!" I stated and was also let through.

I couldn't hear what the First Legion soldiers were

whispering about. I just made out a fragment of something Shoot_to_Kill said:

"... both more or less decent roads to the base in the Eastern Swamp are cut off by the enemy... getting to the fort... will be difficult."

Next to the First Legion soldiers at the weapon counter, I set out three laser pistols, two chameleon cloaks and a scaled thermoregulating Dark Faction suit for Vasiliadi:

"Here is my take from my last game session. And I need a replacement for both of my guns. My Rifles skill is now level thirty-seven." With these words, I set out my shotgun and the Angel Dust PCP-rifle before him together with the remaining rounds and two unopened packs of bullets.

"Well, this is a CTA and weapons are only being issued to..." the stock keeper hadn't finished his phrase before Gerd Tarasov sharply cut him off:

"Give Gnat everything he asks for! The faction needs him at his best! And send that Dark Faction stuff over to the First Legion. I've got recon guys who've been waiting a long time for camo."

Vasiliadi didn't argue with the respected Gerd, and set a gun out before me, still new without a single scratch and glimmering with fragrant gun grease. Beside it, he set two boxes of rounds and four RGD-5 fragmentation grenades to replace the ones I'd used. At that, the huge hirsute stock keeper spread his arms apologetically:

"There are very few nonautomatic weapons in the

warehouse. This is the best I have. After this, you'll either have to order something from the real world or buy it in the Geckho store for crystals. And although it is a hunting rifle and not for combat, it packs a punch. It's twice as powerful as that air rifle. Sure, it probably won't go through a kevlar jacket, but it'll take down a Centaur or Dark Faction Mage in one shot!"

9-mm semiautomatic hunting carbine KCO-9 Krechet

Range: 500 feet.

Damage to unarmored targets: +74%

Chance of dealing critical damage: +2%

Damage to armored targets: -36%

Clip capacity: 10 rounds.

Statistic requirements: Agility 15, Strength 12.

Skill requirements: Rifles 35, Sharpshooter 12.

Attention! You are the first owner of this carbine and may give it a name.

"And also, Gnat, there are two packages waiting for you. One is from Gerd Ustinov, and the other is from Gerd Tamara."

He handed me two cardboard boxes. Plagued by curiosity, I ripped them both open. The first predictably had my light space suit. To my immense relief, it was undamaged. The package from the leader of the Second Legion, meanwhile, contained a quality high-powered radio with lots of settings and two long antennas — geological analyzers for my scanner.

I had to leave right away, because the crowd was pushing me. In a calmer place, I put the carbine into my main weapons lot. I decided not to bust my brains over a name, and just called it Krechet. The object's stats immediately changed slightly:

Chance of losing weapon in case of death reduced by 40%.

Oh! But they said changing the name did nothing! It actually did quite a bit! I placed the Dark Faction paralyzer in my free secondary weapon slot. There was no point putting the Annihilator there, it was out of batteries!

I looked around for Anya and Imran but didn't see my friends in the crowd. I did notice something else though: Dmitry Zheltov's starship flying onto the central square at high speed. My pilot buddy was bringing two green newbies to the Capital. Just then, I hatched a plan. It was a bit undercooked, but I hurried over to the starship pilot.

"Zheltov, didn't you hear about the CTA? Why aren't you helping the fight?" I threw myself at him just after he'd let his passengers out.

"Well, Gnat... I was ordered to pick up newbies after they passed the Labyrinth and bring them to the base. I've been doing it since early this morning. A group of thirty people was supposed to come through today. No one ever ordered me to do anything else."

"Well, lots has changed since then! The Dark Faction is attacking! The Eastern Swamp node is under siege, and the Second Legion is encircled. I'm not surprised you didn't get any more orders. They probably forgot about you. But we could use you for the fight! Let the newbies walk. It's just over a mile to base, and there's nothing too dangerous."

Zheltov removed his old motorcycle helmet and thoughtfully wiped off the mud-streaked face shield.

"Gnat, do you have any ideas?" the pilot enquired, and I nodded:

"As a matter of fact I do! Do the words SMS *Emden* mean anything to you?"

He broke down laughing:

"Gnat, are you kidding?! I went to a military academy. Of course I know the story of the most famous raider of the First World War. The German light cruiser SMS *Emden* harried trade routes on the Indian and Pacific oceans for five whole months, capturing and destroying more than thirty Allied ships! It was fast, so it could evade heavier ships and it always appeared unexpectedly and left just as quickly. Five whole countries had their whole fleets hunting the elusive light cruiser, which weakened the main lines... Uh... wait..." Dmitry Zheltov turned toward his starship. "Am I understanding you correctly, Gnat?"

"Yes, I think you get the idea! Despite its power, the Dark Faction is not elastic. Thousands of their best soldiers are now besieging our base in the Eastern Swamp, and another large division is in Karelia encircling the Second Legion. Those are extremely important missions and I think it's safe to assume all the best Dark Faction soldiers were sent there. There are probably very few defenders left in their territory. The borders are probably being defended by day-two newbies and, deeper in their territory, there's probably nobody. If we make a break past the border and get behind enemy lines, we'll probably only find people who can't even hold a weapon. Then, we can make like a biblical plague, burning fields, destroying infrastructure, blowing up warehouses and laboratories. Our enemy will have no choice but to call fighters off the front! That way, we can help the Second Legion and the defenders of the Eastern Swamp!"

"That's true, Gnat. But as soon as they notice what we're doing, they'll reinforce the border and run us off the road. We'll never be able to get back home. And my antigrav will run out of power eventually. In the end, we'll be captured and taken prisoner..."

"Here!" I extended a fragmentation grenade to the pilot. "So you can always return home."

Zheltov walked up to his racing buggy, got down on one knee and lovingly led a hand over the ornate sparkling word "Starship," inlaid with small pearls on the front spoiler.

"I decided to write it myself so the others would stop scratching it in and messing up my beaut'. I did this just yesterday... Who knew that tonight would be its grand finale.... My girl will show everyone what a starship she really is! Then I'll blow myself up together with her and keep her out of enemy hands... I agree, Gnat! This is a lot better than working as a virtual taxi driver. I'm a space-combat pilot for God's sake! Where are we headed?"

"Wait a bit... We might have two more companions.

Ah, there they are!" I finally saw my friends and waved a hand, drawing their attention.

Well, well. Recently, the Gladiator had leveled to 18, and the Medic to 17. Not bad, not bad at all. My friends, looked at my level 32 with respect, but I saw a certain despondency on their faces. I told my friends my plans. The Gladiator's face immediately lit up:

"Gnat, I was just about to complain that Anna and I weren't being taken to the front. They said: 'your level isn't high enough, you'll just get in the way.' And because all our vehicles are already in use, they're sending us on foot eight and a half miles to the Jungles node to reinforce a border post. Gnat, take me with you! I swear on my mother's life I won't let you down!"

I pointed the Gladiator to one of the back seats, and he hurried to take it before I'd changed my mind. Anya spent some time shaking her head doubtfully:

"It really gets my goat. There's a big battle, but they think I'm useless! But this could land me a smack on the head. Although... I was also ordered to stay by your side, Gnat, so technically I'm following orders. I'm with you!"

The Medic took the last free seat, and the pilot sharply started off, quickly increasing the speed of his starship.

I suggested we go through the neutral Poppy Fields node to reach Dark Faction territory. I figured their border there would have somewhat fewer defenses than where our lands met. That line was probably rife with barbed wire, lasers, concrete fences and bunkers. Zheltov didn't argue, just noted that the closest enemy node to us was named Graveyard, while the one we were going to was called Golden Plain after its vast fields. After that, he gunned the engines and took off to the northwest.

Our border post flickered by. I saw two soldiers up on it looking befuddled. A few seconds later, the driver's radio flickered on:

"This is post three. Zheltov, come in! No one told us you were coming. Do you have a pass to neutral territory?"

The driver was too busy steering between bushes and trees to answer, so I unclipped the radio from his belt and answered for him:

"This is Gnat, number fourteen seventy. We're on a secret mission. You can have the details after completion."

That answer did not satisfy the border guards, and Zheltov's radio, and soon Imran's and Anya's as well started spewing forth angry shouts, orders to return at once and promises of frightful punishment.

Fame increased to 30.

Just then, Anya said in surprise:

"Gnat, I just got a message about fame! Is that supposed to happen?"

"Me too," Imran confirmed. "Fame increased to one."

"Well, my fame just went up to three," our driver boasted. "That means you're doing something outside the norm. The game likes it a lot."

I didn't add anything or brag about my own Fame. I was too occupied with a different question. Why wasn't there any sound coming from my radio?! I had turned in my old one, and the new one from Gerd Tamara just wasn't working. Flying at high speed in the antigrav, it was hard to monkey with the complicated settings. We were changing direction unpredictably and constantly taking sharp turns. But I needed to figure it out right now, because I had to be able to coordinate with the faction.

Finally, I managed to remove the lid and check the battery. Bingo! There was a little piece of paper between the battery and contacts. I removed the obstacle, and my radio sprang to life.

Electronics skill increased to level twenty-four!

I nearly threw the worthless bit of folded paper away, but I spotted some writing and unfolded it. It was a note from the leader of the Second Legion:

"Gnat, I didn't say anything out loud because all conversations under the Dome and at the capital base are recorded, but I am absolutely convinced that someone from the very top of our faction is working for the enemy. Either

Leng Radugin himself, or one of his deputies. Always remember that and never share your true plans with them, because they will very quickly reach the Dark Faction.

Not a word to anyone about this note. Please burn it immediately. Tamara."

Hmm... What a mess... Tamara's message completely confirmed it. Our greatest enemy must have infiltrated our faction at the highest level. They probably knew in advance that the whole Second Legion would be sent to Karelia, for example. That was if I didn't assume the worst. After all, the Dark Faction may have even arranged for them to be there so the two hundred experienced soldiers would be as far from the Eastern Swamp node as possible during their attack.

I thoughtfully hid the letter in my inventory. I wasn't going to burn this note. After all, it served as an excuse for my actions. If the leadership got upset with me, which seemed quite likely, I could play this trump card and explain why I hadn't let the faction leader know about our raid behind enemy lines.

Cartography skill increased to level thirty-eight!

Oh, I was finally in unfamiliar territory! I advised Zheltov not to go near the Dark Faction border yet and head further northwest. We crossed the small field of bright red poppies at immense speed, trying to hold our breath to avoid their intoxicating fumes.

After that, the overloaded starship had to climb a steep hill with a slippery clay surface. It was stalling... and we all gasped in unison. A field of bright red flowers stretched out before us to the very horizon. It would be useless to try and cross it without gas masks. Sure, I could put on my spacesuit and sidestep the pernicious effects of the sleep-inducing poppies, but my companions would all fall asleep. Zheltov stopped the starship, waiting for my instructions.

Cartography skill increased to level thirty-nine!
Mineralogy skill increased to level thirteen!
Eagle Eye skill increased to level thirty-eight!

I noticed a well-trodden road far in the distance through the grass and poppies. It led from the tops of the hills somewhere to the east. That road was far from our territories and clearly could not have been made by our faction. Most likely, the Dark Faction built it to extract clay from this region. Perhaps they needed it for pottery or building materials, or maybe even aluminum extraction.

"Head for that road! We'll take it to the east at maximum speed! Zheltov, push this beaut' for all she's worth. This is her time to shine!" The pilot adjusted his goggles, aimed the antigrav at the road, then gunned it to full speed.

Yikes! Yowee! The speeds and G-forces of my past trips with Zheltov were nothing in comparison with this. I was being tossed about like a rag doll and pressed back into my seat. At every turn, the only thing holding me inside the starship was the seatbelt. With huge effort, I turned my head to the left and looked at the speedometer. I shouldn't have done that! The arrow was tittering on the edge of the scale,

250 mph. We must have been going faster than that.

"Anya's fainted!" Imran's said in fear, but I ordered the pilot not to slow down, because we were near the border.

Danger Sense skill increased to level eleven!

Suddenly, we saw a border post after a sharp turn. Massive barriers blocked the road.

"Turn left off the road hard!" I shouted, and Zheltov miraculously managed to react.

Our racing buggy went off the road and, using a hillock as a jump, flew over a wide water-filled ditch. I saw the amazed gaping faces of Dark Faction soldiers from the air.

"Don't stop!"

We raced through the enemy territory. It was actually quite inhabited and developed. The roads were great, and there were endless fields of grain and incomprehensible signage.

"Let's torch the fields!" I shouted. Zheltov slowed down and came to a complete stop.

While Imran brought the pretty medic back to her senses, the pilot and I fashioned a couple torches from sappy branches and lit them with a signal flare. We tied the flare behind the antigrav on a long cord, then drove at low speed through the fields, throwing the torches and leaving a trail of smoke and burning crops behind us.

We came upon a group of terrified Dark Faction farmers. We didn't touch them or even take the radio helmet from their senior member. We wanted them to alert our enemies.

"Now someone will notice us! Let's keep going!"

We flew deeper into enemy territory, leaving more scorched earth for all to see. We managed to destroy another couple fields, then torch a lumber warehouse and farm vehicle garage. We were totally unimpeded for forty minutes. I even began to worry we weren't doing enough damage to warrant attention. But finally, the enemy responded:

"Gnat, behind us!" Anya and Imran shouted in unison.

A huge metal vehicle somewhere between an antigrav and airplane blocked out the sun, then dove down at us with its huge cannons ready to fire.

Sio-Mi-Dori. Dark Faction shock-landing antigrav.

Danger Sense skill increased to level twelve!

On my order, Zheltov darted aside and increased speed, leaving a whole field of bright explosions behind us. The flying machine passed over us and turned around for a second approach. I got an idea that was either brilliant, or idiotic, but I decided it was worth a try:

"Dmitry, get ready to stop and turn off all electronics as quickly as possible. On my order. We're gonna try to catch them by surprise!"

The single most distinguishing feature of people with military experience is that, when they hear an order, they don't question or dispute it. Even though he clearly didn't understand my idea, the pilot gave a short nod. I placed my scanner on my knee and readied a geological analyzer. Meanwhile, the enemy shock-landing antigrav finished its turn, came at us from behind and quickly caught up. Three, two, one...

"Now!!!"

Our starship braked so suddenly it nearly flipped over. Thankfully, I was ready for it, otherwise I'd never have managed to keep hold of the scanner. As soon as the instrument panel went dim, I activated the antenna. It gave a click and... the enemy antigrav hovering above us lost control and started spiraling downward then crashed into the ground just five hundred feet away!!!

Danger Sense skill increased to level thirteen!

Scanning skill increased to level thirty-seven!

You have reached level thirty-three!

You have received three skill points!

You have reached level thirty-four!

You have received three skill points! (total points accumulated: six)

You have reached level thirty-five!

You have received three skill points! (total points accumulated: nine)

Wow... I wiped the sweat off my face. We had barely made it. Just before the laser cannons turned us to dust, my scanner's EMP deactivated them. As a bonus, it also shut the ships engine down and all other electronics. My plan had worked! And I'd leveled up three times!

"Imran, go check the crashed antigrav. If there's anyone alive, show no mercy. Those are our sworn enemies! Well, first take everything of value, then kill them."

The Gladiator bared his teeth predatorily, took out his fearsome sickle and made it over to the fallen craft in two long bounds.

We found a tall tower and started digging in. Not far from an airfield, it was probably either for dispatching or meteorology, but it didn't look like anything on earth. After taking down the *Sio-Mi-Dori*, we were unable to get Zheltov's antigrav to work. Dmitry spent a long time poking around but was forced to admit it was a serious issue and couldn't be repaired in field conditions. The pilot then pulled all the electronics and wire from his beloved vehicle and, just to make sure, shot through all the antigrav "pancakes."

That cast a long shadow on our raid, but we were all still alive, which meant we could keep fighting and aid our faction. So, weighed down with plunder from the downed aircraft, we reached the tower and got inside. If there had been any enemies here before, they managed to leave it before we arrived.

The main advantage of the tower, which is largely why we chose it as a temporary base, was the forest of antennas on top of it. It was clearly sending and retransmitting signals, so we were hoping to jam the Dark Faction's communications. What was more, Zheltov promised he could use them to contact our faction.

"We have to barricade the door!" Imran said, dragging heavy boxes of equipment in front of them.

The four of us pushed boxes and all the furniture we found up against the doors. Now it wouldn't be quite so easy to get into the tower because the windows were pretty high up.

Strength increased to 13.

Woah! Even the game algorithms thought this was hard work. And so, having more or less blocked the doors, we went up to the top floor. While my friends were figuring out all the technology and handing out weapons captured from the enemy ship, I looked out over enemy territory.

I was most interested in an industrial facility a few miles to the east. It was a large building with huge gas tanks and tall distillation columns. Most likely, it was a gas refinery or petrochemical plant. Another window gave a view over the Dark Faction military airport, though there were no aircraft there. And finally, two miles to the north, there was a massive squat fortress up on a hill. Clearly this was the node's main base.

"Gnat, communications are online," Dmitry Zheltov reported. "You can connect your radio with this plug. Shove it in and go to channel twenty-five — that's the one our faction uses for urgent messages."

I thanked the pilot and set up my radio.

"Attention! This is Gnat, number fourteen-seventy! We have occupied a high vantage point on Dark Faction territory and can spot for long-range heavy artillery. Possible targets: the main fort of the Golden Plain node, a Dark Faction military airport and a petrochemical plant."

Fame increased to 31.

In reply, I got distorted fuzz but, not long after, an unfamiliar voice said:

"You've lost your mind, Gnat..."

But he was immediately interrupted by the familiar voice of our faction leader:

"Cut the crap! This is Radugin. Gnat, turn to channel eighteen and give coordinates to our 152-mm howitzer batteries in the Yellow Mountains. Priority target: enemy fort! Don't waste your time on the plant and airport, they'll stop working automatically if we can destroy the base! And even if we can't fully destroy the fortress, we might be able to bring that node down from level three to two. Then, our enemies will only be able to have five-hundred twenty-two people in the game, which will weaken their assault. Good luck!"

The first group of explosions were very compact, but six hundred feet away from the enemy fortress. I told the artillery they missed and gave adjusted coordinates. The stone and tower fragments that flew up into the air a minute later confirmed that we got it right this time.

Targeting skill increased to level nine!

Targeting skill increased to level ten!

Targeting skill increased to level eleven!

Eagle Eye skill increased to level thirty-nine!

The battery made another few successful volleys, but I didn't notice much serious damage to the massive sturdy fortress. And then, despite Radugin's order, I ordered one of the cannons to fire on the petrochemical plant. And it went off with a bang! Where it once stood, a fountain of flame shot up hundreds of feet into the air. One of the gas tanks took off like a rocket, leaving a trail of fire behind it. The next hit turned the factory into hell on earth.

Targeting skill increased to level twelve!

You have reached level thirty-six!

You have received three skill points! (total points accumulated: twelve)

But then, our one-sided game came to an end. The tower shuddered from a nearby explosion. Glass shattered, and Imran's voice rang out in alarm:

"Dark Faction infantry! Lots of infantry! They're

coming from the airport in armored vehicles! They're unloading! More on the way!"

"Don't let them reach the doors! Use grenades!"

Our tower shook again, and the comms link with the howitzer battery was broken. While Zheltov tried to fix it, I went down a floor and carefully approached the window. Well, well! "Lot of infantry." Imran had put that very lightly. There were at least a crapload of them, if not to use an even more vulgar term! I roughly estimated the number of enemies at around three hundred. But that was good. It meant we had their attention.

Danger Sense skill increased to level fourteen!

A moment after I moved my head away from the window, a few bright flashes came through it. Then Imran's voice rang out in sorrow:

"Anya is dead!!!"

Our beautiful and brave medic was lying on the floor with her head shot through, still squeezing the plundered laser rifle in her hands.

"She'll respawn in fifteen minutes on the base alive and well," I reassured the Gladiator and, one after the other, lobbed two fragmentation grenades out the window. I heard banging on the blocked door below, and I wanted to slow them down a bit.

You have reached level thirty-seven!

You have received three skill points! (total points accumulated: fifteen)

The response flew in almost instantly. A few grenades

came through our broken windows. First a fragmentation grenade. I took shelter behind a fallen metal cabinet. One small bit of shrapnel did hit me in the left wrist, though. Then a smoke grenade...

Medium Armor skill increased to level twenty-three.
Danger Sense skill increased to level fifteen!

That's not any old smoky smoke!!! I changed my jacket and kevlar vest to my light spacesuit before I mentally realized what I was doing or why. And just in the nick of time! The room quickly filled with acrid gray smoke. Imran clenched his throat with both hands and started writhing on the floor. But I had no way of helping him. Five seconds later, my Dagestani friend was on his way to respawn. Before he was gone for good, I realized my Gladiator buddy had hit level twenty-three. Imran went up five whole levels during this raid. What a warrior!

I heard another deafening explosion in the room. Shrapnel ricocheted off the walls with a shrill whistle. Taking advantage of a brief pause, I ran up the stairs, already hearing dozens of boots clomping up the stairs. The enemy had made it through our barricade. I emptied my Krechet's clip, forcing the enemy to take cover. I even hit a few times. Then, I threw down three of the grenades I'd got from the shock antigrav. They were flashbangs, so I didn't kill anyone and just slowed them down.

On the top floor, taking cover behind some broken equipment in the corner, all splashed with blood and caked in cement dust, Dmitry Zheltov was pulling at wires with quivering hands. He was even holding a wire in his teeth. When I appeared, he first grabbed for a grenade, but recognized me and got back to work. The starship pilot's life bar was down in the red. My last ally had less than a quarter of his hitpoints left.

"Gnat, we'll have comms back online in just a couple seconds... Alright, we're up and running! You can use the radio. You got a first aid kit?"

I shook my head no and pointed Dmitry to the stairway, indicating that enemies were close at hand. I stuck the plug back into my radio, took a deep sigh and loudly declared:

"This is Gnat, number one thousand four hundred seventy! The enemy is in the building. There are more than three hundred enemies in my immediate vicinity! Fire on my position! Coordinates..." I opened the map and started distinctly reading out my coordinates, but another voice interrupted me.

"Stop! This is a Leng's order to immediately cease fire! There is a Geckho starship in the combat zone! God forbid we accidentally shoot it down. It would take a lifetime to pay that off!"

Fame increased to 32.

That was the last thing I needed... Who the hell was this?! Zheltov gave a long burst from his fully-auto, gunning down our enemies as they came up to our floor. Then he took another bullet and jumped back, setting his automatic down. Then, my only ally left alive tied a tourniquet above his elbow and reached for the pin of his grenade. I also took out my last remaining grenade and mentally prepared to die.

"Gnat, can you hear me?" The voice clanging out on the radio belonged to our diplomat Ivan Lozovsky beyond a shadow of a doubt. "Those Geckho came for you. It's the Shiamiru. I sent them your coordinates. We've reached a cease-fire with the Dark Faction. They are removing their soldiers from the Eastern Swamp and officially recognizing our rights to the node. We agreed to stop shelling on the Golden Plain and recognized their sovereignty there. There is a one-hundred-step-radius around the comms tower you're inside that has been officially declared a safe zone until the end of the day. Kosta Dykhsh is on his way there to personally guarantee your safety."

Fame increased to 33.

You have reached level thirty-eight!

You have received three skill points! (total points accumulated: eighteen)

I shook my head skeptically. Not about the level-up, of course. That happened automatically based on the game algorithms, so I had no doubt. But a ceasefire with the Dark Faction... that was just too good to be true. Especially considering the alarming note from Gerd Tamara. So, I didn't believe Ivan Lozovsky and even thought the treacherous diplomat may have been trying to trick me into leaving the tower right into enemy hands.

But some time passed, and we weren't attacked. The shots died down. Dmitry Zheltov, not hiding his astonishment, confirmed that the enemy was vacating the tower. And the sound of overdriven thrusters outside could only be one thing. The Shiamiru was landing. My arms stretched out all on their own, reaching for something sturdy before the starship crash landed on the ground.

"Gnat, you there?" the voice of Captain Uraz Tukhsh rang out in my helmet earpiece. I recognized it and was unbelievably happy!

So, everything Ivan Lozovsky said was true?! I mentally apologized to the diplomat for my mistrust and confirmed in Geckho that I was inside the tower and was coming right out.

"There's so much smoke! Everything is burning and exploding... Somehow, I'm not surprised. Gnat, did you break something again?" Uline Tar couldn't hold back a quip.

The sound of the thrusters changed tone and went quiet. The shuttle landed smoothly. I extended a hand to Zheltov and helped him to his feet. Together, supporting one another under the arms, we went down the stairs, stepping over the bodies of our vanquished foes.

There were quite a lot of living Dark Faction soldiers, but they were all far away from the tower, having formed a huge circle. The Shiamiru had landed inside of it. There was a second circle directly around the ship formed by austere Geckho troops.

"Is that... a starship? A real one?" A flame of interest lit up in the eyes of my badly wounded companion. Just a second before, he could barely drag his feet, but now he was walking almost normally.

"Yes, it's a starship," I answered calmly, pretending I wasn't impressed. "Let's go, I'll talk with the captain about you. First, I can't leave you alone surrounded by enemies. Second, you're a Starship Pilot by profession, and the whole crew will be clamoring to take you on board. You'll see."

I headed right for the captain. I was afraid of having to negotiate, but the conversation was very short:

"Tell your friend to come on board. He can be my co-pilot. First for one flight, then we'll see."

Still in disbelief, the denigrated Starship Pilot was finally going to work in a genuine starship. The huge Uline Tar walked up to me, squeezed me and said:

"Gnat, I'm happy to see you! Your Listener's suit is ready and waiting. They even charged the battery. But first give me back the Annihilator!"

We made the trade and I became the happy owner of a matte black armor suit. I checked the requirements and the excitement made my heartbeat pickup! I was just barely too low. My Medium Armor skill was now at twenty-three, but it needed to be forty. But if I put my free points there, I'd have enough. I'd even have one left over. Not wasting time, I invested seventeen points into the Medium Armor skill and donned the dark-colored energy suit.

Fame increased to 34.

Attention!!! Your character has attained significant fame and authority and has now been assigned the rank Gerd. You have received eight stat points.

Attention!!! Your character now has the Authority parameter. Current value: negative eight.

Attention!!! You may change class from Prospector to Listener.

I fell out of time for a second, too swallowed up by the messages before my eyes and the surge of thoughts that followed. I was a Gerd, someone who had proven themselves and stood out from the crowd! And I could change class. I couldn't find a description of the Listener class, but I was intending to eventually figure out the advantages of the rare, and perhaps entirely unique class.

I was brought back to reality by a slap on the shoulder from Uline:

"Accept my congratulations, Gerd Gnat! But with all due respect, get into the ship, it's time for us to take off."

The Shiamiru's thrusters were already grumbling, so I hurried inside. In the doorway, I turned back and took one last look at the many Dark Faction soldiers standing in the distance. I saw among them Leng Thumor-Anhu La-Fin. The fearsome mage somehow sensed that I was looking at him and gave me a slight bow. I acknowledged the authoritative mage in kind.

The ship had already started and was quickly gaining speed when my radio squawked . It was Ivan Lozovsky:

"Gnat, be honest, are you ever coming back? Will you fly off on adventures forever?"

I laughed in reply and answered with all the honesty I could muster:

"The faction won't get rid of me that easy! Our planet won't be kept safe much longer, so this is no time for goofing off. I'll be back! Don't you doubt it!"

End of Book One

Want to be the first to know about our latest LitRPG, sci fi and fantasy titles from your favorite authors?

Subscribe to our **New Releases** newsletter:
http://eepurl.com/b7niIL

Thank you for reading *Reality Benders!*
If you like what you've read, check out other sci-fi, fantasy and LitRPG novels published by Magic Dome Books:

Reality Benders LitRPG series by Michael Atamanov:
Countdown
External Threat
Game Changer
Web of Worlds
A Jump into the Unknown
Aces High

**The Dark Herbalist LitRPG series
by Michael Atamanov:**
Video Game Plotline Tester
Stay on the Wing
A Trap for the Potentate
Finding a Body

Perimeter Defense LitRPG series by Michael Atamanov:
Sector Eight
Beyond Death
New Contract
A Game with No Rules

**League of Losers LitRPG Series
by Michael Atamanov:**
A Cat and his Human

**The Way of the Shaman LitRPG series
by Vasily Mahanenko:**
Survival Quest
The Kartoss Gambit
The Secret of the Dark Forest
The Phantom Castle
The Karmadont Chess Set
Shaman's Revenge
Clans War

The Alchemist LiTRPG series by Vasily Mahanenko:
City of the Dead
Forest of Desire
Tears of Alron

Interworld Network LitRPG Series by Dmitry Bilik:
The Time Master
Avatar of Light
The Dark Champion

Rogue Merchant LitRPG Series by Roman Prokofiev:
The Starlight Sword
The Gene of the Ancients

Project Stellar LitRPG Series by Roman Prokofiev:
The Incarnator
The Enchanter
The Tribute

Clan Dominance LitRPG Series by Dem Mikhailov:
The Sleepless Ones Book One
The Sleepless Ones Book Two
The Sleepless Ones Book Three

The Neuro LitRPG series by Andrei Livadny:
The Crystal Sphere
The Curse of Rion Castle
The Reapers

Phantom Server LitRPG series by Andrei Livadny:
Edge of Reality
The Outlaw
Black Sun

Respawn Trials LitRPG Series by Andrei Livadny:
Edge of the Abyss

**The Expansion (The History of the Galaxy) series
by A. Livadny:**
Blind Punch
The Shadow of Earth
Servobattalion

Point Apocalypse *(a near-future action thriller)*
by Alex Bobl

Moskau by G. Zotov
(a dystopian thriller)

In order to have new books of the series translated faster, we need your help and support! Please consider leaving a review or spread the word by recommending *Reality Benders* to your friends and posting the link on social media. The more people buy the book, the sooner we'll be able to make new translations available.

Thank you!

Till next time!